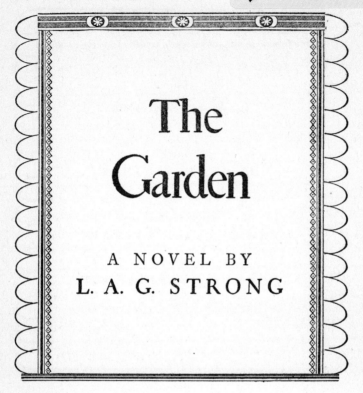

The Garden

A NOVEL BY
L. A. G. STRONG

ALFRED · A · KNOPF

NEW YORK

1931

1952

THE GARDEN

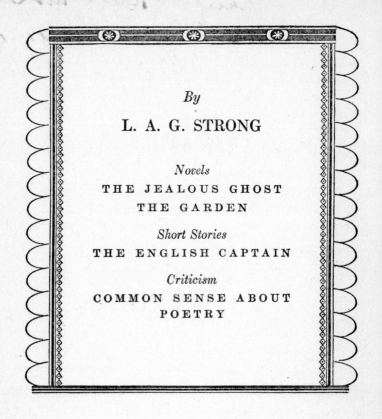

By

L. A. G. STRONG

Novels
THE JEALOUS GHOST
THE GARDEN

Short Stories
THE ENGLISH CAPTAIN

Criticism
COMMON SENSE ABOUT
POETRY

THESE ARE BORZOI BOOKS
PUBLISHED BY
ALFRED A. KNOPF

BOOK I

The Garden

CHAPTER I

THE BRITISH AND IRISH STEAM PACKET COMPANY'S *Lady Hudson-Kinahan* slid gently over the oily water to her place on the North Wall. Holding tightly to his toy monkey, Dermot stood in the safe place where his mother had put him, staring at the quays, the stacks of barrels, and the slowly moving sheds. He was to look out for Granny. Every few seconds he remembered this, and gazed at the little black knot of people who were wavering about on the shore, uncertain at what berth the ship was coming to land. Their faces were small and clear, but somehow unreal: they waved, and their mouths opened, but no cries of welcome could be heard over the noise of the winches. Three or four, who had detached themselves from the main body, hurried along excitedly, keeping pace with the ship. Close to Dermot a sailor, with a big moustache and with wrinkles at the corners of his eyes, was coiling a thick rope, swaying from the hips as he did so. Dermot's gaze fixed on him, and he forgot all else, till suddenly there was a loud hail, and the sound of a rope whizzing in the air. Looking up, he saw the rope fall away into the distance, and land with a thud on the wooden quay. Its bight slipped heavily into the water, and the end on the quay began to slither after it: but an old sailor in a jersey ran with fat agility, got hold of the end, grinned ridiculously up at the ship, and hurried off to make the rope fast.

Then arose a bewildering din. The mysterious little bell

3

rang, the propeller began to thrash in the water, and the ship shivered and throbbed. The shore stood still, then began to approach them sideways. The winches clanked. The faces on the quay grew bigger, and were upturned to the ship. Sailors bustled about the deck, shouting. Unceremoniously two of them cleared a place at the rail, lapped back the big broad polished balustrade, and, between them, lifted a piece of the white railing bodily out. Then, with great confusion and shouts of "Mind yourselves, mind yourselves, now," they ran a gangway along, and fixed it in place. Passengers, their arms full of bags and umbrella cases, fussed back protestingly to give it room.

Remembering his duty with a start, Dermot looked down at the crowd of faces. It was very difficult. He began laboriously eliminating them to himself: "That's not my Granny, and that's not my Granny, and that's not my Granny": but it was very difficult, for as he looked down at the faces, this and that one would catch his attention. A laughing young woman in black, carrying a baby, and making all sorts of signs to someone away on his left somewhere. Dermot looked along the deck to see if the person were making signs back, but could not see past the crowd around the gangway. Then there was an old gentleman on the quay, who had obviously seen the person he was coming to meet, and had gone quite red with pleasure, but evidently did not think it proper to show his delight in public. He kept pulling his mouth straight, and looking down. Then his glance would steal up again, and he would nod very happily, his face working. Dermot could not see who it was he was looking at, either. It was all very difficult. He sighed, and clasped his hot hands tighter than ever on his toy monkey.

Then, very kindly, Granny saved him further trouble by detaching herself from the crowd to ask a question of a sailor. The sailor pointed up at the men holding the gangway in readiness. Yes, there was Granny. Darling Granny: with her black bead cape, and hat tied under her chin with wide black ribbons. He unclasped a hand, waved it, and gave a thin, unheard cry. The ship bumped, the gangways shot out, swooped heavily, blindly, then fell with a crash. The fussy passengers began to fight their way off the ship, entangling one another in their bags and umbrella cases. The sailors shooed them good-naturedly along, as if they had been so many refractory cattle.

Granny had seen Mummy. She was beaming up, her face alight with smiles. There would be tea, and the lovely strange china things on the tea table, and Grandpapa's moustache cup. Then Mummy was upon him, flushed, laughing, still half anxious, and holding him tightly by the hand.

Getting off gangways was one of the things you simply did not dare let yourself experience. You shut your eyes to everything except the exact place you were to put each foot: you clenched your teeth: you did not let yourself think about anything at all until you were safe on the great wide quay that came up to meet you. If you once stopped to think: if you once let yourself feel what crossing a gang-way was *really* like, with all of you: you would never be able to cross one again. A moment of clenched teeth, of stumbling over the high wooden ridges; one sickening glimpse of dark green, oily water; and he was on shore, safe and sound, blinking, with clamour all about him, and Granny stooping from the sky, to kiss him welcome.

He focussed his attention upon her gravely, and was opening his mouth to ask her two very important questions, when she straightened up, and gave her attention to Munny the nurse, who was carrying baby Eithne. Granny began to chuckle and coo, till she realised that, miraculously, the baby was asleep. For a long, long time Dermot stood there, absorbed in thought, surrounded by noise and whirling vague shapes, while the luggage was taken from the hold, recognised, redeemed, and hoisted upon the roof of a gloomy old four-wheeler. Horse and vehicle looked ancient, but the driver, a wild bearded fellow, made up for them with excess of animation. In one sentence he exhorted the porter, re-assured Granny and Dermot's mother, and made impolite re-plies to a disappointed rival and a couple of outside car drivers, who persisted mechanically in offering their services. The mis-givings of the ladies were not allayed. Nothing but the diffi-culty of getting the big trunks down again kept them from changing their mind and seeking a more sober convoy. Finally, when it seemed to Dermot that they must all be going to spend the rest of their lives upon the noisy quay, he was bundled in, and off they started. At once a fresh noise made speech impossible. The iron tyres of the four-wheeler ground deafeningly over the cobbles, and the whole vehicle shook and rattled till the passengers' teeth chattered in their heads. It was like thunder. It was like dogs growling. It was like a hundred stormy nights at once: and out of the window, through the dirty shivering glass, danced distorted, fantastic visions of great ships beside the quay, wobbling and joggling on and on for ever.

Swish—grrr—plonk. The cab swung away to the left, off the cobbles, on to a smooth hard road. The grown-ups smiled at one another in relief, plaintively, and settled themselves in easier positions. It was possible to speak.

Granny beamed lovingly at Dermot.

"Well, little son," she said, "and how are you, after your long journey?"

"Very well, thank you, Granny." Her voice made Der-mot remember his questions. When he wanted to say any-thing of his own accord, he could never get it out straight away. He did not stammer: he paused, looked as if he were going to swallow, and opened his mouth for a moment before the sound came. So Granny, once he had answered, turned to his mother to hear her explain how well the children had weathered the trip. He had to slide off the seat and catch her arm, to make her listen.

"Please, Granny."

"Yes, darling son. What is it—only sick the once, coming

round the Longships. Do you tell me that!— There's me
brave son. Only sick the once."

"Granny."

"Yes, son?"

"Please—how is Paddy?"

"Paddy?" Granny's face went blank for a moment, as
she sorted a host of Paddies. "Oh, *Paddy*! Paddy-monkey!
Is it the monkey ye mean, son?"

"Yes. How is he?"

"Faith, son, he's grand. Full of life and spirits. Too full.
He got away on us the other day, climbed up the pear tree
by the wall, and took your Grandpapa's toothbrush, that
was out drying on the windowsill. Oh, he's well enough.
Well and bold."

Dermot contemplated the monkey's escapade.

"How is Pucker?" he asked next.

Granny beamed.

"She's well. And she has a grand surprise for you."

"A surprise?"

"Yes, a grand surprise. You'd never think it, and she only
a little thing last year, coming in on the bed every morning
to play with you. What do you think—she has a little tiny
kitten of her own!"

"Pucker has a kitten?"

"A little wee kitten, and its eyes only opened just in time
for you."

Dermot's brows drew together.

"Its eyes, Granny?"

But Granny's attention was diverted. They were on
cobbles again, and getting near to Westland Row, where
they must catch the train to Sandycove and Granny's
house. Grandpapa would be at the gate. Grandpapa was
usually at the gate, in Dermot's outdoor memories of him:
either watching for the tram, when he went in to work in
the morning, or coming in from the tram, when it brought
him back in the evening. Dermot had been a very little boy
last year. His memories were not at all continuous.

Then followed more noise and tumult, the dismounting of the luggage, the paying of the cab. The man was gabbling and Granny was saying finally, "Nonsense, me man, nonsense, you're well paid," over and over again, till he retired and climbed on his box, shouting a commiseration to the porter who had undertaken their load. Then, the dark noisome cavern of the station, the yelling, the barrows of luggage: and finally, when they were more or less settled to await the train, the appalling shriek of an engine, which woke the baby and set her crying. All crowded round to comfort her, taking no notice of Dermot, who stood very pale and serious, staring straight before him, with big shining eyes. At last he slipped up close beside his mother. Realising, she squeezed his hand.

"Poor little son," she whispered, half laughing, half sympathetic. "Did the horrid engine frighten him?"

"N-not exactly," he whispered back. "But I didn't like it, very much."

She gave him a reassuring squeeze: and then, before much else could happen, their train came in. Dermot disapproved of the hard, bleak carriages, with their strip of baize nailed on a wooden seat, and the partition which did not go all the way up to the top. The edge of the seat was cold against the inside of his bare knees. He frowned, and wriggled in shocked discomfort. English railway carriages were not like this. His mother, aware of him again, smiled in humorous tenderness. Dermot understood that she was inviting him to laugh at the hard, bare carriage. He smiled dutifully back: then his brow cleared.

Before long, a demented whistling and shouting announced that the train was to start. Granny took a last look out of the window, to make sure that none of the luggage was left behind: the train gave a jerk, and they were off. It clattered past the backs of dingy houses, considerately veiling some of them with puffs of its own steam; then came trees, gardens, open lawns; and soon it was racing along beside the sea. Ca-CLACKET, ca-CLACKET, ca-CLACKET—loud and monotonous the train's noise beat against the low sea wall, echoing back flatly into the carriages. Granny gave up trying to talk. She sat gazing at her daughter and her grandchildren, her face trembling into smile after smile of delight. For a glorious two months she would have them to herself again. And Dermot's mother, exhausted with the long trip, smiled back at her, glad to be in the place she still called home.

CHAPTER II

GRANDPAPA WAS STANDING AT THE GATE, LOOKING OUT FOR
them. He stood with his hands clasped behind his back,
leaning a little forward. He smiled when he saw them, and
then began to look anxiously up and down, to see if a tram
was coming. That was always a difficulty, when the tram-
line went past one's door. Any vehicle delivering luggage
had to make haste about it, or else pull two or three times to
the other side of the road, to let the tram go by. As for delivering furniture—it was a nightmare. Grandpapa would be
irritated and indignant when, in the middle of the unloading,
the great tram came clanking round the curve, and the man
stamped impatiently on his bell: but, as he was above all a
law-abiding man, part of his irritation would be due to being
put in the position of a person distracting the tram's lawful
course. Later on, that same summer, small though he was,
Dermot could feel perfectly his Grandpapa's concern on such
an occasion, and keep watch in a fever of anxiety for the yellow
and blue front appearing round the trees.

But, this time, all was well. In a sort of dream, Dermot
was lifted down, doubling up his legs to avoid the circular
iron step of the cab. He felt the tickle of his Grandpapa's
beard on his cheek, saw the tiny neat garden with its stock
and mignonette, the trim window boxes, the clean wash
of the cottage walls: all in a dream, because his mind was
fixed on Paddy-monkey and Pucker the cat, and because,
though he did not realise it, he was very tired. Finding himself alone, as Grandpapa pressed forward to the others, he
walked up the little stone path, climbed the two high steps, and

went, blinking, into the dark hall. Before his eyes could accustom themselves to the darkness, it was blocked by a stout, chanting figure, holding wide arms of welcome—Bessie, the cook.

"Oh, oh, musha! Master Dermot asthore! The grand big size y'are! The big boy! And Baby Miss Eithne! Well now, well now, indeed."

She hugged him, and put him down, pressing forward to the door.

"Oh, Miss Margaret, ma'am. To see ye agen! Welcome home, welcome home."

Dermot stood, by the big grandfather clock, waiting for the tempest of exclamation to die down. His desire to rush through and out to the back of the house, to greet Paddy-monkey and Pucker, had left him. He felt strange and lost in the dark hall. They were all exclaiming round the baby, blocking out the light, blocking up everything. The man could not get by with the luggage.

Then, abruptly, the assembly awoke to business. Dermot was bundled into the nursery, to be out of the way: and before he could do anything, his nurse Munny took him, and washed his face and hands. She did it instinctively, as the first of many necessary things to be done. While the sponge was obliterating his face, and the towel scrubbling his limp hands, he could hear the heavy steps of the cabman, and the thudding of the boxes. He gave a deep sigh, felt suddenly much better, and smiled up at Munny.

There was a little bit of creeper hanging down outside the window. It had flowers on it. He liked it. He was going to be here for a long, long time.

"Munny."

"Yes, darling."

"May I go and see Paddy-monkey now, and Pucker, and her new kitten?"

"Yes, dear. Go into the kitchen and ask Bessie. You remember the way, don't you."

What a silly question. "Yes."

"Mind that horrid monkey doesn't bite you," Munny called after him. She said it more from duty than anything else: as a kind of protest against the enormity of keeping such a creature. Dermot stopped in the doorway.

"Paddy isn't horrid," he said, frowning. "And he wouldn't ever bite me."

"It's a long time since he saw you. You're bigger now. He may have forgotten you."

As she said it, Munny conjured up for her tired self a real apprehension. She followed him to the door, but was reassured by the sight of Bessie standing at the end of the passage, winking and nodding her head.

"Come on now, Master Dermot, till we go and see Paddy-monkey."

Dermot took her hand, and she led him through the little low kitchen, hung with every sort of shining pot and pan, up a step, into an even smaller white-washed scullery. Out the door, and a couple of steps along the path, to where Paddy-monkey lived, in a big dog kennel against the warm outside kitchen wall. Seeing the kennel, Dermot drew back. Suppose what Munny said was true, and Paddy didn't know him!

Bessie pulled him gently forward.

"Paddy-monkey! Paddy-monkey!"

At the croon of her voice a chain rattled, and a handsome black monkey bounded out from the kennel. A second bound took him to the roof. Seeing Dermot, he pulled himself up stiffly, and stared.

"Paddy-monkey! Here's Master Dermot come back to see you, dear Master Dermot. Sure, you mind him well!"

The monkey made a soft chattering sound. His eyes were fixed on Dermot.

"Go to him now, Master Dermot. Speak to him."

Pushed forward, Dermot advanced to the monkey, with outstretched hand. Very gently, the monkey took hold of it in both his own hands. He looked down at it closely, smelt it, looked up with quick enquiry in Dermot's face: then smelt his hand again, and made a little pleased noise.

"There, you see, Master Dermot! he knows you, sure he knows you."

Emboldened, Dermot reached out his other hand, and began to stroke the monkey. Paddy jumped, and looked up at him sharply again. Dermot smiled, his misgiving quite gone, and went on stroking. The monkey wrinkled his nose, swung down from the apex of the roof, and lay on his back to be tickled. Dermot fell on his knees beside him, and tickled him all over his soft tummy, and under his long arms. The monkey leaned back his head, chuckling and making ecstatic noises.

"There now, Paddy-monkey. Your little friend come back again to play with ye. Isn't that grand?"

Bessie beamed down upon them. She was devoted to the monkey, and all the more delighted by his good behaviour, in that there had been much discussion before the visitors came, and wonder if the monkey's temper could be trusted. Now, her advocacy was triumphantly justified.

"Come on, Master Dermot, and see Pucker. Then you must go in to your tea."

Up the orchard they went, to a little outhouse above the second tiny cottage which served as a lair for Katie, the seamstress. Calling softly, Bessie opened the door, and out of the darkness came the pretty young cat, mewing, glad of a visit.

"Look, till you see now, how she pucks her head, the way she always did."

Pucker's name was due to the ardour of her affectionate nature. Unable to wait till the caressing hand could reach her head, she "pucked" or butted up against it, "for all the world like a little goat," as Bessie had it.

"Look now for the little kitten. Here—there now, Pucker, there now. Sure, we wouldn't hurt it."

Dermot stooped in the gloom, and saw the tiny creature, its dark eyes open, shivering in the straw. He wanted to touch its head, but feared to frighten it. As he watched, it opened its tiny pink mouth in a soundless mew.

"There now, Pucker, there now."

The young mother rubbed anxiously against Bessie's fat arm, which was barring her way to the basket. The moment it was removed, she leaped in.

Bessie straightened up with a maternal grunt.

"Now then, Master Dermot. Your tea."

Dermot turned thankfully. He was hungry enough. The dining-room was reached with one interruption, Munny pouncing out from the nursery and insisting on washing his hands again after "that dirty animal." He was too happy to demur.

Once he caught sight of the big loaded table, his happiness increased. Nothing could so well express the difference between Granny's house and his own. Not only was the china all different, the tea-pot, the jugs, the sugar-basin, the pattern on the plates: but the actual food was different. There were things one never had for tea at home. There was cream, for instance, in a little fat jug with a sky-blue rim. There was brown sugar, as well as white. And, marvel of marvels, there was Grandpapa's place, laid for a mixture of meals so unlike anything Dermot had ever heard of, that it emphasised more than anything else the separateness and the mystery of Grandpapa, confirming his place as a legendary character. Grandpapa took his last meal of the day at six. He would start, as a rule, just after they had finished tea, for he liked to be alone and to have no fuss about him. For some reason, he would be in a state of nervousness when his meal was due, sitting down at the table, getting up again, pretending to read his newspaper, fingering his napkin, till Bessie came in with one of his favourite hot dishes—some stewed thing, to lie light on his stomach—and set it before him, comforting and admonishing him, as though

he were a child. Bessie was always very outspoken with
"the Master." She would often be heard in good-humoured
altercation with him. He grumbled, and rated her for an
ignorant, superstitious woman: but he did as she told
him.

To partake of this meal, Grandpapa needed an equip-
ment which seemed portentous. Dermot's world was small.
Anomalies on a large scale did not worry him. Either he did
not notice them, or they passed easily into the land of wonder, not yet clearly separated from the land of fact: but to
see knife and fork laid at a tea-table, with spoons for helping vegetables, was like the overturning of a kingdom.
Even more wonderful still was Grandpapa's moustache-
cup. Huge, patterned, thick, standing up solid in its wide
saucer: so heavy Dermot needed his two hands to lift it:
with its great bar of china at the top cutting it nearly in
half, and the small hole for the drink to trickle through:
it was as marvellous as any elf-king's goblet. If he had been
told that it had magic properties, and that with its aid
Grandpapa could fly to the moon, he would not have been
surprised.

There it stood, the most vivid, the most magnificent of
his memories, and there, in profusion upon the table, were
the other pieces he so well remembered. One or two—a
squat, heavy salt-cellar, for instance—he had forgotten,
till this moment of seeing them again. Then, as he sat up
on his chair, he was bidden look, there, in his own place,
under his nose. A tiny woollen cosy was whipped off, and
there, in a fat egg-cup, stood the brownest of brown eggs,
and a bone spoon to eat it with. The bone spoon was almost
flat. It made an egg last beautifully long, for you could not
get much on it at a time; and, when you came to the white,
fearful skill was needed, breathless feats of balancing. It
was Dermot's secret ambition to get all the white on his
spoon, in a single unbroken roll. This, he saw, would be impossible in Ireland; but he did not mind a bit. The bone

spoons were enough in themselves to compensate for anything. He sat looking down, in pure happiness.

"Is it the spoon, son? Would you like one of the other kind?"

"No, no—please, Granny." He coloured crimson. "I love this sort best."

"We have the others. (He's not used to them, the son.) Sure, I could get you one in a second."

"No—please."

"Very well then, son."

Hastily he began to eat, lest the change be made. The egg was lovely, with the fingers of soft, cool bread and butter. It took ages to eat, with the beautiful bone spoon.

CHAPTER III

W HEN DERMOT HEARD THE STORY OF THE GARDEN OF EDEN, he decided at once that it must have been just like Granny's garden. Indeed, the two were soon confused in his mind. It was necessary for him to identify any place of which he heard with a place he actually knew. Thus his home at Plymouth and the neighbourhood round Kingstown (as it then was) became the country of Moses, Elijah, Joseph, Jack the Giant Killer, Apollyon, Eric and Russell—for Dermot had encountered Dean Farrar's masterpiece at an earlier age than most small boys.

Granny's garden began with a small orchard. Just outside the back door, under the kitchen window, was a gigantic tub, full of water. Dermot sailed boats on the tub: he slipped, and got his sleeve wet, was scolded, had to come in and be changed, subjected all the while to a running fire of rebuke, which Bessie, fetched out by the commotion, would try to mitigate. Bessie, round and amiable, could be relied upon to sympathise in every misfortune. Beyond the tub, a little stone path on the right led past Paddy's kennel and the out-of-doors lavatory to the scullery door. The main path proceeded up the orchard, past Katie's hut, and a couple of outhouses, to the orchard wall. In the wall was a door, carefully (and quite uselessly) locked each night, which led to the garden proper.

This garden Dermot did not know so well. He spent much of his time this summer learning his way about it. It was very big, and there seemed no end to the marvels it contained. Flowers of every kind grew there, and vegetables.

17

There were innumerable arches, nooks, and seats. There was a greenhouse, a sundial stand, a vast manure heap screened by sycamores and a yew hedge, and an unkept croquet lawn. By this lawn stood two antiquated and long-disused iron posts for holding a tennis net; a swing: and a summerhouse. The whole garden was a thin, uneven oblong. It sloped gently downhill, and ended in a small flat meadow. Across the top, outside the hedge enclosing the orchard, ran a wide path, part paved, part cobbled, and mostly nothing. Then came frames for cucumbers, tomatoes, and vegetable marrows. From here, four paths ran down, till you came to a wide belt of currant and gooseberry bushes. Two-thirds of the space between these paths were devoted to flowers, the rest to vegetables, with a narrow strip of grass supporting a clothes-line. On the left of the garden, level with the currant bushes, was a short yew hedge, with a rustic seat under it, and a heavy metal table, where, on very fine days, they would sit and have tea. Below this level, each of the two middle paths turned sharply off outwards, and ran into the long paths on either side, so that the whole width of the garden could be given to potatoes. Below the potatoes, a last path completed the rectangle, and then there was the lawn and meadow, with its yield of four haycocks. A thick hedge of sycamores marked off the end of the meadow from the big common field beyond, which stretched for a quarter of a mile to the red houses of Glenageary.

Even in daylight Dermot had to get over a certain fear of the garden. If he confused it with the Garden of Eden, it was certainly after the Fall: for the beasts which roamed it were not on idyllic relations with mankind. Into the garden, from the poor districts around, from the fields and the woods, came numbers of cats, semi-wild, offspring of neglected house cats which had taken to the country in despair of getting a living. Fierce, marauding beasts they were, many of them, standing their ground and growling when they encountered the garden's lawful owners: though they had never been known to attack anyone. Dermot had shuddered to hear of these animals, which his imagination at once promoted to be monsters of the jungle, stealthy and terrible, with glaring eyes. To make matters worse, a temporary nursemaid had the year before played a thoughtless trick upon him. One evening, he had been up with her to the top of the orchard, getting the air before he went to bed. She opened the door, and as he peeped out into the perilous land, all huge and golden in the westering sunlight, suddenly, with a laugh, she pushed him through. The great door slammed behind him, and was held fast. He was alone, shut out, in the garden of terrors. At once his horrified eyes peopled the flower beds and bushes with dark prowling forms. He set up scream after scream of terror, but from the other side of the door came only mocking laughter. Then, when his screams sharpened to too wild a note, the girl opened it hastily, and let him in. For days afterwards she and Bessie laboured to reassure him: but they had hard work. His relations, of course, never heard of the incident.

Left to himself, therefore, Dermot did not care to go far from the house. When Mr. Caggen was working, it was different. Mr. Caggen was the gardener. He was lame— "by dint of a blow on the hip," as Bessie explained, "and he a young man." His handsome, saturnine face was covered, from the eyes down, in a long black beard; he wore a battered straw hat, which age and dirt had brought to the colour of brown paper. It was very reassuring to have him in the garden. For one thing, he did not in the least mind company, and was very communicative: for another, he was master of the cats. When one of them had the hardihood to appear, he stooped, and flung a stone at it. The sight of this, and the instant flight of the cat, its quick crouching run through the potatoes, helped mightily to banish Dermot's bogey.

"Them animals," said Mr. Caggen, rubbing the side of his nose with his knuckle, for his hands were all over mould, "I wanted to put down poison for them, but yeer Grandda wouldn't suffer me."

"Grandpapa," asked Dermot, later on in the same day; "why wouldn't you let Mr. Caggen put down poison for the cats?"

Grandpapa turned in the path, and gravely regarded his small grandson.

"Because, me child," he pronounced, in his slow, precise voice, "that would be a very cruel thing to go do."

"Oh."

"The Lord" continued Grandpapa, "has in His wisdom put these animals on the earth with us. As long as they do us no injury, it is our duty to live peaceably alongside with them, as with our neighbours."

"Mr. Caggen"—the voice was very soft, little more than a whisper, for Dermot was in great awe of Grandpapa— "Mr. Caggen says they have the beds destroyed on him."

"Mr. Caggen," replied Grandpapa, "is an ignorant poor man, and I don't wish for you to be copying his ways of speech."

All the same, there was a secret understanding between Dermot and Mr. Caggen on the subject of cats, confirmed with a wink from the gardener, when one evening, as Grandpapa was giving him directions, a cat went by unmolested in full view of them.

The little greenhouse at the top of the garden was not attractive. It was scorchingly hot, and smelled of the dried onions which lay about the shelves. But the summerhouse! No words could express the delights of this place. To begin with, it was very seldom used. Its porch was stone paved, with a roof of creepers, through which, here and there, one could see a tiny chink of sky. This porch was dark, rather damp, and smelt a little musty. The summerhouse proper, a room with tables, chairs, and a bench round the wall, was opened in very fine weather when there were visitors to tea. Sometimes, on a wet afternoon, they would come down themselves in mackintoshes from the house, and have tea there, just for variety. It had a bulging, sagging roof of painted canvas, held up by straps of sailcloth, and thin boards, and was festooned with legends, "Welcome to Ireland," "Cead Mil Failtê," "No Place Like Home," duplicates of those which Bessie put up in the house for the first day of their coming. Dermot had once heard a lady visitor whisper shudderingly to her escort something about earwigs. This he took as a vile aspersion, a horrible example of adult wickedness: the sort of thing the grown-ups who didn't go to church said in *Probable Sons* and in the stories Munny read him from the Sunday Magazine. He had come within an ace of repeating it indignantly to Granny, but a recent experience made him hesitate. Sitting in Granny's little drawing-room, and suddenly realising that the cottage was far, far smaller than Mummy and Daddy's house at home, he had informed Granny of the fact.

"Our house is *much* bigger than yours, Granny. We have lots of rooms, and big stairs. Our drawing-room is twice as big as this one, Granny."

He had said it, not boasting, but as the giver of interesting information. Granny smiled sadly.

"Is it, son?" she said.

Later, in the garden, Dermot's mother had come to him, and told him he had done a very wrong thing.

"But I didn't *mean* it that way at all," he cried, aware of pitfalls he had never suspected. "I didn't *mean* to hurt Granny's feelings."

"I'm sure you didn't, darling. Granny understands, really. You needn't say a word—"

But it was no use. To her private dismay, he broke away from her, rushed in wailing, and hid his face in Granny's ample skirts.

"Granny—I didn't *mean* . . ."

Perhaps, in the light of this dreadful experience, it might be as well to say nothing to Granny about the wicked lady's observation.

CHAPTER IV

THERE WERE AT GRANNY'S HOUSE A MINIMUM OF THE UN-
pleasant things which, in Dermot's experience, had always
to be done, no matter where one found oneself. One, very
definitely, was a walk along the East Pier in the wind. The
East Pier was perhaps three quarters of a mile long. Wide,
with two roads, on different levels, it ran out at an austere
right angle from the Marine Parade, past the dark wooden
mailboat pier, out and out, till even it began to lose its
assurance, looked for its larger brother the West Pier, saw
it, and ran to meet it. Thus thrust out from the shore, which
sloped gently upwards for a quarter of a mile or so, it was
exposed to every sort of wind: and the more boisterous
gusts, which it kept from the vessels in its lee, took their
revenge by whooping down its promenades and harrying
the luckless promenaders. They howled round the bandstand, invaded the shelters, eddied beneath the seats, and,
wherever there might be a gap in the rough coping of uncut
stone, they squirted through at an angle, flinging skirts into
disarray, whisking unguarded boaters into the harbour.
Dermot hated such winds anywhere. On the pier, they made
his walk a misery. To tag along slowly beside the pram,
cold and cross, with the added anguish of grit continually
blown against his bare knees, whipping and stinging them:
he grew to hate the pier, even though, on warm still days, it
afforded so much entertainment.

First, at the foot of it, was Mr. Hogan, a great red-faced
man in a jersey, who hired out boats. Then, parallel with
it, ran the mailboat pier, with the outgoing vessel at its

22

side, one of that slender, graceful quartette, all black and
dazzling white, which looked so beautiful, and were such
villainous sailors. When one tired of looking at her (having
deciphered her name—they were named after the four green
fields of Ireland), there were scores and scores of little boats
to look at, by the life-boat slip. That took one out as far as
the bandstand. Beyond that was moored, almost always, an
old ship of war; not grey, like the new ones, but black and
white and yellow; the *Melampus*, or sometimes—a hard
one to pronounce—the *Call-i-o-pe*. Dermot could say her
name now, thanks to Grandpapa. He read it off, by the
way carelessly, to Munny, every time she was in. In Horse
Show Week, the harbour was full of rich men's yachts,
elegant, slender vessels all in white, with a yellow funnel
and golden scroll-work on the stern. For the most part,
these were drawn up on the other side of the harbour: but
the biggest and loveliest of them all, the *Erin*, which Grandpapa declared to be "the property of Sir Thomas Lipton,"
was moored near the *Melampus*. The only trouble was that
Munny would not stop long enough for him to look at this
wonderful ship, nor allow him to wait by himself, while she
pushed the pram on to the walk's end, and came back.

They never went to the end of the pier, this year. It was
supposed to be too far. At the end was a lighthouse, rocks,
steps, a variety of attractive things, under a high sheltering
wall. Thus the pier walk was an often disagreeable means
which never led to any desirable end.

The other unpleasant thing was going to church on Sunday morning. Dermot had no objection to church as such.
He rather enjoyed it, at home. At home, however, it was
a comparatively simple matter. Here, it was surrounded
with a fearsome degree of ceremonial, which filled the entire morning. First of all, there was the uncomfortable and
inhibiting stiffness of best clothes. Dermot rarely spilled food
over himself: he had a kind of manual daintiness in that
respect: but Sunday breakfast was always spoiled by these

added reasons for not spilling anything. After breakfast, he was kept hanging about in the nursery, till it was time for him to be "got ready." Then—and this was the only nice part of the morning—he was turned into the garden, with strict injunctions not to go beyond the big cross-path outside the orchard, and wait there till he was called. This prohibition did not irk him. Having hitherto associated only with grown-ups, he was very law-abiding. Besides, he enjoyed wandering slowly up and down, trying to go the whole way across the garden treading on the cobbles only: then on the flat stones only: never succeeding, for he would always overbalance somewhere, or set himself too long a jump. The bells of Glenageary added to his entertainment by playing a selection of tunes, their practice for three quarters of an hour before the service. They played "Abide With Me" oftenest, but were hampered in their execution of it by the lack of one of the necessary accidentals. The difficulty was met boldly by substituting the nearest semi-tone. Dermot would look up, and frown, aware of an irregularity for which he could not account. Still, he liked the bells. They were appropriate, somehow, to his one private part of the morning. He stopped, in the middle of his balancing feats, and looked at the tall spire from where they came. It rose behind a terrace of red brick houses, surrounded by heavy trees. Above it, in the distance, was the sweep of the Dublin Mountains. They looked very far away. Wild land, suspect, as being the home of cats even larger and fiercer than those who prowled the alley.

Presently a firm step would sound on the stone path, the orchard door would open, and Granny would issue forth. Granny always carried herself well and boldly; but, on Sundays, she was magnificent. The ribbons of her black but jaunty bonnet, tied beneath her chin, jutted out proudly on her full, broad bosom. Her bead cape seemed to Dermot three or four bead capes, so nobly did it hang: with the rustle of her skirts, the hissing of her satins, the clicking of her beads, and the determination of her gait, she sailed out into the garden like some grand, majestic ship, in undaunted mourning for a lost armada. Even her face seemed set in more resolute lines. It was as if the Sabbath, entering into her, filled her easy-going spirit with an uncommon dignity. Armed with that holy confidence, she feared no man's rebuke. Yet Granny, as even Dermot could see already, was gentle and indulgent to a fault. She had no pride, no thought of self, and was the credulous victim of a whole colony of unfortunates who battened in rotation upon her charity. She was too soft hearted to be a grand lady, except on Sunday morning.

In this high spirit, she would summon Dermot to help her cut some sprigs of lavender from one of the big umbrella bushes half way down the garden. Producing a long scissors from some royal fold, she would with a few imperious waves of it disturb the crowd of butterflies, bees, and other insects which had business about the bush, snip off a few choice flowers, and return to the house. There, she would lay them out upon a table, cut the stalks even, and double them back upon the flower. Each church-goer was presented with one, to put inside his handkerchief. Then—expedition number two—she must go, still with her scissors, to take a sprig of verbena from the wall outside the nursery. This was likewise divided, into single leaves, one for each prayer-book. Towards the end of this operation, Grandpapa would descend from the bedroom, and stand in the hall, brushing his top hat. The hall was never light enough, but he always began brushing the hat there, grumbled, and took it in to the dining-room window.

"Are ye ready, Alfred?"

"I am, Amelia."

"Do you think, is it time we were starting?"

"It wants"—a pause—"it wants but seventeen minutes of eleven, and the tram is not due till the quarter."

Then—as always—Grandpapa would go down to the

gate, and look over it up the road, ready to signal, by urgent and dignified pantomime, the first approach of the tram.

Meanwhile, Dermot's unwilling hands would have been forced into stiff, hateful kid gloves, his sailor hat given a final twist—so that the elastic galled his chin—and his wide silk sailor tie given a final pull. He was "ready." Dermot's mother drifted through all this ritual, which had held good since her childhood, with a humorous acquiescence. She smiled indulgently at Dermot, at Granny, at everybody. That was the way she took things, over here. The responsibility off her shoulders, she relaxed, and watched all about her with an affectionate amusement.

The tram, when it stopped to admit Granny and her party, was seen to be full of old ladies and gentlemen, all likewise on their way to church. Once Granny had seen her charges seated, and could look round, there was a deal of bowing and smiling, and a lifting of silk hats. This little ceremony, for some reason, irritated Grandpapa. He preferred to walk. Only when his gout attacked him, and the half mile was too much, would he perforce endure it, with a very ill grace.

The tram seemed quite different on a Sunday. It was, in fact, the same tram: this Dermot proved to his own satisfaction, by the number: but it, too, seemed transformed by Sunday airs. Probably it was the costume of the travellers, the scent of lavender and leather gloves, defeating the tram's week-day smell, making it for the moment a long drawing-room, an inconvenient salon, where the graces of intercourse were cramped by distance, posture, and the solemnity due to the occasion. Courtly old gentlemen, sitting with their knees wide apart, their hands clasped on the upright walking stick between them, might incline stiffly quarter right, and enquire after the health of "Mrs. Conroy, ma'am": but even that courtesy cost them a painful constriction at the neck. Mercifully, the period of waiting was short. The conductor had barely time to take their pennies when they were at the church. Then, he might rest from the exertion, for twenty old ladies and gentlemen in their Sunday clothes were not to be hustled off a tram in the year nineteen hundred and one. When the tram had well and truly stopped, the church-goers would arise, stiffly, and with some parade of mutual assistance. Next came a polite mutual surrender of precedence, causing, in the narrow gangway, almost as great difficulty as a panic. Only one person could alight from the tram at a time, and all the ladies got down backwards—while to such old gentlemen as had already achieved the conductor's platform was presented the distressing alternative of remaining where they were, in everybody's way, or of getting off before a lady. It all required two minutes, if not three: and the conductor, child of his age and clime, stood in the road, helping the ladies in all friendliness and respect, by the guidance of his arm or the official assurance of his person and uniform; confirming Christian ratepayers in their belief that all was well, and that the tram, marvel of an enlightened age, yet creature of their needs, would not proceed until the last of them had been safely deposited in the road.

To Dermot, all this happened as part of the awful, established order of life. Child as he was, he missed scarcely a detail of it: but for him it meant nothing but Sunday Morning At Granny's. To the very young, if one may borrow a phrase from the theatre, all parts are straight parts. The notion of character comes later. All Dermot's senses were busy, gathering data about his surroundings, in order that he might be able to cope with them: in order that he might know how to behave. Church at home had ceased to be frightening, because he knew, now, what happened there. Church here was different. Timidly, eagerly, he memorised the differences, holding tight to his mother's hand, grateful even to have crossed the road without the need for any action on his own part. The arrival of baby Eithne had thrown him forward upon the world. He was "a big boy" now.

Decisions had to be taken, facts confronted. . . . He shifted his grip of his mother's hand. The kid glove was hot and sticky. They were at the church gates. Remembering from last week, he let go, unwillingly, timidly, and took two steps forward to Granny, just as she was turning to call him. His mother's hand encouraged him, delivered him over with a little squeeze of understanding. He knew, in the moment of letting go her hand, that she was glad he had remembered, of his own accord. Fortified, he braced himself to suffer.

"Ah, Mrs. Conroy!" The speaker seemed afflicted by a permanent hysterical giggle. Her speech shook like a jelly. "And this is yeer little man! I declare to goodness, he's grown—so—*big*! And yeer daughter! She must be proud of him. And another one, too! A girl! Isn't that grand! Margaret, dear, I was saying to yeer mother, you must be proud of the two o' them!"

Fascinated, Dermot watched the agitation of her beads, her cape, and the lilac ribbons which daringly enlaced her poke bonnet. Then he jumped. The spout of her conversation was turned his way.

"And do you like being over here? Do you like your holiday?"

He swallowed, and opened his mouth. Before the words would come, the lady straightened up again, and answered the question herself.

"Indeed, and I'm sure ye do, with yeer dear Grandmother to look after ye all so well. Sure, it's better than being in England, now, isn't it? Ah, sure, Margaret me dear, you only have to see him. He's a proper little Irishman already."

To all this Granny assented graciously, at the same time conveying, by a certain majesty in her demeanour, that a time had come for more serious considerations. Miss O'Killikelly's enthusiasms were always a little deprecated by her. So loud a voice, so buoyant a manner, were considered unsuitable for a church path, and indeed for many another social occasion, but condoned for the sake of the lady's goodness of heart, and her invaluable qualities as church worker.

"Well: I'll see ye all afterwards," giggled Miss O'Killi-kelly, nodding delightedly, and withdrawing into the main door of the church.

Granny's pew was at the side. St. Patrick's was cruciform. At the top of the shaft was the choir, the organ, and the communion table. (Anyone who called it an altar would have been for ever debarred from entering the doors again.) In the cross-piece, facing each other across the chancel, and in the higher part of the shaft, sat the chosen, those who rented pews. Below them sat less exalted parishioners, and, at the very end, were some four or five benches for the accommodation of casual worshippers. When her summer visitors came, Granny had an arrangement whereby she could borrow a couple of seats in the pew in front of hers, from a lady who spent the summer months elsewhere. Dermot did not know in which pew he would rather not sit. To be in front with Granny, in the very front pew of all, was to be conspicuous, marked down as Granny's grandson by the whole host of her friends, his behaviour watched, his fumblings noted; with Grandpapa's voice praying behind him, loud and penetrating, a word after everyone else in the General Confession, in the Litany, in the Creed and at the end of each line in the hymns. This last did not matter so much. Grandpapa was once a fine singer; he had still the melodious ghost of a tenor voice, and it expired, regularly, less a voice than a sigh, the backwash of a smaller wave which has broken after the others. Dermot's mother, who had inherited the gift of song, hardly sang at all in church: and Granny had a habit of swinging gently from side to side when she sang, much as a professional singer turns to give each side of the hall the benefit of her voice— though this, needless to say, was not Granny's motive. On the other hand, Mr. O'Shea the churchwarden would himself carry the plate for the front pew to put in their offerings:

whereas in the second pew it was handed along by the worshippers, a proceeding which filled Dermot with the extremity of nervous anguish. Grandpapa's hand shook so: suppose he were to drop it! Dermot's fears (which impelled him to drop in his own threepence from a height, as if the plate were red hot) increased from Sunday to Sunday, stalking away behind him, following the plate's progress from palsied hand to hand, till at last—oh merciful relief!—Mr. O'Shea's returning footsteps could be heard, and he stood, stiff and pompous, waiting his turn to fall in with the five other gatherers of tribute, and march in virtuous procession to deposit his gleanings upon the vast brass salver extended by Canon M'Gonigal.

The Canon himself, the choir, the organ, and the general conduct of the service, were as yet outside Dermot's range. They existed for him as the constituents of a vague blur of sounds and tableaux: Canon M'Gonigal in the pulpit, a handsome, imposing silhouette: warm floods of tone, lights, attitudes: and above all, the great stained window, showing Jesus walking on the waves. This grew clearer and clearer to the child. He stared at it, never tired of noting its details: the dark, labouring ship, the little green curled waves, more like cauliflowers than the sea as Dermot knew it; the dark green clouds, St. Peter tidily sinking, and in the midst of all, Jesus, in splendid robes of crimson, looking down at St. Peter, with one hand uplifted, and saying—as was written below, on scrolls, at queer angles and levels—"It is I. Be not afraid."

One day, gazing at the window, with the drone of the sermon in his ears, Dermot realised that the moments he dreaded were approaching. Soon Canon M'Gonigal must finish, and then—the ordeal of the plate. Looking up, in a sweat of anguish, he was suddenly struck by the message of the window. "Be not afraid." He stared, his mouth opened—then, in a great cool wave, he understood. It was meant for him too. In his relief he smiled, he looked around upon the worshippers, he almost spoke aloud. He must have moved involuntarily in his seat, for Granny, recalled from some far reverie, put out her hand with a dreamy smile, and touched his arm. He smiled back at her, radiantly. When the plate came, he looked at it, then up from it at the massive contours of Mr. O'Shea, and wondered how he could ever have been afraid.

After church, there was a regular orgy of sociability on the gravel. One after another, beaded and bonneted old ladies exclaimed over him, asking him questions so idiotic, so far removed from his notions of reality, that with the glibbest tongue in the world he could not have known how to answer them.

"Aah, he's shy!" commented the ladies audibly, among themselves: whereupon one added, "Aah, sure, he wouldn't be shy of *me*. Would you now, Dermot? Why—do ye know: I knew your dear Mother when she was no bigger than yourself. Didn't I, Margaret?"

"Indeed, you did, Miss Geoghegan."

"I was telling Dermot here I'd known his mother since she was a little child, smaller than himself."

"Oh, yes, to be sure."

"Aye." Miss O'Killikelly hovered ecstatically on the outskirts of the gathering. She assumed, somehow, a proprietary attitude towards the family's doings, which she mitigated by her extreme humility: alternately intruding and apologising, with a giggle, for her existence. It would be difficult to snub Miss O'Killikelly, even if Granny had the wish or the severity to do so: and she had neither, for the voluble little old lady, in addition to her parochial activities, was a marvellous gossip, with the rarer commendation that there was not in her whole nature one germ of malice. Certain classes, certain countries Miss O'Killikelly lumped together in one fierce damnation; but at the sight of a single member of them, she would instantly forget her principles, and be incapable of anything but an unsparing officious activity of kindness. Dermot did not like her, because she embarrassed him, and spat, quite unintentionally, in his face.

The married ladies of the parish might patronise Letitia O'Killikelly, but they were often dependent on her, for gossip, for friendly help, and, in real trouble, for a sudden shrewdness which sobered the beaming apple face, and revealed an experience of life not to be reconciled with her everyday exterior. Now, they smiled in her direction, and back at Granny, signifying in a glance their understanding, their Christian charity, and their appreciation of Mrs. Conroy's goodness in allowing Miss O'Killikelly to bask within the radiance of her offspring.

These conversations ended, Granny and Dermot's mother went out and joined Grandpapa. In distaste for such reunions, he waited inside the gate of the People's Park until his womenfolk should see fit to join him. Miss O'Killikelly's raptures he found particularly unpleasing. A prejudice against that lady was one of many characteristics with which Granny had to contend in him.

Church did not end the day's solemnities for Dermot. There was still Sunday dinner. To this feast one or two guests were bidden, usually old ladies. Sometimes they would be chosen from among Granny's parochial peers, sometimes from those whom it was "a kindness" to invite. In these latter cases the scale of measurement was financial, not social. The etiquette of both time and place enjoined that, however kindly one might use one's social inferiors elsewhere, they could never be admitted as guests to one's house. When Dermot grew older, he was to perceive that, in reality, his childhood went far, far back into the eighteen-sixties and the eighteen-fifties. In a provincial, decadent form, this era lasted in Dublin well into the early nineteen hundreds. It was maintained by a class numerically and spiritually narrow, a tiny, black-coated incubus, a ruling caste: the Protestant well-to-do, in whose hands was vested all influence, all authority, all patronage: a class so deeply, so instinctively prejudiced that Grandpapa, the most charitable of men, who would pick up a worm from the path for fear it should be trodden, cried out indignantly if a strange Catholic approached his door. Yet his cook, his gardener, all his servants were Catholics. He treated them with the utmost consideration and kindness, and they bore him no ill-will for his opinions, which they found as much a fact as the facts of wealth and poverty, birth and humble living.

The menu for Sunday dinner was selected invariably from a range of three dishes. Boiled chickens with parsley sauce: boiled ham and cabbage: boiled leg of mutton, carrots, and caper sauce. None of these Dermot liked, but worst of all was having to sit still through the interminable meal, listening with distaste to the avid champing of the indigent guests, or the conversation of the well-to-do, with every muscle in his body crying to run out into the garden, to play with Paddy-monkey, to be away out of it all. And, once away, he often got a vicarious revenge, with Paddy-monkey as the unlikely instrument. The outdoor lavatory, added to the old cottage by a more hygienic generation, stood directly opposite the monkey's kennel. Its doorway was well within the range of his chain. Paddy was always resentful of strangers, and played up with redoubled vigour if he saw that they were afraid of him. When, after dinner, guests required to visit the lavatory, Paddy would rush out at the first sound of a strange voice, the first hissing of alien satin, and bar their approach. Therefore, they had to be escorted to the haven. Granny guided them as far as the door, but, as she could hardly hang about outside, Dermot, being too young "to matter," would be charged to restrain the gibbering Paddy till the return journey had been safely made. The first time he was so instructed, and once or twice afterwards, he released Paddy as soon as the visitor was inside, and retreated to wait developments. The sound of the cistern emptying was a signal as well understood by the monkey as by the boy, and the unhappy lady would open the door to find her egress barred by a black leaping shape, holding the threshold with exaggerated demonstrations of ferocity. Dermot would remain deaf to her appeals for aid, till Granny sailed out to see what was the matter: but there was no ignoring her imperious call, and he would come reluctantly to hold the culprit while Miss O'Whoever-she-was made her tremulous escape. Granny was well able to deal with Paddy herself, and he was devoted to her, but she did not wish to pick him up in her Sunday finery. For years afterwards, the image of an old lady holding up her skirts and revealing several inches of lilac petticoat, before a leaping, gibbering monkey, served to solace Dermot for many social sufferings. That Paddy enjoyed the joke, and was not angry at all, was clear from the fact that he never resented Dermot's catching him, nor struggled to escape when caught, though all the time, for the visitor's benefit, he kept up a stream of furious maledictions. As soon as she had gone, he would look up at Dermot with an almost human twinkle, and bound happily enough to the ground. His real rages were quite different.

CHAPTER V

Dermot and Paddy were by now fast friends. By degrees, seeing that the monkey did him no harm, the grown-ups relaxed their hostility. Only Grandpapa made difficulties. Taking Dermot close to the kennel, and then petting him with theatrical expressions of affection—"In order, d'ye see, to show ye the jealousy of the animal"—he risked bringing on what they all feared. Left to himself, Paddy was perfectly good tempered. If ever Dermot went too far, the monkey seized his finger and gripped it tight in his small black paw, uttering a shrill gibber of warning, and staring furiously into Dermot's face. The hint was taken, and harmony prevailed.

Granny had obtained her unlikely pet in an unlikely way. The cottage next door, a lowlier dwelling, went with Granny's. It was entirely separate, with a small garden of its own: and her habit was to let it to some poorer parishioner. One such tenant took as paying guest a negro, and the negro, unused to Irish winters, fell ill with congestion of the lungs. Granny, as a matter of course, ministered unto him. On his departure, cured, in the spring, he came grinning from ear to ear, and begged her to accept the only present he had it in his power to make—a young black monkey. To please him, she took it, intending to get rid of it at the first opportunity. It was affectionate and gentle, and she could not help liking it. Then Bessie entreated that it should stay, and that settled the matter. The formal expostulations of Grandpapa grew more and more formal —"Mark me words, Amelia, that animal won't rest till it

35

has done someone a mischief"—and Paddy stayed. So far, Grandpapa's prophecy remained unfulfilled.

The monkey, a light-hearted little creature, grew healthy and happy. Living out of doors, he kept himself very clean. This was his second summer with Granny. The winter, bane of animals from southern countries, he had survived well. The kitchen wall kept his kennel warm, and Bessie, solicitous as any mother, supplied him with hot-water bottles, round which he curled himself, in his thick bed of straw, and slept through the long, cold nights. Bessie wanted to bring him into the kitchen, but there Granny drew the line. Perhaps because of his youth, Paddy survived, grew strong and hardy, and became an accepted member of the household.

Dermot played with him by the hour. Boy and monkey sat together, quite solemnly, in that satisfying companionship which is the secret of children and young animals. Sometimes they would play with a ball, or romp around together: but, usually, they seemed just to be keeping one another company. Pucker's kitten, when she grew a little bigger, made a third. The monkey lost his heart to her altogether, though his attentions were not always pleasing to the kitten. He would lure her into his range by intriguing motions of his tail and paws, which any self-respecting kitten must at once investigate. Once he had caught her his idea was to nurse her in his arms. This at first suited the kitten very well, but as she grew more active she would resent being held in one position, and mew for release. Then Pucker would approach in a fury. She and Paddy were not on very good terms. When each was small, their well-meaning elders, fearing jealousy, had kept them out of each other's way: and thus the natural alliance between the two had been frustrated. They did not fight, but kept each a wary eye on the other. When the kitchen door was shut, and she was obliged to pass by the kennel to get into the scullery, Pucker quickened her pace to a trot: and Paddy, with his devilish instinct, took to giving his chain a rattle as she passed, so that the trot became an undignified scoot for safety.

The first time she heard the kitten's cries, she flew at Paddy, making him drop his charge and run up the pear-tree above his kennel. By degrees, however, seeing that the little animal was not afraid, and often trotted up to him of her own accord, she ceased to trouble herself. In any case, the kitten was too frisky to be kept out of mischief. Soon she and the monkey were fast friends—their only differences occurring when the kitten protested beneath the analyses to which Paddy from time to time subjected her furry person.

Granny's other dependents, Katie, Mr. Caggen, and his corps of occasional assistants, were all frankly terrified of the monkey, and crossed themselves every time they had to pass up the orchard. Paddy, well aware of this, improved the occasion by rushing to the full limit of his chain, gesticulating, leaping up and down, and flinging his tin mug after their hurrying feet.

Mr. Caggen, being lame, was an especially good target.

"Sacred Heart o' Jasus, Sacred Heart o' Jasus, Sacred Heart o' Ja—" He stopped, out of range, and mopped his brow. "That rompin' divil'll get loose on us one day, Master Dermot—and then where'll we all be?"

"He's quite harmless, Mr. Caggen." Bessie smiled, as she heard the clear deliberate voice through the kitchen window. "He wouldn't do anyone any harm. He only likes to pretend."

"Faix, then, I wouldn't trust him. A haythen sort of an animal, to be havin' about the place."

"Oh no, Mr. Caggen. He's quite friendly. Look."

But Mr. Caggen turned from the sight, and limped off muttering, to exchange comment with his queer subordinate, Jem Neill.

Sunday afternoon had other diversions, however, besides Paddy's inhospitable treatment of the lady visitors. Round about tea-time, Dermot's cousins from Dalkey would come down, accompanied sometimes by Uncle Ben himself.

There were four cousins, but two came more often than the others, and to these two Dermot's adoration was freely given: Con, a great handsome fellow of twenty-one, with the mind and antics of a schoolboy, and Eileen, some four or five years younger, a streeling long-legged girl with delicate features and light, clear-blue eyes. The arrival of these two, whether their father followed them or not, meant tea in the garden. Eileen's first action, on her arrival, was sufficient to stamp her as a goddess in Dermot's eyes. She unhooked Paddy's chain, and went flying off down the garden with him, the delighted monkey gambolling along on all fours beside her, like a dog on a lead. Seldom though she saw him, their understanding was complete. He submitted to her without protest, letting himself be hauled ignominiously from all sorts of pleasing refuges; sitting on her shoulder; running full tilt with her all round the paths; and eating, with the completest trust, whatever she gave him. He seemed to know that he was only out on sufferance, and that such escapes depended on his good behaviour. He knew, too, that his benefactress would stand no nonsense: and confounded the elder members of the party, Grandpapa included, by his demureness and docility. Con, who was quite irresponsible, would attempt privily to excite him, but the monkey paid no attention. Uncle Ben, when he came, late, by himself, bellowing a nautical hail down the garden, would sit down opposite the monkey and at once submit his bald head for inspection. He loved to feel the little paws delicately fingering his scalp. There was in one place a small mole, or stain on the skin. No amount of experience would convince Paddy that this was a fixture, and he would try, gently at first, and then more forcibly, to remove it. As soon as the monkey found this spot, Uncle Ben would begin to laugh. He would shake and splutter, cramming his great red fist into his mouth, until at last he would burst out in a roar which sent Paddy hopping back in affright.

"Oh, there now, me little Paddy boy! Did I scare ye? Come here to me, then. Come on. Sure I didn't mean to scare ye."

Watching him, and chattering gently, the monkey would come slowly back. Uncle Ben would then take him in his arms, tickle him, pat him, and give him a lump of sugar: and Paddy would lie right back, looking up with his bright eyes into the blue of the sky, in perfect happiness.

The whole proceeding so outraged Grandpapa that he would get up and leave the table, and walk about muttering till his indignation had subsided. To let a monkey explore one's head seemed to him contrary to the laws of decency, hygiene, and good sense.

"You're little better than a heathen, Ben," he said severely, seating himself again: "Little better than a heathen; or a black."

"Faith, Alfred," returned his guest, unabashed: "If I've no worse than that on me soul at the Last Day, I won't do too badly."

Grandpapa emptied his cup expressively, and passed it up for more.

"Now, me little Paddy here," pursued Uncle Ben, "is as clean as any one of us, in his way. Not a day passes, but he makes his toilet—and the little cat's too, if he can get a hold on it. There's nothing of the Pharisee about Paddy. He doesn't keep his virtues to himself. Here he'd be, investigating every inch of me, if I were in me pelt—"

"Daddy!" protested Eileen, scandalised.

Dermot's mother laughed her lazy, silvery laugh. Granny made business with the teapot. Dermot, conscious of the embarrassment around him, turned crimson.

"Control yourself, Ben," said Grandpapa severely. "That sort of talk may be all very well among sailor men, but ye should know this is no place for it."

"Forgive me, Amelia." Uncle Ben clasped his big hands in mock contrition, and looked very sorry indeed—for a couple of seconds—then exploded with laughter; exactly as Con did on similar occasions, though Con now sat embarrassed at his father. Yet, strangely enough, as Dermot soon found out, Uncle Ben was of a fanatical Puritanism, and allowed his own family little freedom of speech or action.

He was a man of extraordinary good looks, still in the prime of life, broad, strong, and hearty, with a ringing voice, a big fair moustache, eyebrows like wisps of hay, and the bluest of blue eyes. He had been a captain in the Merchant Service. When he retired, he placed his savings very skilfully in the half-share of a tea and wine merchants' business in Middle Abbey Street, where he now occupied himself, with Con as his assistant. Con had refused the advantages of Trinity College, which his elder brother Brian had embraced, preferring to join his father. Uncle Ben wore hairy tweed suits of green and grey, varied with nautical blue of a Sunday. The only part of him not quite in character was his singing voice. It should have been a rollicking bass: actually, it was a sentimental tenor.

Con was in some ways a replica of his father, though his looks were gentler. He was immensely strong, but had none of his father's bustling alertness. A natural indolence showed in his eyes, which were heavily lidded. It sounded also in his voice. He was capable of violent outbursts of energy, but had as yet little method or staying power.

Now, after watching Dermot idly for a minute or two, he rose from his chair, and led him off to play.

"Uncle Ben," said Dermot, stopping for a moment as he went.

"Yes, son?"

"Paddy has a pre-hensile tail."

He nodded towards the monkey, then turned, and trotted off after Con.

"Glory be to God!" exclaimed the mariner, scratching his head, and staring after him.

With the rest of his family, Con found the child difficult.

Dermot spoke with that clear, pedantic distinctness which some children achieve so effortlessly: he used long words, was aggressively "English," and did not respond to the usual easy gambits. Con, who was genuinely fond of children, and spent much of his free time playing with them, could make nothing of this solemn little owl. He asked him a few perfunctory questions, and received answers so precise and full that he was quite at a loss.

"Will I push you in the swing?" he asked at last.

"Yes, please do."

Dermot sat up, a frail figure, his wrists sticking out thin and white, as he grasped the ropes.

"Not too high, Con," came wavering cries from the ladies round the tea-table.

"No, no, that's all right," he called back impatiently. "Now, then."

With a hand that went all across Dermot's back, he gave him a shove. Not expecting it, Dermot slipped forward on the broad, smooth seat.

"Tell me, when it's high enough."

For an agonised minute Dermot was afraid that he was going to slip right off. He sat as tight as he could, feeling horribly insecure. Then, a stronger push sending him higher, he slipped back. So that was all right. Conscientiously, the fear removed, he tried to enjoy himself. Already his feet were going far, far above the branch of the laburnum which was his own private mark, when he swung himself. Why—gracious—they were almost at the topmost branch, the wildly impossible branch— He began to be frightened. At each swing back the remorseless hand was there to hurl him up still higher. He shut his eyes.

"P—pl—"

The cry would not come. He was sick, dizzy, breathless: the whole world rocked hideously, lunging to and fro, in flashes of green light. Another second, and he would let go —let go—let go—

"Is that high enough?"

Con's voice swung with the great sick lights. He tried to answer, and heard, far off, a clamour from the tea-table.

"All right, all right," called Con, in an offended voice. He caught Dermot, and slowed him down. The world stopped swinging, the lights ceased to leap, and the roaring left his ears. He opened his eyes. All was well and normal. Con was smiling, holding the swing still for him.

Sudden exhilaration and peace filled Dermot. He smiled back radiantly.

"You shouldn't go send the boy that dangerous height," remonstrated Grandpapa. He had left the group, and approached them.

"Ah, sure, Grandpapa, he was all right. You were all right, weren't you, Dermot?"

A glow of masculine pride, of complicity, warmed Dermot's heart.

"Of course I was," he answered.

"That's the boy."

Con and he wandered off through the garden, to the gooseberry bushes. Adult interference had brought them together.

"Ye mustn't mind your Granny too much," admonished Con, his mouth full of fruit. "She's always anxious, that way. She was the same with us, whenever we came here."

"I know. It's only natural for them to be anxious about me, because, you see, I'm not constitutionally very strong. I have to be rather careful."

A frown crossed Con's face.

"I wouldn't go worrying about that sort of thing, if I were you. It doesn't do to be wondering if you're able for this, that, or the other thing. Sure that's the way to make an invalid of yourself. *Do* the things. Then you find you can do them all right. Sure, half the things they tell you you can't do, you find you can do perfectly well, all the time, once ye do them."

Dermot pondered this revolutionary view of things.

"But," he objected, "if your physique won't—"

"Physique! What would anyone your age be doing with a physique!"

"But, Con: *everyone* has one. I mean—don't you see—"

"The less you bother about things of that kind, the better for you. You don't want to be knowing the names of all your parts and diseases."

Dermot, anxious to make the matter clear, adopted his most patronising tone.

"Physique isn't a—"

"Never you mind what it is. Here—" he held out a handful of gooseberries—"put these in your gob, and shut up about your physiques and your constitutions and all your nonsense."

Dermot meekly took the fruit. He was not used to being so addressed, and, as he ate, he eyed Con in some bewilderment. The sun, getting towards the western side of the garden, fell on the big, handsome fellow with soft, golden light. He ate absorbedly, foraging from bush to bush, masticating with enormous movements of his jaws, and shooting out the skins in decisive and powerful reports. Dermot looked past him. Everything in the garden was clear and beautiful. The bushes stood out, each from its own shadow, and Dermot noticed as if for the first time the detail of the prickly stems, the hairs on the fat berries, and, a few paces further off, the brilliant hanging clusters of the red currants. Raising his head, he looked round the garden. A dark, soft shadow, cast by the summerhouse and the laburnum tree beside it, was drooping across the lawn, and approaching the tea party. Soon it would touch the end of his mother's light-coloured dress, where it lay, swished out of harm's way, behind her chair. In a haze by the sundial, midges were beginning to dance. Eileen went up to the group on the lawn. He heard their voices, and then the girl started slowly up the path at the far side, leading Paddy on his chain. Dermot

could see the top of the monkey's head, and the arch of his
back over the dwarf box hedges, as he hopped along by her
side. He made a movement to go and intercept her, but she
disappeared into a big pergola, covered with clematis, and
did not emerge. Evidently she was letting Paddy climb about
upside down on the roof of it.

Con straightened up. Leaning back his head, he sucked
in his cheeks, and shot a gooseberry skin a prodigious distance.

"Them's good," he observed in broad Dublin: and hit his
chest a resounding blow with his great fist.

Then, quite suddenly, as if in response to a signal, the
bells of all the churches began to ring for evening prayer.
Their notes, soft and golden, floated across on the long
slanting beams of sunlight, seeming to hover in the garden,
with its paths, its archways and hedges, the deep glowing
colours of its flowers, as if becalmed there, too dreamily
happy to go further. Dermot stood up very straight. This is
Ireland, he said to himself. This is Granny's garden. I shall
want to remember this. I must learn it by heart.

"A grand evening," exclaimed Con, winking at him
with enormous pleasure. He looked round. "We'll have to be
going. I see me Da on the stir, down there. It must be near
on church time."

"Do you have to go to church twice a day?"

"There's no 'have to'," retorted Con severely. "We
do go. I don't much care for the church down here, though,
I must say," he added.

"I don't like it *very* much either," said Dermot. He felt
full of questions, but, in view of the understanding so happily
established, he judged it wiser to keep quiet.

CHAPTER VI

About once a week, and preferably on a wet day, Dermot had tea with Bessie and Munny in the kitchen. On these occasions he had a boiled egg, which he ate at the smaller of the two kitchen tables, facing the wall, with the stove on his left, and the high wooden dresser on his right. Even with his back so turned to the world, he could gain information as to what was going on, albeit a little distorted, in the row of great bright dish-covers hanging above his head. The window swam, splendid and curvilinear, in every one of these, and nearer, mysteriously shadowed, like some big dusky mushroom, some brown top-heavy egg, swelled up himself, globular, eccentric, liable to strange sudden increase and decrease: with the figure of Bessie making slow semi-circular dips and swings behind him, as she passed across.

Before tea was actually ready, there were a number of entrancing toys and objects of reverence for him to examine. Among the former was an old broken egg-beater. Dermot would get leave, unhook it from its place below the dish-covers, lean his stomach on top of it, and slowly turn the handle, causing the three bent blades to spin jerkily and protestingly around. Among the objects of reverence was Stumpy, Bessie's old odd-purposes knife, which was so far worn down it had hardly any blade left: but a treasure, Bessie averred, worth more to her than she could say. There was also the parsley-cutter, a round short stick with four circular blades projecting all the way round it. This he was rarely allowed to handle, Bessie and Munny both

45

declaring it to be very dangerous. Not to mention the rolling
pins, and the special cork-and-string drawer in the dresser
(with no handle, but a hole into which you thrust your finger).
By the time he had paid his respects to each of these, his
egg would be ready, with horn spoon, by request: Bessie
would "wet the tea," and she and Munny would take opposite ends of the uneven, white, grainy table. Sometimes
Katie the seamstress would be there too, but Dermot did
not care for her. One of a large, poor family, growing
elderly, with little prospect of bettering her lot, she combined Christian fortitude with an expert sycophancy. Her
known unselfishness did not recommend her to her patrons;
she begged for her relations, making resentment more difficult by depriving it of its full justification. When Katie was
present, Dermot had to move down, and make room for her.
Thus he was not opposite his favourite dish-cover, the biggest
and brightest of them all. The meal was further spoiled for
him by Katie's continued thanksgivings for the good fortune
which enabled her to partake of it. She supported these by
naming, with lugubrious relish, those of her relatives and
neighbours who would consider themselves abundantly
blessed to see the half of it. This not only irritated Dermot;
it made him feel guilty. In the face of such cruel poverty,
ought he not to collect and distribute what food he could?
Mingled with dislike of the whining, sing-song voice was this
new sense of responsibility, pressing heavily upon him, especially when he could not get to sleep. One night, his mother
came in, and found him wide awake. He replied to her whispered questions, and the touch of her cool hand, with sudden
tears, surprising himself more than her. She soothed his
trouble: and evidently there was some talk in the family,
with reverberations which reached the kitchen, for Katie next
time maintained a martyred silence, relieving her emotion
with no more than an occasional sniff. In the same week,
Dermot heard a very unflattering description of her from
Con and Eileen: but social conscience, once wakened, was

not to be stifled by discrediting the alarum. Dermot was by nature generous, and though Bessie and Munny between them drew the moral from the wretched creatures, mere animated masses of rags and dirt, who were to be seen everywhere, even in the finest squares of Dublin, festering along the walls, he had from the first a real sense of poverty and misfortune.

One evening, as he walked with Bessie and his nurse, taking a turn towards Glenageary before going to his bed, a poor man blessed him in the road.

"Wouldn't you like to give the poor man a penny?" prompted Bessie, in an eager whisper, as they went past.

"Yes, of course. I didn't understand. Did he want one?"

He ran back after the man, and handed him the penny.

"The blessing o' God on ye, young sir. The blessing o' God on ye."

The voice was hoarse: the unshaven face lit up, with a strange flash.

"There's me good boy."

They received him back with a flutter of praise.

"I'd have given him my whole thirteen pennies, if I'd known," announced Dermot, in entire sincerity. It seemed to him shocking that anyone should be so grateful for a single penny. He earned money, too, and plenty of it. All along one side of the garden grew irises, the long leaves of which concealed hundreds of snails. Dermot collected these, receiving the princely sum of a penny for two hundred. The reckoning, which he kept with pedantic accuracy, was left perforce to his honesty, for Granny had no mind to count the corpses in their reeking pail of salt and water.

The necessity for making money before him, Dermot set to work with extra zeal. Soon snails became perceptibly fewer. Earnings dropped; and it was charity, not avarice, which dictated the business communication presently discovered by Granny in the letter box.

"Walmer Villa,
"August the 27th.

"DEAR GRANNY,

"This is to say, about snails, that it cannot be done any longer at the price.

"Your loving grandson,

"DERMOT."

This letter, though he did not know it, earned Dermot the approval of his Grandpapa, who saw in it the beginnings of a sound business instinct. It pleased his Granny, for she knew why he wanted the money; and a discussion took place in which it was decided that this, perhaps, would be the best way for him to work off the incubus "that foolish woman" Katie had placed upon him.

So Dermot was summoned, and a fresh compact made, by a very business-like Granny, reducing the quantity. She had wished, in her easy rush of generosity, to make it a penny for fifty only, but the others overruled her. It was well that the money should still be hard to earn. The revised rate made it just possible for Dermot to maintain his income at the former figure.

After kitchen tea, Dermont would be allowed to come and talk to Bessie in the scullery while she washed up—always provided he kept clear of what she called "her wicked elba'." She did not like anyone at close quarters while she was working; he was never allowed inside the kitchen when she was at the stove. As the scullery was small, he spent most of the time in the little, cool pantry, with its two windows: one, opening upon the next door garden, always a place of interest as the first home of Paddy-monkey: the other, more surprisingly, into Bessie's bedroom. The convenience of this seemed to Dermot little short of providential.

"Yes, asthore," Bessie would reply, her voice tremulous

with the energy of her ministrations. "It's the way I can keep me eye on them all."

And indeed, there were riches worth keeping an eye on. Strange, goodly objects swathed in white muslin, a palpable ham, a row of delicious jellies all upside down, cooling in moulds: dishes of cold, set gravy: large wet lettuces; clean carrots: all manner of store. Neither really paused to wonder why a watchful eye was needed, for by the time Bessie was in her bedroom, all doors had been doubly fastened; and the window which looked out upon the next door garden was protected by a wire grill, set deep inside the thick wall, able to hold at bay the wildest of marauding cats, the most insinuating of birds. There was nothing else to fear. Even though members of that ill-favoured race known to Granny and Grandpapa as "the corner-boys" broke into the orchard and the next door garden, and by some fiendish cunning succeeded in removing the grill, the whole aperture was too small to let them in, the distance between outside wall and shelf too great for the longest and leanest of avaricious arms. Still, the nearness of her treasures comforted Bessie, and she slept the sounder.

"I do wake sometimes, and the light only starting to come in the little winda'. I do sit up on me arm, and look through, and there they all are, safe and sound, answering back to me, and the birds all starting to twitter in the garden, and I know all's well."

Dermot's quick imagination fixed upon the picture. He could see the pale light filtering in, and hear the birds; he could get up joyously, after an hour's more sleep, to see the first splashes of sunlight on the whitewashed larder wall, and know that another summer day was opening before him. Not for some years did he come to wonder if a bedroom ventilated solely by a small window opening into a place where food was kept might be the ideal arrangement for food or bedroom. He found, then, that the question, so worded, had never occurred to his mother at all. She could never bring a detached eye, from the England into which she had married, to bear upon the only home she could remember.

Bessie's room, once visited, was less interesting than it looked through the pantry window. It had a curious dank smell, all its own, not human at all, something, but not quite, like the smell of a little country church. Nowhere else in the world did Dermot ever find its equal. The room was bare, and as void of colour—walls, carpet, furniture, bed—as a room well could be. Yet it was somehow companionable, for the short times Dermot penetrated to it: times when Bessie was changing her boots, or getting her shawl, to go for a turn round the garden in the evening. In the top left-hand drawer of the chest of drawers lived Bessie's treasures: her everyday rosary, of pale, bony, coffee-coloured beads, and her Sunday best, with elaborate beads of carved black ebony. In the cross of this was a view of St. Peter's, Rome. You held it up to one eye, keeping your hand over the other, and there it was, clear, magnified, and rather yellow. In the biggest bead, likewise equipped with a spy-hole, was a picture of the Sacred Heart. Dermot shied off from this: it distressed him, its suggestion of anatomy recalling a crushed mouse in the garden, whose bright protruding insides had fetched him back, several times, to gaze at them in sick fascination.

Another amusement, after tea, was to play with Pucker and her kitten by the fire. The little animal was becoming very active. It ran about the garden, always with a suggestion of vagueness, as if it were blown off its course by odd gusts of wind. Its hind legs were the stronger, and scampered to such purpose that it often arrived at its destination sideways, or had to pull up and start again. Its tail had not passed the inexpressive state of babyhood, when it pointed away and upwards, and came to a sharp point, like a little pig's. Pucker, delighted to come in to the fire, would lie luxuriously on her side, stretching out her long young legs, and accepting sleepily the caresses and praises of the company. In this state she was often bothered by her offspring, who made attacks upon her from unexpected angles, disturbing her dignity and her repose, if not her lazy good-nature. Dermot would do her a service here, by diverting the kitten's attention to a cork on the end of a string. The little animal would spend perhaps twenty minutes in pursuit of this; then it would trot to its mother, mew, curl up at her side, and fall instantly asleep. As it grew stronger and more expert with the cork, Dermot would roll it over, and tickle its soft little stomach, feeling with delight the vigorous hind legs scampering and kicking to drive away his hand. The kitten now asserted its personality in all directions: even Paddy had to submit. Small though it was, it showed great skill in eluding capture, and understood already the limits of the monkey's chain.

Dermot had a particular reason for rejoicing to see its vigour. One day, when it had not long been able to walk, he was carrying it in his arms, and accidentally dropped it. Instinct made it land upon its feet, but the height was too great, and the little creature, shocked and shaken, crept away into hiding under an empty box. Sick with fear and compassion, Dermot walked about the garden. For a quarter of an hour, perhaps, he was miserably unable to go near and see how the kitten fared. Maybe he would find it mewing, in pain, or dead. At last, able to bear it no longer, calling himself a coward, he went and lifted up the box. The kitten was sitting in a tiny bunch, with its feet tucked underneath it. It looked up at him trustfully, the sky shining blue in its eyes. He picked it up, kissed it, and fondled it, almost wild with relief: but there was still the fear that it might presently develop symptoms, and he did not dare speak of the accident to anyone. Now, however, the kitten's vitality was proof that it had taken no harm. As the weeks went by, it grew exceeding bold, and, being no respecter of persons, had the extreme hardihood to ambush Grandpapa, as he walked up the garden, and jump out upon his trouser leg.

"Gracious sakes above!" the old man exclaimed; and, as soon as he recovered his breath, he delivered a homily to the kitten, which stood, mewing meekly and soundlessly before him. But in a day or so he had come to like the game, and would peer good-humouredly about, in order to spot the ambush beforehand, and be the more emphatically surprised at it. The kitten would follow him a long way down the paths: and Bessie, who always retired reverently to the hedge on the kitchen garden side as soon as "the Master" appeared, would hear him talking to it, and smile happily to herself.

The stroll with Bessie before bedtime became a nightly event for Dermot. He looked forward to it throughout the day with steady happiness. They did not talk much. Bessie walked in front, for the most part, humming to herself, and taking in the sights and scents of the garden. She walked all down the right-hand side, stopping to fondle the tall fronds of the asparagus. She pulled up her heavy skirts, always with the same gesture, to mount the stone steps to "the lawn" in front of the summerhouse. She walked near the laburnum, preferring always in the same place to duck her head, and lean to one side, rather than to walk a yard further away and avoid these necessities. Right down beside the meadow to the very end she walked, stopping at a bunch of mint: and invariably she plucked from it a leaf, which she rubbed between her hands. She was a little, dark, plump woman, with bright sharp eyes, and a vivacious manner. Mystery attended her, in the form of some misfortune or affliction never defined, but always referred to in the household as "her cross, poor soul." All acknowledged that she bore it with astonishing fortitude. Indeed, to see her abroad on these late August evenings, one could divine nothing but a quiet happiness: and she hummed incessantly. The humming did not disturb Dermot. He followed a few steps behind her, looking everywhere: at the houses of Glenageary, their red brick softened by the deepening sunlight: at the great line of the Dublin mountains, turning slowly to purple from dark blue: at the trees, heavy with their foliage, feeling relief in the cool oncoming of night: at the low, sleepy cottage roofs towards the west, with smoke ascending from one or two of their chimneys, smoke faëry and beautiful, the light flooding through it, against a dark belt of trees: at the flowers, turning themselves inside out, it seemed, to give forth the last richness of their colour before they closed for sleep. Far away somewhere, in the meadows, a cow was mooing: and the red-hot-poker flowers, standing up straight and proud, glowed magnificently against the shadow of the hedge.

"I used to be afraid of the garden, Bessie. I'm not, when I come with you."

"Sure, why would you be afraid of it, Master Dermot, dear. There's nothing to hurt ye."

"I was—I was afraid of the wild cats."

"The cats." Bessie voice was dreamy, far away. "Sure, the cats wouldn't touch ye."

"I thought they were fierce cats."

"Ah no. If you'd leave them alone."

"All the same, I think I should still be a bit afraid, Bessie, by myself."

"Sure, you shouldn't. I come down here, many's the time, all these years, and I never seen anything to hurt me."

Dermot pondered.

"But then, you're grown up, and that's different," he said.

"Why is it different, honey?"

Bessie was only half listening.

"Grown-up people aren't afraid of things."

"Maybe that's because they've found out the things do them no harm."

Dermot had not thought of that. He stood still, and opened a snapdragon between finger and thumb, in the way Eileen had shown him.

"There aren't any bees in them now," he said aloud, to

himself. He tried several of the flowers, then trotted to catch up Bessie.

"They *are* afraid of some things, all the same, Bessie."

"Who are, honey?"

"Grown-ups are."

Bessie leaned back her head, and drew a deep breath of the breeze.

"They *are* afraid of some things, Bessie. Mummy's afraid of mice, and spiders, and beetles. So's Granny."

"Beetles?"

Bessie stiffened into momentary attention, and pulled her shawl about her.

"Yes. Granny is afraid of them. And Mummy. And I don't expect Munny likes them very much."

"Ah," said Bessie, relaxing again. "Them's nasty things."

She went slowly on down the path, humming. Dermot watched her. He was very fond of Bessie, and entertained a deep respect for her. She was not at all like anyone else. She was a Roman Catholic, of course, and Granny and Mummy had dark talks sometimes, in low tones, about whether she was trying to pros— pros—something Munny. But, whatever it was, it couldn't be anything bad. Sensitive to character, the boy reacted as quickly and positively to Bessie as to a change in the temperature. Indeed, if an older understanding could have been projected into his mind, there would probably appear, in that early stage of awareness, more correlation between the senses, a less sharp distinction between objects and impressions. Many children include within their everyday range of vision phenomena which they do not realise are not shared by their elders; and, by the time they do begin to realise this, normal fashions of preception influence them, and the extension disappears. Dermot, from his earliest years, could tell instantly the spurious from the genuine in personality. Bluff never deceived him. Plausible himself, and never depending upon reason for his own decisions, he was unimpressed by talk, and began very early to put off asking advice till he had made up his own mind. Bessie, he saw, was in possession of some secret which fortified her and enabled her to meet everything with calm and courage. She had come down the garden for years, without being afraid. Nothing would hurt her, because she was calm, and would go down the garden humming to herself and enjoying the evening. Standing there, his wits half on Bessie and half responsive to the scents and sights and sounds around him, Dermot understood, for a flash of time, that there was really no fear: that there was a state of calm self-possession, of luminous happiness, in which nothing could happen to the self. He was to come back to this knowledge, to need it and to realise it, three or four times later on in life, and always with the memory of Bessie, who introduced it to him.

The garden in the evening, the garden by day: it was a ceaseless source of interest to Dermot, and, truth to tell, his relatives were glad it was so. The baby needed the greater share of attention, and they were only too well pleased to turn him loose and see him absorbed in his own meditations, or in conversation with Mr. Caggen. The bent, straw-hatted figure of the gardener, turning up potatoes, would always have the small form squatting by his side. The long, pink worms, dangling from the turned-up clods, fascinated Dermot. Mr. Caggen would stoop, pick them up, and fling them aside, to avoid cutting them with the fork. It was a most unusual scruple, though Dermot did not realise this. Mr. Caggen had a superstition about them; he believed they were good for the potatoes.

Dermot could not face the idea of picking them up. He watched Mr. Caggen with awe.

"What does it feel like, when you pick up a worm, Mr. Caggen?"

Mr. Caggen considered.

"Soft," he said, finally.

Dermot stared. For some reason, the adjective left him deeply dissatisfied.

CHAPTER VII

U NCLE BEN'S HOUSE WAS ONE OF THE WORLD'S WONDERS. IT
stood on a cliff, which it surpassed in severity of appearance: for the cliff, though undoubtedly a cliff, sloped from
one grassy patch to another, and did not become all rock
till it had only a short way left to go. Even then, it was
climbable at any point except that selected, with comfortable wisdom, for the house's rubbish chute. A good-
natured, easy cliff, it afforded its young explorers plenty of
adventure with a minimum of risk. A path had been cut
down it, enabling all but the infirm and greatly aged to
reach the sea: and yet, when some elderly lady had regained
the top, and stood to get her breath, she could look down
and reflect that, past all doubt, she had negotiated a genuine
cliff.

The house was different. It seemed the architect had felt
very strongly about the cliff, and determined to set it a
proper example, or at least so to continue it as to raise its
status among cliffs. He had accordingly erected a sheer
wall, of enormous height, varying it reluctantly with windows and a severe ledge, termed a balcony, and reached by
a metal ladder. The balcony, one felt, had been added
against his better judgment, and he was determined to make
access to it as difficult and unattractive as he could. Even
the windows seemed a concession to human weakness. They
had no ledges, and stared from the blank wall like lidless
eyes. Below and beside the house were two narrow lawns,
connected by a steep grass slope, and the provision of these
had enabled him further to tone up the cliff by carrying them

as far forward as he dared, and building a supporting wall
to prevent them from falling into the sea. By the time he
had finished, the cliff looked like a mild and peaceful old
elephant surmounted by an armoured howdah. The house,
as far as it could be related to any human style, was bleakly
Georgian: and a succession of occupants had tried with
little success to soften its severity. A path, surrounded by
bushes, had been cut to save visitors the abrupt descent
of the lawns. The slope between these was so steep, and the
lower lawn so narrow, that one could barely pull up from
one's compulsory run in time to avoid falling over the edge,
and being precipitated down the chute. An angular chain,
depending awkwardly from a few metal posts, made this
disaster less likely, without adding much to the amenities
of the place: and a ladder down the face of the wall took one
to the cliff path aforementioned. Uncle Ben had added
a wooden staircase with a balustrade, connecting the balcony with one of the drawing-room windows: but nothing
could humanise the house's sea aspect. It upreared its bleak
grey wall, triumphant, in all weathers, unsoftened by any
light of morning or late evening, a staring example of man's
power to go one worse than Nature.

The view it faced so blankly was one of the most beautiful
in the world. High on the promontory of Dalkey Sound,
with the Island on its left, the house looked full across the
Bay of Killiney to the Wicklow Mountains. The pure line,
the nobility, the ease and grace of that long curving prospect has never been captured in paint or words. It is one of
those which, once seen, remain for ever in the imagination:
yet, since no effort of the memory can summon up the
whole, but is reduced to a loving enumeration, at each return the view sweeps away, with one perfect gesture of its
long curved arm, the piecemeal sketches of memory, and
once more confronts the spirit with a panorama beyond its
compass to build. Those whose houses look out upon it see
it every morning anew. Those who see it for the first time

are apt to be silent. It is liberal, free, and unstaged: no point monopolises it: but from nowhere was it better seen than from the absurd dwelling which the long-dead architect had reared to confront it—Delgany, the home of Uncle Ben. Indeed, there was no fathoming the ways of that architect, for with a fine allowance of ground on which to build, he had deliberately chosen the corner which presented the greatest difficulty, needed the most support, and was nearest to the road: so that one had the paradox of a house in its own grounds standing at the extreme edge of them, for all purposes like an ordinary house with a front door opening on the pavement. A stone path about twenty feet long, and iron railings with a gate, gave the uttermost of privacy he would allow: and, as if regretting that concession, he had so placed the house that the road curved even closer in, and at one place ran almost directly beneath some of the windows.

But indoors—ah, indoors!—it was a different matter. For Dermot, with vague but exciting memories, adventure began with the very opening of the huge front door. The door had a sort of loose wooden lip, which hung down outside it along the ground, as protection against the terrific winds of winter. When the door opened inward, the lip doubled up on its hinge, and dragged along the floor with a queer noise all its own. For years this noise was to be the prelude to rapture, the first welcome back to this extraordinary, lovable house and its extraordinary, lovable inmates.

The hall was unnecessarily high, and rather gloomy. It was covered with a sombre but slippery oilcloth. It contained one or two rugs, which were as rafts sliding about its perilous expanse: a hatstand, shaped curiously like a lighthouse, and endowed with an uncanny ability to drop its burdens, one by one, for no visible cause or disturbance: a long narrow table, highly polished: two shiny wooden chairs, upon which no one ever sat: and the gong. Upon the table was a brass salver, containing dusty visiting cards, and a collecting box, from the mouth of which projected a slip of paper bearing the words "I.O.U. £100,000" in Con's handwriting.

Once past these objects, a visitor turned to the left and saw a passage with rooms opening off it, a staircase up, richly carpeted, a staircase down, not carpeted at all. Over this social distinction presided, butler-like, a grandfather clock, with an aloof appearance and a remote, uninterested tick. The first rooms to which Dermot was conducted, and the most important, were the drawing-room and dining-room. The former had huge, high windows: that was the first thing that struck him. It was also very large. Despite the bric-à-brac and occasional tables of the period, one could go for quite a long walk across its carpeted spaces. One window, as we have said, led to the balcony: in front of the other stood a large brass telescope. Dermot had to be held up, to see through this. The only foretaste of its marvels he received was a gentle bump in the eye and a hazy, swimming view of part of Bray Head, brought astonishingly near. But there were other marvels, easier of inspection. In a glass cupboard lay the dried jaws of a shark, gaping wide and terrifying. It had been captured by Uncle Ben in the South Seas, from over the ship's side, with a bait of rancid pork. In a bottle, half covered with spirit, was coiled a centipede. On the floor, beside the sofa, stood the painted wooden model of a pig, with jointed legs: a creature so cunningly contrived, with so derisive and malign an expression, that generations of dogs had mistrusted it. Their uneasiness had been heightened by the family, who would slide the pig across the uncarpeted edge of the floor, or stand it beside them in a menacing attitude where they lay asleep, and then wake them up with a start. Dermot nursed it, noting with a certain surprise its plebeian expression, and deciding that he could never be fond of it as he was of his toy monkey. This, suffering apparent eclipse before the reality of Paddy, was all the time compensated by an extra flow of private devotion, being taken every night to bed, and joining stiffly in games with Pucker's kitten. One could never take the large hard pig to bed. Besides, the kitten would scamper off at the very sight of it.

Eileen took him upstairs to wash his hands. This ceremony he performed with great care, being on his best behaviour, paying a whole day's visit for the first time by himself: but he was able to note two fresh things. First, that the smell of Uncle Ben's bathroom was quite unlike the smell of the bathroom at home, and second, a matter so strange it had to be brooded over for a long time, that Uncle Ben's bath had no taps! just handles; no place at all, that he could see, for the water to flow in.

"Are you ready, Dermot?" The girl hesitated, standing on one foot. "Do you—"

"I'm quite ready, thank you."

"Come on, then."

They went down. Aunt Patricia was waiting for them at the foot of the stairs. She took Dermot's hand, giving him a smile which wrinkled her eyes and nose. Anne, the elder girl, was standing by the window of the dining-room. She turned as they came in.

"How do you do, Dermot," she said in a hearty voice. It was her manner with children. Towards other people she was quiet, and rather shy. Dermot stared up at her, his brows contracting. She took out a handkerchief hastily, and applied it to her thin, delicate nostrils.

"Come here, Dermot, pet. Sit by me. Can you get up— you can. That's grand. Now where are those others? Where's Father? Where's Con? I had them both in me sight a minute ago, and they're gone off now, Well, I declare."

"He-e-e-re we are, here we are. Punctual to the minute."

Uncle Ben's voice boomed up the uncarpeted stairs from the lower regions. A couple of seconds later, he came in the door, rubbing his hands together. Con followed. He grinned at Dermot, and made a face. These two had been downstairs,

to wash their hands at a tap. For some reason, they preferred this to the bathroom, though there was only cold water
and a chip of hard yellow soap.

"By the holy!" Uncle Ben stopped still, snuffing like a
bloodhound. "Oh, by the holy—that's a grand sniff. What
have you for us to-day, Mother? Sn-oo-oo-ph! I never smelt
a better in all my days."

"Ah, Ben," said his wife, with spirit, "stop your sniffing, and sit down to your food like a Christian. Sure what
way is that to be going on, before the child."

"M-m-m. Never mind, Mother darling. Dermot and I
know what smells good. Don't we, Dermot boy? Faith we do."

Dermot opened his mouth, but the reply was not formu-
lated. That did not matter. Uncle Ben went on happily
without it.

As the meal progressed, Dermot, his eyes wide with wonder,
beheld dietetic variations compared to which Grandpapa's
were as nothing. Lunch at Uncle Ben's was a mix-up
of all the meals together—except possibly breakfast. After
the stewed fruit which was served as a pudding, they ate
bread and jam. They ate cake. They drank tea. Dermot
felt as if the world were coming to an end. He politely refused to partake of these unusual delicacies, but a sense of
excitement, at their very presence, grew in him. It was all
a part of the strangeness of life at Uncle Ben's.

Though he did not know it, he was a subject of some
interest to the family. They knew and liked Dermot's
father, but laughed at his English ways, his precision, his
resentment of their own happy-go-lucky life. They could
not for a long time understand how Margaret had married
him. The fact that he too was of Irish origin—which nobody
would have suspected—only made it seem the queerer.
Legends of Dermot's delicacy, and of the precocity of his
intelligence, they received lightly, as proving only that his
parents made too much fuss of him. He had been too small
for the family to see much of him, before this year, and they

welcomed the first opportunity to study him away from home. He did not talk at his meal, applying himself to its consumption with great care, and a grown-up composure. He ate very slowly, and appeared to notice little: but this appearance, as we know, was deceptive.

After lunch, Uncle Ben took him off by the hand, showed him round the house and garden, told him about the capture of the shark, and of the centipede: took him into the billiard room, and showed him the pictures of his different ships: and explained simply the idea of the game of billiards. Dermot asked question after question, to which the sailor gave precise and detailed replies. The beginning of a long friendship was cemented in that half-hour. Dermot found someone who gave a wealth of information in answer to every question, and who did not seem to mind being questioned, like most grown-ups. Grandpapa was another: but Grandpapa had a way of going on long after the interesting part of the question was answered, and one was dying to interrupt him with a new one. Granny would answer a few questions, but she became absent-minded, and began to think of something else. Daddy would answer them, sometimes: but Daddy at the present time was remote, almost forgotten: not a part of life. Mummy would answer a few, but she often did not know the answers. Or she would laugh, and run her lazy white fingers slowly through his curls, and say:

"What a lot of things my little Dermot wants to know to-day."

Mummy could always bring him round to her mood, and make him smile back at her: but he did not approve of being headed off from what he was seeking.

"You are beautiful, Mummy," he would say sometimes, unwillingly. It was true: he thought her the most beautiful lady in the world. Indeed, when he read the word "lady" he always thought of his mother, with the swish of her long flounces, her perfume, her smile, her slow, musical voice, and her white, lazy hands. Yet, often, her beauty was an interruption, of which he was more than half conscious: distracting him from the pursuit of his thoughts.

Bessie would answer a good many questions, though sometimes there would come a reference to her mysterious "wicked elba'," and he would withdraw, discomfited. Munny lacked the exact knowledge he sought, and tended to reply to all "Why's" with the formula, "Y's a crooked letter, and you can't make it straight"—a reply which, from the very first, seemed to him stupefyingly irrelevant.

"Will you teach me to play billiards one day, Uncle Ben?"

"Faith, I will, son. Many's the game we'll have, please God."

"Uncle Ben—why do you say 'please God' so often?"

"Well, little son—we couldn't have any games, or do anything at all, if it didn't please God to spare us, could we?"

Dermot considered.

"No," he replied, thoughtfully.

"Your Mummy and Daddy have told you all about God, son, haven't they?"

Uncle Ben's voice sharpened ever so little, in suspicion of another and more serious eccentricity.

"Oh yes, ages ago. And I read 'Line Upon Line' for myself, every night. And Munny reads me a hymn always, before I go to bed. And Granny made me learn 'I am only a little Sparrow.' And—"

"That's all right, then, son."

"And I know about Abimelech, and Korah, Dathan, and Abiram. And Jemima, and Keziah, and Karen-Happuch, and—"

"Faith," said Uncle Ben, "that's grand." And he led the way upstairs again.

A little later, they all set out for a picnic to Dalkey Island. Uncle Ben kept his boat, not at the slip beneath the cliff, but in the little harbour of Coliemore, on the Sound, where it was cared for by the fishermen, and had the advantage of a safe shelter in rough weather. The road down the hill was hot and white with dust, but every now and then appeared cool enchanting glimpses, between the trees, of the Sound and Island, to hearten one on. The harbour itself was dazed and blank with sunlight, its row of fishermen sitting half asleep in the shade on the far side of the road. One of them woke to life at a second hail, and slithered across, down the uneven stone causeway, into the clear, green pool on which the painted boats lay dreaming. Very leisurely the process of unmooring seemed to Dermot. The fisherman tumbled into a boat which was lying beside the causeway. A wide, calm ripple started: the boat rocked slightly, and the ripple, when it left the shade, sent a slow, ecstatic tremor of broken light shivering up the inside of the pier. The man stood up, took an oar, laid it in a hollow in the boat's stern, and with a lazy, expert motion of his arm propelled her forward. Reaching the nearest of the row of moored boats, he stepped aboard her, and strode from one to another, setting up an outrageous rocking and smacking of lips, till he reached the boat he was seeking. There followed much loosening and splashing of ropes, after which he steered the boat round to the cool well of the steps, where the party stood waiting for him. There he got out, and squatted on his hunkers, holding the edge of the boat, to steady it.

"Now then, Dermot son. Hop in."

Dermot looked up, from one to another of them.

"Shall I be sick?" he asked, in his clear, high voice.

"Sick?" repeated Uncle Ben. "*Sick?* Why ever would you be sick?"

"I was, a little, on the big boat coming over."

"Oh, the *big* boat!" cried Uncle Ben, waving his head back almost in a circle. "Sure, that's a different matter altogether."

Reassured, Dermot stepped daintily in, and was stowed away in the stern, between Anne and Eileen. Anne moved up a little to make room for him, with a friendly smile. He decided that she was nicer than he had thought.

There was a short dispute as to who should row, a privilege which fell to Con, as the distance was short. He was very strong, and rolled the blue sleeves back from his great golden, powerful arms with self-conscious pride. Uncle Ben kneeled up in the bow, to watch for breakers, as he put it.

Con rowed powerfully, with a great appearance of ease, but Dermot could see that beneath it all he was putting forth all the strength he could, for his colour rose, and his face was a little too calm and unconcerned. The boat slid along fast, with a great clop-clopping of water under her sides: and the big shape of the Island rose up every second before them.

Suddenly Uncle Ben gave an exclamation.

"Look," he cried, "the B. & I. Faith, she's early. She must have had a grand calm passage."

Dermot looked where Eileen was pointing, and saw, a long way away, heading for the Sound, the black bows and funnel of a big steamer. She seemed quite motionless. A dim stain of smoke slanted away behind her, and beneath her bow was fixed a clear white smudge, like a piece of cotton wool.

"We'll be well over, out of her wash," grunted Con.

"There, Dermot son—d'ye see? That's the line you came over on: the B. & I."

"Is that the *Lady Hudson-Kinahan*?"

"It may be—no, I don't think it is. It's one of the others."

"It was the *Lady Hudson-Kinahan* that we came over on."

"Yes, son. We'll see what this one is, when she goes by."

They were now almost at the Island, which lies a bare eight hundred yards from the shore: and when presently Eileen pointed downwards over the side, Dermot could see the monstrous brown forests of the weed, looming suddenly up out of the depths, becoming clearer, waving slow, lazy, rich brown arms—and then Uncle Ben was calling directions, the boat's bow grated gently against a little, uneven landing stage, and they were there.

Dermont was led up to the level ground at the head of the stage, and left there, while the provisions were brought up and the boat moored to the satisfaction of Con and Uncle Ben. When they came back, he looked round, and lo and behold, the great B. & I. boat had somehow leaped across the gap of sea, and was entering the Sound. A faint cheer of welcome came from the houses above the shore: handkerchiefs and white napkins began to be waved from the windows, as the boat, looking huge and noble in the narrow channel, came past the point and breasted her way down the Sound. The cheering grew, the waving doubled: then, as she came fairly under the houses, a faint plume leaped from beside her funnel, and there rang out the stately, musical note known all along the coast, her answer to the welcome. Three times it sounded, three long, full blasts, filling the space between shore and shore, leaping from hill to hill, peopling the lazy afternoon with echoes: and the visitors upon her decks crowded in delight and wonder to see the cool greens of the rocky, wooded shore, the clean colours of the houses rising among the trees, and waved their shrill, fluttering handkerchiefs in answer. The last echo leaped away into the mountains, and the great ship passed by the watchers on the Island, the soft, steady crash of the foam beneath her bows sounding over the still water. Dermot could not read what was on her stern, but Uncle Ben positively declared her to be the *Lady Roberts*, the biggest and newest of the fleet. He knew them all, as he knew every boat that plied along the coast. Next, soon after she had gone by, there was the excitement of her wash. With awe and added delight, Dermot watched the big shining humps of water come slantwise to the shore. They did not break, but came rolling along like disturbances beneath a great smooth, gleaming carpet. When they reached the rocks of the Island they turned out to be far more powerful than they looked, making a great commotion, slapping and flopping up and down at the rocks, making the weed sway heavily, and sending the boat bobbing up and down in great agitation.

When the last of the waves had died, the party set up the slope of the Island to the picnic place. The Island was quietly rocky, and covered with grass. It had no trees. On its highest point, huge, round, and conspicuous, sat a martello tower, like the tower at Sandycove, which Dermot knew well. One could not get inside it. One could only walk round it, getting a crick in one's neck from looking up at its high, smooth sides. The place chosen for the picnic was quite close to this, under a rock to the south of it, from which could be seen the sea on three sides of the Island, besides most of the Sound, the Point, and Killiney Bay. The Wicklow Mountains looked for some reason half as big again as they did from the shore. This afternoon, they were a vast, vague blue: and the miles of thick woods about their feet looked like a darker blue smoke, clinging to the ground, not daring to rise.

At the south end of the Island was a ruined fort. Uncle Ben, at Dermot's loud desire, took him towards it: but the ground was very rocky, and he was not able to get as far as the entrance.

"Another year, son, when you're older," said Uncle Ben: and for some reason that instant remained always a sharp memory with Dermot. Whenever it leaped up in his mind, he heard the precise note of Uncle Ben's voice, saw his head and his green tweed suit against the sleepy blue of the sky, saw the white, sun-parched walls of the fort, and the confusion of sea beyond. And all this, despite the fact that he visited the fort again, several times, and once at least with Uncle Ben, in direct fulfilment of that promise. It was one of a few sharply clear pictures, which he could place definitely in its time, behind a haze of others which had no marked beginning. He could not, after so many Irish summers, say when his memory of this or that place began, when he first saw Miss O'Killikelly or another. They seemed to have been always a part of his life, to have emerged with him into the full daylight of remembered consciousness. But this was one of a few isolated pictures: and it was followed by another.

While they sat picnicking, and Dermot devoured with great care a hard-boiled egg, very much afraid of breaking it and spilling its crumbly and delicious contents, there was a sudden exclamation from Anne, and she pointed up at the rock beneath which they were sitting. All looked up. Craning over the top of the rock, with the benign expanse of Martello tower behind them, looked the heads of a dozen goats. Thin, melancholy, and inquisitive, they stared down upon the invaders. Con shouted, and made a gesture with his arm. A tremor ran along the heads on their thin necks, like stalks shaken by a sudden gust. He shouted again, and again. Each time there was a tremor, but the goats did not run.

"Ah, don't be scaring them, Con," said Aunt Patricia comfortably. ".Sure, the poor things have as good a right as ourselves."

"Better," said Eileen. "It's their Island."

"Ah, hang it all," protested Con, "I don't like being watched at me meals by a crop o' goats."

He took a huge bite, glowering resentfully up at the row of long faces.

The next diversion, when tea was over, was to watch the mailboat come into Kingstown Harbour. She did not come anything like as near as the first boat, passing a good three miles clear of the Island: but brave she showed, with the sun flashing on her white paintwork; growing swiftly from a gleaming little bundle to a ship, lengthening, taking shape and grace, and then gliding stately by, under the Hill of Howth, to slow up, and slide presently between the little piers to her distant berth.

"Tired, little son?" asked Uncle Ben, as he took Dermot down to the boat.

"A little—but in a most lovely way," added Dermot

hastily. "I think it's a lovely feeling, to be tired after nice things: don't you?"

"Faith, son, you're right. None better. But we'll soon be home now. I'm going to take you right down to the tram from the harbour."

"Oh, thank you, Uncle Ben: but Mummy's coming up to call for me at the house."

"Is she? Sure, we might have saved the tramp back there. Never mind. I'll carry you on me back."

"I won't be as tired as that, really, Uncle Ben."

The brief passage across the water was heavenly. He trailed his hand in the cool, bubbling water, and sighed for happiness.

"Now," said Con, as he stepped out, and lifted Dermot on to the stone steps. "Now, were you sick?"

"Of course I wasn't," said Dermot, and entertained a proper scorn for his inexperienced self of three hours back.

"There y'are, ye see," said Con.

CHAPTER VIII

Into the alcove of Granny's dining-room, that recess where lived the sideboard and the cuckoo clock and Grandpapa's books, the new-lit fire threw little timid splashes of warm colour. It twinkled in the silver pieces on the sideboard, which gave it back sleepily, as if summer were their time for hibernating, and they had not expected to be roused so soon. Gaining confidence, it began to leap softly up the wall. The room had grown dark, this overcast September evening. The wind, aware that soon the equinox was coming to give it authority, blustered up the road, harrying small companies of early leaves, and flinging an occasional handful of raindrops against the window. At the first and second of these salutes, Grandpapa had jumped and exclaimed, "God bless my soul." At the third, he had gone to the door, and called for Bessie to light the fire.

"Ah, sir. I thought, now, ye would be wanting the fire, the way it is outside."

"Faith," grumbled Grandpapa, pulling the long lace curtain aside a couple of inches, to peer out into the road, "I don't know what sort of weather this is to go give us. In my young days, ye knew which was the winter, and which was the summer: but nowadays, I declare to me God ye can't tell one from the other."

"Oh, that's right, sir," agreed Bessie, cheerfully busy on her knees by the hearth.

"I'm anxious too, d'ye see, because Miss Margaret and her two children will have to be crossing soon. And if the weather breaks up as early as this—"

"Ah, sir. Sure they could wait a bit, maybe, till it took up."

"The' can do no such thing." Grandpapa turned round, in never-failing irritation at the easy optimism of women. He saw life as obedience to a number of fixed decrees, a kind of enormous public park run in the interests of law and order. It gave him a grim satisfaction to see women brought up against its regulations, and he never failed to point the moral when they indignantly protested against this interference with their own lawless desires.

"The' can do no such thing," he repeated severely. "Don't you know very well that Mr. Gray is coming across in a couple of days, to take a short holiday, and fetch them back along with him?"

"Ah, but, sure, if the weather was agen them—" Bessie kneeled up, and beat her sooty hands together.

"The affairs of a company, such as the company Mr. Gray serves," declared Grandpapa impressively, "are not concerned with the weather—nor with difficult crossings of the Irish Channel—nor with anything of the kind. The' have rules, which must be kept, and are not subject to personal exception. Heh!" He stuck out his beard, and looked down at Bessie with narrowed eyes. "I believe *you* think a company of that kind is run by a lot of old women."

"Oh sir, oh sir," —Bessie rose cheerfully,—"you're terrible hard on us poor women, so y'are. There now: I've lit your fire for ye."

Grandpapa regarded it doubtfully.

"Ta' care, now, would it smoke on us," he observed.

"Ah, sure, a puff or two, in the first fire after the summer, is only what you may expect. It takes the chimney a while to warm up, and get used to the smoke agen."

"Do ye think, now, maybe, there'd be a bird's nest in the chimney? Do ye?"

"And you runnin' a fire on into the month o' May! It'd be the queer bird would live through that."

"Well, well"; Grandpapa waved his hand sideways at her. "Ye may go."

Left to himself, he retreated to the window, and sat, a hand on each knee, watching the fire suspiciously over the tops of his glasses. But the threatened puffs never came, despite the wind, and he was able to resume his reading of *The Irish Times*, murmuring occasionally "Tcha," "The robbers," or "Did ye ever hear the like," until the light from the window became too bad.

By this time the alcove looked cosy indeed. The firelight leaped playfully up the wall, the sideboard winked in a score of places, a great peaked shadow shot up every second above the cuckoo clock, and a faint, warm radiance, reflected from the wall, reached even the old leather backs of Grandpapa's books, which lived in a deep bookcase let into the alcove's darkest corner. So dark was it, that even in ordinary daylight the old man had often to take a book out, and peer at its title, to be sure what it was. For the most part, however, he knew their places by heart. Gazing around the room, thinking of the long winter evenings which he loved, he could not forbear a chuckle of pleasure.

Dermot, entering at that moment, stopped spellbound in the doorway. The room was transfigured. He had not seen its winter self: at least, he had, but when he was too young to remember it consciously. He stared, round-eyed, at the warm soft light and the bobbing shadows.

"Come in, child, come in. Are you frightened, or what is it?"

The stare left the wall, and was fixed on Grandpapa.

"No, Grandpapa. I was only thinking how lovely it looked."

"Eh, well, come in," said Grandpapa, well pleased, "and close the door carefully behind ye. Don't go bang it, now."

The admonition was quite unnecessary. Dermot closed the door with the silent, two-handed care of a child, his tongue curling in concentration over his lower lip.

"That's right. Come on now, to the fire, and warm yourself."

Dermot came on, and copied his grandfather, holding up his thin hands to the blaze. There was a great deal in common between old-fashioned child and old-fashioned gentleman. Both, at their extremes of age and in their different way, loved the same things. The man saw his qualities in the child, and approved with grim good nature: the child as yet could only realise the agreement on rare occasions, since, lack of experience apart, he was generally too much taken up with directly experiencing the new, vivid sensations of life to think about anybody else. When, after some seconds, he looked up from the fire at his Grandfather, and saw the big head nodding and the eyes crinkled with appraisal, he was aware only that Grandpapa was looking at him.

"Isn't it nice, Grandpapa?" he said, and stood a little closer against his knee.

"It is," replied Grandpapa. "It is very nice, as you say." He was thinking to himself that the boy did not look so delicate as when he came: that the visit would have been a benefit to him. He was heartily glad, at the same time, that this delicacy, or the instincts of self protection arising from it, kept Dermot from rough play and noisy companions. Not having been present, he could not take in the fact that Dermot had indeed become very noisy and aggressive soon after Eithne's birth: so much so that his parents had only reduced him to order by sending him to a little kindergarten, where the superior abilities of other children along those lines had, for a time, driven him in upon himself again.

Grandpapa, hearing of the kindergarten and the necessity, had pooh-poohed both. The name kindergarten seemed to him outlandish: some new-fangled idea or other. Characteristically, he did not question the boy directly about it.

"Tell me, now, Dermot," he said gravely, "are ye making good progress with your lessons?"

He pronounced "progress" as if the first syllable rhymed with dog.

"Oh, yes." Dermot looked up at him confidently, for this was a subject upon which they were very much at home. He had been a precocious child, in everything except the power to walk, which came to him very late: the physical delay had been compensated by great activity of mind, and Grandpapa, at an age which would make modern parents throw up their hands in horror and unbelief, had made a beginning by teaching him his letters. Now, he read any book, with ease and confidence. The kindergarten authorities, unprepared for these accomplishments, set him to cut out shapes of coloured paper, and paste them in books; to make islands and isthmuses of sand on tea-trays; to draw ships, etc.: all of which he did with quiet absorption. But he did not call them lessons. Lessons for him meant the continuation, with help from his father, of all he had begun with Grandpapa.

The old man looked at him, and nodded once or twice. Whatever he was going to say was interrupted by the appearance of Bessie, carrying a lamp. Grandpapa's hand rose instinctively, and "Ta' care" formed itself upon his lips; but he knew there was no need to say it.

Bessie always came in the same way, the lamp held firmly in her right hand, her face averted, clear of the big globe, her left hand stretching out for the little mat on which the lamp was to stand. Reaching this from its place on a small side table, she would advance to the centre table, put the mat down, and then with both hands steadily lower the lamp into its place. Then, opening her mouth, and screwing up her eyes, she turned up the wick. There was a steadfastness and strength about her process which reassured Grandpapa in his own despite. He sat back in his chair, one finger tapping his knee, and pushed up his moustache from underneath, till Bessie had gone. Then, after a few seconds' contemplation of the mild, wide light, he rose stiffly from his chair.

"Come over with me here, now, till I find out something I want ye to read to me."

Dermot willingly followed him across to the alcove, giving, as he did so, a single apprehensive glance at the cuckoo clock, lest it startle him by suddenly proclaiming the hour. Last year he would not go into that part of the room without someone to hold his hand. Now, he was getting to love the clock, without fear: only he did not want to be taken by surprise. But there was no fear: the hands said twenty to six.

Grandpapa put a hand on his shoulder, and pointed to a row of volumes with leather backs, standing deep and solemn in the shadow.

"Do you know what those books are, Dermot?" he asked.

"No, Grandpapa. What are they?"

"Those," said Grandpapa reverently, "are the works of Charles Dickens, the greatest novelist who has ever lived."

There was a suitable pause.

"One day, you shall read them. You are not old enough yet."

"Are they interesting?"

"They are more than interesting," replied Grandpapa solemnly. "One of these days, I shall begin to tell you about them, and maybe read a bit to you, here and there. Then, when you are older, you shall read them for yourself."

It was thus that Dermot first heard the name of Dickens— in a far, surviving corner of Dickens' world: in an alcove, with firelight unsteady on the walls, spoken reverently on the lips of one for whom that world was contemporary and real, and those books the newest, the only fiction: somewhere, say, in the year 1860, which had by some mystery been persuaded to stay forty years above its time. It seemed to him afterwards that, by shutting his eyes, he could always slip back into that world, and that he held a real link with it. He knew, with more than an imaginative sympathy, what the books were talking about.

But Grandpapa was looking for something else. Craning back his head, peering (as well he might), he extracted at last a large Prayer Book. Together the pair turned back to the table, where the lamp swam dimly, like the full moon one suddenly sees in summer, some little while after she has taken her place unnoticed in the sky. Sitting down, holding the book forward into the circle of brightest light, Grandpapa opened it, and took from inside its cover a newspaper cutting, yellow with age, and stuck upon a card.

"Now, Dermot," he said. "I want ye to read this to me."

With a slight frown, and a look at the old man, Dermot obediently took it. He had never seen a piece of reading matter of like appearance. In his clear voice, unnecessarily loud, he began to read:

"Henry Francis Lyte, author of the justly celebrated hymn, 'Abide with Me,' passed away on the . . ."

CHAPTER IX

THE ARRIVAL OF DERMOT'S FATHER, THOUGH IT PRESAGED departure, made little impression upon him, so deep was he in the new world. His father belonged, very properly and importantly, to the world of England—to Mutley Park House, Plymouth. Here, he seemed out of place. He lost authority, too. Dermot was quick to notice that, in spite of being who he was in the family, his father was outside the little circle of Walmer Villa. Walmer Villa was Mummy's home. Here she had been born, had grown up, and from here she had married. The house and garden had for her a thousand associations to which her husband must always be a stranger, or an appreciator at second hand. The little circle, which belonged together, most freely opened its enclosure to admit the guest: but a guest he was, and his behaviour showed it. He deferred to the old couple: he asked Grandpapa his opinions, and listened with the appearance of respect. He rose first from the table, and held open the door. To Dermot, accustomed for weeks now to Irish voices, his voice sounded incongruous and strange. He was fallen, most decidedly fallen, from his high estate at home. Dermot disliked to see this, without knowing that he disliked it. His escape from it was to be almost unaware of his father: not to realise his presence until they should all be home again, and he could be given his proper attention in his proper place. So Dermot went about his days, for the most part, as if his father were not there. He shut up his senses from taking any notice of him.

At the same time, he resented very much anything which

77

looked like an attempt to belittle his father. A suspicion
that Uncle Ben and the rest of the Delgany contingent were
laughing at him embarrassed him—though hardly on personal grounds. There was to be no nonsense of that kind.
No one was permitted to overturn the fixed pillars in Dermot's world. On the very evening of his father's arrival, when
Grandpapa had stood at the top of the steps, holding his
hand, and said, chuckling, "That's not your Daddy," Dermot replied coldly, "It *is* my Daddy," and took the joke in
very bad part. He did not consciously side with his father:
but, at home, his father's mightiness was a fact, one of the
facts upon which the world rested, and Dermot, like many
another philosopher, did not like to see his facts lose value.

There was a feeling, too, that besides being always deferential in his behaviour, his father was avoiding certain
subjects. More than once, at meals, came the feeling of a
difficult place avoided. On one occasion, just as he himself
was allowed to "get down" and go out of the room, something had happened—anger from Grandpapa, and, through
the closed door, deprecating and soothing voices from the
rest. Munny, consulted, reproved him for being inquisitive,
but softened later, to remark that she thought it might be
some question of politics. Dermot noticed also that his
father did not accompany the family to church. He enquired
boldly why, and was told by Granny that Daddy was tired
after his journey: leaving him to cogitate on the unusual
rigours of a journey whose effects persisted from Tuesday to
Sunday morning.

The last days flew quickly by, and, before he realised it,
Walmer Villa was loud with preparations for departure.
Uncle Ben called and said good-bye on his way in to Dublin:
Aunt Patricia, Con, and the girls came in late the same afternoon. Seeing them, hearing their voices, Dermot felt a sudden
tugging at his heart-strings. He wanted to go again to the
big cliff of a house, to take part in the strange meals, to go
across in the boat to Dalkey Island, and see the ships, and

the goats. He clung suddenly to Aunt Patricia's hand, and said so.

All bent down to reassure and comfort him.

"Ah, sure, little son, when ye come again next year, ye must come up and see us lots of times."

"Yes, Dermot. We'll go over to the Island, and have a grand time. There'll be twice as many goats."

"We'll teach you to fish, too."

"Yes—listen, Dermot—you sit in the back of the boat, and hold a line in your hand as we're going along—we'll show him the way, won't we, Eileen?"

"—Oh, sure we will—"

"—And you'll catch big, shining mackerel!"

The tears were delayed a moment.

"What are mackerel?"

"Oh, grand fish. They pull hard, and, when you get them in, they flop about all over the place. And they're the loveliest colours—"

"Yes. All like a rainbow, where the light comes on their side."

He looked mournfully from one to another, only half comforted.

"You wouldn't be able to do these things much longer, this year, anyhow," put in Con, with real understanding. "It'll be too rough and cold. But next year, now—"

Between them, they managed to distract him for a while. Eileen took him out into the garden. She loosed Paddy-monkey, and the three roamed round the walks. Whether from compassion—for she thought him a queer little freak —or because she was setting herself a task, she did everything in her power to charm and divert Dermot: and made him her slave for life. Paddy, unconscious of the coming separation, gambolled happily along. When they ran, he galloped ahead, throwing up his behind like a frisky cat. When they stopped, he turned and looked up at them with human, intelligent eyes.

The walk was all too short. Anne appeared at the top of the garden, waving and calling. Eileen had to go.

At the actual good-byes, Dermot shed tears. They were all so kind, so lively—they came from a world which seemed to him exciting and delicious and strange: a world of shark's teeth and centipedes and telescopes and wooden pigs and queer meals and bathrooms without taps and sea and boats and outings and front doors that made a queer noise. The detailed memory was too much for him: he shook himself free from the comforting ministrations of Munny and Bessie, and crept out into the garden.

Paddy sat on top of his kennel, eating his supper. Bessie had filled his tin mug with stewed apple. He looked up as Dermot appeared, made a little friendly noise, and went on eating.

For several minutes Dermot stood watching him, brooding upon the separation that was coming: watching him hungrily, taking in every movement, every look of his friend, staring at the kennel, the tree, the little path that ducked suddenly and dodged into the scullery: learning it all by heart, to remember during the long winter months which were coming. A year—a whole year! It was more than he could grasp. He *could* remember last year, of course, but only as a sort of dream, dim broken pieces. A year! Why, the time he had been over here, that great, long, wonderful time—that was only two months and a bit. A year was twelve months! No, that wasn't quite right: you had to take away the two months and a bit. That left ten—nine months and a bit. More than four times as much as the time he had been over here must go by before he saw Paddy again, and Bessie, and Mr. Caggen, and—everybody and everything.

He put his arms round the monkey, who had finished eating, and held him tight.

"Oh, Paddy, darling Paddy," he whispered.

Puzzled, the monkey stared for a second. Then, aware of his distress, it snuggled close to him, with crooning, comforting noises.

CHAPTER X

THE ACTUAL DEPARTURE WAS FEARFUL, EXCEPT THAT IT HAD about it the excitement of strange and unusual doings. Sitting up to an early tea, eating an egg with a bone spoon for the last time, taking, whenever he could spare the time, a surreptitious glance around the room—

"—Hurry up, Dermot. There's not time to go mooning around. Get on with your egg."

—to fix its darling details once more in his mind: that was awful. There was a sick, heavy feeling in his chest, which would hardly move aside to let the food go down. He had not cried. There was a sort of numbness—the sorrow was too big: and, at the same time, though he knew he was going, that in one hour he would be gone, and Walmer Villa be empty, but for Grandpapa and Bessie, and Paddy rattling his chain (tears suddenly welled up, but he choked them back): though he knew all this, and the pictures of that knowledge came flashing up, every now and then, like stabs of pain: yet some queer sort of strength had somehow come up inside him, putting an excitement underneath the sorrow, and making him at moments almost callous. He had said good-bye in an almost jaunty spirit to Paddy, to Pucker, and to the kitten—who was in a most inappropriate mood, and would not come to be petted, but thought the pursuit was a game. Bessie's continual saga of "the days we'll have next year, please God": and "Sure the time won't be long passing. Christmas'll be on us before we know where we are, and then, sure, in a month or two, we'll be making ready to welcome yez all again," was curiously invigorating. He had come in to his early tea almost cheerful: but the stabs of realisation came up again.

Watching him, hard put to it, indeed, to hide her own grief, Granny made one of her very few mistakes.

"Would you like to take one of the bone spoons with you, Dermot dear, to eat your eggs at home?"

The boy's face darkened in repudiation of such a blasphemous thought.

"No, thank you—" he got out somehow, and stopped short, blinking hard: for the separateness, the difference of Walmer Villa, of everything in Ireland, was the strongest of his secret pleasures.

Then, suddenly, came the bustle of leaving. A last glimpse of Paddy, snatched on the pretext of wanting to go to the lavatory, a preoccupied Paddy, playing with his chain: something put into his hand: his father's voice, impatient, "Come on, come *on*": the tickle of Grandpapa's beard: the brave show of flowers in the tiny front garden, suddenly noticed, as if especially bright: Bessie waving her hand merrily from the steps, crying "Next year, next year," and his own hand, laboriously freed, to wave back: the darkness of the cab, the loud clatter of its wheels: they were gone.

The B. & I. boat took a long time to get from the North Wall to Dalkey Sound. The evening was overcast: there was a chill air: all the land, the trees so soon to lose their tired foliage, looked dark and cold. The boat went down the Sound almost in silence. As one who has suffered too much, and can feel no more, Dermot stared at the little harbour of Coliemore, where Uncle Ben's boat lay. He got a quick glimpse of boats at anchor, but could not see *the* boat: it was moored too far round. Then they cleared the point, and Delgany itself showed gaunt above the curving shoulder of the land.

Uncle Ben and Company had arranged to be down on the boatslip. They were to wave a sheet.

"Look, Dermot, look. There! There they are!"

Mummy was pointing over his shoulder. He looked, and there, sure enough, were two or three tiny figures, waving what looked like a napkin. He waved back, mechanically.

When they had finished waving, Uncle Ben's party climbed the path up to the house, and turned the telescope upon the boat. They saw through it a picture which they described to Dermot in later years, so convincingly that he always seemed to see it himself. At the stern of the boat, clearly visible, so that they could even see the expression on his face, he stood, in his sailor cap, his blue reefer coat buttoned across, gazing vaguely back towards Dalkey, solemn, lost in thought. The telescope was so powerful that they could see him for quite a long time, dwindling slowly eastward into the dusk.

INTERLUDE

THE INTERVAL WHICH FOLLOWED DESERVES SOME RECORD, because, though Ireland became more and more important to Dermot, he did not visit it again for two years. These two years marked the development of Baby Eithne from a helpless and noisy little animal into a person, obliging Dermot to adjust his singular existence to admit her. Remembering his first hostility, his parents kept anxious watch; but they were reassured. The opening of her eyes to the world roused Dermot's interest. She was a new and exciting plaything. He became much attached to her, and took a grave pride in fetching and carrying for her, and directing her first steps. Strange feelings came over him, when he stood in the nursery, holding out his hands, and the baby, her own hands outstretched, took her unsteady way across the floor, caught his hands, and sighed with the satisfaction of an accomplished journey. Soon she was walking all over the place, with the dour, valiant tread of the very small child, stopping still, every now and then, with great virtuosity, and turning her head to smile at her escort. She was a purposeful baby, and when, as frequently happened, she fell on her face, she was not so much frightened as resentful of the interruption to her progress; and would be set on her feet again, her face dark with anger, which she immediately forgot.

A memory which came often to Dermot was of sitting with Eithne in the big nursery window, watching down Oxford Avenue for his parents to come back from the town. Oxford Avenue marked the end of civilisation, the end of

streets and lamps. Their house stood in a garden, not nearly
as big as Granny's, but of a decent size: and, beyond its
southernmost fence, rough, broken ground sloped down
to the top of Oxford Avenue. This broken ground opened
into a small wood, which ran beside the eastern fence of the
garden: a piece of waste land, still more than half wild,
with a stream running through its midst: too small, and
too near civilisation, to give much pleasure: spoiled by an
occasional rubbish dump, and the haunt of small armies of
street boys. Each successive tenant of Mutley Park House
put up a higher fence to exclude these armies and pre-
serve his garden from their inspection. The waste land was
bounded on the far side by a steep rise in the ground, which
was let out to market gardeners. Happily, the little wood
concealed this from the house. On the north ran a lane,
which also bounded the garden, and curved round the
meadow and clump of trees at the back of the house.

It was a wild November evening. Over Plymouth Sound,
a great opening had been torn in the ragged sky. The evening light shone through it, grand and mournful, and the
wind roared in from the sea, whirling down the narrow
streets from the Hoe, leaping impatiently across the pit of
the town, and shaking the regiments of houses upon North
Hill. It leaped at the great high nursery window, again and
again. One could almost see it coming: but the two children did not heed it. Dermot's gaze was fixed intently
upon as much as could be seen of Oxford Avenue. Eithne,
too young to concentrate on any intellectual purpose, sat,
her short legs sticking straight out in front of her, pulling at
her toes, and chanting to herself an interminable song of
pleasure. Every now and again, moved by an imperious
shaking of the glass, she would look wonderingly up at the
window; but she did not stop her song. Drawing his brows
together, Dermot watched. The avenue was empty; its
very lamps appeared fitful in the wind. Suddenly a strong
gust flung a handful of drops against the window. They

trickled slowly down, and the light of the lamps dazzled into stars. The window became a drizzle and a blur: fresh drops were flung upon it, splashing out at first into little rings, which drooped and became part of a general descending sadness. Then the assault ceased: the pane dried quickly in the wind, save where a few big drops clung shivering. Dermot moved his head so as to see the street lamps through the drops, and each light became to his imagination a fairy, with a big radiant head and shooting, dancing limbs. In less time than it takes to tell he knew the name, the history, and the habits of these iridescent creatures. They lived on a hill above the town. As soon as he had gone, or the drops had dried from the window, they would drift slowly away to it, like thistledown, like dandelion feathers. Dandelion feathers on their stalk—only more splintery; and with exactly that same transparency, like the daytime shell of the moon; drifting along in flocks and companies over the heads of the admiring townspeople. Only—the townspeople would not admire. They did not know. He alone knew: he had the lovely sight and knowledge and friendliness of them, all to himself. He alone knew—and, of course, Eithne.

"Baby!" he said, pointing at the nearest dazzle. "Look, Baby! Look at the Goombies!"

Eithne gave a crow of delight. She agreed to everything. Rapturously, she rocked herself up and down, beating the palms of her hands on her upturned toes.

Dermot was not quite satisfied that she understood.

"Look, Baby. Look—there in the light, all dancing. Fairies. Goombies."

"Ee-eee-ee-ee," sang Eithne, and jumped herself up and down on her behind. She gave him one of her quick delighted glances, and laughed with glee.

"Goombies," repeated Dermot to himself, solemnly. It was a good word to say. He said it with relish. "Goombees": those would be the big, fat, grandfather ones? No, he decided, he liked it best said quickly, so as to make them sound little and lively: "Goombies."

Hullo. There were Mummy and Daddy, waving to them from the gate. He had forgotten all about keeping watch. He pointed excitedly, and Eithne, looking everywhere and nowhere, waved her hand in welcome to the whole world.

This memory recalled an incident, which must have happened the following winter, for Eithne was able to run all over the place, and the two watched now, not from the nursery window, but from a small side window in the hall. Eithne, a solemn looking little thing, except for the quick crinkle of a smile she had kept from babyhood, stood close beside him, watching down the Avenue. It was earlier in the year, or earlier in the afternoon: anyway, not so dark.

"Here they come," cried Dermot, suddenly catching sight of the two tall figures. He always felt a quick thrill of thankfulness and recognition, even now that he was bigger, and knew no harm was likely to happen to them in the town.

"Oo. Where? Oo."

Eithne pushed impetuously forward, and, as she did so, bumped against a stool, on which stood an enormous yellow vase. Aware of the collision, she spun round; and both watched with horrified eyes the huge vase topple, slip, and fall with a reverberating crash upon the floor.

For a few seconds Eithne gazed appalled. Then, uttering a little bubble of sound, she fled from the wreck as fast as her fat little legs would carry her, out of the hall, into the night nursery, and far, far in, under the remotest corner of Munny's bed: whence her mother had the greatest difficulty in coaxing her. Besides the shock of the crash, she had an intellectual cause for terror. Some days before, she had heard her father in high indignation over the careless breaking of a valuable teacup: and, contrasting the size of this with the vase, she supposed that nothing short of death could atone for so enormous a misdeed. An hour was needed, and all manner of comfortings, before she sobbed herself to sleep.

Soon after the return from Ireland, Dermot left the
kindergarten, but not before the marvellous and unexpected
pleasure of a visit from Uncle Ben. The mariner arrived
unheralded at breakfast time. With shouts of laughter,
opening his arms wide, he lifted their mother off her feet,
wrung their father by the hand, and filled the house with
the uproar of his delight. Feeling a little "mousey," as he
put it, he had taken a week off, boarded his beloved B. & I.,
and made the voyage to Plymouth. Here he would stay
two days "if you'll have me, Mar, me child," and catch the
boat on her return journey, to arrive home set up, with all
the mousiness blown out of him. Dermot heard the noise
from the nursery, and thought the world must be turned upside down. When he appeared, stupefied, hardly able to
believe his ears, he was seized and held right up in the air,
high over Uncle Ben's head.

"Ben, you madman," laughed Dermot's father presently,
"what on earth time were you up this morning?"

"Oh, faith, Ernest boy, the usual time. The usual time.
Six o'clock—when they're swabbing down the decks."

"And the hose on you?"

Margaret wrinkled up her nose in mock horror.

"*And* the hose on me," said Uncle Ben, with complacency.
"Sure, where would I be without me bath?"

Strange and wonderful it was, to have Uncle Ben in the
house. He was not like the bone spoon, all wrong out of his
own place. He brought himself, a real bit of Ireland, unchallenged, triumphant, into the foreign land. That very
morning, he insisted on accompanying Dermot to the kindergarten. Dermot hesitated for a moment whether to take his
toy monkey with him as usual. Uncle Ben might laugh at him.
But the toy monkey was a link with Paddy, and Paddy
meant Ireland: so the toy monkey went, and, far from
laughing, Uncle Ben took the liveliest interest in disposing of
him, during lesson-time, in his hiding place: a kind of box,
built into the wall, so that the front door key should not

chip a hole in it when the door swung back. It was wonderful, walking down beside Uncle Ben in the sunny October morning, hearing about Ireland.

"Have you been to Walmer Villa, Uncle Ben?"

"Yes, yes, Dermot boy. I took a cup of tea with them, only last Friday."

Only last Friday.

"Was the fire all bright over the wall: all twinkly in the things on the sideboard?"

Uncle Ben stared.

"Faith, son—oh yes, bedad, so it was. So it was. Till Bessie brought the lamp in."

Dermot stopped still in the road, with parted lips, seeing it all so vividly that it hurt. Then they walked for a minute in silence, Uncle Ben stroking his moustache, and glancing down curiously at Dermot.

"Did you see Paddy?"

"Oho, faith, I did." Uncle Ben threw back his head, and his voice echoed in the prim road. "I never go there but I have a word with me little Paddy-boy."

"Was he very well?"

"He was. He was glad to see me, too, the little chap. He hasn't anyone to play with, d'ye see."

That brought back another sad thing, Bessie's letter, written only ten days after they left. "Paddy-monkey does be missing you dreadful." Poor Paddy-monkey. Still, he had to get used to it, as Mummy said. He had no one but Bessie and Granny, for nearly all the year.

It was hard not to be terribly proud, in the kindergarten, of his wonderful uncle. None of the other children had such an uncle. One little girl, indeed, put forward claims for a father in India, who had killed a cobra: but even he, as she was forced to admit, did not allow a monkey to tickle his head. The legend made so great an impression that, when Uncle Ben came again to fetch him home, he was greeted by a little crowd of silent, staring children. No whit daunted, he addressed them all boisterously, smiled at their Nannies, lifted his cap to their mothers, laid siege to the heart of poor Miss Simpson with a brace of rolling compliments—there was something entirely irresistible in his voice and the twinkle of his eye: and led off Dermot amidst an admiring silence, every eye following his broad back up the road.

Uncle Ben took him there the next morning too, and added to his feats by leaping up and snatching off a spray of flowers that was growing down a wall, for Dermot to give to Miss Simpson. There was something so utterly unlike his father, unlike England, about a big man jumping up and pulling down a spray of flowers off a wall, that Dermot never forgot it. Miss Simpson was not herself for twenty minutes after the presentation.

But soon, dreadfully soon, came the time for Uncle Ben to go. He left as cheerfully as he came, with shouts of laughter, and waving of the hand. Happy, lovely Uncle Ben: able to sail back to Ireland. The place seemed all dull and empty after he had gone.

CHAPTER XII

Since the months immediately following Eithne's birth, Dermot had been quiet and law-abiding, and seldom got into trouble. Indeed, from all his Mutley Park House days, he could only remember two large transgressions, both harmless in intention. The first, and the more serious, concerned the plumber. There was a path running down beside the sloping lawn to the little gate which led to Oxford Avenue, and under this path the plumber was laying a pipe. When he and his assistants had excavated the path to their satisfaction, they went away for their midday meal, leaving the pipe, which was of small diameter, lying in a coil beside one of the garden trees. The coil was a most inviting, a most suggestive object. Dermot contemplated it. Then he went off to get his tool box. He had not many tools, but they were enough for the purpose.

The coil was tied together in several places with thick, coarse twine. This was easy. He simply put the blade of the chisel against the twine, and hit the chisel with a mallet until the twine was cut through. Once all the twine was cut, he began to uncoil the pipe. The lead was surprisingly soft and pliable: he uncoiled several yards of pipe, before he stopped, panting, for a rest. The plumber, who bore the homely name of Boggis, had omitted to mark his piping with it. Dermot repaired this oversight, in several places, cutting the letters with bradawl, chisel, and mallet, and adding a pedantic full stop after each inscription. The principle, if not the occasion, would have delighted Grandpapa. Then, the fancy gaining on him, he fashioned the

end of the pipe into the head of a boa constrictor, whose
eyes, like those of a plaice, occurred irregularly on the top
of its head, and proceeded to wind it round the tree. This
was arduous work, and it was perhaps as well that the
plumber's assistant should return and interrupt it at about
the third coil.

The plumber's assistant stood still in amazement. Dermot
faced him shyly, conscious of having done him a good turn
by uncoiling the pipe, but of having exceeded instructions
a little in winding it round the tree. He expected thanks,
with possibly a good-humoured admonition, a wag of the
finger in mock reproof.

"I've been making a boa constrictor," he said, in a tone
to which self-consciousness gave a superior sound. "Or an
anaconda. I'm not quite sure."

The plumber's assistant's sallow face went all dark.

"Aaaaaah—you—bliddy—little—toad—" he began:
but Dermot did not stop to hear the rest. Hastily, and in
great surprise, he sought another part of the garden. Here
he walked up and down, composing lordly speeches, imagining himself a potentate—the Dermot of Celebes—sitting
upon a throne in a high room, into which his trusty slaves
dragged the plumber's assistant, a grovelling captive, to sue
for mercy at his feet. The Dermot of Celebes was a new
creation. He had read of Celebes in his geography, and, being
much taken with the name, constituted himself its absolute
ruler. To-day's was the first practical use of the new dignity.

When he went in for his tea, avoiding with haughty care
the south end of the garden, he saw that the pipe had been
laid. Mr. Boggis and two assistants were stamping and
patting down the earth by the side of the path. He was glad
of this, despite his lofty mood, and decided not to mention
the incident to anyone: since it was possible, just possible,
that other adults might take the same attitude as the plumber's assistant. In any case, it was usually unwise to repeat

incidents in which the lower orders had a share. He had had an instance of that only a couple of Sundays ago. There were two visitors, and, doing his best to make interesting conversation, he had narrated the strange behaviour of the street boys in the waste land, during repairs to the fence. They had climbed a tree which enabled them to over-look the garden, and had engaged him in conversation.

"They would insist," he told the visitors, laughing at the memory of such stupidity, "they would insist that my sur-name was * * * *."

Instructed by this incident, therefore, he kept his own counsel.

But, a few days later, something happened which brought back disturbing memories.

"I can't think," said his father to his mother, "why that path is getting in such a swamp. We've hardly had any rain. It wasn't like it all the winter."

"Swamp, darling?" said his mother vaguely, recalled from abstraction.

"Swamp," he repeated sharply. "It's my belief old Boggis has made a mess of it again. If it turns out so, this is the last time I'll employ him."

That was all: but it was enough to fill Dermot with sick uneasiness. He remembered his carving: he remembered his full stops: and, for the first time, he faced the idea that he might have pierced the pipe. Any little quiver of anxiety he had felt on the afternoon itself had been lulled to rest once the pipe was safely underground. Out of sight, out of mind: only, unfortunately, the pipe would not play up to this comforting maxim. The starkness with which his fear now confronted him showed that it had not been buried very deep. Indeed, with Dermot, fear was never buried deep. For all the look of confidence which misled grown-ups about him, his soul was riddled and undermined with fears. Certain things did not frighten him, because he knew very well that they would not do him any harm. But the un-

known was always a source of terror. Had he been old enough
to formulate a philosophy of life, it would have seemed a
narrow, precarious path, trodden on sufferance, in the midst
of perils.

For two miserable days he crept about with his secret.
No adult would have inflicted on him a tithe of the punishment he gave himself. Half an hour's fear is an age to a
child: and Dermot very soon showed the toll. He would not
eat: he looked white and drawn, spoke hardly at all, and,
when anyone spoke to him, began his reply unnecessarily
loud, and let his voice die away before he had finished. Thinking he was upset inside, they gave him Gregory's Powder, a
bestial and nauseating medicine then in high favour. This
did him no good—except in so far as strong emotions always
upset him, and it may therefore have been needed. On the
evening of the second day, his mother took him on her knee,
and asked what was the matter. Her voice was very gentle,
almost playful. It held a note so near to laughter that no
trouble could be really very terrible. Hiding his face against
her breast, he whispered his fear—begging her above all
things not to tell his father. She looked a little serious at that.
She could hardly promise, she explained softly, stroking his
hair. But, very likely, what he had done had not pierced the
pipe. It might all easily be a mistake of Mr. Boggis. He had
done a job all wrong before.

"Oh, but don't, don't tell Daddy. He'll be so angry.
He'll—he'll shout at me."

The voice trembled into tears.

"Darling, he won't. He won't, really. Daddy isn't at all a
cross sort of man."

"Oh, but I've heard him, when he *is* cross—"

"Never fear, darling. He'll see perfectly well that you
didn't mean to do it."

"B-but, you remember, Mummy, the time I broke the
water jug. I didn't mean to do that—and he was dreadfully
cross."

"But you had no business to be playing with that, had you, little son? You see—"

"He'll say I had no b-b-business to be playing with this."

"That happened straight in front of him, and made him start. And you *had* been rather tiresome, fidgeting about, darling. This is different. He'll have time to think about this."

"Oh, darling Mummy, don't, don't, *don't* tell him."

"Well," she temporised, looking down at him in some concern, "I won't unless it becomes absolutely necessary, darling. More than that I can't promise, even to you. But I do promise, whatever happens, it will be all right."

Luckily the ordeal was not prolonged much further. When Dermot's father came home that same evening, the swamp had grown alarmingly, and water was trickling on the surface of the path. Accordingly, on the next morning an aggrieved Mr. Boggis arrived, surveyed the swamp, and went off discomfited, to return after lunch with his two assistants. The water made its first appearance two thirds of the way up the slope: therefore, being Devonians, they began their excavations at the bottom. Thus it was not till Dermot's father had returned from the office, and was going the round of his greenhouse, that Mr. Boggis appeared dramatically in the doorway.

"I've found the cause of the trouble, Mr. Gray," he announced, in deep and solemn tones.

"Oh—that's good. What is it?"

"Your Son."

Mr. Boggis held up eighteen inches of lead piping, which he had been concealing behind his back.

"Your Son, Mr. Gray, sir. That's what it is. That's the cause. Your Son. A-writin' of my name on the pipe with a sharp pointed objeck. Pokin' 'oles."

He thrust the evidence into Mr. Gray's hand.

"You see for yourself, sir, what 'avoc 'e done."

"I do indeed." Dermot's father took the disclosure very

well. "I can't say how sorry I am, Mr. Boggis, that you should have been put to all this trouble."

"No *trouble*, sir," replied Mr. Boggis gloomily. "No *trouble*."

"Well," amended Mr. Gray, "I'm sorry you have had to come here again, through no fault of yours. I'll keep this, and speak to my son: and—I don't expect anything of the sort will occur again."

"Yes, sir," said Mr. Boggis, after thought.

How it was managed, or what took place behind the scenes, Dermot never knew. All he knew was that, next morning, after breakfast, his father called him down to the dining-room, and was extraordinarily gentle and kind. He just pointed out the trouble and expense which had been caused, and said it would turn out a very good investment if Dermot learned from it never to interfere with what did not concern him. He held Dermot on his knee, and talked to him quietly and reasonably, as if he were grown-up too. Finally, he gave Dermot the piece of pipe, to keep as a memento, and a reminder not to tamper again with anything he did not understand.

After that, it seemed evidence of some strange perversity on Dermot's part that the second row should happen a bare week afterwards. He had learned from his governess how to draw a horse's head, and accordingly decorated the wall of the house with a series of horses' heads in chalk, all the way up beside the hall door steps, as a surprise for his father, and a proof of his newly acquired skill. The surprise was badly received, however; and Dermot came out wide-eyed to the summons of an angry voice. "Guttersnipe," "street cad," "little vulgarian," —terms of severe abuse broke like fireworks round his startled ears. He had let down the prestige of the house: he had befouled its aspect: he had disgraced his parents and himself.

"I was very gentle with you, when you did a damnfool

silly thing last week: and now you think you can do what you like with the place. It isn't even as if the rotten things were decently drawn. Go and get a sponge and basin, and sponge them off."

Very silent, and with shaking hands, Dermot crept out again from the scullery. Even the maids were awed by the thunder from above. Cook gave him the basin hastily, as a person handing something to a leper. His father was still standing on the gravel, his mackintosh over his arm, when Dermot emerged.

"Good. Now—don't let there be a sign of that when I come out again."

He went up, passing Dermot on the steps. The boy shut his eyes, and cowered against the wall: but nothing happened.

The despised heads were soon erased, and Dermot slunk off with his basin and grey, dirty sponge. As he passed under the drawing-room window, he heard his Mother's low tone, and the raised voice answering.

"My dear, we can't have him thinking he can do just as he likes. You and Maud—"

Maud. That was Munny. Mummy and Munny. You and Maud. How different, like the voice Moses heard out of the mountain, angry and terrible. Mummy and Munny. You and Maud. The Old Testament was at this time very near to Dermot. With its outbursts and its terrors, it was the supernatural counterpart of his view of life. His daily walks took him into the midst of it. The pleasure ground on top of Compton Hill was Mount Sinai. From its highest point Moses looked over to Egg Buckland, Lee Moor, and the Dartmoor heights, viewing the Promised Land. The same height did duty for other mountains. In the little gateway on the far side of the ground sat David, and heard of Saul's death on Gilboa, a hundred yards up the slope. Eli also sat there, presently falling back and breaking his neck. Gideon, on the other hand, put to flight an enemy encamped in Granny's meadow, his army hiding their lights

in washstand jugs with bright pink rims (like Munny's) or—
this in the secrecy of his mind—in chamber pots. These
last Dermot arrived at, not from any spirit of levity, but
because they were so obviously suited to the purpose. Besides, there would not be enough jugs to go round.

"What will happen when God comes next time, Munny?"

"Next time," Munny would reply, in a hushed whisper,
"God won't come with water. He'll come with fire, and
burn up all the world, and all the wicked people."

The answer never varied, and Dermot would have been
much upset if it had. Munny was not often consulted upon
religious matters. A couple of years ago, she had taken over
from his mother the duty of hearing him say his prayers.

"Our Father, Which art in Heaven—" she intoned.

"Our Father, Which art in Heaven—"

"—'allowed be Thy Name."

"No."

"Come on, Dermot, darling. Don't be naughty. Say it
after Munny. ''Allowed be Thy Name.'''

"No."

With childish pedantry, he would not countenance the
dropped aspirate: and his mother had to be called in before
he would finish the prayer. Nowadays, he said his prayers
silently, to himself. His mother would come in, once he was
in bed, and read a hymn to him. He became quickly expert
in the Irish Hymnal, from which she read, and requested
certain favourites so often that she felt obliged to impose a
rule, restricting the appearance of the same hymn to once a
week. Once a week, therefore, with unfailing regularity,
Dermot demanded his favourite of all:

> *Weary of earth, and laden with my sin,*
> *I look at Heaven and long to enter in.*

This was accompanied in his mind by a picture from a
magazine, of a ship labouring to her death in stormy seas,
while overhead, clear above the wreck, floated the Celestial

City—envisaged by the artist as a cross between St. Paul's and the Crystal Palace. As the hymn progressed, this quite inappropriate picture was succeeded by others. All the hymns were mentally illustrated in this manner, so that each became a very real journey through well-known country. Like almost every child, Dermot loved ritual, and the vividness of his imagination enlarged and complicated it to a high degree. It was love of ritual which prompted him to ask of Munny the question which could only have one answer,

"Next time God won't come with water. He'll come with fire, and burn up all the world, and all the wicked people."

This, and the peculiar expression on Munny's face as she said it, made a definite part of the furniture of life: those constant entities which it was good and reassuring to take out and verify, like the money in one's money-box. One knew how much there was, and one knew it was there. Taking it out and counting it was a proof that the world was still the world: and this sort of reassurance was very necessary to Dermot. For the world was not always the world. It needed watching. Soon after the affairs of Mr. Boggis and the horses' heads, the world gave an ugly and terrifying demonstration of its instability. Dermot's father fell violently ill, and was put to bed with agonising pains in his stomach. The doctor diagnosed appendicitis. It was before the days of ready operation, though both the disease and this way of treating it had become known. Dr. Garfield applied poultices and belladonna, and held his hand. Forty-eight hours of agony followed; then the disease fortunately cured itself. The patient survived the fever, the inflamed appendix sloughed away, and Dr. Garfield was able to assure Dermot's mother that, though very weak, her husband was on the way to health. The danger had been near, and the case a lucky one: but such natural recovery, the doctor maintained, was more valuable and more complete than the results of an operation. Whether he was right or not, the recovery was complete, and Mr. Gray had no more trouble of the kind.

The idea that anyone so tall, so authoritative and permanent should be struck down was a staggering shock to Dermot. He was not allowed to see his father for ten days, and then the shock was increased. The thin, pale, worn face, with the sprouting beard and tired, dull eyes: the kind, husky whisper of a voice, the smile that seemed a physical effort, leaving him more tired than before: it was all awful to Dermot, and he shed tears as soon as he was taken out of the room. The tears were not all compassion for the undreamed-of suffering which must have been necessary to reduce his masterful father to that poor, tired, gentle thing: they were partly compassion for himself, long since frightened of what the world might do to him, and now made aware of even more terrifying powers. When he was a very small boy, before Eithne was born, he well remembered coming crying into that very bedroom, where his mother was getting ready to go out to a concert or a theatre. He was always afraid she and Daddy would be run over and killed outside the big Guildhall, or at the corner by the theatre. People *were* killed in the streets—Munny would read about it from the papers: and, as he had never himself been out at night, he imagined that the streets were then more dangerous. It had taken him a long time to get out of that particular fear: and here it was, swooping down again unexpectedly, in another form.

"Aha!" said the world, nodding and grinning at him sardonically. "You've had a narrow escape, young fella-me-lad, that's what you've had."

For, if Daddy had died, what would have become of them all?

He sat again with Daddy a few days later, and watched him eat his first solid food: an egg. He knew better this time than to ask for the top, which was usually his portion: realising somehow, so upset, so shocking had the world become, that the invalid would fight with the last of his feeble strength for every morsel of that precious food, and lie back weeping, in the abyss of all defeat, if it were taken from him. So vivid was the imagination that he burst into tears, and fled from the room. Then, shame of shames, they thought at first that he was crying because he had not been given the top of the egg as usual!

The cruelty of this misunderstanding so humiliated and outraged him that he buried himself deep in his bed, and would not be comforted for an hour or more. But Mummy understood. She always did.

BOOK II

BOOK II

Huge, overshadowing, and vivid, so full of dark massed colour that they seemed closer than the coast beneath their feet, the Dublin Mountains slid swiftly over the satin waters to meet the mailboat. From one dominant peak, of an intense, clear blue, they humped off in rich, uncouth profusion, huddling over the city which lay under their shelter in a silver haze of smoke: guarding it from the wilder, more arrogant peaks of Wicklow to the South. Beneath them, all was dark and vague, till a shaft of sun, falling on the spires of Kingstown, pulled them forth brilliantly from their brooding background, like a cluster of stiff, spiky flowers, rising suddenly above the water. And all the time the land came nearer, nearer. Soon the wide arms of Dublin Bay would open to let in the mailboat: the shapeless hill to the north-east would reach out past her, and take on the remembered contours of the Hill of Howth. Already that dim, insignificant mound near the spires had grown its tiny obelisk. It was Killiney Hill, which, once located, gave a clue to the changed shapes around it. Soon one would see the woods and rocks of Dalkey—and there, marvel, the shaft of sun struck nearer, and caught a low-lying green strip, crowned with a short fat pepper-pot: Dalkey Island!

Dermot stood by the rail, close to the bow. Every now and then he took a deep breath, and looked down from the land at the calm sliding water. It almost made him dizzy, the ease and speed with which the gleaming silver sheet slid past. It was the sea and the land that were moving, not the boat. She was still, a bright and spotless universe, with steady decks, and white paint brilliant in the sun. Her tall masts soared up motionless, her black majestic funnels leaned back into the sky. They were eternal. The afternoon in flux dreamed its way past them. Giddy, Dermot tightened his hold on the rail, and blinked at the dark splendour of the mountains. Now, as they drew nearer, their mass was even nobler than before. Now the Wicklow Mountains began to slope away astern, the Dublin Mountains drew further aloof from them. Now the spires of Kingstown shot up effortless ahead, and now could be seen the low short-bread arms of the harbour for which the boat was heading. And, at last, to complete the spectacle, the sun overcame the cloud above the coast, and sent a great soft shaft towards the mountains. Gratefully, gently, yet still magnificently, they responded. Underneath their changing line the masses crumbled into new formation. Fresh humps, fresh shoulders burgeoned forth, new shadows fell across the valleys: slow colours flooded the vast, smooth curves and sides: for an instant, as the wide light poured between them and the boat, they looked like piles of giant fruit: then they became clear again, alive and angry, with deep shades of blue and purple, and on their lowest slopes the tiny fields showed emerald. And all the time, all the time, Ireland was drawing near: Ireland, so long unvisited: Ireland, with Granny's cottage, Granny's garden, Paddy-monkey, Bessie—with Delgany, and Uncle Ben—all, all marvellously in front of him, stretching ahead for days, for weeks, for two whole months: Ireland, real, *there*, before his eyes: there still, when he shut and opened them again: not just looked back to, called from memory, but there.

"Wait a minyit, Dermot darling. Hold hard for a minyit, now, till I come with you."

Dermot paused, and looked back, surprised.

"Why, Bessie? I'm only going to see Paddy."

"Sure I know, honey. But you'd better wait. Here now"
—she wiped her hands hastily on a cloth—"Now I'm ready."

"Why couldn't I go by myself, Bessie?"

"Sure, he's older, d'ye see, and he hasn't seen ye for a
long time." Her voice fell to the old, familiar coo. "Paddy-
monkey! Paddy-monkey!"

There was a rattle of the chain, and the monkey sprang
out from his kennel. The sight of him gave Dermot a shock.
Not that he was unrecognisable: he was instantly and
clearly Paddy: but he had grown, and coarsened. His black
hair had turned in places almost to brown: his whole
appearance was fiercer, more alert: and he was nearly half
as big again. He sat up very straight on the back of the
kennel, eyeing Dermot with keen, suspicious eyes.

"Paddy," said Dermot. He took a step forward, and held
out his hand.

"Here," Bessie pushed by, and surreptitiously gave him a
little carrot. "Here, Paddy, honey. Up to me."

With a single, swift bound, the monkey leaped to her
shoulder, and rested, one arm about her neck, still staring
at Dermot.

"Here," Bessie coaxed him, "sure it's your little friend
Dermot, who used to play with you. Sure you remember
him. Oh, indeed ye do, now. Give him the carrot, honey,"
she added, in a low voice.

Dermot went closer, and held out the carrot. A change
came over the monkey's demeanour. Very gingerly and
softly he put out his hand, took the carrot, and began to
eat, glancing up quickly every now and then at the giver.

"That's the boy," cried Bessie, when it was finished.
"That's me little darling Paddy boy. Now, Dermot honey:
give him your hand to look at."

Unafraid, Dermot put up his hand. Paddy drew back
suspiciously: frowned down his nose at it: looked more
searchingly into Dermot's face: then took it, and began gently
to examine it. There was a tiny dark spot, like a freckle,

near the thumb. He pulled, gibbered suddenly to himself —the first sound he had made—and tried it with his teeth.

As soon as she judged the introduction made, Bessie took Dermot away.

"Ye want to be a bit careful with him, at first," she said. "You see, it's the way he's older and stronger in himself. He's got away on us lately once or twice, and he defies your Grandfather and the Mistress. Only for yous coming, they'd have got rid of him."

"Got rid of him!"

Dermot stopped blankly. Such a thought was sheer blasphemy. He could not understand it.

"Got rid of him!" he repeated. "But why—how silly! —how—"

"Well, you see, honey," Bessie glanced round anxiously, lest anyone should hear: "he's a bit noisy, in the night time, and he wakes your Grandfather: and the neighbours do be complaining, sometimes."

"Noisy! At night! What does he do?"

"He does be banging his tin mug on the flags, and rattlin' his chain. Don't say too much about him, in the house, now." Bessie's anxious face creased into rueful smiles. "We had a terrible to-do on the head of him, only last Sunday."

"What was it about?"

"He wouldn't let the old ladies into the closet. Your Granny had to take the cane to him."

Dermot considered this.

"I expect I'll have to hold him again."

The anxious look reappeared.

"Be careful how ye thwart him. He's a bit wicked, when he gets excited. Sure ye'll mind him, honey?"

"I will," Dermot promised.

The subject was a live one, as he found when he sat down to his tea.

"The ape," declared Grandpapa (he pronounced it "the yape")—"the ape does be getting very savage. Ye'd do well not to approach him at all close. Ye'd want to mind yourself, for fear he'd do you some sort of mischief."

"I was with him just now," ventured Dermot, "and he didn't do me any harm. Bessie was there too," he added hastily, seeing his Grandpapa's face.

"It would be well, Margaret," said Grandpapa, "it would be well—Margaret, do ye hear me—it would be well, I'm saying, not to let the children near the ape."

Eithne, fortunately, showed no disposition to go near Paddy. Dermot hobnobbed with him more or less surreptitiously for a day or so, and then, as no harm befell, he did not bother to hide their conversations. Paddy, if more independent, was as friendly as ever: in fact, he visibly improved in disposition. Maybe it was solitude and lack of a playmate which had aged him. Grandpapa shook his head gravely, when he saw Dermot by the kennel, but he did not interfere: and the matter rested.

For one thing, the family were only too pleased to see Dermot happily engaged. A new problem had arisen, the problem of filling his days. He was too big to be contented walking after the pram when Eithne rode, and her pace was too slow for him when she walked. Unaware of the problem himself, but making it plain to others, he found his own solution. Munny had left them; she liked very young children, and there was no further prospect of them with the Grays. Her successor, a young and goodlooking girl called Annie, often took the two down to the Sea Wall, which, though now shorn of its glory by the new promenade, is still a feature of Dun Laoghaire. Below the Sea Wall is an enchanting half mile of rocks and pools and inlets, and here, sitting resentfully beside the pram, Dermot saw scores of boys, ragged and gentle, but mostly ragged, fishing, hunting for shrimps, digging for bait, busied in all the hundred ways which such a paradise afforded. He watched with growing envy, and went home with the one idea fixed in his head. It took about a week to get his way, but Dermot, once his imagination was roused, proceeded with unremitting obstinacy in the one direction. The new desire ousted all others. He moped about the garden, he grew bilious, he would not eat. In the end, his unhappiness carried the point. Objections were many. He would fall into the water. He would take cold. He would catch fleas, or diseases, from the little ragged boys. They would molest him. He would pick up vulgar accents and expressions. He would run the fish-hooks into his fingers. To all these Dermot replied with unhappiness and the reiterated assertion of his desire.

"Lots of the other boys are no bigger than me, Granny. Some are much smaller. Why mayn't I go?"

Granny looked helplessly round.

"Ah well, ye see, son, it's—I don't think it'd be very nice for ye."

"But it would, it would. Granny, I want to go *so* much. Other boys are allowed to. Why can't I be like other boys?"

"You see, darling," put in his mother, "you're not very strong. You have to be careful."

"But the sea air is good for me. You said it was, yourself. Mummy—you did say it was. You know you did."

By Friday afternoon, the resistance was weakening. Then, in happy time, Uncle Ben called in for tea, and blew away the remnant of it with his gusty scorn. On Saturday morning, therefore, Dermot set out, self-conscious but determined, beside the pram, his thin bare legs tapering into a pair of brand-new canvas sandshoes, and in his hand a brand-new ready-made line, bought from M'Gurk the ironmonger's, and personally recommended to Granny by the proprietor. There had been talk, at home, of cutting the barb off the hook; but the practical difficulty of accomplishing this led to the point being waived, until the first accident should have occurred. Yet Dermot, though vague and unpractical, was better able to take care of himself than they supposed. In all his fishing years he never ran a hook into his hand: and he only fell in the water twice—both times on the same day. He had no liking for risks, and never took them. His few deeds of daring were not recognised by him as such: and he had an unfailing instinct for his own safety. He was unadventurous.

The first morning's fishing was not a success. Dermot broke periwinkles for bait, as he had seen other boys do, but his ready-made line was cumbrous and unsuited to the weedy, rocky bottom. Its wire gears kept catching in things, and the plop of its ring sinker scared the little fish. After a barren hour, Dermot edged away from Annie and the pram towards a group of boys on a big rock who were evidently having much sport. They said nothing, so finally he climbed beside them.

Their apparatus was much more primitive than his. In most cases they had nothing but a hook on the end of a length of thin twine. But they were amazingly successful. The little fish seemed to fight for the privilege of swallowing their baits. Several times Dermot's hand went towards his own line: but he saw that the ragged boys were all packed closely on the good side of the rock, and that the manipulations of his own elaborate line would probably get in their way. Chagrined, beginning to perspire with mental conflict, he took a place as near them as he could, laboriously broke a winkle, and cast in his line. They looked round quickly at the splash, sniffed, and jeered among themselves. Sure enough, the line got caught. He tugged at it, but it would not come free. Furtively, he looked out of the sides of his eyes at the ragged boys, half afraid that they would see, half longing for their help. Suddenly one of them, a spectator only, caught his eye, and came across.

"Ay, Jack. Is yer line cotcht?"

A year ago, Dermot would have set the stranger right. His name was not Jack. To-day he gulped, and answered to it gratefully.

"Y-yes. I'm rather afraid it has."

"Show."

The stranger took it. He was exceedingly ragged, exceedingly dirty, and in urgent need of a pocket handkerchief. He jagged twice at the line, then sprang down, with an agility incredible to Dermot, to a lower point of rock, at right angles to the direction in which they had been pulling. Crouching, getting a purchase with his bare feet, he grasped the line in both hands, and, after violent tugging, jerked it free.

"There y'are, Jack."

"Thank you. Thank you very much."

The deliverer climbed up and stood close behind Dermot, looking over his shoulder at the line, and sniffing. Dermot could not help drawing away, but his action was unnoticed.

"Yer huke is broke," announced the stranger.

It was.

"Yer gears is jairked."

Dermot could not corroborate him there, for want of technical knowledge: but the line was manifestly out of action. He saw himself going home empty-handed. A temptation as old as fishing woke in his mind.

Interest over, the ragged boy was moving off. Dermot put a hand in his pocket. He had fivepence.

"I say. Do you think those boys would give me any of their fish for fivepence?"

"For wha'?"

Dermot produced the pence. The rescuer's eyes goggled. He turned to the fishers.

"Ay, ay! here's a young lad wants to buy fish for fivepence."

In an instant Dermot was surrounded. Hot acrid bodies crowded on top of him: dirty eager faces bawled into his: slimy hands thrust fish upon him. He was suffocated, bewildered, stunned by the clamour.

"That's all I have," he kept repeating, his voice loud in his own ears. "That's all I have. Share it out between you."

Quickly, as if they feared he would repent of his bargain,

as if they feared the police would be after them, the ragged
boys took up their lines and scuttled off, leaving him in
sole possession. The pudder of their bare feet sounded on
the rocks, and they were gone, rushing off as fast as they
could in the direction of the town. Dermot looked down at
the little pile of fish. They were useless to eat: even he knew
that much. "Stingoes," the boys called them. They had big
heads, and silly blunt faces: the biggest of them was about
six inches long. He looked around him. There was no
way of carrying them. There were too many for his bare
hands: besides, one or two of them were still alive. In the
end, he took off his shoes, filled them with the fish, and made
his perilous way back to Annie. She regarded him blandly.

"That was a much better place, over there, Annie."

"Did you catch any?"

"Look." Even now that he was committed to it, the lie
stuck in his throat.

"Oo my. Did you catch all those?"

"My line's broken, so I had to stop and come back."

"Or did those little boys give them to you?"

"Of course not." That could be answered indignantly,
and with perfect truth. They had not given them. They
had sold them.

Annie looked into the shoes, wrinkling her nose. She had
large nostrils, which Dermot disliked.

"Oo my. What will you do with them? You can't eat
little fish like that."

"It isn't the size, Annie. It's the species. This species of
fish is not good to eat."

"I should think not, indeed. Ugly, horrid little things."

Dermot was offended, without precise reason.

"What will you do with them?" harped the ingenuous
Annie. "You're never going to take them home with you!"

"Of course I shall take them home."

"What's the good of them, if you can't eat them?"

"They—I—" Dermot groped for words which would

not come. "I shall show them to Granny," he concluded lamely.

"She won't want to see them," said Annie relentlessly. "Dirty, ugly little things."

Dermot decided that there were moments when he hated Annie. He usually felt obliged to put on a patronising air in dealing with her, but the good-natured Devon girl seemed quite unaware of it. Sometimes, when he was extra superior, she would laugh, as if he were being amusing especially for her benefit.

"Well." She began to gather up her belongings. "It's time we were off."

Dermot went round to the side of the pram.

"Look, Eithne," he said ingratiatingly. "Look at the pretty little fish."

Eithne looked at them, and gave a mechanical smile. Her mind was busy with other concerns.

"Master Dermot. There's your Daddy, on the wall, beckoning to you."

There, sure enough, stood the tall figure, clad in grey, aloof from the activities of the Sea Wall. Something, a sort of graceful stiffness, proclaimed that he had not come there for his own pleasure, but to encourage or retrieve his son.

There was an interval of care, loud breathing, of bare feet on wet, slippery weed, and hard, warm rock: then Dermot climbed up beside his father. At just the right distance short of him, he looked up, with a smile of eager, modest triumph.

"Look, Daddy."

Mr. Gray looked.

"H'm," he said. "Several."

"Yes."

Dermot stood beside him, a shoe in each hand, waiting to start for home.

"You don't propose to bring them home, do you?" asked his father.

Dermot looked up blankly.

"Yes," he said.

"What for?"

"T—to show Granny. You see, she bought me the line," he added, with sudden cunning.

"How will you carry them?"

"Like this—in my shoes."

"That you won't," said Mr. Gray, with decision. "I'm not going to walk home with you padding along in your bare feet, like one of those street boys. Throw them away," he went on, as Dermot hesitated. "I'll tell your Granny how well the line worked."

With disappointment, yet with a sort of secret relief, Dermot tipped out the clammy load into a pool. He sat down on the wall, and dutifully pulled on his shoes. His growing sense of guilt was somehow lessened by the loss of the fish. The corpses were no longer on his hands. He trotted along beside his father, perfect image of the disappointed yet docile little son. This picture, with the faintest suspicion of injury, perceptible to the women and winning its full meed of unspoken sympathy, he kept up till about three that afternoon: when it was effectually shattered.

Grandpapa, when at home, spent a good deal of his time looking out of the parlour window. If a caller excited his disapproval, as not infrequently happened, he would bustle out to the door himself. The habit was a source of much concern to Granny, since the old gentleman did not mince his words, and often sent people off with a flea in their ear. Dermot loved to listen on these occasions: and so, hearing Grandpapa muttering and storming his way to the door, he put his head outside the nursery where he was supposed to be resting, and cocked his ear.

The latch clicked, and the heavy door creaked back.

"What do ye mean," cried the angry voice, "coming up this way to me door, ye little ragamuffins, ye?"

"I' ye plaze, sir," murmured a low voice, punctuated by sniffs, which Dermot in horror recognised. "We cem to see would the young lad buy the big fish."

"Buy the fish! 'The young lad'!" Grandpapa almost choked. "And for what, do ye think, would a person want —"

But Dermot waited for no more. Burning with shame, he fled to the furthest part of the garden, and there remained till he was called for tea.

CHAPTER XIV

On the Monday Dermot was down at the sea wall again, with two new hooks. He doubted his ability ever to catch a fish, but a sort of obstinate bitterness drove him on. Separating himself as soon as possible from the pram, he chose a place all alone, on the edge of the wall. There, laboriously, he baited both his hooks, and dropped in his line. The ragged boys were far away. He could hear their brawling. He prayed they might not see him. It was in case of fresh offers of fish that he had gone well away from Annie.

He sat for a long time, forlornly holding his line, the object of amused glances from passers-by. Even at high tide, the wall was an unusual place for fishing. The rocks below it were only covered for a bare two hours, and he was fishing in three feet of water.

At some time unnoticed by him, a figure sat down some distance on his left: and Dermot presently began to realise that he was being watched. He went hot, and pretended to be absorbed in the important technique of his line. Stealing a glance round, he saw that the result of his efforts was to produce a wide, friendly smile.

The stranger was a young man of about twenty-eight. He had a broad, honest face, and blue eyes. He had a straggly little moustache, was decently though poorly dressed, and his legs hung rather queerly over the edge of the wall.

Dermot took several glances at him, and, meeting each time the same wide smile, at last smiled back.

"Are you Mrs. Conroy's young lad?" asked the stranger.

"I—She's my Granny."

119

"A grand lady, Mrs. Conroy. Terrible kind. Glasthule'd be the worse without her."

"Oh yes. She's very kind, I know."

"She does be looking after a lot of the poor, and finding work for them. Many's the job she gev me, where others wouldn't."

He glanced down expressively at his legs, and swung them in humorous contempt. Dermot followed the glance with interest.

"Why wouldn't they?" he asked.

"It's the way I'm crippled," replied the stranger cheerfully.

Dermot shrank back at once, afraid he had asked a painful question.

"I'm sorry," he murmured.

"Oh, faith," said the stranger, "it's no matter. I do get about grand. First Monda' in August, I do often win a prize in the sports. I'm terrible strong. And I play football, too. Wing-man Kennedy, they call me."

"Wing-man! What a funny name! Is it your Christian name?"

"Ah no. It means, d'ye see, I do play on the wing."

"I see," said Dermot blankly.

"On the wing of the field, d'ye see." The stranger was anxious that his point should be correctly taken. "On the wing. The side. Way out be the line."

"I think I see."

"That's right." He paused, and spat into the sea. "Ah, no. Sure you couldn't be called Wing-man for yer Christian name. Me Christian name is Patrick. Born on St. Patrick's Day."

"Patrick. Oh, I know. You're Paddy Kennedy, that used to help Mr. Caggen in the garden, when Jem Neill was ill."

Paddy nodded in delight.

"Yis, yis, that's right. Did you hear me name, then? Did your Grandmother—"

"Mr. Caggen told me. And Granny, I think. Yes. I'm sure I heard Granny say it."

"Ah, yer Grandmother is a fine lady. A grand lady. We'd all be the worse off without her. Sure everybody says that."

There was a pause. Paddy transferred his attention to the line.

"Did you catch anythin'?" he enquired.

"Not yet."

"That's not a good place for your line."

"N—no. Perhaps it isn't."

Paddy put down his great hands on the wall, and with astounding agility levered himself along to where Dermot was sitting.

"Show," he said, holding out a hand.

Dermot willingly transferred the line, noticing as he did so that Paddy's hands were deformed, the fingers and thumb all bent in upon themselves. Paddy grasped the line, and felt it. His eyebrows rose comically.

"Be the holies!" he cried: and pulled up *two* little fish, one on each hook.

Several passers-by stopped to look at the scene, Dermot dancing with excitement and joy, then squatting down over the captives, and Paddy rolling about, bellowing with laughter.

"Two on the line—and you holdin' on to them all the time," he cried. "Did yez ever hear the like o' that. Two on the line, and you holdin' on to them all the time. Oh, Janey, that's a quare one. Two on the line—"

He was too much amused to unhook the exhausted fish: while Dermot kept exclaiming, between his hops,

"I caught them myself, Paddy, didn't I? I caught them myself!"

"Oh, faith, ye did." Paddy sat up, and wiped his eyes with a dirty brown handkerchief. "Faith, ye did, and no one else at all."

The two were now on the most intimate terms. At last Paddy unhooked the fish. To point the coincidence still further, they were of different kinds.

"That one's a stingo," he said, "but this is a young rock brame. It's this sort you should be fishing for—the big ones—not stingoes."

He put such scorn into the word that Dermot was abashed.

"Why don't you fish for the big brame?" pursued Paddy.

"I don't know how to."

Paddy considered the downcast figure, and his own eyes lit.

"Will I learn ye?" he enquired. "Will I come down every day, and learn ye how to catch every sort of fish?"

Dermot looked up, and clasped his hands in rapture.

"Oh, Paddy, *do!*"

Paddy nodded solemnly several times.

"I will so. But ye must ask your Granny."

Dermot asked his Granny—and she jumped at the chance. Here was the solution to all the family's difficulty. She knew Paddy well, a trustworthy, honest fellow, unable to get regular work. It would be a godsend to him, and a godsend for Dermot. So Paddy was summoned, and took on the not too arduous duties of gilly and guide for the sum of sixpence a day. He added, of his own goodwill, those of philosopher and friend: and so began for Dermot a friendship which taught him more perhaps than any other in his life.

The new interest came in good time, to take the place of an old: for the accession of Paddy the Second was swiftly followed by the deposition of Paddy the First. Not that Dermot was fickle, or to blame. The deposition was literal. Granny took the step she had so often threatened, and got rid of Paddy-monkey.

The return of a playmate had humanised him, but Dermot could not help seeing, again and again, that he had not really improved with age. He was wilful, and sudden in his moods: one had to go carefully with him. When he flung his tin mug at Mr. Caggen and Jem Neill, dancing up and down to see them hurry and cross themselves, there was a note of real savagery in his noise. If he were free, he would have bitten them. He was at open war with Pucker, too, though there was an armistice now and then, if she had a kitten. He sat on the roof of his kennel, facing the way she must come when the kitchen door was shut, feigning to be asleep, watching her through a wicked, gleaming slit of his yellow eyes. The cat crept up the path, looking balefully up at him, wondering if she dare risk the run past his kennel. A pause—then, crouching low, she ran. With a leap, perfectly timed, the monkey landed on the path beside her, gave her tail a vicious tug, and in the same movement bounded back again to his roof, the fraction of a second clear of her avenging claw. He learned also, whether by chance or bad example, to throw water over her from his mug.

Besides his self-appointed post as door-keeper to the lavatory, Paddy made a nuisance of himself by dismantling the little rockery which stood against its wall. Over this he showed less intelligence than usual. The stones at the top were small, the size of half bricks and upwards. He could easily detach them; but no amount of experience taught him that it was dangerous to pull at them directly. He never actually succeeded in crushing his paws, but would often leap away just in time, shooting across to his kennel, and dashing as far as he could up the pear-tree, there to hang, swearing and chattering, for several minutes. The rockery became an obsession with him. Despite all punishment, he could not keep away from it.

"Aaah!" Bessie cried threateningly, seeing him there. He started, but remained, not daring to take his eye from those resourceful enemies, the loose stones on top, which might at any moment roll down and attack him.

The only good his attentions did the rockery was to keep one side of it free from snails. As, however, he would delicately remove his captives' shells, and leave them crawling about in agony on the path, his gardening was not appreciated. After finding the rockery dismantled for the third time in a week, they shortened his chain.

This privation instantly transformed Paddy-monkey into a wild beast. Leaping, gibbering, gnashing his teeth, his eyes gleaming with bile, he tugged, he strained, he rolled on his back, he screeched and fought and cursed. No one, not even Bessie, dare go near him. Grandpapa stood at a safe distance, moralising on the fulfilment of his oft-repeated prophecy. Mr. Caggen, watching with sardonic eye, wagged his beard malignantly at the prisoner. Jem Neill goggled, and said "Bedam." The slither of his hobnails maddened the monkey. He leaped up with a shriek so envenomed that the man's face mottled, and he made off up the garden at a run. Katie the seamstress shook her head, looking sadly over the tops of her steel-rimmed glasses at everyone in turn, ready with whatever commentary should be required. No one spoke to her, so she withdrew, sucking in her thin lips and still shaking her head.

For a few moments they all stood, gazing at the monkey. Then, a little shame-facedly, the gathering dispersed. They preferred not to contemplate for too long the results of their disciplinary action.

"We're only exciting him, by staying."

"He's only carrying on like that because we're here."

"He'll soon calm down, once we're gone."

Only Dermot stayed, in a place where Paddy could not see him. As soon as he found himself alone, the monkey ceased raging. He sat up, and looked around. Then, with all his strength and cunning, he strove upon the chain. He worked in bursts of silent, terrific energy: straining, arching himself over backwards, wrinkling his face into a little demon's mask. Then, suddenly, he gave one or two high leaps into the air, shaking the loose chain. It was no use. He rested, panting, baring his teeth from time to time, like a navvy on a hot day. Then, with a sort of controlled frenzy, he began throwing himself about again, leaping from side to side, making movements that would have been laughable but for the despair upon his face.

Dermot went up the garden. There should be nothing troublesome in the sight of a disobedient monkey justly shorn of freedom: but there was. Dermot felt unhappy and ashamed. There were things in the world he had not suspected.

After that, Granny acted with decision. Dermot heard nothing, till the afternoon when he came in to find the kennel empty, and was shown, in explanation, a brief notice in the personal column of the *Irish Times*. Printed, unbelievable words stared into his eyes, and were lost. "Thanks to Mrs. Conroy, for monkey . . . The Dublin Zoological Society." Thanks . . . for monkey. . . .

Happily for Dermot, there came a distraction that very evening, to take his sorrow off himself. Anne and Eileen came down from Delgany, with an invitation for Dermot from their mother. Eileen, who had heard of the monkey's disgrace, went straight out to commiserate with him, and was confronted by the empty kennel.

Then and there, her childhood ended. Brushing aside poor tearful Bessie's efforts at propitiation, she burst into the parlour, and faced her startled elders.

"Where is he?" she cried fiercely. "Answer me! Where is he? *What have you done with him?*"

The words were flung in their faces like hailstones at a window. She was transformed. Her lithe, long-limbed body trembled with passion. She advanced on Granny, as if to shake the answer out of her.

Granny's jaw dropped in amazement and consternation. "Gracious, Eileen child, how ye startled me," died on her lips. She had never, as she said afterwards, "seen the child that way before."

"Oh, *answer* me, someone! What have you done with Paddy?"

There was dead silence for a couple of seconds. Then Grandpapa spoke.

"The ape," he observed with satisfaction, "is in the custody of the Royal Dublin Zoological Society, to whom he should have been sent in the beginning: to whom, if Amelia had been said by me, he *would* have been sent in the beginning."

Eileen gazed at him, in wild incredulity.

"What's more," continued the old man, turning further towards her in his chair, "this is no way to come rush into a room, and downface your elders. If your father were here, he'd be highly displeased with ye."

Eileen paid no attention to the rebuke.

"You've—sent him—to the Zoo!" she gasped at length. "You've sent him—oh, how cruel! How *could* you!"

Words left her. With a miserable gesture, she flung out of the room, and slammed the door behind her, leaving a circle of faces blank with amazement.

"Merciful hour!" ejaculated Granny at last. "What's come over the child?"

Dermot left them discussing the matter, the ladies quickly concerting to combat Grandpapa's diagnosis that Eileen was just "a bold girl" and needed correction. For some time he was afraid to follow her down the garden: then, feeling justified by his undoubted position of second mourner, he went timidly after her.

She was more composed, and had got rid of her tears, but she was in high rage. To comfort himself, Dermot urged feebly that Paddy would be well looked after.

"Yes, yes," she interrupted him. "But, can't you see, he'll absolutely *hate* it. He's been by himself, and a pet, all his life: and then, to be put in a great cage, with a crowd of other monkeys—" she turned her back on Dermot, and blew her nose. "He won't live," she said, after a few seconds. "He won't live a month: you see if he does."

About ten days after Paddy's departure, they went in

to visit him. At first he was not to be seen in the big cage. Bessie, mournful, dumpy, wearing her boa, her big hat, and her funny little in-and-out costume, leaned back her head and peered up into the gloom.

"Paddy-monkey!" she called. "Paddy-monkey! Paddy-monkey!"

There was a flash of movement, and the distraught thin figure was at the bars, his face alight, his lips moving in rapturous greeting. When they held out the food to him, other monkeys rushed down, and Paddy cowered pitifully away to one side. With valiant cries and gestures Bessie routed the intruders; and Paddy partook for the last time of carrot and apple from his own garden. For some minutes they talked to him, and with every minute he grew happier, more confident, more like himself. He chattered gently, holding out his hand through the bars, delicately taking the morsels, snuggling up close while Dermot poked a finger in to tickle him. When at last they turned to go, and he realised that they would not take him with them, his little face went cold. Mournful, incredulous, unprotesting, he watched them go. Bessie kept waving to him, encouraging him. "Paddy-monkey. Paddy-monkey." They would come to see him again, yes, soon again. She hurried after the others, tears streaming down her cheeks. Dermot turned back in the doorway, and saw Paddy still clinging there, looking after them.

No one spoke for a while. Bessie lagged behind, sobbing openly, and soon Granny too had to stop and lift her veil.

"Ah, the poor animal," she said, "you couldn't but be fond of him. He was a great pet. But sure, what could we do? It wouldn't have been safe to keep him: let alone the trouble he gave. All the same, I don't like to think of him, shut up there."

Dermot's father began to tell her how well he would be looked after, and what fun he would have, once he got used to the other monkeys. Granny sniffed, and smiled weakly.

"I expect you're right, Ernest," she said, "but I can't but be worried for the poor animal."

But Paddy did not keep his mistress anxious for long. Three days after their visit, he was dead.

"Broke his heart, ma'am," said the keeper. "Broke his heart. Ah, the' will, ye know, when they've had it all their own way, and been med a pet of."

CHAPTER XV

PADDY-MONKEY'S DEATH WAS ONE OF THE LAST DEFINITE dates in Dermot's memories of Ireland. From this time on, when he looked back upon his Irish summers, he began to lose count of them, to be unable to distinguish one from another. He could class them roughly into two periods, the summers before he went to a public school, and the summers afterwards: but even that distinction had blurred edges. Coming back each year to the same scenes and to the same people, taking up life exactly where he had left it the year before, he had an Irish memory, quite separate from his English memory. The Irish memory was qualitative. It had its own time, its own space, its own emotions.

Dermot was happy at home, and only occasionally unhappy at his preparatory school in Plymouth; yet he lived the whole year through in the hope of Ireland. He saw the year as a great curved track, not circular, but completing an irregular ring. The Autumn was the terrible time, that slightly curving part of the run when one was leaving the wonderful days further and further behind. Then, with the new year, one curved sharply, swinging a wide arc through January and February to March, when, for the first time, one's eyes caught sight of the golden patch ahead. From then on one sped faster and faster, making straight for Heaven: eight weeks of dazzling gold: so on and on, for always.

The worst flaw in Heaven was still the Sunday. By a law of compensation, the period before Church in the morning had become one of the week's best joys: the time, above all others, for deliberately realising that he was in Ireland. The

129

walk up and down at the top of the garden, balancing on the uneven stones, had become a ritual. Time and again, at the end of a passage, he would look round intently upon the landscape, letting it soak in to the very back of his eyes: looking down the garden, taking in each seat, each tree, each clump of flowers; taking in the big fields beyond, the houses of Glenageary, the steeple where the bells still played their same old tunes. He pressed his feet hard on the ground, gripping on tight to the edge of the hot wooden cucumber frame, and repeating to himself again and again and again, "This is *Ireland*. This is *Ireland*."

He usually walked to Church with Grandpapa now, instead of going with the others in the tram. Grandpapa walked very slowly, but he was always good-humoured towards the boy, and to walk with him meant part-escaping from the attentions of Granny's old lady friends. Besides, he hated taking the tram for so short a journey. Tram-rides were lovely, exciting things. You rode on top, and watched everything. The only drawback was that, even from the very front, you couldn't watch both sides of the street properly at the same time. To clank along half a mile of perfectly well-known road, sitting inside the tram with your back to the window, was a travesty of a tram-ride.

"Your Granny," Grandpapa observed, as they went slowly along between St. Joseph's and Sandycove Station, "your Granny is always one for the talk. To meet with her friends outside the church, and say 'How d'ye do' to this one, and 'How d'ye do' to that one, and nod her head to each of them in turn, and they to nod back with their bonnets bobbing up and down—Heh!" He chuckled, and turned half left, to look down at his grandson. "What sort of a way is that to be going on, eh?"

"I don't know, Grandpapa."

"Faith, you may well say so. I've been married to your Grandmother these eight-and-thirty years, and I'm no nearer to putting sense in her head than I was at the start.

With her fussing and bowing here, and her fussing and bowing there, her talk and her comether and her how-d'ye-do—"

"Then there's Miss O'Killikelly, to make it worse," put
in Dermot skilfully.

"Miss O'Killikelly!" Grandpapa stopped in the road
and searched his mind for epithets to fit her. "That one!"
he said finally. "That one would have a man in his grave,
that had to sit listening to her. She comes in" (Dermot had
heard all this dozens of times) "at any hour of the day or
night, and a very late inconvenient hour for choice, and
down she sits"—Grandpapa made a gesture as of a man
setting down a big basket—"and flounces herself, and
waggles her head, and 'Oh, me dear,' says she, 'do you know
what I'm after hearing now?'"

The falsetto squeak was so penetrating that Dermot
glanced uneasily at the other churchgoers on the pavement.

"'No, Letitia,' says your Granny, 'I do not.' And that's
invitation enough to me fine lady to sit there an hour and
maybe two or three, pouring nonsense out of her like a
barrel."

He paused, and stood still a moment to get his breath.

"I go up to me bed: for there's no man's ears could endure
the torment of that woman's tongue. When I'm half-way
undressed, I do open the door, and throw down me boots
into the hall, one after the other. That does be apt to startle
their ladyships; and, maybe, it'll only take Miss O'Killikelly, as you call her"—Grandpapa always affected to treat
her name as a jest, or an imposture—"it'll only take her a
matter of ten minutes to be out of the house: and the last
five of them spent on the doorstep, and calling back from
the gate. But some nights," he started walking again, "it'll
take more than the one pair of boots. I've had the hall full
of them, before this, and their two ladyships tripping over
them, and they saying good-bye."

Dermot gasped, contemplating a vision of the hall filled
with boots, like snails and slugs come out after the rain.

"One time," pursued Grandpapa, with unregenerate chuckles, "she didn't go till I threw down the poker and tongs."

"Whatever did Granny say when she came up?"

"She was wild with me," replied Grandpapa complacently. "But, sure, I don't mind her." He chuckled again. "It's not only the start they get with a boot, d'ye see, it's knowing there's more to come, and waiting for the next bump."

"The fire-irons must have frightened them," said Dermot, half in awe.

"Aye. I never had to throw them, only the once."

They turned the corner, and reached the church gates. Dermot felt almost grown up, half a conspirator with Grandpapa. The old man had the knack of rousing masculine freemasonry. Courtly and decorous to a degree, flattering the sex of even the youngest girl, he took a very simple view of the relationship between men and women. His was the philosophy expressed in a song of Samuel Lover, which he used often to sing, sitting by himself in the dark parlour, waiting for Bessie to bring in the light, in his faded lain-in-lavender ghost of a voice.

> *Now the pretty flowers were made to bloom, dear,*
> *And the pretty stars were made to shine,*
> *And the pretty girls were made for the boys, dear,*
> *And maybe you were made for mine.*

"Do you never be looking after the young ladies, Dermot?" Grandpapa sometimes asked him in public: and when Granny took him up warmly, for "putting ideas into the child's head," Grandpapa gave him a wink of delightful complicity. Dermot adored his Granny: yet, so sure was the old man's appeal, that although he did not like being quizzed about little girls, he was enlisted by the wink on Grandpapa's side.

The service at the church did not grow any more interesting with repeated hearing. The hymns were usually the

same: he soon came to know the choir's rendering of them,
and the balootherums (Grandpapa's word) with which the
too exuberant organist accompanied their course. The
lessons were naturally more or less the same. Certain episodes
Dermot came to know almost by heart, and could never
afterwards hear without the intonation of Canon M'Gonigal
sounding in his head. The reverend gentleman, good-looking,
portly, and easy of manner, read in a perfunctory good-
humoured sort of way, swaying his body from side to side
(like Granny) and eyeing his congregation. "Jurr'bome,"
"Rheobome," and his "charyut": a smile came over Dermot's face at any allusion, during the rest of the year, to
these properties of Canon M'Gonigal's discourse. Better,
even, he liked, "Thur is but WAN left, Muy-CAA-yah, the
son of Imla: but I hate'm." Dermot already practised to
himself various styles of utterance, though semi-consciously,
with no intention of burlesque or mockery. His copying of
Paddy was at first involuntary, and brought severe censure
from Grandpapa. Not until he came out in front of Con with
an imitation of the Canon, and Con, who had suffered much
from compulsory boyhood visits to that church, threw back
his head and gave a shout of laughter, bidding him do it
again, and again, did Dermot realise in the faculty a potential
source of credit and entertainment.

Thenceforward he studied Paddy and his friends. Soon
he could not only reproduce, but extemporise, the adenoidal
snuffle of the ragged boys, the gross bawling accent of the
jarveys by the pier, the comfortable, almost motherly tones
of the old fishermen. . . .

Thoughts of fishing, ideas for imitation, long spells of
gazing at the window in which Christ walked upon the
waters: these filled most of church time, till, after two or
three years, a more urgent interest took their place. When
he first noticed her he could never tell. She seemed to have
happened, to have been there always. Perhaps it was that
she (and her relations) had changed their pew. All that

mattered was that there, every Sunday, she now sat, almost
facing him, but mercifully at some distance off.

Everyone was agreed upon her beauty. She was, when he
first saw her, eleven or twelve. A pure, oval face, most
delicately coloured, too beautiful to last: wide, grey-blue
eyes: long golden ringlets, hanging down on either side
over her shoulders; dressed always in soft, foamy white:
she was the perfect idol, and received the perfect adoration.
It was so disinterested, so cloud-high, that for a year Dermot never dreamed of meeting her. He was content to live
unnoticed in a different world: to gaze where the lovely
head and shoulders blossomed on the church's darkness, to
see of all the rows of faces only one face, swimming lightly
in his vision, like a water-lily on turbid waters: his spirit
filled with the pure sense of holiness: hearing and recognising still, but only as in a dream, Jurr'bome, Rheobome
and Muy-CAA-yah the son of Imla: knowing that here,
vouchsafed to him, living before his eyes, was perfect beauty.
When the service was over, he would hurry home, if he could,
before the others, post himself behind the drawing-room cur-
tains, and watch the lovely figure go by. She walked with a
fine swinging step: and she lived only a few doors up the
road. Paddy volunteered her name: he had done odd jobs for
her mother: but Dermot kept privately to the name he had
given her in his heart. He called her Mona. It was a whole
year before the others learned his secret, before their knowledge and his self-defence could vulgarise it, before it reached
even the semblance of a personal desire. The immediate gain,
besides these riches of the spirit, was that Sunday morning
ceased to be a penance. Even its travesty of a tram-ride
could be borne, if necessary, now.

Of real tram-rides, there were many. One fine evening,
maybe half an hour from bedtime, Dermot was playing by
himself in the garden, waiting for Bessie to take her little
walk. He played hidden away somewhere in the bushes,
deeply absorbed, when there floated down the garden the

clear, liquid "Cuckoo" with which his mother always called
the children. Frowning, afraid some caller had arrived, he
emerged, and trotted up the path.

His mother stood at the top, smiling at him. She wore
a flowered muslin dress. Very beautiful and cool she looked,
standing there, idly stroking a big trailing flower, and smiling
her smile of lazy endearment.

"Darling," she said, as he came near. "I've a bit of a
headache, and thought I'd go for a short tram-ride. Will
you come?"

His mouth opened silently, and "Yes, please," shot out
with very little hesitation.

"Get your hat and coat, then."

"*Coat*, Mummy?"

"Yes. It will be cool on top of the tram, especially coming
back. I'm wearing mine."

How strangely Mummy gave one orders, he reflected,
running in ahead of her for his coat. She hardly ever *told* him
to do a thing, as Munny used to, or as Annie did, or Grandpapa—or Daddy. She always said it as if she were only a
little older than he, as if it were something she supposed
ought to be done, but personally did not believe in. Look,
she seemed to say, I'm doing it too. He frowned fearfully
with the effort of his thoughts. Yes; that was what she was
like, when he and she were alone together. Just occasionally she was different, severe, grieved, somebody else. That
was when Daddy was angry. Not on her own account. Yes.
Daddy made a big difference.

When he came out, she was not ready. He had to wait
five minutes before she came slowly down the stairs from
Granny's room. She used it to save her going across the road
to Miss Tarbet's, the house where Daddy and she and Dermot slept. There was only the one spare bedroom in the
cottage, and that was now given over to Annie and to Eithne.

"Now," she smiled at him, and they went out of the narrow, dark little hall, down the brilliant white garden path,

into the road. Dermot held out his hand stiffly till the big, blue-and-cream tram ground to a standstill. In another minute they were seated right in front, on top, the breeze on their foreheads, heading for Dublin and the western sky.

"Monkstown, please," said Dermot's mother, when the conductor came.

"Monkstown? Wan and a half? Yis, Miss."

It still pleased her to be called Miss, as often she was. There was an irresponsible grace about her, a remoteness, which did not go with Mrs. and maternity.

Leaning her head back in the cool breeze, Dermot's mother began to talk. She pointed out this house, and that house: told stories of the people who had lived in them: explained the changes that had taken place since she was a little girl. They were not many. So vividly did she talk, that Dermot saw the far-off days as clearly as the passing scene.

"Look, Dermot. That big house in the grounds. That was where I went to my first ball."

"Along that road poor old General O'Donovan was chased by a mad donkey."

"Three old ladies had that house, for years and years. One died, and the other two went on as if she were still there. They had her place laid at table, her bed turned down every night: and every morning the maid had to go with hot water, and call the old sister who wasn't there. This went on for years, and then the second one died. The poor old one that was left—she was wonderfully handsome, a little, proud, slim thing, with white hair, and rather a big nose—she went on with the same ceremony."

"What—both places laid, and calling them both in the mornings?"

"Yes. Just the same. At last she herself fell ill: nothing much, a cold, or something. But she had to stay in her bed. It was the chambermaid's evening out, and the poor old thing got the idea into her head that the rooms were not properly ready, nor the beds turned down. She wouldn't call the cook. I suppose she thought they laughed at her, and she was too proud. Anyway, when the chambermaid came back, in time to let the doctor in for his bedtime visit, they found the poor old thing in bed, nearly fainting, with her legs terribly scalded. She had been filling the hot water bottles for her dead sisters, and had upset the boiling water over herself. But she'd somehow filled the bottles and got round to each of the rooms. The beds were turned down, the nightgowns laid out, and the bottles were in the beds."

Dermot was staring straight in front of him.

"Did—did she get better?" he asked.

"No. She died of the shock, that same night."

There was a silence, and, seeing that she had distressed him, she began to talk of other things.

"That house I showed you just now, where I went to my first ball—"

She paused, and Dermot, recalled to the present world, held his breath: for they were reaching Monkstown, and the strange towers of the church swung into view. The collector came up, shaking his bag of pennies, as a hint to them.

"Shall we go on?" said Dermot's mother, looking down at him with her smile.

"Oh, Mummy, *do* let's. It's so lovely."

"We'll go on," she looked for the coins in her purse, "we'll go on to Merrion, please."

Dermot gasped. He had thought of Blackrock as the farthest possible limit.

"Just to get a glimpse of the sands," she said. "We oughtn't to, really. It's terribly naughty of us."

Dermot thrilled, and wriggled himself closer to her on the seat.

"Go on telling me about your first ball," he besought her.

"Well, you can imagine the excitement I was in, for weeks beforehand. A first ball meant something, in those days. There was my dress to be made, and this and that little change: it drove poor Katie nearly out of her mind. I was in and out of her little house all day."

Dermot frowned.

"Did Katie come, even in those days?"

"Yes," said his mother, "she did." She sat up straighter on the seat, and spoke with more decision. "Katie is a very old, faithful servant to us all, and you mustn't think unkindly about her. You must be nice to her, always."

Dermot fidgeted.

"She's so—so sort of oily. She's always cadging for things," he muttered.

"She has a terribly hard life: and she never asks a thing for herself. Whatever she gets goes to her sister's family. You're *not* to speak unkindly of her. It's wrong, and uncharitable."

"Uncle Ben and Aunt—"

"They've always had a spite against her. Who do you think are likely to know best? Granny and I, who have always had her here: or people who only see her at odd times?"

"Oh, well, I—"

"Who, Dermot?"

"Oh, well, you and Granny, I suppose."

"There's no 'suppose' about it." Her tone changed. "Be fair to her, Dermot. She was always very kind to me."

The boy swung his feet, and wriggled. This was the only unpleasant part of the ride. He looked away, and saw the solid, grey, Georgian houses slide by, with their clumps of thick chestnut trees, their dreaming beeches, shafted by the sunlight: the people sitting in their gardens, the children running, the tennis lawns, sounding with gay voices: a full and comfortable peace, stately, grown on security and long unanxious tenure. The character of it all impressed him, catching his senses right away from Katie and the tram. Then, as usually after a sudden, complete perception, they turned abruptly back again.

"Go on telling me about your first ball."

She smiled straight in front of her, without looking at him.

"When at last the day came, Granny had a cold, and couldn't go with me. I was in despair. We tried to get hold of friends—Amelia O'Farrell, Mrs. ffrench: none of them could come. Then, in the afternoon, who should come in to call but Cousin Corny."

"Cousin—?"

"You know—Cornelius O'Dowda. *The* O'Dowda."

"Oh—him. I've seen pictures of him."

"Yes. The big photo in the drawing-room. In he came, and, as soon as he heard of the trouble, nothing would do him but he must go, and chaperon me. He wouldn't hear of a single objection. He insisted. Dermot—you should have seen him, when he came to call for me!"

Her eyes were shining like a girl's. She clasped her hands in front of her, on her knee.

"He is very handsome in the picture," said Dermot.

"Nothing to what he was then. He came—he is six foot two, at least—stepping out of the carriage, in his long black cloak, and the ribbons of all his foreign orders flashing across his chest . . ." She broke off. "And there was I, a young silly girl at her first ball, escorted by the handsomest nobleman in Ireland: and all the others eating off their heads in envy."

"Did he dance well?"

Dermot had a practical taste for exploring all the aspects of a situation.

"He danced most wonderfully. He still does. And he treated me all the evening as if I were a queen. That's one of the most wonderful things about him. He's terribly selfish in some ways, and goes off anywhere the moment the fit takes him: but he treats every woman, young or old, as if she were a queen. I'll never forget that night. He made me feel—I *knew*, all the time, of course, how kind he was being to me—but he made me really believe that he was enjoying it all, and thought himself lucky to have been able to dance with me."

She turned and looked at Dermot, a half-humorous look in her eye.

"Men like that are very dangerous to us poor women, Dermot, as you'll learn one day."

Dermot looked up, surprised.

"Dangerous? But you said he was so kind."

"So he was. So he always is. That's just why. It would be so hard to refuse him anything."

Dermot frowned.

"Well, what would he want?" he asked prosaically: imagining his noble cousin coming back at the end of the evening, and asking an ornament off the mantelpiece for his services.

His mother interpreted the question correctly, and laughed.

"Fortunately he didn't want anything." She drummed with her fingers on the rail . . . "I meant that girls lose their hearts to him. He wouldn't value that, you see, he gets so many."

"You mean, he has lots of people in love with him?"

"Lots," replied his mother lightly. "Lots and lots."

The tram clanked along between the trees, and came out by Booterstown into full sight of the sea. The tide was low, and, beyond the railway wall, the sands ran out, flat, wet, gleaming, so far that one could hardly tell where the sea began. Dotted over them, far apart, with rolled-up clothes, stooped the dark figures of the cockle gatherers. Nearer the City, in the soft haze of smoke and sinking sun, the tall chimney-stacks by the river rose with a kind of lonely grace, bewitched by distance and the evening. The long arm of Howth, running low by Clontarf, and swelling up slowly into the Hill, was dim and faint, as if it had gone off somewhere by itself, further off from the City and the Bay, and had forgotten them in a private dream. The tram hurried over the clear long curve towards Merrion, and the whole Hill came into view: then, as they looked, its soft obscurity was pricked by the sharp gleam of the Bailey Light. Further on, they could look back, and see the long awkward ˌelbow of Kingstown Harbour, the less familiar, seldom seen West Pier, with the queer jumbled forest of masts and funnels sticking up above it.

"Good day to you, Miss," said the conductor, touching his cap and grinning, as they got off.

CHAPTER XVI

"MARAUDERIN' DIVILS!" SAID MR. CAGGEN, SPITTING VEN-
omously sideways through a gap in his yellow teeth. He
looked up, and saw Mr. Gray coming up the path to join
them. "It's poison is wanted, sir," he said, touching the brim
of his old straw hat. "Poison, and no stint of it."

Mr. Gray raised his eyebrows.

"Cats again?" he asked.

Mr. Caggen made a sweeping gesture with his arm.

"Wild, murderous divils from the woods beyant," he
replied, "comin' down and stravagin' all over me beds."

Mr. Gray whistled.

"I say—they have made a mess. What a wicked shame.
Can't you—do anything?"

"Th'ould gintleman," growled Mr. Caggen respectfully
—he always alluded to Grandpapa thus, "Th'ould gintleman: he won't suffer me to raise a hand agen them. It's
a curse to the whole neighbourhood they are. Carryin' off
chickens, and young hens. Sure there's none to withstand
them."

"Those two big toms are the worst?"

"Aye, sir. Them big toms. The black wan and the yella
wan. Faix," he raised his hat, and rubbed the top of his
head with his knuckles, "I'd like to take a dart at them two
myself."

Dermot's father looked thoughtful.

"I wonder," he said. "I have a little rifle . . . a neat
enough little thing. Possibly, one day, when the old gentleman is out of the way . . ."

"Oh, bedad, sir, it's time. It's time. They have the whole place destroyed on me."

"Well, if you think we could . . . ? It shouldn't take long. If you'll have a little grave prepared somewhere, handy, we could have the victim out of sight inside a couple of minutes."

"Never could work come sweeter to me two hands, sir," declared Mr. Caggen, spitting on both of them.

"Good. Then we'll wait our chance."

The chance did not come for some days, but fresh occasion was given for the plan. Of the biggest cats, one was nicknamed Black Tom, for obvious reasons, and the other Lord Spencer, for his ginger colour and his lordly mien. The name was Mr. Gray's, and was lost on Dermot, though he used it gladly: it was appropriate, even without its reference. The two were not leagued together, but rivalled one another in daring, as if each felt bound to outdo the other's latest feat: and their efforts culminated in the rapid entry of Lord Spencer into the kitchen, while Bessie was absent a few seconds in the scullery, and his successful abstraction of one of Sunday's two boiled chickens. He was positively seen, by Bessie, leaping off the table with the bird in his strong jaws. Horrorstruck, she recovered instantly, and gave chase: but the animal bounded off up the garden, and made good his escape, leaving a thin spattered trail of parsley sauce on the flagstones.

This deed roused the household, and even Grandpapa found difficulty in defending it.

"It's the cruel way people do be acting," he complained presently, "turning away their poor cats from the door, and leaving them to starve. Sure, who could blame—"

"That animal," cut in Granny with decision, "that animal takes very good care it doesn't starve. Mrs. Geraghty, below in the cottages, was telling me it's worse than a fox, the way it does be taking their chickens."

"Mrs. Geraghty. Sure, who'd believe Mrs. Geraghty?"

"Now, Alfred, don't be talking nonsense. It's your own fault, more than another's. You're always encouraging every sort of stray animal into the garden, and here's what comes of it. Half me nice dinner gone: and everyone obliged to go short."

"It's your dinner you're thinking of, not the cat at all."

"Of course it's me dinner I'm thinking of. Sure who wouldn't think of their dinner, and it snatched away from under their nose?"

Grandpapa looked around the table.

"Do you hear me old woman—" he began, with a chuckle; but he got no support.

"It's time a stop was put to those cats. They'll hurt one of the children, one of these days."

"They *are* nasty creatures."

"I must say, sir," observed Mr. Gray, "I agree with your lady. If anyone tried to stop one of them taking something, he or she might be very badly mauled."

Grandpapa looked round upon them.

"Faith, you're a nice lot," he said, "afraid of a cat."

The matter came up again, as soon as he was out of the room, and Dermot's father met with great approval when, emboldened by Granny's decisive words, he suggested he might, quite painlessly, get rid of the pests.

Dermot missed the end of Black Tom. He arrived in time to see the great body lying by the side of the grave into which it was quickly bundled. The great scowling beast looked less terrible in death. His eyes were shut, his mouth open, the white teeth showing in an expression of perplexity—pathetic rather than savage. His death had been savage enough. Mr. Gray had stalked and shot him, from behind a tree, in among the cabbages. The shot was clean and true. Mr. Caggen vowed he saw it hit the ground on the other side. The big brute fought like a tiger, tearing up the soil for a circle of six feet around: but he could neither rise nor run: he could only struggle furiously, blindly, without purpose. It took a second bullet, and a third, to still the body that leaped and pulsed like a mad furry engine.

In some way that he could not explain, Dermot was sorry to see the limp thick form shovelled into its ignominious grave by the dungheap. Soft in death, its teeth showing beneath its twisted lip, it seemed no more than a poor ordinary cat, stricken down suddenly for no cause that it could understand. There was something furtive, almost cowardly in the uneasy haste with which they huddled and stamped it out of sight. Only just in time, too. Grandpapa appeared, his dark blue cloth cap pulled down over his nose, sniffing the air of the garden, as was his wont.

"Th'ould gintleman, sir," said Mr. Caggen out of the side of his mouth.

With a whistle of surprise and complicity, Mr. Gray put the elder trees between him and the garden's lawful owner, dodging him round the little greenhouse, and getting his rifle back into the house unseen.

Lord Spencer ranged for several days longer. His death, when he met it, was fierce and splendid, calling for no pity. Lean and raking, a greyhound, a racehorse of a cat, he stalked in aristocratic nonchalance where his colleague crouched and ran. Lord Spencer disdained his enemies. He did not spit and growl, like Black Tom. He looked with haughty hostility out of pale lemon eyes, and passed on his way, barely deigning to hurry. He seemed to know that the threat was angry air, that the flung stone would miss him. His appearances had not the apparent criminal purpose of Black Tom's. Yet, for all his languor, he was hard to catch. Whether he noticed his rival's disappearance, or whether his instinct warned him, he was not to be found when Mr. Gray stalked the garden for him. This was the more provoking, as Grandpapa had a way of coming out, just when they thought he was deep into the *Irish Times*, for all the world as if he suspected something. The rifle had to be concealed in a number of unlikely places.

But the chance came at last. At the end of a glorious, long, hot day, Lord Spencer woke from sleep, which he had discreetly enjoyed, at full stretch, on the roof of a little outhouse by the orchard wall. He had been invisible all day, high above people's heads, and surrounded by trees. Waking with a vague sense of loss, he found that the wheeling sun had left him. To enjoy its last mellow rays, he must move forward a little, and sit up. This he did, and would still have been invisible, had not Dermot, climbing in a tree some fifty yards away, caught sight of his ginger fur among the leaves.

Quickly Dermot descended. It took five minutes to get his father out, and he dreaded lest the enemy should have taken the alarm and fled. But no, there he was, sitting splendidly upright on the apex of the little roof, blinking sleepily into the sun. On his right, the roof sloped a little way into a sycamore tree, at the top of the orchard. On his left, it was soon lost in a great elderberry, which overhung far out into the garden proper, threatening to push out the loose top of the old crumbling wall. At the foot of the wall, deep under the trees' branches, stood a vast tub, from which Mr. Caggen filled his cans to water that side of the garden.

The tree in which Dermot had climbed was too distant for a shot, and from the ground Lord Spencer was still invisible. Hastily and stealthily, Dermot's father brought up a high garden chair, and placed it carefully in a flower bed, about fifteen yards from the wall. Then, moving as slowly as he dared, he mounted it—and found himself face to face with his quarry.

If he saw him, the great cat did not move. The lazy, benign sunshine, the mellow gold of the late afternoon rayed him round; the sleepy buzz of bees rose from the garden, mingled with the smell of the warm, contented earth, and the fragrance of flowers. It was an evening of such peace that even the wild creature, sitting there on the hot slates, soaked through and through with sun, must have felt too lazy to apprehend a threat. He sat, blinking and smiling, facing his murderer.

Dermot's father himself felt the power of the scene, and hesitated for a moment to take the sitting shot at his enemy. Then, reproving himself sternly for a sentimentalist, he raised the rifle to his shoulder. There was a long moment of silence. Dermot looked around the garden, screwing up his eyes into the sun. Two butterflies, silhouetted against the dark hedge, danced leisurely over the top of a great puff of lavender. Alight—flit; alight—flit; one chasing the other, yet too lazy to catch her. Then there was a sound like a cracked whip, and a terrible commotion broke out on the roof of the outhouse. The great cat, shot squarely through the lung, slid scrabbling down the roof and fell, fighting like a devil, into the elder tree. The tree vibrated and quivered, as the heavy thrashing body tore its way downward through the branches: it seemed impossible that one creature could set up such agitation. Then, as they watched with staring eyes, the lower branches drooped, discharged their lacerating burden, and the frantic body fell with a flash of ginger fur into the water tub!

Dermot and his father rushed up, the latter pausing, with a shout of warning, to reload. But Lord Spencer did not emerge from the tub. They waited for a few seconds, then tiptoed to the edge and looked in. The cat was half sitting, half standing, on his haunches, his eyes tight shut, his fore-paws held out stiffly together. With regular efforts, rhythmic as a pulse, he lunged upwards through the water, his face almost reaching the surface at each lunge; and then sank back. There was something remote about his efforts: they were not like a savage creature's last fierce struggle for his life. They were vague, unreal: his pale yellow body bloomed languidly up like a flower through the dark, stagnant water. As they watched, his rise and fall grew slower, more dream-like. One last effort brought him floating up into distinctness: his outstretched paws broke the surface, his mouth and nostrils touched it, hesitated, hung a second: then, slowly, he sank for the last time.

An instinct made Dermot avert his eyes from the lank, forlorn, draggled body that was fished out five minutes later. He preferred to remember Lord Spencer as he had been, proud, fierce, and magnificent. It did not do to see cat-marauders when they were dead.

If Grandpapa noted the disappearance of the garden's two chief enemies, he said nothing about it. An occasional gleam of suspicion and baffled enquiry, from under his grey bristling eyebrows: eyebrows so thick and deep that they almost hid the gleam which was the more disquieting when it pierced through them: that was all. With his sturdy wisdom, his sharp common sense, both trained in the practice of the law, Grandpapa was not going to give himself away, nor distress himself with a catastrophe of which he could so easily stay ignorant.

CHAPTER XVII

"P-LAY UP THE MUSIC" SANG PADDY, "AND I WILL TELL YEZ all, The way we used to sing and dance, Down in Donegal. . . ."

He looked up, knitting his brows and baring his teeth at the horizon. "'Way ou' o' that—rain! Who toult ye? It'll be a grand evening."

"The barometer," said Dermot uncomfortably. "The weatherglass."

"Well now, bazometers and weather glasses, or no bazometers and weather glasses; it's going to be a fine evenin'."

"I'm glad," said Dermot meekly. The lore of home and kindred, quoted against Paddy, and listened to by that gentleman with respectful awe when he did not understand it, collapsed very quickly before his assault as soon as it touched his own province. At first, Dermot argued fiercely: but he was no match for Paddy. Paddy's technique in such matters was to brush aside all that was argued against him, and shatter his opponent with a series of rhetorical questions, each one referring to a great and usually an unheard-of authority.

"Bazometers!" repeated Paddy, scornfully, to the line he was labouring to disentangle. "Would John Rogan ever use a bazometer? Would Mike McGuiness, was the best judge o' the weather ever sailed a yacht? Would Shaun Rooney? Did yez ever hear tell Dark Jim Magee used a bazometer—him that could sail his little boat from the Coliemore to the Hill o' Howth in a black fog? Bazometer, me a—."

Dermot blinked under the rebuke. On this occasion, he felt he had hardly earned it.

"I'll tell you what it is, Master Dermot." Paddy paused, and made a perfectly appalling face as he pulled out a knot with teeth and both hands. "To be a good fisher, ye want to learn the way of things for yourself. Ye want to watch the weather, and see the way it will be goin'. Ye want to dig your own bait, and make your own lines. Amn't I after showing you the way to make lines? Well—and aren't the' better than them rotten old things you'll get ready-made up above in the shops? Aren't the'?"

"Yes, Paddy. Lots better."

"I'm not sayin' that be way of boastin' meself," pursued Paddy earnestly. "Sure, any fella along the shore here could show you the way of a line. I'm only sayin' it, the way is, ye see—" he hesitated, carried into deeper conversational waters than usual. "You want to rely on yourself, the way, if anything goes wrong, ye can set it right."

Oh dear, thought Dermot, in a small voice: oh dear. Everyone kept telling him that: Daddy; Uncle Ben (very kindly, very gently, which made it even worse); Eileen; Con; and now Paddy. It was true, of course: but he hated having to be competent and self reliant, and having to *do* things. He liked, when he first knew Paddy, to fish till the line went tangled, or there were no more fish in that spot, and then to take on again when Paddy had put matters right. But Paddy had not inclined to that view at all. Bit by bit, he obliged his pupil to act on his own. Dermot was intelligent, and Paddy had the tireless patience of the uneducated. It was easy to learn from Paddy. Yet being with Paddy was an asylum, a protection from the hard world. Uncle Ben, Con; and the rest were not content to take him out in the boat, give him the mackerel line, and land an awkward fish for him. After the first time or two, they made him do it all himself. He hated having to do things himself—except the easy things, which he knew he could do. Yet, in his heart, he acknowledged the wisdom of it all. A great many of the things he could now do easily he had been unable to do a little while before. When I'm grown up, he thought, I'll have people to do everything for me: I won't ever let myself be left on my own. Even the few things he was able to do gave him no thrill of satisfaction. He would sooner have been spared the necessity of doing them. Not till an achievement had become mechanical could he cease to worry over it.

Once, in the first two or three summers, competence in an emergency gave him a thrill of pride. This was not with Paddy, but with Con. The two were out in the boat, in Dalkey Sound. Con rowed easily, leaning back, looking round upon the reflected hills, and letting his magnificent voice escape him in little spouts and swills of sound, as rich, as deep as the live, glistening pits left swirling in the water where the oars had been. Dermot, in the stern, managed the two mackerel lines, each crooked over a sensitive fore-finger. Slim, growing tall, his face in shadow, he sat up, watching his companion: ten years old, perhaps, or eleven, with great promise of good looks, but solemn, attentive, old for his years. The sun beat down around and behind him: it splashed his white sun hat, and his erect, thin shoulders: it made large plaques and pools that sprawled and leaped and grimaced on the dizzy waters. It gleamed in the sweat on Con's forehead: it flung into relief every feature of his conventionally handsome face. It called all the colour from his pale pink shirt and the little bow at his neck; it winked from the buckle of his braces, and played gossamer hide-and-seek among the soft golden hairs on his great forearms. It summoned from the old friendly boat every smell she ever had in her: paint, warm varnish, fish, rotten bait that had slipped under the boards, and a sort of composite, com-panionable air that was none and all of these and something else as well: the smell of boats and harbours on hot August afternoons.

Suddenly looking over the side, as they went vaguely along, Dermot saw with horror the long wicked tongues, the wide flat streamers of the weed, close underneath. Shallow water—the lines—danger! Like a nerve responding, he cried his warning, took in yards of one line frantically, then of the other. The boat bounded forward, making the long lead sinkers rise with the pull: and they were over the danger, in deep water again, spinners and gut intact.

"Bravo, Dermot," cried Con. "Bravo, boy. You saved that well."

But would it always be so? Was he really competent, and quick, like other boys? Was this an act of the real Dermot, or an inspired fluke only? He had no confidence. He still preferred to look on.

For the first years with Paddy, and for long intervals in the later years, the Sea Wall satisfied all his desires. He soon outgrew the stingoes: but it boasted other fish. First and foremost, it was rich in "rock brame" (wrasse) of every possible variety, from the multicoloured, delicate little ones to the bright yellow-bellied brame that lived in the tangle, and their softer, silver-bellied cousins who preferred the patches of white sand. From the biggest of these patches, that in front of Doyle's Rock, were sometimes to be taken little flatfish—if one had the right bait. Round many of the rocks, at high tide, small pollack swam, in nervous, darting motion. Dermot loved these, with their slim green and silver, the pliant grace of their limp, dead bodies. To handle and look at them was an inexhaustible delight. He even let it outweigh more practical considerations, for, to be nice for table, they had to be gutted at once. That spoiled their symmetry, and he always delayed the operation as long as he could, despite Paddy's remonstrances. More wonderful than the pollack, sometimes on drowsy, glittering August afternoons the grey mullet would come in on a full tide, swimming gracefully and lazily just below the surface, their back fins and tails rippling the still silk of the water. Those,

Paddy said, one shot, or took with the bait of a cabbage:
but, as nobody knew when they were coming, the requisite
floating tackle was never rigged, and they remained unattainable, symbol of dreamed achievement, fish of the
Hesperides.

"And next year, please God, we'll have a dart at the
mullets," Paddy would say, when that hateful morning in
September came round once more, and the pair took their
farewell walk on the Sea Wall, from Ballygihen to New
Town Smith, back again, and up Burdett Avenue, where
Dermot would turn around, to let Paddy clipper-clopper a
little way ahead of him, so that he might privily clasp his
fingers and pray, "Dear God, bring me back safe to the Sea
Wall again, for Jesus Christ's sake, Amen": and so that
he might whisper, "Dear Sea Wall; good-bye." It became a
formula, repeated every sad last morning, "Next year, please
God, we'll have a dart at the mullets." And why not? What
might not happen, when the long dark circuit had been once
more completed, and they stood at the beginning of their
time again, with the days stretching golden all before them?
Not, as now, a bare hour that was not an hour, with Dermot
in his travelling clothes. More pain than pleasure, that last
ceremonial round brought them: but it had to be done. It
was the last real time with Paddy. True, he would shuffle
down with Dermot to the boat, if they went direct, or to the
station, if they went by the South: but that was a short,
unhappy walk, charged with a misery which neither tried to
hide. Once there, Paddy became a poor, humble, waving
figure, well in the background.

But, besides the enchanted "Mullets," as Paddy called
them, there were other accessible creatures. At low tide,
Dermot caught little eating crabs, under the loose rocks.
With breathless care, his tongue curling out over his lip, he
stalked the wary prawns, and caught them, convulsed and
clicking, in his net. Cunning, idiotic creatures! their cunning and their idiocy so mixed, their suspicion so inopportune,

their serenity so misplaced. Like the wicked, they fled
when no man pursued them: and by the time the net was
cleverly sunk behind them, they were drifting along, in
a sort of dark green dream, and fell victims to the most
obvious of hostile manœuvres. Then, in the meshes of the
net, how perverse and unavailing their agitation! Dermot
would take a whole minute, sometimes, to extricate one
without injury. This was not only tenderness for the prawn.
It was a profound feeling that to hurry, and break it, was
illegitimate and clumsy, like cutting the string from a
parcel, or forcing a puzzle. Still, he did not wish the prawns
to suffer unnecessary hurt. When, more out of curiosity than
cruelty, he took one by the proboscis and dipped its tail into
the saucepan, and the creature with an agonised flip sent
a splash of boiling water up his sleeve, he accepted the
perfect justice of the pain, even while he was still hopping
about and holding his wrist in anguish. He had done a cruel
thing, and been well served. There was no cause for com-
plaint.

Prawns (Paddy called them "swimps") were more profitable than the little eating crabs, not one in ten of which could
be eaten. These Dermot hunted for the thrill of finding them,
and in the hope that he might one day unearth a really big
one.

Another unprofitable captive, prized only for its rarity,
was the Horny Cobbler. This creature, shaped like a small
fat kite without a tail, had a number of spines, reputed to be
full of the direst venom. It had also a vast mouth, and insisted on swallowing hook and half the gut. Paddy was
always needed to detach it from the line, with boot, jack-
knife, and volleys of theological oaths. On the few occasions
when Dermot, fishing by himself, got one on his rod, he
was obliged to go home, dangling the unwelcome captive at the end of it. He hated Horny Cobblers: but, there
was no denying, they gave an air to one's fish book, when
the catches were added up. An unusual fish always de-

lighted Dermot: the day he first caught a young ling, he was beside himself with joy.

The Sea Wall thus offered excellent training to the novice, going far to equip him for more ambitious fishing, when he must put away childish things and take his place among men, fishing in deadly earnest for their families. Moreover, not all its game was on a small scale. Along its humble rocks, at the ends of its little channels, under its trees of weed, was to be found the most fearsome fish of the whole coast—the conger. Paddy and Dermot, looking intently on the patch of water before them, would often hiss an exclamation, and point simultaneously to a blue shadow waving among the weeds— losing itself—then emerging, a bar of purest azure, taking its lazy way, sometimes so near that they could see its little soulless eye; watching it breathlessly till it disappeared under the gleam or ruffle upon the water. Paddy had begun to talk of making a line for conger, and getting leave for Dermot to sit up after dinner, since conger took best at night: and Dermot had gone so far as to purchase a huge conger hook, which he carried about in his pocket, king of the cork in which his hooks were muzzled, but as yet serving no more practical purpose. He did not dream in what circumstances, and how soon, he was to find a use for it.

CHAPTER XVIII

Meanwhile the friendship with paddy grew steadily, and to it in due time were added Paddy's friends. Of these two stood out, chiefly because they were most often there: one having nothing to do, and the other very little. Long Mike Hogan, a tall, seedily handsome man of about forty, clad always in a navy blue suit, a dirty yachting cap, and even dirtier white shoes, needed to pursue no calling, since his mother did a small but steady business in fried fish. The only work she ever laid on him was to attend and persecute the meetings of the Salvation Army. The opening of this sect's Glasthule branch had given rise to lively scenes. Local zealots, incensed at what even Bessie termed "a street mock of our Blessed Lord," had surrounded the premises and interrupted the singing by the projection of a large paving stone through the plate glass window. The Salvationists were rescued from the back of the building by the police: and ever since that date, a policeman followed the dreary exiguous band everywhere about the town, to protect them from further violence. It was never offered, nor did the meetings cause any disturbance. About the only attendant was Long Mike, who, keeping to the far side of the road, and with a wary eye on the policeman, repeated at intervals, "Hoormongers. Hoormongers. Hoormongers," in low but penetrating tones, for so long as the group held together. He would follow them implacably from pitch to pitch, keeping up his monotonous chant, never so happy as when their leader crossed to remonstrate with him, or when the policeman told him to move on. The latter event happened seldom, the policeman maintaining, if the Salvationists invoked his aid, that Long Mike "had as good a right to his opinions" as themselves. Only when Mike's devotion showed signs of attracting a crowd, or when some high-up Protestant was taking note, the law stepped in. Vainly did the Salvationists change their evening, and their route: Mike always got wind of their plans, and they would convene secretly at some remote place, only to find the long, melancholy form of their critic leaning against the nearest wall awaiting them. Nothing shook him. Not even when the meeting, abandoning its general programme, prayed loudly for his personal salvation, did his expression change or his voice vary. He would return to the Sea Wall exhausted after his labours, lowering himself limply to the rock without a word.

"Have ye been after the mockers, Mike?"

"I have." Mike fumbled in his pocket, brought out some tobacco, and proceeded languidly to cut it in the palm of his hand. "Bad scran to them. The' have me pretty near wore out. I believe it's in Booterstown they'll be meetin' next, the b—." He here received a vigorous nudge, followed by a jerk of Paddy's thumb towards Dermot, who pretended not to listen. About to protest, he found the effort too much, and spat instead.

"Well," said Paddy, "ye do be a great thorn in their side, and no mistake. A great thorn."

Mike was understood to mutter through his quid that they were a worse thorn in his.

"Only for me Ma," he said presently, "I'd give over, and leave them be."

"Oh, sure, ye couldn't do that."

Paddy was shocked, for Mike's activity had won him great renown as a defender of the faith. Many a soft job came his way, which could be attributed to no other cause. Mike did not like jobs, even of the softest: but he took one now and again, when his needs outpaced his pocket.

"You couldn't leave them be," continued Paddy, in

the same shocked tone. "Sure, the' couldn't be let mock our Blessed Lord, and no one to say a word agen them."

"Let someone else say the word," replied Mike morosely: but even Dermot knew that the protest was only for form's sake, and that, next evening, he would be found at his post.

Peg-leg, the second of Paddy's friends—his real name was Dan O'Shea—was a different proposition. A little quick, furtive man, clean shaven, dark as a flue brush, with wide nostrils like sooty chimneys, he got his nickname from a stiffness in his right leg, which did not however incapacitate him from great activity. A fast walker by habit, he walked also in races, and had in his time won many prizes. His furtive air, and the quick nervous glances he darted from side to side as he scuttled along the street, were quite misleading: he was a mild, honest little man, with no worse vice than laziness. Peg-leg was a skilled carpenter, and could on a single day make enough money to last him for the week. He was a bachelor, living with his eldest sister, to whom he handed over three quarters of his earnings as a matter of course. Like Paddy and Long Mike, he desired nothing better than to sit in the sun, to smoke and spit and talk: and, as he had none of Mike's fanaticism, he led a most enjoyable life. His few long spells of work occurred when the parish priest laid some carving or carpentering on him as a duty. Then he gave his labour freely, but grudged his time. If kept too long at work, he would turn sulky. No other circumstance bothered him, or elicited anything but harmless laughter, which his satanic appearance transformed into a villainous snigger. When he laughed, his nostrils, big enough already, were so drawn up that they seemed to turn inside out: his lips were pulled back from his yellow tobacco-stained teeth, his shoulders hunched up to his ears, and his whole frame convulsed with mean and ignoble spasms. Poor Peg-leg. He would be cast for First Murderer, for Spanish Traitor, for Poisoner, or Copper's Nark, in any theatre in the world: and he was an inoffensive, kind, shrewd little

man, generous and patient, and one of the best heel-and-toe
walkers in Leinster.

Many a morning and afternoon dreamed its way along,
with Dermot fishing by the water, and these three close
above him. So still did he sit, so little attention did he seem
to give them, that they soon came to forget him and talk
as if he were not there. Thus, all the time, he was picking
up rare and valuable knowledge. The poor as seen from
Granny's doorstep were one thing: the poor, overheard
talking together, in their own territory, were another. He
ceased to see their lives as the lives of animals on show. He
ceased, at once, to pity them. Listening, he found himself
at home in a world full as his own, but quite unlike it: a
world of wonderful kindness and sympathy, narrowing
down savagely to intolerance of anything outside its code or
ken: a world on the defensive, enjoying its happiness instantly and eagerly, as the good hours of an ague: a world
united, just and unjust alike, in hatred of one enemy, the
Law: a world which laid all its fatalism and belief upon the
shoulders of one Power, and acknowledged the representative
of that Power, the parish priest, as king. The parish priest,
Paddy assured Dermot, could strike a man dead: and there
was no doubt that he believed it. Interpreter of the God in
Whom they trusted, medicine-man, judge and law-giver, he
ruled them with a despot's power: pattern of the Hebrews'
Jahveh, mirror of a Father Who chastened those He loved.
They were slaves, childlike, sinful, and uncomplaining. Half
the time, they did not know from where their next meal
was coming: nor did they care. "Sure, God won't let us
starve." "The Lord won't suffer the poor man and his children to die." There was fear in the voices, but there was also
a slave's faith in his master: and there was submission. To
realise, almost unconsciously, a way of life different from one's
own, is as salutary a lesson as can be learned. Dermot minded
his fishing, but a part of him was drinking in all he heard, and
learning not only to talk but to think in the second language.

Peg-leg was the most articulate and the most intelligent of the three, and it was he who explained such ethical and theoretical questions as arose between the new world and the old. Dermot sometimes gave Paddy small presents of his own money. When, one day, he had seemed to presume on one of these, and the threepenny bit had been flung on the rock at his feet, it was Peg-leg who gravely explained the source of offence and recommended the apology that put all straight again. When Bartley Grogan attempted to kill his wife in the dwellings, believing her to have been unfaithful, it was Peg-leg who contrived to explain the grievance without recourse to more worldly knowledge than that implied in the laws of possession: saving a situation which had turned Paddy brick red and moved Mike to hollow and derisive chuckles. A year later, when the worldly knowledge had been theoretically acquired, the trio sighed with relief, and permitted themselves a licence which much enriched their local gossip. Dermot's innocence had been a restriction, loyally observed. Its removal was due to a fashionable preparatory school, not to three illiterate men whose normal vocabulary was so richly coarse that they spoke like foreigners without it. Of their personal morality, there was no doubt at all. One evening, when a good-looking, blowsy girl in red laughed a remark to the three, Paddy threatened her with the back of his hand, Peg-leg spat on the ground, and Long Mike crossed himself and uttered a pious oath. One lesson at least their faith and their priest had taught them, a lesson Ireland knew well.

If Peg-leg was the most voluble, Paddy had a gift of phrase which enlivened many a story. He had once seen a small child decapitated by a tram.

"I seen the wheel go acrost the neck, and the blood bursted out, and the little head lepped on the pavement."

In like mortuary vein was his tale of a disaster at the Forty Foot.

"He was only the week married, and he and she on their

honeymoon. So he ups and off with him to the Forty Foot, and she goes up to this seat here, to look down and see how fine he could dive and swim. Out he comes presently, and the man at the Forty Foot tries to stop him, be reason of the waves, that was runnin' big. Oh no, says me fine boyo, sure, that's all right, says he. He wasn't goin' back on it, and his wife up there on the hill to watch him. So he dives in, bold and fine, off o' the top board, and swam out to that rock—looka, that one there—wasn't it, Peg-leg?—and stud up for to wave his hand."

"Aye," pronounced the dark one, after satanic consideration, "that was the rock, Paddy. The second one, there. That was the rock."

"He stud up," pursued the narrator, gesticulating in the air, "and wave his hand: and, with his head turned, he got the lick of a big wave, and she seen'm swep off o' the rock and threw up agen that rock beside it, and go limp, and g'down. She run down to try and save him, like a mad one, the poor thing. The roars of her was onmerciful."

Such narratives, chosen from a wide store, whetted Dermot's appetite for the morbid. When a man was drowned at the Forty Foot, and his body picked up fourteen days later and stuck in the mortuary, he hovered near the place all day, eagerly questioning the boys of the Sea Wall, as they returned with gleaming eyes and bright wet lips from their view, but afraid to go in himself.

The pair, with occasional assistance from Mike and Peg-leg, dug their own bait; but they could only get lug at certain tides. Sometimes it had to be bought. For this Dermot learned to seek out one Mrs. Ryan, who lived in the Fishbank, then one of the foulest slums in Ireland. It looked clean enough, from a little way off: row upon row of uneven, lopsided whitewashed cottages, some roofed, some thatched, spilling crazily about the hill between the tram-lines and the water. Some of them gave points to Paddy's home, for they had, at least, stone floors: but the filth and degradation of the inhabitants needed to be seen and smelt. Children, clad in one garment, or in nothing at all, rolled and sprawled in the festering gutters. The first time Dermot went there alone, he saw a woman reach out over the half door of her house, to get a jug of milk. With one hand she was holding up a sack in front of herself. As she stooped, one great breast fell out and dangled. Straightening up, she caught the boy's look of horror, leered and put out her tongue. When she turned round, he saw that she had no clothing but the sack.

Another time, there was a screech of laughter from one of the cottages, and a woman some fifty years old, quite naked, ran across from one cottage to another, jumping over a group of children to get by. Jeers and catcalls came from the men sitting in the gutter, which she answered from the depths with a screech like a jay. While Dermot stood transfixed, a man staggered to the door from which she had fled grinning fatuously, and reaching out fumbling, amorous paws to detain her.

"Aw, aw, aw, c'm on," he babbled, and stood swaying, holding on to the doorpost, toppling forward, as if a hinge were broken in his middle. "C'm on, c'm on," and the spittle drooled down in ropes over his stubbly chin.

Clasping his tin of lug, Dermot fled.

"Paddy," he gasped, when he joined his faithful comrade, "I *can't* go there again. They're awful people. I saw—"

He didn't say what he saw: but Paddy was very matter-of-fact and soothing. They were poor people, his explanation ran, who knew no better: Dermot was not to tell his grandparents. The caution was unnecessary. Dermot knew better than to imperil his own freedom. There were too many efforts to wean him from Paddy already. On three separate occasions Granny had found "Such a nice boy, Dermot darling, to play with you." Each foredoomed occasion had been a failure. Two of the visitors had been prigs, and the third of so aggressive and violent a temper that the effort was given up as a bad job. He compelled Dermot to climb a tree, and hurt his arm, challenged him to wrestle, punched him in the chest, and tweaked him black and blue. Even Granny could not blink the unsuitability of such a companion.

"You'd better leave him as he is," counselled Dermot's father. "This Paddy seems a very decent sort of a fellow."

"Oh, he's decent enough," said Granny with spirit, "or I wouldn't have employed him. I was only thinking, was it bad for the boy, only to be with a poor ignorant creature . . ."

Her voice died away, and she sighed.

"Dear old lady." He laid a hand in her lap. "You want the best for all of us, don't you?"

"Well, Ernest, I do. Though I can't often give it ye, I'm afraid."

"Indeed, you spoil us," declared her son-in-law. "You absolutely spoil us."

"Ah, no, Ernest. I can't content meself. I do often be ashamed . . ."

. . . "But, seriously," he was saying, a little later, "the boy will take no harm. He's happy, and in the open air all day long. It does him a world of good—and he's none too easy to content, either physically or mentally."

So Paddy's sway remained unchallenged, and Dermot went quietly on his path. Soon the Fishbank lost its terrors, and seeds of initiative grew in the timid spirit. No one can say when a quality is born. We can only record the first time it appears. The first time Dermot found it was on the occasion prophesied a few pages back: his first encounter with a conger eel.

CHAPTER XIX

Near the newtown smith end of the sea wall, a sewer ran out into the sea, built like a tiny pier. Paddy and his kind referred to it always as Kelly Shore. The end of it was a famous place for prawns, and Dermot, at low tide one afternoon, was busy catching them. Peg-leg, Paddy and Mike sat fifty yards further up, on the dry rock, smoking, spitting, and watching the mailboat glide swiftly in across the bay. The sun shone upon her white paint. She would be full: it was the start of Horse Show Week. There would be a power of high-up persons aboard of her. They gazed, spitting appreciatively.

The tide was a little high still for Dermot to reach his best point of vantage, a low, flat stone commanding a tiny bay. Opposite this was a big rock, hollow underneath. As the tide dropped, prawns in great numbers drifted from beneath this rock, across the little bay, and out through a passage which Dermot, standing on his flat stone, could command. Pulling up his trousers as far as they would go, he stood frowning, prepared for the leap across, but doubting its value, as the water was slightly ruffled, and still too deep. He would not be able to see what he was doing.

Deciding to wait till the mailboat rounded the pier, he controlled his impatience, and watched her, biting his underlip. Then, resolutely, he made the long stride, slipped half an inch, made a wild gesture, and regained his balance. He frowned, and looked quickly inshore, but Paddy and Co. were not visible. Then, bending down—it was still to deep to squat, without wetting his behind—he shaded his eyes, and peered into his hunting ground. Intent, careful, alert, he surveyed it over, inch by inch—then suddenly he stiffened.

Bang opposite him, a foot below the surface, projecting from under the hollow rock, half hidden by a streamer of weed, hung a motionless blue cylinder. Its blue was as virulent as the green of oxydised metal. It was solid and thick. It was close to him, in the same water as his bare shins. He knew exactly what it was.

At the first instant of recognition a thrill went all through him. His eyes clouded, and he began to tremble. He stood up abruptly, looking fascinated at the thick blue bar, which, with the laziest of motions, was beginning to slide slowly out. That movement decided him. Without pausing to think, he reversed his prawn net, and prodded the bar with the butt end of the long cane handle. He prodded gently at first, then harder. The bar gave a little, like solid india-rubber: then, with a lazy wriggle, it withdrew under the hollow rock, giving him a glimpse of its long sloping snout and opaque, glassy eye.

Then Dermot moved very quickly indeed. An observer might have supposed that he had been stung by a hornet. He leaped up to the highest rock close to him, and began to wave frantically, calling to Paddy and his friends in that shrill, overcharged voice which burst from him when he was excited. The faces of the group turned towards him: but they did not stir. After his third cry, Paddy called something back.

"A great—big—conger!" Dermot screamed again. "Oh—" and a sob of eagerness rose in his throat, as he climbed down to his place of vantage—only just in time. The blue bar, moving more decisively, was sliding out again between the dark weeds, Another jab, and another—vicious, excited jabs, delivered against a proclaimed enemy: and with an angry twist the eel once more retreated, turning slightly, showing the grey of its belly.

"Paddy! Peg-leg! *Do* come! A great big eel. On my honour; I'm not codding you."

Strange the local words sounded, when Dermot incorporated them in his talk, without imitating them. They laughed at him up at Uncle Ben's about it, saying "begawrah" at him, and the like. Dermot did not mind. He could deliver speeches heard on the Fishbank with full voice, and knew it. One of these days . . . ! For the present, taught by Granny's and Grandpapa's distaste for such performances, he did not venture.

Paddy said something to his companions, and started cloppering down the little pier, with that exaggerated swing of his arms which he used to ferry himself along. Dermot darted back to his place, and stood trembling, the cane grasped tightly in both hands, watching for a fresh sortie. The tide was running down fast. Upon his own quick breathing gained the scrabbling of Paddy's boots, and the series of grunts with which he negotiated the slippery rocks.

"Now then. What's this ye're sayin' about an eel?"

"Truly, Paddy. Really and truly. He tried to come out, and I prodded him with my cane. I— There! Look at him!"

"Faith." Paddy slipped and slithered. "I see no eel. Where do you—Oh, I see'm. Oh—be Jasus! Hey!— quick!"

Dermot jabbed, setting his teeth. The great steel spring of a body squirmed against the cane, and jerked sharply back. They heard it splash, deep under the hollow rock.

"The curse and flames!" Paddy floundered across to where Dermot was standing. "The tide's runnin' low on'm. He won't wait there long. He'll have a dart at it."

"Oh Paddy! What a pity we've no bait. I've got the conger hook here, and a bit of line."

"Bait! He'd touch no bait. It's his excape he's thinkin' of. Oh, be the holy! I've a plan. Have ye the hook? And the snood? Han' them over quick. Peg-leg! Mike!" He let such a bellow that Dermot jumped, and almost fell off the stone. "Ay! Ay! C'm on the two o' ye, quick!" He levered himself, monkey-like, on to a rock close by. "Here. Gi' me the cane."

"The cane! But I'll have nothing to keep him back with."

"Han' it up quick, I'm tellin' you, now, without you want us to lose him."

"But he's getting— Ah! Go back, back, back, you brute!"

Passionately, his face contorted, Dermot stabbed at the eel, which had tried to rush him.

"That's it. Give him a hell of a puck, and han' it up quick while he's still sore."

There was no further sign of the eel, so Dermot reluctantly handed up his weapon.

"What will I frighten him back with now?" he asked disconsolately.

"Yeer fut," grunted Paddy, already furiously at work. He had seized the cane, and was lashing the big conger hook to its end with the snood of line, pulling with hands and teeth, letting fall a string of muttered curses, and eyeing the lessening space of water. Bending down and away, to get a purchase, he heard a determined splashing, and looked up to see Dermot dancing in the water in front of the hole. With a grunt of approval, he once more applied himself to his task.

"Oh, Paddy, hurry! He's splashing about under there."

"Amn't I—workin'—as hard as I can. Where's them fellas. Here, you'll have to come here a minyit. Put yeer thumb on this— Oh, here y'are!"

Peg-leg was advancing lazily down the slip.

"What ails yez?" he enquired good-humouredly. "Why are ye baalin'?"

"A bloody big eel, inunder the rock beyant," explained Paddy briefly. "That's what ails me. That's why am I baalin'. Here—put yeer thumb on tha'. Grand. Now— Is he there yet, Dermot?"

"He is. He tried again, to come out."

"Well." Mr. Kennedy grasped his weapon, and slid grimly over the rock, to the scene of action. "Let him try now, the b—, all he pleases."

The eel obliged, Paddy stabbed his gaff into the water, struck savagely, and missed. With a furious writhe the eel shot back into its retreat.

Paddy knelt down on the now bare stone.

"Oh, bedam, I see'm! A b— big b—."

Dermot stooped too. There were now only a few inches of water beneath the hollow rock. The tide was running its last lap like water draining from a basin. Deep underneath, with no escape but the way they guarded, the eel lay half in, half out of the water, regarding them with cold, malevolent eyes. His iridescent blue had left him. He was a dull, dirty grey, covered with patches of slime.

"Le' me see." Peg-leg scrambled down, elbowing Dermot aside. "Oh, be the holies! That's a big lad, Wing-Man. That's a terrible big lad."

Paddy did not reply. He was cursing softly, in a kind of ecstasy. The appearance of a formidable opponent, animal or human, wrought him always to a frenzy. When, once in two years maybe, Wing-Man Kennedy was roused to fight, the battle was short and desperate. To use his full strength, all of it, at once: to hate and destroy, and in the violence to purge off all hatred and destruction: that was the way Paddy worked.

Suddenly, Dermot did not see how, the fight began. There was a terrific scrabbling and groping, a yell from Peg-leg, and the eel was out in the open, leaping and lashing about at the end of the cane, with the hook deep in its neck. The savage, demented pulsations were almost shaking Paddy's great arms from their sockets. His face was set and terrible, as if it had boiled over and gone cold: the muscles about his jaw stood out like thick round cords. Leaping up clumsily with a cry, Peg-leg rushed to him from behind, and flung his arms round him. Long Mike was slithering and ejaculating somewhere in the background. Dermot stared, the scene flaring vividly in his sight, so tense, so charged with a vicious power that the figures stood out as in a stereoscope. He, perceiving them, seemed to move on a different plane of time: their movements, quick and jerky with the strain of rigid muscles, were yet arrested: he saw each movement as a series of still poses, in a glaring and terrifying dream. The purpose of Peg-leg's embrace, which at first gave a grotesque note of horror to the scene, became soon apparent; for the eel, grasping a projection in his tail, with a lightning convulsion jerked both men on top of him. A yell arose, horrifying in its fear, its uncontrolled animal fury. For a moment the two men grovelled helplessly: then Peg-leg, yellow, spitting with fury, rolled off and leaped to his feet, revealing Paddy right on top of the eel, holding away with one hand the flat evil head that was only a few inches from his own. Like a gorilla, with the sheer power of his long arms, he raised himself, his brow a network, his mouth open like a gorilla's, bellowing his fury and loathing. Another second, and he was on his feet, staggering away to one side. The eel slid over and tried to escape, but the long gaff galled it: it flung itself about, and the cane handle slid and whacked on the rock.

Before Paddy could get a hold on himself, for the sudden proximity of the eel had filled him with nausea, Long Mike stepped coolly across and put his foot on the cane. Then, going down on one knee, and propping his left hip against a buttress in the rock, he took hold of it, and jerked the eel out of the crevice on to a comparatively flat surface. There, keeping the cane low down against the rock, he contrived to hold it, as it leaped and writhed, unable to get a purchase for resistance.

"The gaff is tearin' loose," he warned them suddenly. "Hurry up, or he'll be away on yez."

This speech shook Paddy into activity. Planting his legs

square, and bending down between them, he put forth the full strength of his back and his long misshapen arms. When he rose, he held by the edges a huge flat stone, with weeds and water dripping from it. Grunting from the effort, he swung it up to the flat rock beside the eel, and climbed up after it. As he beheld the eel, and contemplated his blow, his face became once more terrifying. The lower jaw projected, the brows drew low, the blood came down in a dark cloud between the eyes. Then, quickly as if galvanised, he stooped, raised the great stone high above his head, and crashed it down upon the leaping eel.

The effect was devastating. The stone lay all across its victim: the leapings ceased. Only a slow, shivering writhe of the tail marked the remnant of vitality which survived the blow.

It was a full minute before Paddy tipped the stone off the eel. He did it warily, for he had once been bitten by an eel, apparently dead, which he was carrying from a hook. In a last effort, it had leaped and fixed its serrated rows of teeth in his knuckle. But for his promptitude in forcing his whole hand inside the weakening jaws, he would have suffered badly. As it was, the teeth met in his flesh.

But this eel was past doing harm—past any conscious action. The blow had smashed its spine in a dozen places. Its head was flattened, its gills crushed outwards: one eye bulged loose from the socket. Even as they watched, its slow writhing ceased. It stiffened. Tremors, so quick, so small that Dermot thought his eye was tricking him, began to chase each other under its skin. They grew: the long, slimy sides, scarred grey, shimmered in a kind of ecstasy: a broken, choking cough rose in the crushed throat, and with a last effort the eel rolled over on its side, then relaxed upon its back, its grey belly bulging upwards to the sky.

"God mend his like," said Long Mike piously. He picked up his pipe, a clay with a tin protector, which he had laid down in a cranny of the rock, and pulled at it anxiously.

Presently he gave a grunt of contentment. It had not gone
out. Mike hated having to use matches. They were his
economy, his mania. To see them spilt, or wasted, or thrown
away before every possible pipe had been lit, was physical
hurt to him. No Vestal Virgin tended her sacred flame with
greater personal zeal than Mike the dottle in his pipe.

Up through the town they went, exhibiting their famous
catch. Everyone said, "Be the holies!" and "How did
yez catch that lad?" and to each had to be explained, with
laughter and oaths, in shaky voices, the quite unheard of
way in which they *had* caught him. Everyone said, "G'way
ou' of that. Yez are coddin' me": and received in reply,
"It's God's truth. Ask the young lad." Everyone then said,
"Jasus": or "Did yez ever hear the like o' that?" and
the concourse, increasing every five yards, agreed that
begob, ye never did. By the time they reached Walmer
Villa, there was quite a crowd in attendance. The first cold
water was cast on the exploit by Grandpapa, who came
fuming to the door, apparently under the impression that
all the "Cath'lic blagyards" of the place were in insur-
rection and had chosen him as their first victim. Hailed by
the crowd in terms of high respect, and called upon to
admire the magnificent catch, he was little appeased, but
let the captors in, if only to be rid of their followers.

"Mind now, mind now." He stood, tetchy and fidgety,
on the step. "Hold it clear, hold it clear. Don't let it be
touching anything, now."

"Oh, damn the fear, sir," said Mike, unexpectedly: and
received a kick from his scandalised chief.

So, edging their way along, backing and sliding, they
steered their inert burden down the hall, round the corner
by the kitchen—"Tch, tch, tch," exclaimed Bessie, standing with disgusted face by the door—and into the garden.
There they laid it, beside the tub, and stood back to contemplate it in admiration.

Grandpapa followed them.

"I declare to me God," he complained, "to go bring . . . Tchah . . . What did you want to go bring that thing in here?"

"Sure, sir," said Paddy in scandalised tones, "we couldn't be leaving it on the shore, and we after catching it. It was Master Dermot seen it," he added proudly, "an' kep' it from escaping, the way we could come at it with the gaff."

Grandpapa's manner softened a little. Inconvenient though the captive was, he did not wish to dishearten his grandson.

"Well, well," he said. "Don't go making a mess with it, now. Well, well."

The battle seemed to have set free Mike's spirit. For the second time, he burst into unaccustomed speech.

"Them fish," he observed, addressing Grandpapa, and designating the eel with his pipe, which he had removed from his mouth: "them fish gets a good price on the fishmongers. High up people do be eating them. In hotels. They do boil them, for to make soup."

Grandpapa stared in astonishment. This ragamuffin of a fellow, to go lifting up his voice, and lecturing him. Then good-humour overcame him. He smiled grimly.

"Well, well," he said. "You'll soon be done:" and, turning his back, he clasped his hands behind it, and went away slowly up the path.

"Hould yer whisht, Mike, ye bloody fool," said Paddy, *sotto voce*, as the majestic back receded. "Don't you know that's the way to anger the old gentleman? With yeer soups, and yeer hotels, and yeer high up people! Wouldn't Mr. Conroy know, better nor you, what high up people are apt to eat?"

"Be easy," replied Mike, replacing his pipe. "Be easy, now."

CHAPTER XX

THE FINISH OF THE EEL WAS NOT ON A LEVEL WITH ITS CAP-
ture. Bessie firmly refused to make soup, or anything else, of
it. Like all the people round about, she looked upon eels as
serpents, and felt a superstitious horror at the thought of
eating them. So the eel—four foot six in length, sixteen
pounds and eight ounces on the scales—was cast out to rot
on Mr. Caggen's dunghill.

This anticlimax in no way chilled Dermot's zeal for the
new sport. After such an excitement, ordinary fishing seemed
tame. Nothing would do him but that they purchase the
materials for a real conger line. Leave for the requisite
night-fishing, however, was not yet to be had. He had to be
content with fishing by day, and setting the line in a convenient place at night.

In underground but natural ways, the exploit, and the
praises he received for it, so fired his imagination that for
the first time he envisaged a personal relationship between
himself and Mona. From the distant worshipper, who did
not aspire even to be a suppliant, he rose to be a possible
champion, winning not only acquaintanceship, but homage.
A success in the field of action revealed how deeply and
how secretly he coveted such success. He longed now above
all things to perform some feat before Mona's eyes: to
catch a huge, savage eel with her for spectator: even (since
that, he had to admit, was unlikely) to be seen carrying
his captive past her door. The girl left the cloisters of his
mind, and walked openly in the sunlit street. By coincidence, he saw her several times, out of doors, in her front

173

garden, and once, oh choking, suffocating thrill, on the Sea Wall itself. So ardently did his eyes follow her white frock along under the grey masonry, that Paddy noticed.

"Do you know who that is?" he enquired. "That's Miss Scanlon."

"You know her?" Dermot turned, in dark amazement.

"Surely I know her. A very nice, pretty young gerrl. I do be often doing jobs for her mother in the garden. A nice spoken, friendly young lady."

Paddy eyed his companion narrowly. The white frock flitted along, soared over the steps of Kelly Shore, dipped, was hidden behind a rock, appeared triumphant, then swung off up the steps of Newtown Smith.

"Would you like for to meet her?"

From anyone else in the world, the question would have been an outrage. To anyone else he would have shot out an indignant, shamed refusal. But Paddy was Paddy, before whom he had no shame. Dermot turned to him an awed, shining face.

"Oh, Paddy, could I?"

Paddy shifted his feet, in a businesslike manner.

"Faith," he said. "Easy."

"But how, Paddy?"

"Faith, me knowin' her well, an' all, d'ye see: I goes to her and tells her the young gentleman I do be with would like for to meet with her down by the gate—"

"Oh, but not anywhere near the house. They might see."

"Well then. Forenint Burdett Avena'. I'll tell her," predicted the match-maker confidently. "She'll come, and glad. You'll see, now."

Something deep down in Dermot distrusted this simple plan, but he was only too eager for it to be tried. His desire was sharpened, that very afternoon. Looking up as he went home alone, he saw Mona approaching, a few yards away. It was too late to cross the road. The pavement was empty. They had to pass. A miserable, sweet pang ran through him,

a mixture of pride and utter shame. The moment lasted a
lifetime: it had a landscape and a climate of its own. Crimson,
he dared to raise his eyes, and saw that she was looking down,
trying not to laugh. His heart gave a sudden wild leap, and
he smiled too: and so they passed, smiling away from one
another, the girl all self possessed, Dermot in an extraordinary perplexity of relief and feelings he could not understand.

All promised well: but strange, capricious are the ways
of women. Poor Paddy's embassy, discharged in husky
secrecy by the back door, received with smiles and blushes,
went all awry. The faithless Mona told her mother, who
summoned the ambassador, and soundly rated him. How
dare he? What did he mean? She never heard the like.

"You forget, Mr. Kennedy: my daughter is only a child."

"So is Master Dermot, ma'am," spoke up Paddy sturdily.
"What is he, only a child too. What harrm, ma'am, the childer
to be playing together. Sure, isn't it only natural—"

"I don't like such a way of doing things," said Mrs.
Scanlon. She was a big, over-ripe woman, and had perhaps
some reason for being extra particular. "It's not the right
way, nor the way I've been accustomed to."

"You know Mrs. Conroy, ma'am, and you know Mr.
Conroy. Sure, there can be no harrm there. Such a fine,
well-respected lady and gentleman—"

"No harm at all, I'm sure," conceded the lady. "I know
as well as you do who they are. But it's not a thing I like,
and it's not a thing I will have, Mr. Kennedy: you to be
making assignations with my daughter, for anyone's behalf,
at the age she is, and putting ideas into her head."

"'Putting ideas into her head,'" repeated the discomfited one venomously, when he came to report his ill-luck.
"As if it wasn't stuffed full of them already, and she with
half the schools runnin' after her in the road. She's a nice
little girl, mind ye: but she well knows who looks after her,
and she passing by. Maybe she doesn't well know the way to
lead them on, either!"

When next Dermot saw Mona, she tossed her head, and went by with her beautiful chin held high in the air. Next year, it was too late. She was crazy about athletics. She went to cricket matches, and, in September, to the football: the object of her regard being a curly-headed hero with the improbable name of Lambkin, whose prowess was remarkable in both. If she had other suitors, he ousted them all: and the day came when Paddy reported that he "seen young Lambkin pinnin' her up agen the wall at the butt of Ballygihen Avena', and he kissin' the face off of her." From that day, Dermot set her down as unattainable. She became once more a wraith, a vision: and remained embedded in his prayers, last of that list, nearly all relations, whom, after saying the Lord's Prayer, he called on God to bless. Banished even from daydreams, there she stayed; subject of a mechanical petition: sometimes remembered, with a smile, but causing no resentment, nor regret. To have had her, and lost her to Lambkin, would have meant disillusionment. Mona was not meant for the trials of actual acquaintance. She was a vision, in a white drifting frock, a creature from the land of myth. His first instinct had been right. She was only for the eyes. And, alas, when a few years had gone by, no longer even for them. She flowered too early.

But, before all this happened, there came a second deed of derring do. Another eel was captured: and though Mona was not there to see it, others were. Plenty of little girls, from fourteen downwards, caught prawns along the Wall, sailed boats, built castles (to the fishermen's indignation, since the only sandy places were sacred to the digging of bait), paddled, and occupied themselves busily day in, day out. One of these, a handsome sturdy laughing creature, two years older than Dermot, much approved by Paddy, believed in going for what she wanted. She wanted Dermot, who attracted her by contrast. He, as soon as he found that her eager questions were not really prompted by an intense desire to learn about fishing, received them coldly. She asked him the same questions too often. But Marjorie was assiduous. Flushed and sunburned, she waylaid him one evening, and pinned him against the wall, hemming him in with her strong arms and legs, gazing enthusiastically into his eyes.

"I expect you'll catch lots of lovely big fish," she proclaimed.

Dermot wriggled, averting his eyes uncomfortably from her face. Past her straw hat, her thick dazzling plait of hair, and her pink-sleeved shoulder, he saw the wide calm bay and the elbow of the pier.

"Oh," he said.

"*I* think so," she repeated. Her face was closer. He felt her breath.

"Don't come sprawling all on top of me," he said with sudden irritation, and pushed against her chest. She held firm, smiling at him.

"I'm stronger than you," she said.

He stared into her face, his own wrinkling in distaste. Some other little girls were looking on, and laughing. If he struggled, she might win. It would be too undignified.

"*Do* let me go. I've got to hurry home. I shall be late."

Marjorie took her reverse good-naturedly. She stood back, and let him go.

"Oh, well," she said, smiling right into him in a large way that made him feel very uncomfortable. He ran up the steps, to join Paddy, who was leaning over the top, looking down. "Good-bye," she called after him.

"Oho," said Paddy, at the top. "Oho, boy! Looka, Master Dermot: the young girl is waving good-bye to you."

"Oh, good-bye."

He turned and waved.

"Good-bye, Dermot."

She went to join the others, waving and smiling.

"Oho, boy," chuckled Paddy again, as they fell into step, "ye were very near gettin' kissed that time."

Dermot stopped short.

"Good Lord," he exclaimed, "was *that* what—"

He went on again, saying nothing, while queer hot waves of feeling went over him. He had had no idea: and wondered, now, whether he would have liked or hated it, if she had.

He might try again, go near her, and see if she would. Paddy's shameless enjoyment made him look at the matter differently. Paddy—and Grandpapa: that was the one point on which they both agreed. Girls were to be admired, and run after, and—Dermot's imagination stopped. The active rôle, as yet, was outside his range.

When he next did meet Marjorie, he received fresh evidence of feminine instability. The conger line, fitted up at last, had been set for the second time, below high water mark, lashed to the iron stanchion on the left hand rock at the foot of Ballygihen Avenue. An eel had been seen there, and one afternoon, on the rising tide, they had fished him. What a clumsy, unlikely instrument of capture the line looked! how garishly the thick white twine showed up, lying lumpily along the bottom, with half a new herring transfixed on the great hook. Scarcely had they flung it in, when a little crab, marvelling at his good fortune, had flung himself upon the bait. Paddy swore, and jerked on the line: the little crab hung on. Paddy pulled up the line: just below the surface, the little crab let go, and sank regretfully back, his legs and claws outspread, like some eccentric flower. Paddy put out the line again, in a different place: but the scent of the herring was strong, and the little crab, capering over the tussocks of brown weed, found it again with joy, and fastened on.

"Holy Mother of Divine God," cried Paddy, in high wrath, "will you look if this bloody little divil isn't at me bait again."

He was about to move the line a second time, when Dermot caught his arm, and pointed. Coming in languidly, on the far side of the little bay, nosing his sinuous way along—the eel. Instantly, with a great scutter and slithering of boots, Paddy lay flat on his belly upon the rock: and his pupil followed him. Tense, hardly daring to breathe, they watched the eel's progress. Waving his way along, like a streamer, a long blue weed, he was in no hurry. Once he disappeared into a hole. Then, when he emerged, the light upon the water hid him. For a long time he was out of their sight; and Dermot was just about to raise himself cautiously upon one elbow, when a sharp hiss from Paddy stopped him, and he saw the eel, close to them, cutting straight across and making a beeline for the bait. Three seconds, perhaps, and the little crab let go of the bait as if it had been red hot, scampering wildly, with all his legs, to bury himself under the protecting weed. But the long lean snout did not concern itself with him. Delicately, warily, it nuzzled the bait: delicately, warily, it picked it up, and began lightly to chew. The veins stood out on Paddy's forehead. His very muscles and tendons seemed to creak. His hand shook: but he held the line loose.

"Chuck, Paddy," breathed Dermot. "Oh, now, now."

"No. Lave it to'm."

"Chuck!"

"No, I'm tellin' you."

Gaining confidence, the eel began to bite in real earnest. He worried the bait, shaking it, turning up his underside.

"Now! Oh, Paddy, you'll lose him."

"Will you lave me be!" came back the furious whisper. "Do you want to lose'm on me?"

"Oh, oh, oh, look! Oh Paddy—I'm sure it's time."

"Divil mend you, then!"

Paddy struck, with the full force of his arm. The blow spun the eel clean over, tearing the bait out of his mouth. Then, with a single stroke of his long tail, he was off like an arrow, frightened irretrievably; and the power of the stroke sent up a ripple to writhe resentfully on the calm surface of the water.

Paddy rose.

"Now then," he adjured the crestfallen Dermot, "maybe
you're satisfied. Now maybe ye're pleased with what ye
done."

He pulled in the line.

"Another minyit, and I had'm. He was bitin' on it grand.
Only for you fussin' me, and goin' on at me, I had'm here,
now. Do you know more about fishin' for eels: or do I?"

"Well," protested Dermot ignobly. "If you know such
a lot, why did you take any notice of me?"

"Now then, Master Dermot," said Paddy, very properly,
"if ye're going to talk *that* way, ye can get someone else to
fish with ye."

Receiving no reply, he gave his pupil a long lecture, of
such admirable sense that even a small and disingenuous
boy could not but feel the justice of it. The incident concluded well, and it was with complete submission to Paddy's
science that the line had been laid down, which they were
now to take up.

The tide ebbed slowly. By infinitesimal degrees, it seemed
to sigh its way down the rocks, and out of the small weedy
bay. Bright yellow the weed drooped, as if exhausted by the
burden of the waters: like a hostess who collapses into a
chair when her guests have gone. Ripples upon the shiny
surface darkened, broke, became the tops of rocks: rose into
little polls: and soon were casting a shadow. In a few minutes,
if he rolled up his shorts into tight rings around his thighs,
Dermot would be able to wade across and reach the rock
with the stanchion. They could see the stanchion. It had
been uncovered for some time, and they could just see the
butt of the line. It *looked* taut, but one couldn't really tell,
at that distance, whether there were anything on it or not.
If the eel had been at it, Paddy explained, the line would be
taut anyhow. He would have dragged the bait off into the
weeds, to worry it undisturbed.

A number of little girls, with Marjorie at their centre,
had gathered on the Wall. Dermot, feeling important,

strolled over, and explained to them what was afoot. Far
from being properly impressed, Marjorie scoffed at the idea
that there could be an eel on the line.

"Pooh," she laughed. "You couldn't catch an eel."

Dermot drew himself up, deeply offended.

"I caught one the other day," he asserted.

"You mean those men caught it for you."

"I don't. I mean—"

"Did you catch it all by yourself: or were they there?"

"They were there. But I kept it—"

"There you are, you see." She would not let him explain.
All the girls sided with her, and laughed at him. Worst
of all, he saw Annie and Eithne on the rocks, not far off.

Hurt and puzzled, he turned away, and went back to
Paddy. Paddy looked at him.

"I think you can get across now," he said.

Biting his lip, Dermot bent to tighten the rolls of his
turned-up shorts, and began to wade across. The water
rose high and cool inside his thighs. In one place, it touched
the roll. Then the floor sloped upwards: a stride or two, and
he was upon the rock, the water squelching out of his sandshoes. As he crossed, he heard a murmur from the girls.
They were watching, intently enough. He half realised that
they were really interested, but were belittling him for some
mysterious reason of their own.

The line was drawn down tight from the stanchion. Shading
his eyes, he peered down into the forest of upstanding weed.
A shock hit him right under his ribs, tangible as a real blow.
There, beneath him, a little to one side, just above the bottom, keeping level with faint languid movements of his tail,
the outstretched line leading straight into his jaws, he saw
the eel, suspended, a prisoner.

"Is he in it?" came Paddy's voice.

Dermot turned, over his shoulder.

"Yes."

There was a stir among the audience, an excited murmur.

This was the moment. So swiftly that he gave himself no time to hesitate, and the exhausted eel no time to resist, Dermot stooped, seized the line, and with a couple of frenzied tugs had the captive leaping on the rock beside him. Then, and then only, did he realise how little of the rock was out of water: a small, irregular platform, close quarters for four foot six of galvanized indiarubber, with vicious teeth, and a solitary, bare-legged captor.

Happily, the eel was caught, all right. Even supposing it got back into the water, it could not escape. Dermot watched it. It was quite close, a yard away, perhaps, but there was a reassuring aimlessness about its leaps. Either it did not see Dermot, or else it did not connect him with its predicament. The unhappy brute had probably been caught on the evening tide, and been left high and dry for several hours. This it could easily survive, for eels will spend a long time out of the water of their own accord; and the wet weed, in which it would have sulked, would keep it going. But this, and its long struggles to escape the great pitiless hook, had weakened it. Even now, as Dermot watched, the eel ceased leaping, and lay still a moment on its belly. Then, with smooth insinuating purpose, it wormed its way into a crevice. The stiff, hard snout scraped harshly against the rough surface of the rock.

What to do now? Impossible to carry the captive back in triumph. Dermot could not hold it high enough. Besides, the beast would probably attack him. He had heard enough tales of eels' ferocity to assist his natural caution. Still, something had to be done. He could not stand helpless there, in front of Marjorie and the rest. Stooping down, he took hold gingerly on the line, and gave it a timid chuck. A discontented writhe was the answer, as the eel wormed deeper into the crevice.

Then, to his surprise, he heard a splash behind him, and turned to behold Mike. The longshoreman had removed his shoes and stockings, and rolled up his trousers, revealing a pair of unprepossessing hairy shins, and toes so warped and discoloured that they looked like roots.

"Undo the butt," he advised, turning a lack-lustre eye upon the eel.

Dermot stared for a second in bewilderment, then understood, and hastened to untie the end of the line.

"I sent Mrs. Crotty's young lad to borry the lend of a coal hammer," Mike vouchsafed, as Dermot fumbled at the cold, swollen knots. "We'll jairk him above on the Wall."

Dermot nodded. Blood was pumping and singing behind his ears. He coveted Mike's approbation. What a good thing Mike was there. Ah—the knots were coming.

"It's—nearly—undone," he panted: but Mike had straightened up, and was gazing intently at a passer-by upon the Wall. Sudden dread chilled Dermot. Supposing it should be someone from the Salvation Army! Then, Mike would at once forsake him. At the call of conscience, he would leave any gathering, any occupation, and stalk off, muttering his one word of ill-omen. But the passer-by proved innocent. Mike sighed, and looked back at the eel.

"Have ye it undone yet?" he asked mildly.

"Yes." Dermot straightened his aching back, and handed the line to his companion. Mike took two turns on it.

"Hel' up," he exclaimed, and savagely jerked the eel out of its crevice. It flapped, but feebly, and they realised how grievously exhausted it was: for after a convulsion or two, it lay upon its back, arching up its belly slowly from the rock, dropping back again, and twisting into a slow, stiff arc.

"Way ou' o' that!"

Mike dragged it along the rock. Then, reaching the water, he shortened his grip upon the line, and swung the eel away, high and wide. He kept it swinging, so that its own weight should keep the line taut, and prevent its jumping up and biting him in the hand. Dermot followed. In the short time, the water had sunk almost to his knees.

They dragged the eel up on the Wall, just as Mrs. Crotty's

little boy arrived with the hammer. A gasp went up from the crowd as Paddy dealt the executioner's blow. Some of the little girls screamed faintly, and hid their eyes. With her arms about a couple of them, Marjorie looked steadfastly upon the deed, her lower lip stuck out, her face flushed.

As soon as he could slip away, Dermot strolled casually over to her. Now, she would recant. Now, she would admit that he could catch an eel. His face stiffened into patronising lines.

To his amazement, she assailed him roundly. He was a coward. He was afraid of the eel. He stood there, like a baby, on the rock, with his thumb in his mouth, for all to see. He could do nothing. He couldn't even bring the eel back. The poor man had to take off his shoes and stockings, and go across to him, just like a nanny.

"You were afraid," she charged him, boldly and contemptuously. "You were afraid of the eel." And all the other little girls joined in, and chanted, "Afraid of the eel. You were afraid of the eel."

Crimson with mortification and bewilderment, Dermot faced them.

"I pulled it up, anyway," he kept repeating, almost humbly.

"Coo," said good-natured Annie afterwards. "They didn't half give it to you."

Dermot turned angrily away. That Annie should have seen, and should sympathise, was the last humiliation. His heart was full of resentment against Marjorie, and all her satellites. Girls! Never again would he have anything to do with them. Walking back with Paddy and Mike, his triumph gone sour in his mouth, he imagined scenes of fierce humiliation for Marjorie. His imagination, darkening, like a thunderous sky, grew lurid and alarming. He pictured himself beating her with a cane. For a moment he could hardly see where he was going. Paddy had to ask him a question twice, and he stammered as he replied. His throat seemed to have swollen.

Later, his mood grew cold. He would ignore her. It was well for his peace of mind that her holiday ended soon after, for she would have beckoned to him one day, and, to his own complete surprise, he would have gone to her. Let her speak nicely to him once, and his resentment would be all forgotten. It was as well, perhaps, he should not find this out.

A further annoyance was to be lectured by his father upon unnecessarily taking life. The eel was useless for food: why kill it? This Dermot felt to be a sort of blasphemy, a base, unfair contradiction of that gospel of the chase to which Paddy had brought him up, which fortified and raised to ritual his normal boy's instinct. A rebuke from his father always outwardly abashed him. It filled him with a strange embarrassment, which had nothing to do with his transgression, and imparted a sort of anger to any defence he might put up.

"You shoot cats," he muttered at last, shifting from one foot to another, and looking on the ground.

"Only when they do harm," replied his father. "That is a very different matter, as well you know."

"Well—eels do harm."

"What harm?" enquired the cold voice.

"A lot of harm. Paddy says so."

"It seems to me you are more ready to believe what Paddy says than what your parents tell you." There was a slight emphasis upon "Paddy" which stung the boy. "I'm not sure you are not too much with him and his friends. However—" Mr. Gray paused. "If you must kill fish you do not want, need you bring it here, to be thrown out?"

He paused, and, receiving no answer, walked away. He was wearing a white panama hat. Dermot raised his eyes, and stared resentfully after the dignified figure. He found something a little ridiculous in it, though he dared not admit as much to himself. Why bring the eel home! Why, to show, of course. Any reasonable parent would be proud of him: would sympathise. . . . Dermot turned, and hurried off in consternation. His eyes had filled with tears: tears of anger, but humiliating enough.

He wandered down the garden, and related his exploit to Mr. Caggen. The gardener gave him all the applause he craved, plus a totally unexpected chance to score against his father. Mr. Caggen knew of a poor Protestant family who had no prejudice against "sarpints," and would be glad of all the eels they could get. With a real satisfaction, and no little cunning, Dermot contrived to tell Granny this, in front of his father, in such a way that it appeared his bounden duty to catch them eels.

"Yes, yes, darling," beamed Granny, in all innocence, "Ye'll be doing the poor souls a real kindness."

Delightful, neat revenge! He carefully avoided looking at his father: and, as soon as he could, withdrew from the room. Scoring like this was a new experience. It brought a sense of fear, almost of sacrilege. To stay in the room after it was more than he could manage. With his mother Dermot got on perfectly. She checked him sometimes, but always in a language he could understand. Left to herself, she was easy-going: she never fussed: she was languidly unconventional. His father would lecture her, would urge her to be more systematic, would interfere sometimes, and overrule their delightful, intimate schemes. Then, and only then, would she lose her composure, and strike out in sudden attacks of nerves which Dermot could understand and allow for. Mr. Gray was beginning to be worried about Dermot's good—at least, it was becoming apparent to Dermot that he did: the worrying had started long before. One thing he could find no fault with. Dermot's progress with his lessons was all the most exacting father could desire. In this respect, Mr. Gray was delighted with him: but a very natural and proper fear of making the boy conceited led him to withhold all but the most guarded praise, and gave Dermot the idea

that his father did not care about him. So a natural anta-
gonism drew nourishment. The two got on well enough on
many occasions—far better at home than in Ireland: but
there was a wariness on Dermot's side. The old simple relationship was gone.

CHAPTER XXI

THE FIRE FLICKERED DROWSILY OVER THE WIDE, LOADED sideboard. Silver and fat Waterford glass, caught at odd angles, winked back indulgently. Their shadows, bobbing up and down on the wall behind them, forbad them to be staid. Dermot, watching them, was reminded of a number of fat old women bathing, holding on to a rope, and bobbing up and down: a sight often to be enjoyed, from a respectful distance, at the new Victoria Baths, or at Sandycove. Vision displaced reality: he forgot where he was, till the entry of Bessie, lamp in hand, recalled him.

Grandpapa folded the *Irish Times*, rose, laid it on the table, and peered over the tops of his glasses at Bessie: ready to admonish, should she show any sign of prematurely raising the wick. "Tang-hoo-hoo! Tang-hoo-hoo! Tang-hoo-hoo!" —the cuckoo clock played its punctual part in the performance. One could just see the dark little space inside the doors, as they opened. Six. Bessie turned up the lamp: stooped for a moment, eying it anxiously: turned it up further: smiled at Dermot, raising her eyes in a comical, expressive gesture; and withdrew.

Grandpapa gave a grunt of satisfaction. He looked for a couple of seconds at the closed door. Then, starting with the deliberate effort of the aged, he went over stiffly to the bookcase. Adjusting his spectacles, and peering upward, he selected, lovingly and carefully, a leather-backed volume. Dermot watched him with vague, passive pleasure. He was getting to know the books and their positions pretty well. At the bottom left-hand side, *Charles O'Malley*, and other works of the same author: the *Self-Made Merchant*—Dermot did not greatly care for him: the poetical works of Sir Samuel Ferguson: a large volume of the Irish Wits, from which Grandpapa read him, with much relish, the escapades and drolleries of Vousden, for whom the old gentleman cherished especial admiration. Then, a long row of bound church magazines, and Lecky's *History of European Morals*.

The next row he knew rather vaguely. It was complicated by the situation in it of a biscuit box, cunningly contrived to resemble a row of books. Deceived by this in earlier days, and bitterly mortified by the deception, Dermot fought shy of the second row. All he knew, besides the biscuit box, was that it contained *The Cloister and the Hearth*, the *Speeches* of Curran, and a volume, referred to by Grandpapa in tones of solemn piety, recording the briefs and other legal activities of James Mongan, barrister-at-law, and illustrious connection of the family.

The third row contained the works of Charles Dickens, with a Thackeray or two, in larger binding, at the right-hand end, to fill up. It was to this row that Grandpapa now addressed himself. The fourth row—smaller books—was occupied by a whole set of *Comic Offerings*. Each contained much letterpress, and a variety of illustrated puns: "A 'Heavy Swell' at Weymouth"—depicting a large gentleman dressed in the height of fashion: and so on, and so forth, after the manner of their time. They did not seem so amusing now as when he was five or six. There was also a long poem, in three books of manuscript, called *St. Pierre*, composed between the years 1810 and 1817 by a relative of Grandpapa, and exhibiting in full flower the poetical fashions of its period. It had a hero, a villain (dark and Byronic), and an innocent heroine (who lost her innocence in the third canto):

> *The final aid was lent by thee*
> *Thou Demon—OPPORTUNITY!*

Dermot was not very clear about this part of the poem,

which he had read hurriedly on one occasion because he gathered it was unsuitable for him; taking advantage of Grandpapa's short absence from the room. Other parts of it admitted of no doubt. There were murders, discovered and bewailed by a chorus of drooping ladies:

> *Don Diego sought in language brief*
> *The reasons for this scene of grief—*

Grandpapa's voice read on, in complete solemnity and absorption. He found the poem extremely edifying. Finally, for no reason clear to Dermot, there was a sort of general massacre in a glen, the sight of which was too much for the villain whose machinations had brought it about. He lost his reason:

> *And sudden, with terrific yell,*
> *He fled from the ensanguin'd dell.*

The conclusion sounded very moral, but its precise application was not at once apparent. Dermot thought that, on the whole, Dickens was clearer.

Opening the book, making great play with a long yellow marker, Grandpapa proceeded with the adventures, begun overnight, of Mrs. Gamp, as that redoubtable lady entered upon her duties in connection with the fever at the Bull. Listening, the boy saw it all: the long, dark passage, the frightened, scurrying maid, the tray, and Mrs. Gamp's repast: her nose sliding along the rail of the fireguard, her watchman's cloak, her enormous shadow on the wall: later, the room growing dark and chill: her awakening: and then, after hours of darkness, the coming of day.

"It was bright morning the next time Mrs. Gamp looked out of the window, and the sun was rising cheerfully. Lighter and lighter grew the sky, and noisier the streets; and high into the summer air uprose the smoke of newly kindled fires, until the busy day was broad awake."

He saw it all, with that sharp, conscious vision, that ex-

tending of the bounds of knowledge, which we experience
from imaginative writing of the highest class: saw, with
knowledge not his own, the colours of the walls, the baggy,
faded satins, the queer dark furniture: heard the soft noises
of the fire: and then, when morning came to banish the
fears and stuffy darkness of the sickroom, he looked out
with Mrs. Gamp, over the parapidges and crazy roofs of a
London he had never seen, through the clear morning air to
the green wooded hills: he drew the air deep into his lungs:
he heard the cries, the wheels that rumbled on the cobble-
stones. . . .

Grandpapa shut the book, with the phrase that always
followed his reading, sure as the amen following a prayer:
"Charles Dickens: a great master of literature." And Dermot, the clear colours fading slowly from his mind, looked
at Grandpapa, looked round the room, and knew, somehow,
that here, in this one place of all the world, that era still
lived on. The world whose beginnings Dickens had celebrated stuck somehow here, its growth arrested. Like
branches, borne down a river into a deep pool, and there
caught in an eddy, the eighteen-sixties circled slowly round
and round; their time stood still. Some changes had come:
the long greyhound mailboat had displaced the paddle boat,
and Dublin's new electric trams were the admiration of
Europe, but they ran garishly over the old dirty cobbled
streets of a Victorian city. The pool was stagnant; it smelled
like the Liffey at low tide; and the captive eighteen-sixties
were decaying. Development clogged with dirt and cobwebs:
Dickens their living author, the scruples and gallantry of a
lost period their conviction: Dr. O'Donovan their fashionable
doctor, driving to visit his patients in a carriage and pair,
pulling off his silk hat and lavender gloves to cross their
parlour door: in Dublin City, a hundred offices from Dickens'
world, with their old musty ledgers, their high desks and
stools, their low yellow windows looking out on gloomy
streets. Here, for a few years more, one might live in two

worlds. Here one might turn backwards, and take a walk down the last century. Realisation of this grew in Dermot, year by year, as a landscape emerges from a fog. Grandpapa was born in 1828! He could remember back, right back, easily, into it all. He had seen Tom Moore, and heard the Wicklow Sand-man, with his sack over his shoulder, crying his cry down Grafton Street. When the Famine came Grandpapa was a young man. The old fine head, bending in the lamplight—those eyes had seen Tom Moore! those old ears, with the hair sprouting from them, had heard his voice! Tom Moore was as much a hero to Dermot as Dickens was. The great, green, leather-bound *Irish Melodies*, with its brass clasp, which was the only book in the drawing-room besides the Bible, was equally sacred in his eyes. He was allowed to read it on special occasions, after washing his hands. The old flowery words, the old flowery pictures by Maclise— how well he knew and loved them. All, even Walmer Villa itself, belonged to an age which collapsed rather than passed: like an old, old woman who defies the years and is snuffed out in a morning. Dickens the only novelist and historian, Moore the only poet: Dr. O'Donovan the only doctor: the *Irish Times* the only newspaper: John Jamieson's the only whiskey: Protestantism the only faith, and the voice of Empire re-echoed, in a genteel brogue, from Dublin Castle. Outside the house, in Dublin, great, airy, rushing trams, and foul, clogged gutters: fine coloured ladies driving in high fashion to the Horse Show past rows of ragamuffins spitting on the pavement: great silver churches soaring over filthy hovels, like tall flowers from a dungheap: a world of wild contrasts and contradictions, where the thoughtful few turned bitter and derisive, where it was wiser to belong to the entrenched party, and never think at all. Dermot knew only the graces of that world, the long summer evenings, the light-heartedness, the uncouth characters and the violent incidents that seemed to belong to a play: Dublin, the great, warm, gloomy, friendly city: Grandpapa,

Granny, Walmer Villa, and the garden: Delgany, with Eileen, Con, and Uncle Ben: the Sea Wall, the harbour, Paddy, Peg-leg, Mike: happy patches from the great crazy quilt, all lit with the magic light of holiday. This light gave even the cruel and brutal things he saw a look of unreality: a woman, in the streets of Dalkey, her front teeth knocked in, jabbing her husband in the face with a broken bottle: a drunken father, on the Fish Bank, tearing the skirt off his sixteen-year-old daughter and slashing her bare buttocks with his belt: a boy kicked off the Sea Wall on to the rocks below: the screeches of an old woman in the cottages near Walmer Villa, the howls of dogs, beaten insensible so that their owners could say that they were dead and avoid paying the licence for them: all that was savage and bestial never came between him and his joy in the place, because of that magic holiday light, which made everything that was not happy seem unreal. One thing only shook him, and made him angry and miserable for days. A woman in Dublin threw some kittens from the top window of a house into the road. He read of it in the *Irish Times*. "One or two were killed outright: others lay writhing in agony, or tried feebly to crawl away." Dermot, who had seen the dirty, blubbering girl beaten with shock, but without pity, cried himself to sleep for several nights over the sufferings of creatures from his own nursery world. To hurt a kitten seemed to him the ultimate unkindness. Another Dublin woman, who knocked out her half-witted servant girl's teeth one by one with a hammer, seemed to him nothing in comparison. The people in the slums and on the Fish Bank were monsters: he could not take their sufferings seriously. But kittens!

Dermot's visits to the city itself were not many. He went once a year to the Zoo. Two or three times Granny took them shopping. They would visit Mrs. O'This in Stephen's Green, Mrs. McThat in Merrion Square. They would walk up Grafton Street, down Sackville Street, and round by Dame Street. They would look at the Post Office, the front of

Trinity, and the Bank of Ireland. Then, tired and foot-sore, they would have tea at Mitchell's, and catch the tram home. The tram was the most exciting part of it. Eagerly, as they approached the city, Dermot would note the different trams, with their marvellous, poetic destinations: Drum-condra, Glasnevin, Terenure: Sandymount—that would be a little, funny tram, without a top: Donnybrook—an old, rickety type of tram, with no shelter for the driver or con-ductor. Besides these, there were the queer, exciting trams-that-were-no-trams: the water-cart tram, and the tram that squirted sand. There was the tram-shed at Blackrock: and, then, at the foot of Nelson Pillar, surely the greatest and noblest concourse of trams ever assembled in a single place.

Very occasionally, he would visit Uncle Ben and Con at their office in Middle Abbey Street. The lower part of the windows was protected with a sort of wire, or gauze, on which the title of the firm was written in faded yellow letters. The top part seemed permanently discoloured, to resemble the little saucers of cold tea that stood in rows in the tasting room upstairs. It was queer old office. It would have well become the brothers Cheeryble: Dermot all the time ex-pected to see some such figure emerge from its inner gloom, a condensed, idealised, indescribable atmosphere like the brown of a moth's wing. Everything was brown: the desks, the ledgers, the floor, the walls, the very light that filtered in through the windows: brown, tired, and goodnatured. The smell of the tea upstairs was sharp, clean brown. The smell of the cellars and wine bins was old, rich, sleepy brown. The smell of the beer and porter casks was cool, thick, wet brown. Even Uncle Ben himself, with his lively colours and his ringing voice, seemed mellowed and subdued. Con's voice, that rich, golden sound, was darkened, like brown treacle. The clerks spoke quietly, in faded, Dublin voices. Even old Ned, the messenger, whose voice was a garrulous quack outside, softened down in the office to the sort of muffled gobbling ducks make with their bills in the water. Brownness dyed everything—the clear stain of tea, the musty stain of ledgers and old furniture, the warm stain of beer, the rich stain of old sherry—all nourished, aged, and mellowed in the brown Dublin air that rose from the brown Liffey water, settled over the old streets, and fell asleep.

Uncle Ben did not fall asleep. He talked and laughed quietly, by the way not to disturb the other workers, but really, as did they all, deferring to the old brown atmosphere. Con quite often went to sleep. He sat at his desk, and dreamed of the long wild roads by Glendalough, the thin white ribbon winding over the hills to Sally Gap, and all the other magic places he could reach on his new motor bike. He dreamed of the cool ride home in the evening, with the sweet air rushing upon his eyes and forehead, and the quiet, exultant lapping of the waves upon the rocks below the garden. Then, rousing himself, he would go down into the cellar, and help shift: lifting the smaller barrels in his enormous arms, and handing them up through the trapdoor to Ned and his fellow.

"It's a gran' shtrenth ye have, Mr. Con," Ned would gabble softly: "A gran' shtrenth. Gran' muscles. Damn the lie in that."

Ned was clean-shaven, red-headed, birdlike. His walk was a scuttle, his salute an incredibly rapid raising of his finger to the end of his big birdlike nose. He was married, but had, in his own parlance, "chose a bad wan." They lived apart: Mrs. Ned supported herself by selling fish on the quays. She was there of a morning before Ned, who passed her on his way to work. Every time, by his own account, he would salute her and say politely, "Good mornin' to ye, ma'am." Every time, with grim good humour, she would reply, "To hell with ye." She had a fearsome tongue, as Con could witness. He had been down there one day when she and certain ladies of her trade were busy gutting cod.

An altercation had arisen, and continued till Mrs. Ned, seizing a handful, had cried to her opponent:

"Hould yer whisht, Sarah Dooley, hould yer whisht, or I'll gie ye a powltice o' hot guts in the gob."

"Oh, bedad, sir, she would," Ned corroborated, "She would, Mr. Con, sir, and damn the lie." He spat, and rubbed his hands nervously together. "She would, so. I'm well shut o' that wan. Terrible wicked, Mr. Con, sir, with hand and tongue."

He was a wonderful little man, Ned, full of resource, and a humour so apparently innocent that people seldom gave him credit for it. Many laughed patronisingly at him, whose measure he had long ago taken. Once, years before, when Con hurt his leg—Con's boyhood was spent hurting the various parts of his anatomy in succession—Ned was deputed to wheel him about the streets in a bathchair. All jobs came alike to Ned. Adjuring his passenger to "steer careful, Mr. Con, sir, for the love o' God," he grasped the handle, put his head down, and charged along the pavement. The invalid, well pleased, did his best, and with a series of alarming swerves and lurches they sped along in the direction of the Hill of Howth.

All went well till, at a sharp corner, they ran down an old gentleman of military appearance, in silk hat and morning coat. Con tried to clear him, but he received a glancing blow, and the off wheel ran over his immaculate boot.

"Confound you, fellow," roared the military gentleman. "Where the hell are you going?"

Ned looked up at him, birdlike:

"To the Hill o' Howth, sir," he replied, ducked his head, and scuttled on at the same pace as before.

CHAPTER XXII

"C'M ON, DERMOT," CON WAS SAYING, AS HE LED THE WAY UP to the tasting room. "We'll play a trick on your Granny and Grandpapa. I'll mix up a sample of tea—"

"They won't take it," interrupted Dermot. "They've been had too many times already. I made a jelly of mint and lavender only this summer, and Granny had to go out of the room to spit out her mouthful. And you heard what Eithne did?"

"No. What did she do?"

"She made a blancmange—it looked perfectly all right, as pink as the best of them: only she put pepper, and salt, and washing soda in it. Granny wouldn't try it. Daddy did, though. He knew there was something shady about it, and he pretended to take some to encourage the others. Several people took some, but they all sat waiting for each other to begin, so Daddy had to try a bit: and it was *so* beastly he couldn't pretend. Then Eithne took it into the kitchen. Bessie tried a bit, and rushed into the scullery, and spat it out in the bucket. Eithne cornered Katie, and made her eat a whole plateful. She was so afraid of offending Eithne that she ate it all."

"Serve her right," pronounced Con, with a huge grin. "The dirty, time-serving old screw."

"And Bessie warning her, in a loud whisper, all the time, from the scullery," laughed Dermot. "I should have burst out laughing: but Eithne kept an absolutely straight face. She can."

"She's a grand girl, that sister of yours. A grand girl: and you ought to be six times as proud of her as you are."

197

"Yes."

"'Yes,'" Con mimicked him. "Now listen to me. That girl—"

"So you see, they'll be very suspicious, now."

"Eh?" Con's wits did not always move very rapidly. "Eh? Wha'?"

"They'll be very suspicious. Granny and Grandpapa. We won't be able to play a trick on them."

"Oh, ah." Con brightened at the reminder of his stratagem. "Wait now, till I tell you. I've put up two samples, d'you see. One of them is fit for a king. That's the top one. Do you give it to them, from me. They'll be suspicious, as you say. Your Granny will say, 'Thank you, me dear,' and put it away in the cupboard. Leave it for a bit, and then say, I was asking how did they like it. Go on at that a bit; and then, one day, I'll ask: or *I'll* say, Father wanted to know how they liked the sample. Then, at long last, they'll try it. It's marvellous stuff: they'll enjoy it, and feel ashamed of ever having suspected anything. *Then*"—he beamed with satisfaction—"they'll try Sample Number two."

"What's that like? asked Dermot, beginning to grin.

"The most awful stuff that ever cut the back teeth out of a mule," replied Con, beginning to shake with laughter. "Half of it is a flavouring you'd only put a pinch of into a ten-pound tea chest. They'll make an occasion of it: perhaps even give a sup to the old man: they—"

Contemplation of the scene robbed him of speech. His great laugh rang along the shelves with their rows of saucers.

The trick fell out exactly according to plan. It was ten days before Granny could be induced to brew the first sample. Dermot did nothing to allay her suspicions: it was essential that she should have many doubts to be ashamed of. He was not there when she and his mother warily tried the tea.

"That was wonderful tea Con sent us," admitted the repentant old lady, when Dermot returned for his supper.

"Wonderful tea. I must thank him for sending it. It was a great treat."

"We told you it was very nice," said Dermot, as one unjustly suspected, who sweetly hides the hurt to his feelings.

"Indeed, ye did, me child. Ye did."

Dermot tapped her arm.

"*I* believe you thought we were playing a trick on you, Granny."

A slow smile spread a score of kindly wrinkles on the old lady's face.

"Well now, to tell ye the truth, Dermot, that's just what I did think."

The second sample was brewed with great ceremony.

"Alfred," said Granny, "I want ye to take a cup of this splendid tea Ben is after sending us. We had some the other day: and delicious it was."

The old man looked up at her from his *Irish Times*.

"Heh," he said. "Ye're a great one for making a fuss, Amelia."

"Well, fuss or no fuss, now: I'm going to give ye a cup of it."

"Oh, ye'll do as ye please. I'm sure of that," he replied, going back to his paper.

A few minutes later, the tea was brought in, and poured out. Grandpapa was given the first cup. Putting down his paper, he took it up, in his shaking hand: he stirred it, blew on it, stirred it again: took a generous sip: spat it out: set down the cup: and delivered a long speech, beginning, "I declare to me God."

Abashed and confounded, Granny tasted her cup. A slow expression of horror and disgust congealed on her face.

"Aaaaah!" she cried. "Ye bad child": and then, rolling her eyes towards her husband, she began helplessly to shake with laughter.

"Ye took us in well," she said to Dermot afterwards, with a kind of melancholy admiration, adding, as a matter of form, "Ye bad boy."

But Grandpapa did not forget the episode, and assailed the astonished Uncle Ben, on the next occasion he dropped in, with bitter reproaches upon the quality of his wares.

Soon afterwards, to Dermot's surprise, Grandpapa declared his intention of taking him to the Exhibition. Dublin had burst out into one of those White Cities which were to spring up so gaily in the waste places of many a metropolis, and was losing money with every outward appearance of delight. The Exhibition was situated at Ballsbridge. It was to attract visitors from all over Europe. Unfortunately, Irish exhibits, eked out with water-chutes and switchbacks, while they delighted the Irish public, left the Continent unmoved. The Irish public enjoyed itself enormously, and was most indignant when rumours began to spread that the backers were losing money. Sure, and wasn't the place packed! Will ye look at the queues do be waitin' for a ride on the water-chute! It took years to convince the public that the Exhibition had been a disaster, and many of them still attribute its natural failure to dishonesty.

Dermot, who had somehow got the idea that Grandpapa was very old and needed looking after, stood solicitously aside, and held open the gate.

"Have you got the money, Grandpapa?" he asked, merely as a gentle reminder.

The old man stopped, and looked at him quizzically.

"Heh," he said. "Ye must think I'm the funny old fella."

"Not a bit, Grandpapa," protested Dermot, flushing. "I only wondered if—"

"The funny old fella—to be starting out without the money. Wait now—there's the tram. Run out to the post and signal the man to stop."

Dermot did so, glad to escape for a moment. He stood beside the post, and, as the tram approached, he made a shy, half-hearted gesture with his left hand. He did it merely because he had been told, for he knew that, all the time, Grandpapa would be executing behind him the gesture

which Con called "poking the tram man's eye out": i.e.
standing, with outstretched umbrella, and only lowering it
as the tram ground indulgently to a standstill. All the
drivers knew Grandpapa. They smiled, as the advancing
glass almost hit the end of the umbrella. Grandpapa was
still really suspicious of electric trams. He ignored the
human element in their direction, and believed that, if he
took his attention off them for an instant, they would
devilishly gather speed and rush past him. Grimly watchful,
he stood, holding out his umbrella, shooting out his trimly
clipped moustache in little puffs: then made all haste to
scramble aboard, before the machine could run on again.

"Good mornin', Mr. Conroy, sir," exclaimed the conductor, taking his elbow, and helping him in, with a wink
at Dermot.

"Good mornin' to ye," returned Grandpapa, still preoccupied with the need to find a seat and get safely into it.

A minute later, as the tram rattled down Glasthule, and
Dermot peered anxiously out, in case Paddy were there to
be waved at—Paddy, on such days, sat disconsolate in the
street—Grandpapa took out a shilling from his pocket, and
said, "Two to Ballsbridge, if ye please"—and the expedition
was begun.

It was a grand day they had together. The old man, far
out of touch with boyhood though he was, proved excellent
company: and Dermot, whose quick sympathies responded
at once to the friendly mood of another, was at his best.
He could be very charming, when he was perfectly at ease.
His mixture of deference and enthusiasm was exactly right.
It was not artificial, nor calculated: it came naturally enough
from a personality which lack of confidence put on the defensive, and which, for all its unconscious inward arrogance,
and its clear-cut tastes, was desperately anxious to get
on well with people and grasped at every outstretched hand.
Dermot was quite naturally a different person with different
people. He was not a hypocrite. Deep inside him, he knew

what was what: sometimes he knew that he knew: but a
confident assertion daunted him at once. Other people's
personalities seemed to him so much stronger, so much surer
than his own. He was really afraid of Grandpapa, as of all
grown-ups (except, perhaps, Granny); and he took hold
with both hands on his opportunity. Grandpapa unbent
more and more. He sent Dermot on the switchback railway,
and stood below, amid the crowd, waving to him, and smiling
his grim smile. He took him in to see the Indian conjurers.
The conjurers did impossible, appalling things. They put a
boy in a basket, and stuck swords savagely in and out through
it, from every angle. Then they opened the basket, and the
boy got out, smiling, and salaamed to the people. Grandpapa
laughed contemptuously throughout the performance. He
not only refused to consider how it was done: he hardly admitted that anything had been done at all.

"Black fellas," he repeated, as they came blinking out
of the booth into the brilliant sunshine. "Sure, they'd believe
anything."

They sat down to lunch at a little open-air table, which
they were lucky to secure. Even so, they had to share it
with a large, purple lady who was evidently feeling the
heat. She had a husky voice, and apologised amiably for
disturbing them. Grandpapa made a courtly reply. The
lady commented upon the weather. Grandpapa made another courtly reply. Mopping herself, and breathing loudly,
the lady essayed another opening. Grandpapa stared straight
in front of him. Dermot wriggled, and finally drew his attention.

"I beg your pardon, ma'am": he emerged from his statue-
like attitude, and inclined a courtly ear. The lady repeated
her observation.

"Yes, indeed, ma'am": and he once more became a
statue. The lady eyed him doubtfully, and tried no more
openings. After a suitable interval, Grandpapa began dis-
coursing very amiably to Dermot. He showed a further un-

expected awareness of boyish needs by ordering him a large
glass of lemonade. The companionship of Grandpapa, and
the suggestion of complicity in his snubbing of the purple
lady, warmed Dermot's heart. He had forgotten what fun
it could be to spend a time with Grandpapa. The evenings
of Dickens worship were different. There, Grandpapa was
high priest, and himself an acolyte. But here they sat, two
males, taking their meal together, having repulsed politely,
but unmistakably, a female's effort at intrusion. Still, the
score was not all on their side. It was impossible to be unaware of the lady, and her heavy, hot lunch. Purple face
downcast, she ate with sulky gusto, like a penitent under-
going his pains. She ate aloud. Dermot's cool maleness
began to desert him. He became embarrassed. He looked
almost imploringly at Grandpapa. The old gentleman gave
no sign. He took his food with grave and fastidious care:
and, in the intervals, poured out a grave, even stream of
comment upon progress with a short o.

It was curious, Grandpapa's insistence upon progress:
for he appeared to dislike almost every manifestation of it.
Motor cars, trams, telephones—he anathematised them all.
Evidently he had imbibed some idea of progress in the
abstract, some ascetic enthusiasm, from the days of Ruskin
and Carlyle, and applauded in theory what he disliked in
fact. Grandpapa's own learning was immense, but curiously
impractical. His amazing memory had grown from servant
to master, and a passion for statistics to a notaryship in
Cloud-Cuckoo-Land. A few years back, Dermot's father,
half in joke, had made the old man a birthday present of
the time-table of every railway with a London terminus.
This unusual gift earned him the warmest and most delighted letter of thanks he had ever received. Grandpapa
spent hundreds of hours plotting and executing in his mind
improbable journeys, memorising routes, and tracing precarious connections, until he had acquired a familiar, if
out of date, acquaintance with the entire railway system

of the United Kingdom. Seeing in the paper that His Majesty
the King was about to journey from Windsor to Balmoral,
he would produce his volumes; there would be great licking
of thumbs and turning of thin, rustling pages; and then,
after five minutes, he would look up at the others in the
room.

"His Majesty—if he would be said by me—would do
well to take the 4.15 p.m. from Windsor as far as Slough.
There he would . . ."

No one was so tactless as to point out that the Royal
Train had a private schedule: though Dermot, as soon as
this occurred to him, had pointed it out in a stage whisper
to his mother, and been silenced into understanding.

Listening to Grandpapa, and letting his eyes wander
around the brilliant scene, with its sunlight, its colours, the
dazzling white of the minarets, the happy, moving crowds,
Dermot became aware of a sharp pressure against his leg
under the table. At first he thought it was Grandpapa, calling his attention privily to something. He looked up and
smiled uneasily, but Grandpapa's eyes were not upon him.
Then the pressure grew so intense that it hurt. It began to
vibrate, to jerk uncontrollably. Frightened, Dermot tried
to draw his leg away. It must be the purple lady. She was
trying to make him look, so that she could start talking
again. As he struggled, with bent head, trying to push back
his chair, she gave a sudden coughing sound. Lowering his
eyes obstinately, he received a sharp kick on the shin. Then
he heard Grandpapa's voice.

"Merciful God!"

Dermot's chair fell over backwards with a crash, and he
sprang away in horror. The purple lady was lying stretched
back, rigid, her mouth wide open, her eyes rolled up so
that he could only see the whites. She was making a horrible
snoring noise, and, as he stared wildly, her stiff body was
racked by a series of violent jerks and spasm. Slowly her
chair began to tilt back, and the side of the table to rise.

A glass rolled, and crashed upon the ground. Recovering his presence of mind, Grandpapa seized the table, and pressed on it with both hands. For a moment the purple lady projected, stiff as a board: then she collapsed, and became a heap of twitching dusty finery.

"The poor lady is in a fit," Grandpapa kept repeating, as people rushed up, and knelt round the sufferer. No one took any notice of him: they all shouted confusedly, advocating this or that remedy. They grappled with her garments, to loosen them. They threw water over her. Fresh people came crowding up, with blank, eager faces.

"Wha's happened? Wha's happened?" they exclaimed.

"Make way there! Make way there!"

The deep authoritative voice calmed the crowd at once. They parted, docile and quiet, as a huge R.I.C. sergeant, a handsome, brown fellow with a moustache, shouldered through to the victim, followed by a doctor. The doctor knelt: examined: then looked up, and said something to the sergeant.

"Stretcher! Amb'lance!" the cry went through the crowd, pattering, murmuring away into the distance: and in a surprisingly short time a couple of men in uniform trotted up, laid down a canvas stretcher on the ground, and carried off the purple lady, now limp and moaning, out of the crowds, out of the lives of Grandpapa and Dermot, but not from Dermot's memory, where she remained for ever.

CHAPTER XXIII

THAT YEAR OF THE EXHIBITION AUTUMN CAME DOWN QUICKLY, adding a sharper pang to the sorrow of departure. Flocks of dismayed leaves, torn from the branches while they had another month of life in them, were whirled up the curve in the road before Walmer Villa, took refuge underneath the wall by Sea Bank and St. Helen's, were sought out, and driven helter skelter, up the short hill, past Mona's door, to be scattered and forgotten in the gutters along the desolated tramway on to Dalkey. In a day, the whole aspect of the place was changed. Grey, cloudy skies hurried over Kingstown, as if charged with mournful news for the mountains. These they passed, stooping every now and then in a rain shower or a gloomy pall of mist, and sped over the great central plain of Ireland. Half way across, they met incomers from the West, messengers more urgent, more determined than themselves. The sky over the great plain became congested and thronged with clouds. The westward rush was checked, but its sheer weight held up the charge of the invaders. Like bullocks at a fair, the jostling clouds mounted on each other's backs. Higher and higher the great sulky mass rose in the air. Then the invaders won, the clouds that had gone westward were pushed back, weeping, and the great depression moved slowly East. Softly, with dull persistent fall, tons of rain came greyly down on the bogs, the fields, the cabins, with their dripping thatch. In a night, it turned the farmyards to malodorous quagmires. It flooded the gutters of the little dead-alive towns, and sent down, outside their tap-room windows, thin, quivering palisades of silver. It turned the slack, surly rivers into muddy torrents, thick with eddies, rolling, just underneath their excited surface, rubbish, worms, and branches. Reaching the mountains, it hid them, and prepared them, privately, to be sponges once again: a skill they had forgotten. Reaching Kingstown it poured, in melancholy, foul cascades down the sloping streets, and into the sea. There, slowly, a grey cloud thickened and rolled out from the shore, fifty, a hundred, five hundred yards, opaque and sluggish, curling stupidly under the pock-marked waters. The rain emptied the Sea Wall and made it a desert; no feet slid and slithered over the twice-slippery weed. Passing further over, crossing the Bay, it advanced dully on the Hill of Howth, and sent its stupid curse after the last brood of swallows that sped and dipped, and sped and dipped, in pursuit of the sun.

Many memories of departure were crowded together in Dermot's mind. Sometimes the family went South, by Rosslare. They would travel sadly into Dublin, to Kingsbridge, and rattle away into the gathering dusk, till the trees became dark as crêpe, and presently, over the hazy fields, the enormous harvest moon arose, and stared changelessly in the carriage window. Later, he would look out, and see the roofs of Kilkenny shining in the green moonlight. Other times, they would go by the morning mail from Kingstown. The streets would be clean and empty as they went down, with the heavenly early morning smell to make parting a worse agony. Everyone they met would be smiling and cheerful, going about their business for another day. A milkman, jumping from his float, would sing out some remark in the darling tongue Dermot was to hear no more for ten whole months. Half an hour of confusion, and stiff smiles, and they would be standing out splendidly across the Bay, looking at the houses all shining in the morning sun, at the Island, Dalkey Hill, the Sound—and Delgany itself, standing up clean and pure upon its hill. Deliberately, he would look down for a minute at the hissing, creaming wave that rushed away from the ship's side—just to prove that, by lifting his eyes again, he could still actually feast them upon the loveliest and dearest place in all the world. He would watch, as in duty bound, till his eyes ached, till he could no longer pick out houses, till the spires were dim astern, and Killiney Hill itself a brown knoll on the horizon: till, when at last one looked ahead with a sigh, the cold unwelcoming cliffs of Wales stood up, and Ireland was lost in a smoky cloud on the edge of the sky.

Once, they went all down the coast to Waterford. This was heartrending for a while, though not perhaps as bad as leaving by the mailboat. All got in at Sandycove, and the train puffed maddeningly along to Dalkey, past Dalkey, below the road to Delgany, and then, after a short tunnel, past the very windows of Delgany itself; and rushed off down the coast to Killiney. That far, one could pretend, tantalisingly, horribly, that they were just going for a picnic to Killiney Strand. Indeed, Mr. Gray, with ghastly jocularity, teased them by saying as much: but, as Eithne collapsed at once into tears, and Dermot scowled furiously, he was not encouraged. Granny came as far as Bray with them. Even Dermot felt this to be a mistake, a prolonging of the agony. All along the coast from Killiney to Bray, one could watch Delgany, clear upon its cliff, retreating, growing tinier. One could watch, and turn to see the great tireless waves crashing in upon the Strand. It looked forlorn already, with, here and there, a person walking alone, holding a hat on against the evening breeze. Great, curling waves. In half an hour, when he was miles down the coast, they would still be falling; breaking, creaming, subsiding, hissing: like that wave now. It was hard to realise that all would go on just the same. He had never seen the country except in summer, and could not picture it.

Presently, down the coast, dusk would fall. Eithne and he would have to give up counting donkeys and goats. They

sat together, in the window, doing this, eating their supper—eating the last dear food of Walmer Villa, the last
picnic basket. It was a sad pastime, but it was part of the
ritual. Besides—and here was its real value—though every
clockety-clock of the wheels was taking them further and
further from the dear places, there would come a day when
the train would bear them upward again, when they would
joyfully count goats and donkeys. Swallowing the ache in
his throat, Dermot repeated almost savagely his favourite
text, "Heaviness may endure for a night; but joy cometh
in the morning."

BOOK III

CHAPTER XXIV

THE TREAT OF THE WHOLE HOLIDAY, THE VERY SUMMIT OF happiness, was the week Dermot spent at Delgany. Aunt Patricia's invitation had been grudgingly accepted at first, for both Granny and Dermot's mother were afraid that the un-accustomed diet would upset him, that he would be kept up late, and that efforts to keep pace with Con would over-tax his strength. But Dermot pleaded so hard they let him go: and the precedent, once established, might not be broken. Indeed, as soon as Eithne was nine, she was asked too. It was *the* week of the year, the summit of all joy, and, blessed circumstance, not right at the end of their time, but a good fortnight or so before, so that their farewell, when they had to leave the house, was not final. They knew they would soon be up again, for a day. It was good-bye by easy stages.

He went up to Delgany in the morning. Paddy, subdued at the prospect of a week's loneliness, took the old Gladstone bag. Eileen opened the door, gave him a hug, and in a few minutes was helping him unpack in a high airy room that smelt of the sea. After that, there was time to rush down the steep path, joyously waving a towel, and get a glorious bathe and a sunbathe before lunch. Dermot would have to go round and undress by himself in a queer little cave. A former owner of Delgany, a crippled man, with an in-veterate love of bathing, had caused a wall to be built across the mouth of this cave, enclosing a small bath of water, some twenty feet long, by six or seven across. Into this his attendants lowered him, on a stretcher, so that he could still gasp and tingle in the cold, live element. All

213

shook their heads, and called it suicide: but he lived six years to enjoy his bath, and the doctors could not say it had shortened his life: so he got good value for his money. Nowadays, the bath was not inviting, for no one troubled to clean it. Uncle Ben, who bathed before breakfast the whole year round, might well have used it: but, after one glance, he preferred to walk the half mile to Vico, and bathe there. He was wise, for the walk back warmed him up. The cave would be very damp and depressing on a wet winter day.

But winter was far off. This was high September, that marvellous time when the sun shines all day, rising to find the grasses white with dew; when there is a tang of early frost in the morning air, clearer than the air of full summer; when the sea sparkles with fresh life, and mackerel pull stronger on the hook, and there is a joyous rush to use the boats that must soon be beached and housed. Soon after Uncle Ben returned, singing, from his bathe, there would be a furious sound of razor strops, followed by the mellow uproar of the gong: and Dermot would come down to breakfast. He would find, in the dining-room, most of the party, speaking in hushed voices. Chairs would be set out, in odd, constrained positions. After a few brief civilities, silence would fall, broken at last by a slip-slopping hurricane of sound, as though a young elephant were falling down the stairs; and Con, in slippers, hastily doing up the last button of his waistcoat, would burst in, exclaiming, "Sorry, Mother. Sorry, Dad," and collapse into a chair. Then Uncle Ben, looking over the tops of his spectacles at nothing, would go across to the door and cough a tenor "ahem." At the signal, there would be a clippering of heels on the oilcloth, and in came the maids, self conscious, looking down their noses, to take their place stiffly on two chairs apart, against the wall. Coughing once more, Uncle Ben began to read. He read always one of the lessons for the day. When he had finished, everyone rose stiffly, and kneeled down. Dermot

at first covered his eyes with his hands. Later, finding that as
he knelt against the low window seat, he faced Vico Hill
and the Bay, he took unashamedly to gazing out. This did
not take his mind off the prayers. The whole picture, the
rise and fall of the sea on the gleaming weed, the clean colours
of the houses on the hill, the pale blue plumes of smoke that
rose into the morning air, wooded Killiney, and, beyond, the
great line of the mountains, were all blended with the earnest,
emphatic tones of Uncle Ben's voice, that special voice in
which he read the prayers, which was yet so recognisably
his own. Here, Dermot felt, one *did* pray. The prayers
startled him at first. They were family prayers, read from a
special manual, quite unlike the prayers to which he was
accustomed. To hear God called upon to sanctify the work
and pleasures of each individual, to safeguard business
dealings, watch over jokes and private conversations, and
take a benevolent hand in family disputes, used at first to
shock him. Then, catching the spirit of this amazing household, and realising that in it all they were in deadly earnest,
he began to feel the warmth of their devotion. He was glad
his father was not there, nor his mother. They did not take
their faith like this. Their worship was not so simple, or so
demonstrative. Their voices did not alter when they prayed.
They would have felt uncomfortable, tried, politely, to
laugh it off. Without a word spoken, he knew that. What
was more, he knew that one day he would have to choose
between this way and theirs. It was some time before he
decided. When the day came, he found that he had decided
to follow the way of Delgany: laying up for himself much
trouble in this temporal world, and staging yet another
conflict for a nature that was to fight a good many already.

The moment prayers were over, the family all began to
talk in their normal voices. Con would leap upon Dermot,
make a hideous face at him, and lift him into the air.

"G'd marnin' to ye, old sober gob," he would bawl.

"How aarre yez? Have ye no tongue in yer head, boy? Wha', wha', wha'?"

Each question would be punctuated by a shake, so that Dermot could not answer.

"Con! Sit down to your food, like a Christian."

"All right, Mother, all right. Dermot—d'ye hear—sit down to your food like a Christian."

And breakfast began. Three or four times during the meal Eileen screwed round in her chair, to look out over the gleaming expanse of the bay.

"That's a grand day. What would you like to do, Dermot, son?"

"Aah, Eileen! don't be goin' on about the day. What good is it to poor divils like Dad and myself, has to be goin' in to earn money by the sweat of our two brows?"

"Keep your divils to yourself," said his father equably, hunting for his napkin ring. "Now where, now where in the world—oh, here it is. But ye're right, son. It's too good a day to be going into the city."

"Money!" said Con melodramatically, rolling an eye towards his father, for this was a beloved gambit. "Take heed, Dermot. Be warned in time. It's greed for money has us slavin' away like this. Money is the root of all evil."

Uncle Ben, who had risen from his chair, looked down at him in mild reproof.

"No, son," he corrected. "The *love* of money."

"Oh, sorry, Dad." Unable to control himself, Con burst into a guffaw, with the endearing candour of a sheepdog which knows it has been naughty, but cannot feel repentant. His father took no notice, but went about the room, patting his pockets, and peering on the mantelpiece.

"What is it you want, Ben. Is it your pipe?"

"It is, darling. It is me pipe. Me little pipe. Oh, me pipe, where are ye. Where are—Golly Mass! Here it is, under me nose, all the time."

After breakfast, which was quite a leisurely affair, the

whole house seemed suddenly to go mad. Uncle Ben, looking out of the window, caught sight of his train somewhere
between Bray and Killiney, and broke into wild lamenta-
tions. From his outcry, and the scurry it caused, one would
surmise that he had lost everything he possessed. The
commotion always ended in his running out of the gate,
blowing huge kisses back at Aunt Patricia, and paying no
attention to the recommendations she was screaming after
him. Dermot had never before seen people whose moods
varied from instant to instant. At one moment, in the
hall, Uncle Ben, separated from some important belong-
ing, would be crying his woes to Heaven. Irretrievable disaster, to judge from his tones, would be overhanging the
house. In another moment, on the doorstep, he would be
beaming, encircling, with a vast bear's hug, everyone there
to see him off, and rush off, trumpeting with laughter.
Con, who all this time had been sedulously brushing his
teeth (another eccentricity, in Dermot's eyes. He brushed
his when he first got up)—Con would become infected with
the same madness, and plunge bellowing through the house,
down to the mysterious and utterly delightful cellar where
he kept his motor bike. One of the pioneers of this sport, he
rode in trials for a large manufacturing company, and received from them a new machine each year at a nominal cost.

"Here, Con, Con, Con! Your parcel!"

"It's no good, mother, it's no good. I can't stop. I can't
stop."

"Ah, Con! Here, Eileen. Run out and catch him."

Seizing his beloved machine, Con would charge out
with it, across the narrow space between the lawns, through
a small gate, and into the path which led to the shore. Up
this, with his exceptional strength, he was able to push
the bicycle: but, once started, he could not stop until,
panting and crimson, he reached the level of the road.

"Get away, girl, get away, girl, get away. Thank ye.
D'ye know what ye are? C'm here till I tell ye. Ye're a pet."

An overalled arm would encircle her, and she would receive an enormous kiss.

"Aah, Con, let go. You're making me all dusty."

"I tell ye wha'," bellowed her brother, over the roar of the engine. "That fella Cecil" (or Patrick, or Denis, or Freddie, or Joe)—"he doesn't deserve ye. No. He's not good enough."

"Aah, Con. Will you shut up."

And, her eyes sparkling, Eileen returned to the house.

For Dermot, the day stretched ahead, with all its enchantment. Anne and Eileen had their various tasks to do for a while, but they would be sure to join him at half past eleven for a bathe, or to troll for mackerel up and down the Sound. Till then, he was left to himself. He could go down on the shore, and fish—more for form's sake than for any practical result, for the place was a mass of weeds. He could potter about the pools, or play upon the lawn, listening with one ear to Anne practising in the drawing-room. He could pop discreetly into the greenhouse, where Eileen was tending her vines: the hot, mossy greenhouse, so queer after the sparkle and sunshine outside: quite a different world. Anne's playing, softened by distance, wove itself deeply into the spell of those mornings. He could never afterwards hear Sinding's "Rustle of Spring" without a rush of memories and sights and sounds; the sigh of the waves, the brightness and bustle of the sunny morning, the bees in the bushes, and, abrupt and sudden, the rushing of a train out of the tunnel, filling the bay with its noise and its general air of flustered unpunctuality. The light notes of the music, cheerful and shallow, leaped out of the window like a school of little fishes: Anne put into her piece the gaiety and vigour of the morning. Then, more assertive, more majestic, the strong left hand went crashing down into the bass, in full and sufficient assertion of the animal spirits proper to such sunlight and such a shining sea.

In the afternoon there would be a row in the boat, or a

picnic on the Hill. Any odd few minutes, any cold or wet time, Dermot would put in on the billiard table. Under the tuition of Con and Uncle Ben, he was practising assiduously. The trouble about Con and Uncle Ben as coaches was that, being possessed of an excellent eye and much natural games ability, they played for the individual shot rather than for the leave, and so encouraged Dermot into a virtuosity to which he was by nature only too prone. When Brian came in—he lived in rooms in Dublin, for his work—he was very scornful of their teaching. Dermot was resentful at first; but, seeing Brian defeat them easily, without ever appearing to make a difficult shot, he had to admit privately that there was something in it. Con could never stand being beaten.

"Look at the leaves the fella gets," he would mutter angrily.

He could not be brought to see that these were provided by Brian's skill. Con would never admit the possibility of a skill beyond his own understanding: though, as he did some things very well indeed, this was not so grave a limitation as it sounds. Con had a magnificent voice, and would not believe that it could be the better for training. He was amazingly strong, and professed to laugh at all systems of exercise. He had robust health, and could hardly help looking upon the care that others took as fear and faddiness. Finding that by nature he could excel the majority of his fellow men, he despised the means by which they sought to better themselves. "Brains" was the only attribute he respected. "One of those clever fellas," he would say, and an expression of reverence would come over his face: for "brains" Con lacked. He read his motor-cycling journal, but little else: and, typically, since this was the only mount he could afford, he believed quite sincerely that a cycle was in all respects superior to a car. Dermot would go down to the cellar, as soon as the snorting of the machine advertised Con's return in the evening, and stare at the great engine, there fitly housed, amid walls whose whitewash was covered six feet above the ground with cuttings and photographs of similar wonderful engines and their godlike drivers. Dermot had no natural aptitude for machines. He valued them because Con did, and for the pleasures they gave, their roar, their speed, the marvellous rides they took one, flying away in no time over the hot road he would need hours to walk, rushing up the little roads into the mountains, escaping by Sally Gap or Glen Macnass to the airy top of the world. They would go up there when Con came back early from the city. Later on, when Dermot was older, he would go in to Dublin on the tram, and call for Con at Middle Abbey Street, to save time. In half an hour, they would be whizzing up a steep hill, and presently they would look down on a little clear toy city, with miniature spires shooting up alert out of the haze of grey and blue, and tiny piers jutting out on the pale, looking-glass sea: upon the Hill of Howth, squat, sulky, mutinous, blue: away past Dublin into infinite flat distance, rich, sweetly wooded country which speedily became like smoke, fading out at the horizon's rim. Then they would turn to the near shoulders of the mountains, and greet the breeze that blew across the great smooth billows of peat and heather. Those swift escapes from the city to the mountains, the rush of air upon one's face, the roar behind and beneath one, the dogs that scampered soundlessly out to attack, tore along level for a second, and fell behind: what joy they held! Sometimes Dermot rode in the sidecar, but usually on a cushion strapped to the carrier. This he much preferred—holding on to Con's broad back, his feet on the shivering rests, feeling every motion, as the machine leaned over, swooped, or powerfully charged a hill: craning round to get the fierce rush of the wind, or stretching back as far as he dared, to hear the clamorous echoes behind them, as they sped down the Rocky Valley on their too-swift journey home in the sunset.

Once, on a wild, far-flung evening before rain, as they stood by the side of the mountain road, Con filling his huge chest with breaths of the living air, a tall figure approached them carrying a gun over his shoulder. Looking at him, they saw a handsome man, evidently a game keeper, walking easily, sure of himself upon the mountain.

"A grand evening," he called, when still some yards away.

"It is that," answered Con.

"It won't last," said the stranger. "Still, we must thank God for what we can get." He laughed, and eyed Con with his head on one side.

"I'm not complaining," said Con, shortly.

"Faith, no more am I. No more am I." He looked away to the North, shading his eyes. "But, if ye have to be outdoors all the day, ye prefer the fine to the wet; though, faith, ye're used to both."

"Now, that's where I envy you. I'd give me eyes to be outdoors all day."

"Aye." He looked at Con, appreciatively. "Dublin, is it? Well. There's many would be glad of a dry desk to sit at, in the bad weather. Sure, we all want the opposite of what we have. Isn't that so?"

He grinned at Dermot, showing all his teeth.

Dermot frowned. He was unprepared for the question, and afraid of displeasing Con if he answered it wrongly.

"I suppose so," he said at last.

"Oh, indeed we do. Well"—he turned to Con—"you can have my job: and I'll have yours."

"Faith," said Con, "I wish the world was as easy arranged as that."

"Ye'd have a right—if ye had nine childer waitin' on ye when ye got home."

"Nine, eh?"

"Nine. And I wouldn't wish one of them off my hands. No, sir. Not one. Only it's hard to stretch your pocket, sometimes." He looked again to the North. "There now; if ye look, ye'll see something worth looking at."

They turned where he pointed, and there, on the farthest horizon, under a long slit of saffron sky, appeared a line of tiny mountains, of pure innocent blue, so frail, so delicate, they might have been painted by some miniaturist upon china.

"Them," said the gamekeeper, "is the Mountains of Mourne, one hundred and ten miles from where ye stand. And, by the same token, I'll be goin' on home, for when ye see them the rain is not far off."

Con turned abruptly, and fished something out of a flap pocket on his machine.

"Here," he said. "Wish us luck, before you go."

He handed over a small flat bottle, a whisky sample. The stranger's face lit up like a candle.

"Faith, and I will," he said. Uncorking the bottle, he took a mouthful, and then climbed down a few feet to where a spring chuckled out from the hillside.

"Don't spill it," called Con.

"Oh, damn the fear." The man's manner had changed entirely. His air of foxy sententiousness had left him. 'Why didn't ye say that at first?' his expression seemed to say.

"Well"; he reached the spring, carefully filled the bottle, and held it up to them. "May it be to your good health and your good luck."

He drank, and wiped his mouth on his tweed coatsleeve. In a few seconds, he was beside them again. As he handed back the bottle, he looked at it, and his eyes gleamed.

"Now blast the bellas of the divil that blew out that bit o' glass," he said. "That he didn't get a better breath, and blow it bigger. Wha'?"

He shook them both by the hand.

"Well, be good to yourselves."

A kick, a roar, and they were off, turning perilously, on the rough road, to answer his wave of farewell.

"That was a queer chap," shouted Con presently. "Did ye notice how we had to give him the drink to find out what sort he was? There's too many of them like that. Handing you out stuff, and watching you out of the corner of their eye to see how are you taking it. I hate that."

"Then—why did you give him the whisky?"

"Ah, what good is it, to stand talking rubbish to one another, instead of sense."

The machine, swooping down a narrow glen, put up a flight of rooks with its noise.

"That chap, d'ye see," resumed Con presently, over his shoulder, "has two faces. One for the priests and gentry, one for his friends. Didn't you like him better at the end than the beginning?"

"Yes."

"Well, then."

Twenty minutes later, they ran into the rain.

CHAPTER XXV

BEST OF ALL DAYS AT DELGANY WAS SATURDAY. FIRST OF ALL, Con got out early from town, and was always ready to do something delightful: a long ride into Wicklow, a row in the boat, a picnic; and, after that, when one had had dinner, there was the band in the evening. The band played in Sorrento Park, across the road. One could either listen from the house, or cross over, walk about among the lamps and people, or climb up to a nook in the rocks at the top, and look out over the great moonlit bay, with the dark shapes of the mountains, and the twinkling lights of Bray upon the waterline, four miles across, on the other side.

Eileen met her gallants at the band. They treated Dermot goodnaturedly, and he, dumb with a queer kind of jealousy, kept at her side. He did not properly understand the situation, and it never occurred to him, as it would to many boys, to make an excuse and run away. All he knew was that he loved being with Eileen, that she had come over with him to the band—Anne preferred to listen from the house— and that now this man was here, spoiling his evening, and would not go away. He kept by Eileen not from obstinacy, but because he felt bewildered, and that was his place, anyway. Maybe she enjoyed the chance to tease Hughie or Cecil or Denis or Patrick or John. They, for their part, took the matter with great goodhumour.

"See here—What's his name?—Dermot—See here, Dermot, will you be a true man, and go away for a few minutes?"

The boy looked at him rebelliously, unhappily.

"Why should I?"

"Sure, I want to whisper sweet nothings to Eileen here."
Dermot pressed against Eileen's arm. She gave no sign.

"I dare say you do," he said heavily.

The suitor sighed goodhumouredly.

"Ah," he said, "you're no true man."

On other occasions, when Con was present, visits to the band were different. Con became impatient of the music after forty minutes or so, and Dermot, though normally he hated to miss a note, was so readily infected by the other's mood that he got up without a word, and joined in a hunt for that salt of life which Con vaguely and variously termed "divarsion." Divarsion, at the band, consisted in hunting about among the rocks, and inconveniencing lovers: getting behind respectable citizens, and making remarks about the music in vulgar Dublin voices: throwing missiles from the shelter of the rocks at prominent and pompous individuals below on the promenade: and, richest joke of all, surreptitiously introducing foreign substances into the interstices of wind instruments, during the intervals between the music. To do this, under the full glare of the bandstand lights, without being detected by public or musicians, required great skill. Needless to say, it was always Con who essayed it. He was a fine actor. He would saunter round the very edge of the bandstand, feigning intense interest in all to do with it, or wearing an air of bland and slightly sorrowful abstraction, which served as cover if he roused suspicion. This air he even succeeded in maintaining when an indignant musician caught him in the act of inserting a nail into his bassoon. Nothing was said on either side, Con bestowing on his bristling victim a gaze of innocent and sad affection, as he wandered out of range.

Con's finest coup at this particular spot was brought off, not at the band, but in the theatre. Sitting in the front row of the parterre, he saw presented to him the top of a double-bass, leaning against the rail which enclosed the orchestra. Under cover of darkness, and with many a suppressed guffaw, he managed to turn the keys, and twist all the strings hopelessly out of tune. His convulsions during the remainder of the act were a source of some annoyance to the people near him: but they were nothing to the happy bellow he let when the trick reached its denouement. The orchestra filed in for the interval: the conductor raised his baton: and then as the first chord crashed down, there broke from the maltreated instrument a sort of unearthly belch, making the conductor jump as if there were a pin in his trousers, and glare furiously at the bewildered player. Con bawled so loud that Dermot's own joy was swamped in self-consciousness. But Con was always uproarious in the theatre. He took Dermot to see "When Knights Were Bold," and laughed so loud that even Jimmy Welch began to laugh too. The only comfort was (for Dermot) that Con's was such a vast, generous laugh, it made everyone else want to join. Even if they thought the stimulus insufficient they had not the heart to spoil such enormous and innocent enjoyment. Dermot's father, Con's complete antithesis, to whom all these practices were "childish nonsense the great fellow should have grown out of long ago," could seldom resist him, but must begin unwillingly to laugh too.

Another happy-hunting-ground for diversion was the Pavilion, at Kingstown, where travelling pierrot troupes spent a week at a time. Dermot often visited this place on his own account, but not entirely for pleasure. Mr. Gray's attack of appendicitis had made real to the boy a fear which had haunted him since childhood. Mr. Gray's own father had died young, leaving a widow and a boy of twelve completely penniless. The boy of twelve had perforce entered as office boy the first firm that would accept him. He had risen swiftly, after a hard struggle which had taken from him some of his capacity for youth, which had in fact caused that punctiliousness and tendency to worry, so ridiculous to the folk at Delgany. Dermot did not know about this. What he did know—now—was that the same fate might be in store

for him. At any moment, so he feared, he might be called
upon to support his mother, and Eithne. Accordingly he set
himself to develop and make ready his one commercial
talent—mimicry. Then, if the disaster came, he could earn
a living as a comedian. Every gag and joke, all he could remember of every song, went down in a fat black exercise
book, and was learned by heart. Sometimes two visits to
the same show would be necessary, in order to get hold of
something peculiarly attractive. Dermot sat through the
vocalists and the pianists and the violinists and the con-
certed numbers, for the sake of those minutes when the
comedian held the stage. Every company carried a comedian:
some carried a "light comedian" as well. Light comedians
were seldom profitable. They were but foils to their middle or
heavy-weight colleagues, and their solo numbers usually
amounted only to a song and a step dance. So, year by year,
Dermot with endless care and labour amassed a fund of
middle class facetiæ and vulgarities which stood him in fine
stead at school, but were fortunately never called upon for
the purpose with which they had been compiled.

When Con came, however, he could allow himself a holiday.
Con soon tired of the entertainment. He would laugh, suddenly and loudly, once or twice, at the comedian, comment
unfavourably on the soubrette, dislike the soprano, and
declare, of the baritone, that sure, he could do as well as
that himself. At the interval, therefore, they would leave
their seats, and walk on the Pavilion's outer decks, drawing
in the fresh sea air and looking with satisfaction over the
lights of the harbour. Then the sound of a drunken brawl
between two navvies, breaking out round a corner of that
respectable and select enclosure, would bring a couple of
scandalised officials at the run: but they would only find a
boy and a grave, good-looking young gentleman leaning over
the balcony and looking out to sea.

"Wasn't it here we haird them?"

"Faith, I'd have swore to it."

Pause; suspicious glances directed at the two unconcerned backs: and a slow withdrawal of official feet.

More dangerous was the discharge of small bombs which, in those early days, were sold for motor cyclists to throw at the dogs that rushed out to molest them. Each exploded with a loud report on hitting the ground, and was further equipped with a nucleus of small pebbles, to act as shrapnel. When thrown underneath or near an oncoming dog, they routed him, without inflicting any harm. Dropped from a height, into the crowds of the dispersing audience, they produced "divarsion" of the liveliest kind. Too lively, indeed. One night Con flung down a handful of them from the topmost deck of all, and caused a small panic. Eileen, who was still inside the building, heard the bang. The two offenders bolted downstairs as hard as they could go, almost running into an attendant who was charging up.

"What was that bang?" cried Con instantly, as if he were blaming the man for it. The attendant stopped and looked at him.

"Some bloody young blagyards up above," he muttered, and ran on.

"Begob," said Con presently, when they were safely mingled with the crowd, "we were only just in time. We'd better go easy a bit."

And, though neither referred to the fact, bombs were not used again.

One night, when Dermot was staying at Delgany, Eileen refused to join them, and the two went to the Pavilion by themselves. When they came back, Con led Dermot into Eileen's bedroom, flashing an electric torch on her as she lay in bed.

"Here," he cried, "here's Dermot come in to kiss you good-night."

"I haven't," protested Dermot, horrified.

"Ah, get away, the two of you," cried the girl irritably, screwing up her eyes against the light.

"Snubbed, me lad," observed Con, shutting the door after them: and Dermot hurried off to his room, hurried into bed, and hid his face in the pillow. To say it all openly, laughing, out loud like that—oh, oh, oh! Probably, had he asked himself the question, he would have said that he loved Eileen. He might even have said that, when he grew up, he would marry her; but he would have meant it as a child means such declarations. For years he had adored and worshipped Eileen. When they first met, on his first rapturous visit of the summer to Delgany, she would kiss him. The same happened when they said good-bye. And so, because he would so terribly have liked to kiss her more often, and because he did not discover the fact till Con so ruthlessly showed *he* knew it already, Dermot was much troubled. He brooded, waited his chance, grew self-conscious, and shy of Eileen: symptoms noted with affectionate amusement by the girl herself.

On the last night of that same visit, he did not say good-night as usual to her on the landing, but made some pretext to follow her into her room. She lit the candle, and stood at her dressing table with her back to him. When she turned round, he saw in the dim light that she was smiling.

"Well, son," she said, in tones of friendly mockery. "What are you doing here? You want a kiss—is that it?"

He looked at her sorrowfully, almost indignantly, for he had followed her with no set thought in his mind, but by instinct, because it was his last night; to be with her, near her, a minute longer.

"No," he said, "I didn't come for that."

She crossed over to him, and laid a hand on each shoulder.

"Ah, never mind, Dermot," she said. "You're a decent sort. Good night," and with affectionate firmness she pushed him out of the door.

He wandered into Con's room, and stood fidgeting about for a while, uncertain what to make of this, but sure she was not really angry. Why, then—? He crossed to the mantelpiece, and frowned thoughtfully at the range of exhibits upon it. Con kept a great and fascinating variety of objects on his mantelpiece: innumerable picture postcards, most of them representing little girls with enormous eyes: dance programmes, invitations, Boileau and Gibson girls: grotesque china bulldogs: a series of photographs, taken at school, showing the various stages of a fight: calendars, and two or three booby prizes, with personal and appropriate labels. Dermot knew them all by heart, but inspected each with elaborate care, as if he were seeing it for the first time.

"What ails ye?" asked Con, flinging back his braces, his shadow enormous on the ceiling.

"Nothing. I don't know. That is—"

"Are ye feeling mousey?"

Mousey was Con's portmanteau word of condemnation. Compounded of lousy and mildewed, it was employed by him to describe both physical and spiritual conditions, with equal freedom.

"No," replied Dermot, "I'm not feeling mousey."

"Well then, don't go gawkin' about with a mousey mug on ye."

Dermot smiled. He could sometimes look as old as Con.

"I'll go to bed, I think," he said.

Next morning, he met Eileen on the steps outside the front door, where they all gathered to exclaim over the morning. She slid her arm through his, and kissed him affectionately on the lips.

"Morning, son," she said.

So it was all right. Hooray. She wasn't angry with him. Darling Eileen. Tears came into his eyes, he loved her so.

After that, Dermot frankly kissed her whenever he could, disregarding such observations as Con saw fit to make.

CHAPTER XXVI

CERTAIN PLACES, CERTAIN HOUSES, SEEM LUCKY FOR US. Nothing unpleasant happens to us while we are in their shelter: we cannot be unhappy, we cannot even be unwell. We thrive in them, like plants in favourable soil. For Dermot and Eithne, Delgany was one of these lucky places. It provided them with romance, excitement, and surprise. Thus it was only fitting that at Delgany Dermot met the man he always considered the most remarkable figure he had ever known. He met him, perhaps, in all his life, three times; but the figure, in appearance and manifestation more impressive even than the legend which surrounded him, remained perfect in his mind. Most marvellous of all, this strange, dazzling man was related to him: his cousin.

It was in that capacity that Dermot was introduced to him, one night when he and Con returned just in time for dinner from a ride in the mountains. Eileen came out into the hall, a sparkle of excitement in her eyes, and shut the drawing-room door behind her. She said something to Con which Dermot could not catch, and then, to Dermot,

"Come and meet your cousin."

"My cousin?"

"Yes, my lad. Your cousin. And don't you forget it."

Dermot looked from one to the other in such bewilderment that both burst out laughing.

"Run up and wash yourself, quick. Then you'll just have time to meet him before we go in to dinner. It's the O'Dowda," she added, with a touch of excitement she could not suppress. "You've surely heard about him, haven't you?"

231

"Oh yes. I've heard about him."

"Go on, then. Quick."

Dermot climbed the stairs soberly. He had indeed heard of this legendary figure, who, after a brilliant career in the diplomatic service, suddenly threw up his post, left, almost contemptuously, his beautiful wife (who was glad to be rid of him), and became a globe-trotter, a cosmopolitan; more at home, like so many of his ancestors, in the salons of Paris and Vienna than in the wild lands of which they had been dispossessed. Dermot, never having seen him, had not bothered his head much with a person so far outside the known world. He remembered his mother's story of how the O'Dowda had taken her to her first ball, but even that had not served to make him a real figure. Nor was Dermot alone there, for the list of his cousin's attributes seemed to belong rather to a romantic opera than to life. Hereditary chieftain of Connaught, diplomat, amateur of the arts, he went his way, surrounded by a popularity and adoration he did not value, never putting himself out a fraction of an inch, yet entirely subjugating all he met. Dermot's mother and Granny, though they often agreed he had treated poor Felicia "very badly, my dear," were thrown into an instant flutter of delight if they heard he was in Ireland: and when he called (as he invariably did) they hardly knew what to do, for hours afterwards. Even Mr. Gray, who, when he first heard the legend, pronounced that the man could be "little better than a cad," capitulated altogether after ten minutes' conversation, and "had to admit" that there was "something remarkably charming about him." The fact was, the O'Dowda possessed, to his own life-long comfort, the gift of instantly and carelessly flattering every person whom he met. It cost him no trouble to be charming. He enjoyed it, without being greatly concerned to secure the invariable effect. When he came to Kingstown, he visited without fail every relative and every friend, bringing palpitations to the dullest of old ladies, quickening the blood of the most lethargic of old gentlemen. He knew, without thinking, precisely what to say to each of them. He made every woman feel a queen, every man a fellow of high consequence. And he did not care a damn for anyone. Small wonder that all this, added to his magnificent appearance, won him slaves wherever he went. Indeed, the only undignified or commonplace thing about him was the diminutive to which his relatives possessively shortened his Christian name. They called him Corny.

Creeping downstairs, hands washed, hair brushed, Dermot hesitated at the drawing-room door, wondering what he would see; what new thing would have happened to him, once he opened it. He heard a burst of delighted feminine laughter, blown like streamers round the deep laugh of a man. Biting his lower lip, he grasped the handle and pushed open the door.

The light of the big room dazzled him for a moment, but he saw the tall figure that turned, in the midst of the laughter, to see who had come in. The figure did not come forward, or stop laughing: yet, somehow, Dermot was instantly included in the laugh, invited, though late, to join it. He stood, staring at the most handsome man he had ever seen.

Cornelius Conlon O'Dowda, in the late summer of 1910, was past his prime, but still magnificent. Standing six feet two, yet so proportioned that he did not seem unusually tall, he gazed upon lesser beings like an eagle. His thick hair was turning iron grey. His black eyes flashed, like an eagle's, under wide dark brows. His lean, shaven face was brown with the tan of travel and endurance. His teeth were strong and white. His whole head, with its bold beak of a nose, its lofty carriage, and the way it moved quickly on the muscular lean neck, was like an eagle's. The mouth was hard, the expression, in repose, cold and disinterested. It was one of the paradoxes of the face that, scrutinised item by item, it was not handsome: yet, in life and motion,

the O'Dowda was one of the handsomest men imaginable.
Now, as Dermot was introduced to him, his face eased into
a wonderful smile. Lazily, he moved one step forward, taking
Dermot's in his own long, sinewy hand.

"So this is Cousin Dermot," he said, admitting Dermot
instantly, as if by right of birth, to full intimacy. That was
the secret of his charm. He appeared to treat all those whom
he met as if they belonged to the same world as himself:
and since that world seemed to them remote and wonderful, far above their own, they were flattered beyond
expression. Con and Uncle Ben were both fine looking men,
but beside him they seemed ordinary, and unfinished. He
caught more than his share of the room's light. He was
more arresting, more vivid: yet there was no tension in his
manner, and he moved languidly, with muscles at ease.

At dinner he held them with the force and colour of his
talk. He told them of adventures in strange cities, of dawns
on cold, wild frontiers, the buzz and riot of bazaars, the
slow intoxicated whisper of tropic seas, the steep narrow
streets of Italian towns, the glaring, windy roads of Spain.
He spoke of Jew dealers outwitted in Morocco, of murderers
pursued by motor-boat across the Lake of Zürich: of the
earthquake in Oakland and San Francisco; of bull-fights in
Mexico, and contests of guitar players in Vienna: of Parnell,
Foli, Lina Cavalieri, Wilde—here Uncle Ben began to look
anxiously down at the table—and of Buck-Shot Foster.
There was a lull, after the mention of the last worthy,
and Dermot, who in each lull had been longing to attract
that wonderful attention, suddenly seized hold of his courage.

"I know a story about Buck-Shot Foster," he heard
himself say.

For a terrible instant it seemed as if his remark was to
pass unheard. Then he saw that the black eyes were looking
down into his own.

"You do, do you. Come on, then. Let's hear it."

Everyone looked at Dermot. The blood rushed up to his

cheeks, and the faces swam like pink ballons around him. Keeping his eyes fixed desperately on those dark, amused eyes, he opened his mouth, fumbled, and found speech.

"My other uncle was passing a public house, when a great big huge man l-lurched out and caught him by the shoulder. He said to my uncle, 'Where's Buck-Shot Foster?'"

The veracity of the four words, their thick wheezing utterance, startled the company. But the black eyes looking into Dermot's showed no gleam of surprise. That was the way a man would tell the story he had set out to tell: the right way.

"The big man looked very threatening, so my uncle said 'Why, I saw him go into Mooney's below, only a minute back.''Thank ye,' said the big man, and let my uncle go. When he'd gone a step or two towards Mooney's, my uncle called after him, 'What do you want him for?' The big man turned round and said 'Ta puck the bowels out of 'm.'"

There was a laugh, but Dermot cared for nothing except the eyes into which he was gazing. They twinkled just so much quiet approval as one man might give another without patronage.

"Bravo," said the O'Dowda; and the talk broke out again. Dermot sat, feeling the rush of blood ebb away and leave him very, very cold, but very happy. He had ventured, and succeeded. His instinct was far too sound to let him try again.

After dinner, when they went into the drawing-room, the full moon had risen in the south-east, and made a wonderful wide path across the waters. When they had admired it, all turned to the O'Dowda, and begged him to sing. He, in turn, begged Con to sing. In the end, both sang. Con's choice was Lambert's setting of "She is far from the land." He sang it with great feeling, and his voice was naturally richer, warmer in tone than the O'Dowda's: but it sounded gusty and ill-regulated beside the perfect schooling of the other.

The O'Dowda, accompanying himself on his guitar, sang first Moore's "When he who adores thee." No more pointed contrast to Con's performance could be imagined. Con sang of the bereaved girl with a contemporary, almost impersonal sorrow, as would any young fellow whose heart was in the right place. The O'Dowda's song, though the singer bewailed his own sad fate, was every note addressed personally and intimately to the woman. To point the difference still further, he sang a passionate Spanish love-song. Settling down, seated beside the open window, with the moon at his elbow, he sang a score of songs, of every kind, of every nationality. Just when they had decided that he could sing nothing better than a Bohemian lullaby, his guitar crashed out the stirring chords of an old Swiss peasant song of revolt; his voice went black and taut; it sank to a whisper, the voice of desperate, controlled determination. "Wir zogen in das Veld . . . Wir zogen in das Veld." Next, he was a Hungarian ne'er-do-weel who had lost his possessions and his sweetheart. Lines of bitterness and indolence seamed the handsome face; the voice drawled, spat, flashed out for one terrifying second into rage, and sank back on a sneer. The next minute, with a leap too wide to be accidental, he was broad country Irish, singing "Kitty me love, will ye marry me?" to the painted wooden pig.

Dermot saw him once more that year, at Walmer Villa: a less satisfactory experience, because it puzzled him, and put him in the wrong with himself. He came in from Paddy and the Sea Wall and went straight down the garden, to the swing. For some reason, he took the right hand side, brushing by the tall leaning asparagus, and passing directly in front of the summer house window. As he went by, he heard with amazement the deep, caressing laugh of the O'Dowda. There was an answering laugh, and then his mother's voice.

"Ah, Conlon," it said lightly, "we're past all that nonsense."

There was a rumble of amused protest, and then Dermot's mother appeared in the door. She did not start when she saw Dermot. She brushed back a tendril of hair with the back of her hand, and went on smiling serenely. He thought he had never seen her look so beautiful. The tall form appeared behind her, sardonic for a second in the shadow, then smiling in full sunlight. He too showed no surprise. The black eyes twinkled indulgently into Dermot's, inviting his tolerant, man-of-the-world complicity in—what?

"Well, little son," said his mother, smiling at him.

"Well, cousin," said the O'Dowda.

Dermot still stared. Then he found a smile, and ran away to the end of the garden. They looked after him, and he heard their voices, talking of him with affectionate amusement. But what . . . ?

For weeks afterwards, he dreamed of passing the summerhouse, hearing the voices, with all their original shock of something unprecedented. Neither he nor his mother ever spoke of the meeting again.

Dermot's attitude towards his parents grew more and more mechanical, less clearly defined. He learned this whenever he saw them at Delgany. Even Eithne, who was now nine, felt the same, and disliked the one day of their visit when the parents came up to dinner or to spend the afternoon. Free for a week at least from the world in which they were brought up, under a roof where another set of values held, they did not want the two confused. They wanted it all the less, since the atmosphere of Delgany brought out in both the parents all that was most discordant from it. Mr. Gray's punctiliousness it exacerbated into priggishness, his love of order into fuss: while the Delgany crowd were impelled to exaggerate their own opposite characteristics, and so call forth the excess of both. This drove Margaret to her husband's side, against Delgany. She lost her easy, light airs, and was further embarrassed by realising that they noted this, and remarked among themselves how her marriage—"though, mind ye, he's very decent fella, is Cousin Ernest"—had tarred her with his brush. Dermot saw that this was the one bad turn his father had done his mother. She had acquired her self-possession as a defence against the circumstances of her home, for both her parents were given to worry. Her husband, weakening this, had broken down her strongest defence. Now, when she was tired, on journeys, or when driven by him to act against her judgment, she became anxious and irritable, she lost poise. At Walmer Villa, Margaret was quintessentially herself, for there it was she had painfully forged her silvery armour. Seeing her unperturbed, her parents were soothed and calmed. Ernest was her weakness. Attack her there, and she was like a woman who has lost her coolness on a hot day.

Dermot knew this; but life, to rub the lesson in, gave him fresh evidence. In an unfortunate moment, before the holiday began, he repeated to his father an old "howler," saying that it had occurred in class at his little Plymouth school. He said this not to deceive, but to make the joke more interesting. Mr. Gray had been delighted: the joke was anti-clerical, and years of choir-singing had given him a satiric turn of mind. He therefore recited it far and wide. What was his mortification to be told, by perhaps the thirteenth recipient, that the story was a chestnut.

"Heard it when I was at school, man," said the business friend.

Mr. Gray stiffened.

"Indeed," he said. "I beg your pardon, I am sure. I repeated it in all good faith. It was—er—it was told me by my son, who assured me that it actually took place in his hearing."

"Pulled your leg, he did," diagnosed the friend, with a grin.

Mr. Gray did not smile. He sat very erect, with heightened colour, looking straight in front of him.

"Pulled it proper," added the friend.

This was a few days before he joined his family in Ireland. When he arrived, Dermot and Eithne were at Delgany. Mr. Gray had a serious talk with Margaret, and, when they came up to dine, Dermot saw at once by their faces that something was wrong. The greetings took place in public, so there was no chance for more than a display of stern rectitude by his father—it was quite marvellous how much he managed to convey in the customary kiss—and a sad, reserved embrace from his mother. Uncle Ben took his father off for a talk, so *that* was all right. As soon as he could, Dermot made for his mother alone. Sick at heart, in the chill of unexplained foreboding, he ran up to her, bursting with demonstrative enthusiasm.

It was no good: he knew it wouldn't be. She took him away to one side. For a long time he could make nothing of her string of low-toned reproaches.

"Deceiving your Father . . . wicked, wanton lies . . . humiliating him before all his friends . . . deeply pained . . . so hurt. To think a son of mine could wilfully lie. . . ."

"But, Mummy," he cried, bewildered. "What is it all about? What have I done?"

She stopped on the narrow lawn, and looked at him.

"Do you mean to say you don't know? Do you mean to say you don't remember telling your Father that wicked story? Saying it happened at the Hoe? In class, with Mr. Melsom?"

Recollection woke, sudden, dim, with vague nausea.

"Oh—*that!*"

"Yes. *That.*" She was very angry: nervous, resentful anger, burning up inside her. "I see you think nothing of it. I see you hardly remember it at all. Am I to suppose you so frequently deceive us that you can barely remember one falsehood from another?"

Poor Margaret! Remembering the conversation a few years later, he saw she was a gramophone, reeling off the righteous records of Ernest. At the moment, he was too stunned, confused by the sense of sudden injustice. To do wrong, suffer the tortures of conscience, and then be blamed: that he could understand. But to find that a thing to which one had barely given a second thought was, in these people's eyes, just as bad—why, that meant that at any moment enemies could leap at him out of the past. That meant you could hardly be sure when you were doing right, or—

"What possessed you to do it? What could you gain by deceiving your Father?"

Exactly, cried Dermot's heart bitterly: what could I gain? I gained nothing: therefore I did no wrong.

The others came up at this point, so that the reproaches could go no further. Watching keenly, and noting in particular Ernest's air of pained reserve, the Delgany contingent saw that the two were displeased with Dermot over something, and sided instantly with Dermot. They sang his praises heartily, but to no visible effect.

The dinner was not a success. All sounded forced. In Dermot, misery, choking him so that he could scarcely eat, began to sharpen into anger. Coming up here, when he was so wonderfully happy, the two of them, pulling their long, grieved faces at him. . . .

When Uncle Ben at last bluntly broached the matter, Dermot was ready.

"Sure," said the mariner, wrinkling his bald brow in lines of quizzical enquiry, "what is it ails ye both? And you, Dermot? There's not a word to be got out of ye. What's the boy done, Margaret?"

Mr. Gray's eyebrows rose. Visibly, in stiff, pained surprise, they deplored Ben's lack of taste. He was about to reply, when Dermot forestalled him.

"I'll tell you what it is, Uncle Ben." The boy had suddenly put on five years. He shook with passion. "Some time ago, I told Daddy a story, and said it happened at school, just for fun. He's been telling it to people, and at last he's found out it's an old one. That made him feel foolish. So he says I told him a deliberate lie."

There was a dead silence. All the air in the room pressed upon Dermot's face, pricking him with a thousand needles. Blood pumped in his ears.

Uncle Ben laughed.

"Ah, sure, Ernest," he said, "he was just codding you. You wouldn't call that a lie. He was just codding you."

And that line the entire household at once adopted. It was useless for the half-mollified Ernest to explain afterwards, "You see, Ben, it's the principle I'm anxious about": he was not taken seriously, and suffered the further humiliation of being told how good a boy Dermot was: "as if I didn't know my own son," he complained, when he and Margaret walked to the tram afterwards.

Dermot lay that night with a fierce conflict inside him. He felt by turns ashamed, for having sought allies against his parents: by turns elated, for having rebelled and won. Ah, dear understanding people of this house! Yet, in so many ways, they were strange to him, much as he loved them. Some day, some day, the choice would have to be made. It did not enter his head that he might choose neither.

But he was fortified in spirit. When, after he went back to Walmer Villa, his Father reproved him for trying to let his parents down in front of the Delgany folk, he had his answer ready.

"If you were in the right, how could it hurt you for me to tell the facts."

Mr. Gray tried to explain the scene away.

"You made it very awkward for them. Of course Uncle Ben had to make light of it."

"He told me himself, the next day, that it wasn't what he would call a lie."

"He wouldn't have said that, if it had been one of his own children."

"Oh, yes," said Dermot bitterly, "I suppose we are the only honest people in the world": and, with unheard of boldness, he got up, and went out of the room.

CHAPTER XXVII

Even when he was not staying there, the influence of Delgany went deep. It was Delgany, through Con, that suggested a deliverance from the Sunday morning ordeal of St. Patrick's. Con did not greatly care for the church where his parents worshipped, and had found another, up at the back of Killiney Hill, which he liked better. He got leave to take Dermot there one morning, and the mischief was done. Dermot was then twelve, and he did not receive the rapturous attentions of Miss O'Killikelly and her like with too good a grace. He stood frowning, biting his lip, and kicking the gravel with the toe of his shiny brown boot, making short replies.

"Dermot, darling."

A sweet smile would come his way from his Mother or Granny, a public smile, ending with a glance at the boot. Sometimes even, there would be a laughing, deprecating apology on his behalf.

"He's shy. The school age," his Granny would murmur: and all the ladies, with their nodding bonnets, their black, their lilac, and their mauve, their beads that glittered shrilly in the sun, would draw delightedly together, looking at him as if he were some rare and precious animal, and exclaim:

"Aaah, he's shy. That's what it is. Sure, you could see it in a minute. It's shy he is, the poor boy."

"He'll be going away to his public school in a year," said his Mother, in a kind of dream.

"His public school. D'ye tell me that now. And only the other day, he was just *so* high."

242

"When I was *that* high," said Dermot on one occasion, merely meaning to join humorously in the discussion, "I shouldn't have thought I could stand upright at all."

The remark was received with laughter and flutterings, but Dermot was afterwards told he had been rude.

No. St. Patrick's had lost its hold. He loved, privately, to get just one sight of the window with Jesus walking upon the waters, on the first Sunday of the new holiday, so that he could gaze upon it (it seemed he had only left it the Sunday before) and thank God for having brought him safe again. He liked, also, to say goodbye to it at the end, as he did to Killiney Bay. When you walked to Delgany, just before you reached the house, you came clear of a belt of trees, and the whole panorama opened in its perfect finality before you. That, of all moments in the year, was the moment to stand and thank God for bringing you back again. In the same way, when the glorious weeks were over, on the last day, coming up mournfully to Delgany to bid them all goodbye, he crept off by himself to Con's room, which looked out over the bay, kneeled up in the window, and prayed that he might be brought back to see the view again. Soon, the view took the place of the stained-glass window. So Dermot fought hard to go with Con on the motor-bike to the church on the hill, and rush afterwards through the villages of the Vale of Shanganagh—Ballybrack, Cabinteely, Loughlinstown and Little Bray—and back by Cobawn Lane and the sea, past the stooks of yellow corn, with Con, moved always to the same memory of his school-days at St. Columba's, bawling his part in the anthem: "The valleys stand so thick with corn, that THEY laugh and sing, that THEY laugh and sing"—ending in an enormous laugh of excitement and happiness. First, Dermot's parents let him once or twice desert St. Patrick's. Next year, he demanded to go always with Con. There were recriminations at the top of the garden.

"Your poor Granny is so sad. She loves to have you with her—"

"And show me off to a lot of beastly old women."

"Your Granny does everything she can to make your time here happy." (It was so true. Dermot felt the barb.) "I think you might at least do this to please her."

"I thought," he muttered sulkily, "one went to church to please God, not one's Granny."

"Now you're being impertinent," said Margaret coldly, drawing herself up. She went away, leaving Dermot angry and miserable. As he approached his cub years, and was rude to her, he could see all the time that she, the beautiful lady his mother, should never suffer rudeness. It was impossible, in her true character. He resented darkly the soilure and wickedness of the world which brought it about. He could not feel all in the wrong. She, left to herself, was not wrong either. It was only when circumstances drove her. Circumstances, and Daddy.

Finally, it was settled that he should go definitely once a summer to St. Patrick's, and that, for the rest of the time, he might worship where he pleased. This was a large and rather surprising concession, and the strongest factor in it, curiously, was Dermot's father. From being embittered by association with a long succession of clergymen, he was finally moved, through a dispute with the vicar at home, to forsake churchgoing altogether. In this new mood of large-mindedness he startled Margaret by declaring that he wished Dermot left free to choose for himself: adding that to sit under such a fool as the present vicar could do no one any good. Dermot jumped at the chance, and spent his Sunday mornings at home in long walks with his father, upon which the pair got on very well indeed. But the mind of a boy grows strangely. Since he was six or seven, Dermot had feared rather than loved his father. Now, the new companionship, the delightful conspiracy against churchgoing, while it banished a deal of the fear, banished a deal of respect with it. This decay did not manifest itself till later: the real point was that religion for Dermot became divorced from his home and parents, and associated altogether with Delgany. So deep an impression did those simple spirits make upon him, that when the development of his intelligence and his education offered him difficulties which for them did not exist: when he perceived that there were problems and crises in the contemporary world to which their declaration could not in its simplicity be adjusted: he felt all the time, not that he was trying to make the necessary new adjustment of faith to intellect, but that he was degenerating from the simplicity of a golden world.

Mr. Gray, perceiving this, and disliking the Delgany philosophy, gave Dermot, as he grew older, the full weight of his mind. All the doubts and problems which had been stirring so long beneath his churchwarden exterior were imparted, logically and persuasively, to the boy. Dermot seized upon them. He was just at the logical age, and to disprove the faith of his mother and his Granny was a fascinating game. He caused much trouble to the more conscientious and orthodox of his school friends, who were unable to answer him, except with Uncle Ben's argument that there were some things with which the human intellect was never intended to cope. This argument, in the pleasure of using his intellect, Dermot pushed on one side: but he could never profess agnosticism at Delgany. That was the one place which made him feel uneasy. He would conveniently forget it there, or, after tentative discussion, almost agree with Con that *the* temptation for a clever man was to use his intellect upon questions of religion. But we are getting ahead of our tale, which at the moment is lodged somewhere about the end of Dermot's last holiday as a preparatory schoolboy.

At this point Anne sprang a surprise upon her family. She had always been the conventional one, insisting upon a good education, a finishing school in England, and the piano: and her behaviour had shown the influence of these additions. She was quieter than Eileen, more devout, more talented. Alone of the family, she liked going away from home, paying long visits to friends in England. She spoke French, and stayed two months in Paris, with a family of unimpeachable respectability, to perfect it. She took herself altogether more seriously than the others, but no one could resent this, because she was sweet-natured, and not at all conceited. A deep humility, rather, led her to better her abilities. Dermot made little of her. He liked her, for she was always kind to him: but she was more and more away from Delgany, more deeply busied with her own concerns —which included "social work" in Dublin—and he soon ceased to include her in the Delgany scheme.

Then she went for a holiday to Switzerland, with a girl friend, and returned, engaged to a Swiss! The parents of the girl friend were much concerned. They wrote to Aunt Patricia in a tone of mingled apology and glee, for the Swiss was very well off. He was, they declared, a gentleman, in every sense of the word: polite, kind-hearted, very religious: in fact, "a great dear." Anne was transfigured. To her parents' remonstrances and queries she presented a sort of radiant obstinacy.

"*What* do ye call the fella?" asked Uncle Ben again, wrinkling his brows.

"Topje," said Anne defiantly. "That's his nickname. That's what he's called at home."

"Topsy!" cried the scandalised mariner.

Anne laughed happily.

"No, Daddy darling, Topje."

"Topyee." Uncle Ben made a face. "That's a queer sort of a name, for a man. That has a Dutch sound, to me."

"I can't help it, Daddy."

"Are you sure, now, he's not a Dutchman?"

"Quite sure, Daddy. He's a Swiss, and he lives in Bern."

"Well." Uncle Ben looked round the room. "It's the funniest sort of a do I ever heard."

"Oh, Daddy." She sat herself beside him on the floor, and put her arm on his knees. "Do be nice about him."

"Faith, pet," he looked down at her in amused perplexity. "I want to be nice. But—but—you've taken the wind clean out of me sails. All of us. I mean, pet, it's a bit of a surprise, d'ye see."

"I know it is, Daddy. It's rather a surprise to me. But wait till you've seen Topje. You'll like him: you'll all like him. He's an absolute darling. Do write and ask him to come, Mother darling?"

"Oh, faith," Ben answered for her. "We'll ask him to come, all right. We must have a look at your Topyee, anyway."

So Topje was invited, and replied in beautiful archaic English, disclosing a mind of great simplicity. Even Aunt Patricia had to admit it was a very nice letter. Privately, she was very downcast at the idea of "a foreigner," the term implying for her all manner of laxity and license.

"Still, I'd rather it were a Swiss than a Frenchman," she confided to Dermot; for she knew nothing against the Swiss: nothing at all about them, indeed, except that they made watches.

Everyone was curious to see Topje, and in due time he arrived. He was a success from the first.

"Ah, you couldn't help liking him," Granny said, after he had visited Walmer Villa. Topje did not seem to mind how many people he had to meet. He smiled amiably, and was nice to them all. He was, certainly, not much to look at. Short, fair, nearly bald, about thirty-four or five, holding himself stiffly; with a fresh colour, an innocent expression, and rather unusual blue eyes, he was no match for the quite beautiful Anne. Yet everyone liked him at sight. The simplicity of his character, his child-like good nature, was apparent at once: and there was something in the eyes that suggested strength behind the simplicity. For all his innocence, Topje did not miss much. Delgany soon admitted he was no fool.

Con and he got on famously. To Con, he was like a new toy, to be exploited and played with in every conceivable fashion. He pulled Topje's leg right royally.

"Please?" Topje would say, smiling amiably, as roars of laughter exploded round him. "Please?" And Con would put a great paw on his shoulder, trying to explain between his guffaws: whereupon Topje would beam, and pat Con on the back, with the greatest good humour. Anne was at first cross and apprehensive, and Aunt Patricia joined her.

"He'll think you're laughing at him. You'll hurt his feelings. He won't understand."

But Topje understood all right. Nothing disconcerted him. The horseplay and practical jokes which formed the staple part of initiation to the Delgany household he received with every appearance of pleasure. Finally, after he had been in the house a week, he retaliated upon Con with a practical joke of such ingenuity and efficiency that Con was completely won, and ready to embrace him as a brother-in-law.

"Please," said Topje one morning after breakfast, "we can get married now, yes?"

Aunt Patricia gasped. She had hoped next year, at the soonest. . . . But Anne and Topje laid siege to her, and, before an hour was passed, she had given in. Uncle Ben raised no objection either, when he came home.

"But your trousseau," protested Aunt Patricia feebly. "How will you—"

Topje turned to her.

"We have honeymoon in Anne's country, like we say this morning. Then, after honeymoon, we make our shoppings, and go home."

"Aaah," said Aunt Patricia, sadly. "I never expected to lose you so soon."

"Not lose," said Topje, patting her hand. "Not lose. Every year, you come and see us: we come and see you."

He was now master of the situation, and had taken charge of the whole family. They sat back, half in a dream, while Topje arranged everything. He even interviewed the Vicar, who called afterwards, simply spluttering with his praises.

"Upon me soul," said Uncle Ben one evening, when the two had gone out together: "Upon me soul, I'm beginning to admire that fella. He's got a head on his shoulders."

"Anne's done uncommon well for herself, if you ask *me*," said Con.

"Indeed, he's very nice," conceded Aunt Patricia mournfully. Now that the banns were up, and the affair out of her hands, she had fallen back on resignation. "All the same," she would protest, to her friends, "it's not what I looked for, for her, at all."

"Ah, but he's so *nice*," they all comforted her. "He adores her. Sure, ye can see it. He'll make her a splendid husband."

Yes, Aunt Patricia admitted, there were comforts, certainly. And, there was no denying, Topje was very well off: very well off indeed.

The wedding took place at half-past eight on a wet September morning. Anne, now that the day had come, looked pale and miserable: Topje, resolute and concerned. The church was chilly and damp: the Vicar had a cold in his nose. Everyone looked as if they had just been roused from sleep, and, by an unwilling and desperate effort, reached the church in time. Con and Dermot were the only people in form. While the register was being signed, they turned their attention to the bridal car. Con, guffawing, tied an assortment of old boots to the back axle, while Dermot plastered the wet shiny surface of the car with confetti, which stuck grimly everywhere. Before the pair started, Granny hurried to the driver, spoke to him in a low voice, and pressed something into his hand. Then, to the accompaniment of feeble cheering, the pair drove off, the boots hopping and dangling behind, at which spectacle Con slapped his knees and bawled with laughter.

When the car had gone a quarter of a mile, it stopped, and the driver, following Granny's instructions, got out and cut off the boots. Con and Dermot, returning home, were indignant to discover them lying in the gutter. Despite Aunt

Patricia's protests, they retrieved them, and brought them home.

"For ye never know," proclaimed Con, leering at Eileen, "how soon they'd be wanted again."

"Well, if they are," retorted his sister, "it won't be at half-past eight on a wet morning, I can promise you that. I'm not going to the altar blue with the cold, and a red nose on me, for any man."

"Ah, me poor little Anne," said Uncle Ben. "She was hardly her best."

"Hardly her best! Sure, I never saw her look worse in me life."

"Ah, Eileen, pet, no. That's an unkind thing to say."

"Well, God defend me from looking that way, when I'm married, that's all."

"Ta' care," said Con, "you ever are married. Don't be too sure."

"If I'm not, you won't want the boots. Unless it's for yourself."

"Or Dermot here. Will you look at him. Musha, Dermot, I tell you, when the girls get hold of that mouth of yours—"

"Shut up."

"Yes," said Eileen, "shut up. We've had enough of you, for one morning. Weddings are bad enough anyway, without you hee-hawing all over the place."

"Ta' care, or I won't honour yours with me presence."

"Indeed, and I devoutly hope you won't."

"Now then," admonished Uncle Ben. "Order there, me hearties! Order there!"

CHAPTER XXVIII

Autumn had set its promise early on the country. Gales blew in the first week of September, and a couple of days sufficed to turn lazy, full-fed summer into something wilder, more aware. The gales passed, and kindlier days followed them, but there was a new smell in the air, a new spirit, alert and passionate, upon the mountains, the thickets, and the bracken-covered slopes of the hills.

One wild, splendid evening, after a day of showers, Dermot and Paddy walked past Glenageary along "the metals," the old discarded track long since used only as a walk. It ran by the backs of fields and hedges, and the two found it far preferable to the road. In front of them, Dalkey Hill stood up in the wet, low sunlight, its cliff scarred with long dark shadows, its wall and castle reared heroically to face the West and give back to the dying day a look as desolate and splendid as its own. A single window in the castle burned with liquid yellow fire, pale but indomitable. Dermot gazed up at it in awe and delight. The castle and wall, visible from so far away—one caught sight of it on the home-bound tram as soon as one was clear of Merrion Gates—had always enchanted him. Even a close view of it, from the road above the station, with its rabble of forlorn little cottages underneath the cliff, failed to harm it in his eyes: a view reducing its proportions, turning it into a stark quarry surmounted by an irregular wall and flat, blank tower. From a distance, from the street of Dalkey itself, it looked so fine, domineering over the little huddled town: and, all the time, it was not even the height of Killiney Hill behind it.

251

They walked slowly, for there was plenty of time. Clup-clup, clup-clup, sounded Paddy's feet: he hobbled along, swinging his arms, humming to himself, in high glee: for they were going to see the circus. The circus came once a year to Dalkey, and camped in a field beside the church. Dermot always took Paddy, ostensibly as escort, though he was not needed in that capacity, as they sat in the better seats. Paddy enjoyed the show so wholeheartedly, it was a treat to be with him: but, in any case, Dermot would not have cared to go without him. Circuses and Paddy were right, just as theatres and Con were right.

"*I'm coming . . . I'm coming . . .*" (sang Paddy)
"*And my . . . headdiz . . . bending . . . low. . . .
I . . . hear them . . . darkie . . . voices . . . calleeng . . .
Poor . . . ould . . . Jow.*"

The gaps in his song were filled with a variety of extraordinary noises: whistlings, intakes of the breath, snorts, and an occasional expectoration. He varied this—when he was not talking—by a sort of cheerful growling noise, working his arms extra vigorously, and puffing out his moustache like a seal; executing all the time the remarkably efficient shuffle that served him for a walk. It was tireless, and little handicap in speed. Paddy could maintain an ordinary man's walking pace, albeit at the expense of much to-do and working of the arms: but his ordinary shuffle was a bit slower. He insisted on his ability to walk any distance. Every summer he and Dermot went for a ceremonial walk, always referred to by Paddy as "the Loughlinstown Walk." They went past Mona's door—Mona, no more a trouble to Dermot, though lodged for all time in his prayers, from which nothing, not even her death, could bring erasure: past Mona's door, up the long white dusty stretch of the Albert Road, on by Ballybrack to the Big Tree of Loughlinstown; down past the Union (object of great dread to Paddy), looking dubiously into the brook, wondering if it held fish, turning

off left, and going home through high hedges near the sea. Dermot met two boys and a master from his preparatory school
one day on this walk. The boys coughed derisively at his
ragged henchman, but the master shook hands with Paddy,
and seemed to notice nothing. Next year Dermot felt an
apprehension rise in him as they reached the spot, but the
meeting, needless to say, was not repeated. He was not a
snob: he had been at first annoyed, then angrily despised the
boys. It was the sense of discord which he hated, the intrusion
into his Irish life of something from England which did not
belong to it. . . .

He walked slowly, balancing himself on the old metal
rail. There were a few clear stretches of them: then they
would all be overgrown with low, dense bushes, and he
would have to walk round till he could get on again. The pair
were perfect company, each absorbed in his own thoughts.

Suddenly Paddy's song broke off.

"There's Mike," he exclaimed.

Dermot looked up, and saw the long, dejected figure
slouching along in company with a group of others. A whippet
tagged after them.

"I haven't seen him for ages," said Dermot. "Where's
he been?"

"He's been very busy, over th'Army," said Paddy,
sucking his teeth. "There's a second branch of them now."

Dermot grinned.

"Poor Mike!"

"They have him very near wore out," said Paddy. "He
won't be able for them much longer, by the way he's going."

Dermot watched the dispirited figure of the fanatic.

"He's taking a holiday to-night, anyway," he said.

They were approaching the field in which the circus
people had their caravans. The church field was not large
enough to hold more than the tent and the wild beast cages.
All the rest was spaced out comfortably a quarter of a
mile away. Dermot stared at the clean, gaudily painted vans.

The back doors of several were open, and the last of the
sun illumined weakly the spick and span interiors, with
their polish, their brass-work, their incredible, small neatness. On the steps of one a fat, dark woman sat sewing.
She looked up from time to time at the setting sun, pursed
her lips, and went on with her work. They passed on to
another van. A girl came down the steps, swilling some liquid
round in a blue enamel basin. When she reached the grass,
she jerked the liquid out with an expert twist of her two
hands. She stood up, sniffed, and rubbed her shapely brown
nose with the back of her forefinger. She was good-looking,
and rather dirty to come out of so bright a van. Catching
sight of Dermot, she returned his stare, and smiled. The
suddenness of the dark, soft smile made Dermot jump with
a sense of physical shock. He had been looking at her as a
part of the scene, and she had startled him by coming to
life and being aware of him. Paddy, seeing the smile out
of the tail of his eye, quickened his step and crossed himself.
But Paddy was over-zealous. It was not that sort of a smile.

The sun disappeared as they were reaching the church.
It flung a last random shaft on the winding street of the
queer little town, and fixed upon the castle in its last despair.
There it would hold a few minutes longer: but Dermot and
Paddy were now one of a crowd, treading the uneven cobbles,
pressing forward to the field where the great tent rose like
some pale growth sprung up uneasily in the dusk, hoping
that the tall stiff church would not turn around and order
it to be off. The pay-booth stood at the entrance to the field:
a loud man with great red moustaches was lighting the
naphtha flares which illumined garishly the giving and taking
of money. Hissing, leaping, exploding perpetually in a series
of tiny spits at the air around them, they transformed the
crowd into monsters, throwing their shape out of all propor-
tion, distorting their countenance with unnatural shadows,
pulling their features uncouthly into prominence: turning
the mysterious dusk into cheerful, bellowing night.

The two were in their places early, long before the show began. For a while they sat isolated, the cheaper seats filling rapidly with a happy, cat-calling crowd. Then, some ten minutes before the show was due to start, "the quality" began filing in: and, not more than five minutes late, the circus band climbed unsteadily into their bedizened waggon and filled the tent with sounds to match its lighting and its decoration: sounds which, somehow, were the last touch required to release in the expectant crowd the magic which only a circus can excite.

The circus was like all other circuses. It was even exactly like itself of the year before, and the year before that: but who cared? The same characters, the same feats, the same favourites—these were precisely what they had all come to see. They would not miss a single item of it. There was Captain Foster, the black who put his curly poll right into the lion's mouth. There was Little May, who did a number of incredible (and some quite credible) exercises on the rings and trapeze. Dermot thought her very beautiful, invested her with a character of great queenliness and reserve, and enacted in his mind many romantic scenes between her and himself, for days afterwards. There was Pansy, the world's most wonderful performing horse: Bimbo, the World's Wisest Elephant: Mademoiselle Fazzetti, the lovely equestrienne: and, greatest of all, those two favourites, whom Paddy, striking his knee, averred to be the best he ever seen: Young Hannaford, the bareback rider, and Johnny Quinn, Ireland's Own Singing Clown. Young Hannaford does not now visit Dalkey: he has risen to the peaks of the circus world, and metropolitan audiences have rewarded him with that firm, insistent, yet reserved applause which ripples from tier to tier, till the whole house is alight: the steady, well-bred tribute of a cosmopolitan enthusiasm. Yet even that, the summit of his ambitions, could not kindle him to greater pleasure than he felt, in the little tent at Dalkey, as he leaped down sweating from his horse, to a raucous storm of joy. "More power to you, boy! More power! More power!" It took no urban skill to see the difference between the work of the brown, stocky, smiling figure and that of his colleagues. Light as a gull, swift and merry as a blackbird—failing at one terrific feat, smiling, putting the horse back—try again—Holy Mary!— seven hundred hearts slipping a beat—he's done it! A great roar of joy, a roar of love, for the lad who has shown them victory. Victory; that was what the circus stood for. Victory over difficult things, over aching muscles, over creaky thews: over ugliness, over despair: over the stubbornness of tame beasts, the ferocity of lions: victory over fear, over rags and dirt, over every human limitation. Try, try, the smiles of Young Hannaford and Little May seemed to encourage them: look, it is easy: try, and you will do it. Look, drawled Captain Foster of the flashing teeth and eyes, I only a big buck niggah, I go into de lion's den, put my head in his mouf, you see, pah! Other lion he snarl, reach out paw, no get me. Ha ha! Human peoples bettah than lions, aftah all. You see! Oh, yes, sure, everything was easy, if ye only went at it the right way, with your heart up. "More power, Young Hannaford! More power to ye! More power."

And Johnny Quinn—king of his troupe of clowns—what could you say to him? His retinue did not seem to Dermot as funny as the rest of the house knew beforehand they were going to be. At the very sight of them, Paddy went off into screams of laughter. "Errah, the Handy-Andies! Will ye look at the Handy-Andies!" he cried, and began to jeer at them delightedly. "Yeee-ow!" he yelled. "Yeee-ow!" as they ran about, tripping over large objects endeavouring to assist in the movement of properties, and getting explosively slapped for their pains. When they had nothing better to do, they joined hands and gambolled ungracefully round in a ring. "Yee-ow! Yee-ow!" screamed the crowd. The clowns became greatly excited. They exaggerated all their antics, they howled and wailed, they guffawed with

the vacant, loutish laughter of idiot boys. Paddy writhed in
an ecstasy of delight.

No one noticed just when Johnny Quinn came in. He
was suddenly there; wandering about in the ring, paying
no attention to the audience or anything else. No sooner
had the crowd noticed him, than the rest of the clowns
tumbled out of the arena, with a last baa-haaing and volley
of slaps on the buttocks, leaving Johnny all alone. A sudden
hush fell over the tent. Johnny did not appear to notice
that either. He took off his pointed hat with an ungainly
circular gesture of his arm, and held it in his two hands
about the level of his chest. There was a sudden laborious
burst of melody from the band, their music sounding crude
and garish in the stillness, as they tried their best to hush it,
to make it comely for the occasion. Then, with an un-
expectedness which sent a cold shiver down Dermot's spine,
a voice was singing in the tent—a clear tenor, worn, but soft
and true.

"Ha-as sorrow thy you-ung days shaded . . ."

The melancholy, graceful song rose like a flower against
the incongruous background, the smoky, flare-lit tent, the
rows and rows of faces: faces astonished, spellbound, empty
of expression, their mood abruptly changed by a will and
authority not their own. From the uncomprehending street
boys squatted on the grass nearest the ring, staring up at
him with open mouths and goggle eyes: from the arrested
faces of the louts and larrikins, the bewildered faces of such
as Paddy, to the vaguely uncomfortably, down-my-nose
faces of "the quality": all acknowledged and obeyed the
power of the man who stood there alone, taking no notice of
them, shutting his eyes, holding his pointed hat tight against
his chest, singing in the voice that did not seem to come from
him. After the stupefaction of the first verse, the audience
stirred. They were warming to him. Has sorra thy young
days shaded. Aye. That was a good tune.

> *"Has hope, like the bird in the story*
> *That flitted from tree to tree . . ."*

Oh, bedam, that was true. Who hadn't the wish for something was just out of his reach? Is there e'er a man satisfied? "Has hope been that bird to thee?" Line after line, the song bade them all bring their sorrows to a pool, and make common lamentation. Bring their sorrows to Johnny Quinn. Everyone had a sorrow of some kind. Here, bring them all, everything that ever went wrong on ye in your life. Come on, the whole lot of ye. The melancholy, impersonal feeling in the voice caught at their souls. Tears smarted in their eyes. They could barely keep still. They wanted to howl, like dogs.

> *"O child of misfortune, come hither,*
> *I'll weep with thee tear for tear."*

Silence—then, to release their emotions, they burst into frantic cheering, more as an excuse for themselves than a tribute to the singer. Again, again, again! they could not have enough of this, they cried to one another. But Johnny knew them. He was not fool enough to repeat himself. So the band struck up one of Paddy's songs, "Down in Donegal," and the great roar of relief that went up told Johnny how well he knew his people. After this, they could look at each other again. Wholeheartedly they joined in the chorus, leaving nothing for Johnny to do but watch them, grinning on one side of his face.

> *"So—p-lay up the music*
> *And I will show yez all*
> *The way we used to sing and dance*
> *Down in Donegal . . ."*

"Oh boys, oh boys, that was grand," said Paddy, as they swung out into gusts of cold night air. "That was great valya. That was grand."

They headed for the metals, putting their heads down into the quick onsets of the wind. There were lights in the caravans. Dermot peered up for the one where the girl lived who had smiled at him. Yes, that was it. A dim light in the tiny window, like the others.

Paddy huddled down into his jacket, and drew a whistling breath through his teeth.

"It'll rain to-morra," he observed.

CHAPTER XXIX

THERE HAS BEEN LITTLE ABOUT EITHNE SO FAR, FOR THE good reason that in Dermot's summer life she played no part at all. After the first years at home, when she had been fascinating as Baby, the two grew apart. There were four years between them, and, though it was Eithne's one desire to accompany and resemble her brother, he had only occasional use for her society. It was the time when brothers really tended to despise their smaller sisters; but, apart from questions of fashion, Dermot played by himself when he was at home, and was most of the day away at school. They fought, inevitably, since Eithne's desire to resemble her brother led her to appropriate his toys when he was out of the way. As, in the resultant quarrels, grown-ups invariably took her part, he speedily learned a technique for quieting her before they arrived. Immediately the first piercing scream announced her defeat, Dermot would hold out his hand. The furious little girl hit it with all her might, whereupon Dermot feigned to be doubled up in the last extremities of pain. This sight afforded Eithne such rapture that she forgot her own sufferings: and by the time the avenger dashed breathless into the room, with the formula, "Whatever have you been doing to your poor little sister *now*?" the little sister was beaming in manifest delight.

Their friendly hours occurred usually on a Sunday after tea. Dermot's talent for story-telling, exercised upon her without restraint—although, fearing fresh charges of "lying," he swore her to secrecy—found a most appreciative listener. He persuaded Eithne that the spirits of a whole hagiology of wizards, witches, and elves could in succession inhabit his body: and the gift of mimicry helped him out. Their procedure was always the same.

"Well"; he stood importantly in front of the nursery fire. "Who would you like to see to-night?"

"I'd like to see Nikoota."

Nikoota was a witch, old, brusque, but kind-hearted: one of the "bless me, child" school. Eithne liked her.

"D'you think you can get Nikoota?", she pleaded, anxiously.

"I *think* so," Dermot replied, in the tone of a bank manager royally conceding an overdraft. "But I expect it'll mean seeing Miboosha too."

"Yes. I'm 'fraid so."

"You see, you didn't ask for him last time. And we don't want to hurt his feelings, do we?"

"No."

"Besides, Nikoota will notice, if you get out of seeing him twice running. She's a bit sensitive about people not wanting to see him."

Eithne sighed.

"Oh, yes," she said. "I suppose he'd better come."

Miboosha was the oafish and loutish husband of Nikoota. His manners were deplorable, his tongue was too big for his mouth, and he was exceedingly greedy. The pair had numerous children, but managed somehow to achieve greater reality and consistency than their family. Nikoota was said to inhabit occasionally a quarry hole a mile from the house. Eithne used to leave ginger biscuits there, which duly disappeared, and would find under her pillow charred acknowledgments. The fact that these were scribbled on torn pieces of paper with burnt edges was accepted as final and indubitable proof of their authenticity.

"Very well, then," said Dermot. He drew himself up to his full height, and stuck out his chest. "You go out of the room and count a hundred, to give me time to get to the Pyramids."

His real self, he explained, went to Egypt and stayed inside a Pyramid, in order that the wizard folk might make use of his body to appear to her.

"Good-bye," he added, as she was closing the door.

She looked in again, her face set with awe and expectation.

"Good-bye," she said. "But you won't be long away, will you?"

He shrugged his shoulders.

"All depends," he answered. "It's difficult, sometimes. Perhaps you'd better not come in till Nikoota raps on the table. I'll tell her, as we pass."

Eithne nodded, and went out. Dermot allowed a good minute and a half to pass before he rapped on the table. He huddled himself, as he did so, into a bent misshapen form, and his face creased in querulous wrinkles.

"Good evening, my dear," croaked an old voice, as Eithne came tiptoeing in. The voice had the shake of some of the old St. Patrick's ladies, but their Irish accent was overlaid with something more theatrical.

Five minutes later Eithne was once again in the dim hall, holding the door handle, waiting for the blundering sounds which would announce Miboosha. She found him hungry, and more uncouth than ever.

"Wha', wha', wha'," the ogre complained, pawing his way about the room. "Ugg! Gunnuck! Nuyce!"

He picked up her favourite doll, and made as if to eat it.

Then indeed Dermot had to admire the presence of mind of his little sister. No trace of horror or panic showed itself on her face: she wore only an expression of polite concern.

"I'm 'fraid," she said, and stopped short. "I hardly recommend that. I'm 'fraid it wouldn't be good for your digestion. You have to be careful, don't you?"

While he hesitated, she took the doll firmly out of his hands, and put it in safety.

"Here, Miboosha," she said, "I thought you might be hungry, and I kept these."

She produced a small piece of cake, a piece of bread-and-butter, and two biscuits—secreted during tea. Cunning little thing, he thought, for he had never seen her take them.

Miboosha, falling on the viands with ferocious joy, discovered speedily that he was not as hungry as he had thought.

"Well," said Dermot presently, as, restored to his proper form, he rubbed his hands at the fire. "How were they? How did you get on?"

"Oh, it was all right. It was lovely some of the time. Only—" She hurried over, as if to make sure that the doll was still safe. "One thing was rather awful. Miboosha wanted to eat poor Ethelfreda. But I managed to get her away from him, and 'stract his attention."

"Oh? tell me."

He went on rubbing his hands, expressing great approval of her tact.

"Whew," he said presently. "It was pretty cold, on that staircase, in the Pyramids."

Now that Eithne was asked with him to Delgany, however, she began perforce to take a share in his holiday life. She was one of the party, and, away from home, she sparkled. The journeys into the mountains involved the sidecar now: or, if the route were to be too rough, Con took the two in turns. This went on all through the holiday, for he came often to Walmer Villa, on his free day, to pick up one or the other of them. Dermot, without resentment, but with a sort of wonder, had to step back from the exclusive possession of Con, and look at his sister with a fresh respect. If Con did not find her company tiresome; if Con sought her out for hours at a time, there must be something in her. And there was. Appreciation brought her on like a spring tide, and she discovered to the astonished Con a personality ready made and mature, the existence of which he had never suspected. The small girl, neat, pretty, brown, presided delightfully at their picnics and the teas they ate in lonely mountain cottages. She poured out for them, she kept Con in order, happily rebuking his more outrageous outbursts of flirtation, twinkling from one of them to the other till Dermot, his nose in his teacup, wondered half dazed who this changeling was that had suddenly come to life in the quiet and unregarded person of his little sister.

Every Sunday afternoon Con came down to Walmer Villa to play with them. Soon, obviously, he came to play with Eithne: but Dermot was quite happy to assist at the games. Con was the royal source of all exciting things, all feats, and all "divarsion." Everything he did was right. Dermot felt no jealousy, and his first bewilderment soon passed. His conceit and self-consciousness were ignorance, more than the vices themselves. Like many an only son, he had his own way, and did not at first realise that there were others. Parents and relations had put him first so long that the first place seemed only natural. Once enlightened, he was almost pathetically ready to play second fiddle.

"Well, Dermot." Con sat in the hay, his collar undone, his hair tousled, puffing. "So you're going away to a boarding school after this, wha'?"

"Yes."

"Will ye—Eithne, ye little divil, if you put any more hay down me neck, I'll have the hide off ye. G'way. Will ye like that?"

"I don't know. I shall feel very strange at first, I expect."

"And it's some sort of a scholarship thing ye got?"

"Yes."

"For what ah, no, Eithne pet. I'm too hot. Easy a minute. Easy. Oh, glory!"

The indefatigable maiden, dodging cleverly, had put a last handful down between his collar and skin.

"Now I'll leave you in peace," she announced.

"That's one thousand seven hundred and seventy two you owe me, mind," threatened Con, laughing.

"Poo," replied Eithne, loftily; and allowed herself an

unrepentant grin. This formidable score represented kisses due, as penalties for misdemeanours, to be claimed at some indefinite date in the future. The creditor occasionally took one or two on account.

"What were we sayin'—Eithne, ye ill-mannered little gomm! Here was I having an important conversation with your brother, and you've put it all out of me head."

"About my scholarship," said Dermot awkwardly.

"Oh yes, bedad. What was it for, exactly?"

"For Classics."

"For Classics, eh." Con sighed. "I was never a hand for me books. More power to you, son! Eithne"—his great arm shot out like lightning, grabbing her ankle. "C'm here. Do you realise what a grand, learned brother ye have?" He shook her so hard that she could not reply. "You don't? Very well—*I'll* show ye."

And he took a full revenge for the handful of hay, rolling her over and over, cramming it into her mouth, and maltreating her generally.

"Pfoo—pfff—pfoo. You beast!"

She ran away, and stood, crying with laughter, spitting hayseeds out of her mouth.

"What did I hear you say? WHA'?"

He rose, and galumphed after her, like some enormous dog, to a far corner of the garden. Dermot watched, smiling, but made no move to follow.

An hour later, the three sat quiet, under the spell of evening. Grandpapa had come down, talked to Con a while, and retired, one hand held open behind him, in the small of his back. Smoke from the cottages rose frail and straight into the musing air. They saw it against the trees of Sandycove; higher, it was gone. The shadow of the summerhouse and its laburnums streamed towards them across the little lawn. Standing up straight in the rich slanting rays, with the blue hazy darkness of the hedge behind them, the red-hot pokers glowed, deep flaming suns, feeding furiously on their living core. The bells of Kingstown had begun to fill the sky with their music. This was Ireland. Soon, soon Dermot would be gone: gone to he knew not what.

"Sing, Con," he said suddenly.

"Yes," said Eithne, nestling up closer to him. "Please."

"What will I sing?"

She wriggled on the seat.

"You know."

Con was silent for a moment. Then, lifting up his face into the sunset, and shutting his eyes, he began the first deep note startling them, as it always did, with the full quality they could never quite remember, which no experience could teach them to expect.

> "*She is far from the land where her young hero sleeps,*
> *And lovers around her are sighing,*
> *But coldly she turns from their gaze and weeps,*
> *For her heart in his grave is lying.*"

Gazing across the garden, held by the small suns of the poker flowers, they abandoned themselves to the sweet melancholy of the song. Yes, yes: they were soon to go, to leave Ireland for a whole long year. Yes, yes. The very seat beneath them thrilled with some of the deep notes, like a church pew thrilling to the organ. Dermot considered, in a wonder he never outgrew, the phenomenon of a human being with a Voice: a real voice, rich, powerful, something which welled up from the depths of life: something which Con, god-like, turned on at will: with which he could exult in a fine summer morning, filling the bathroom with sounds free as the sunlight, sounds which threatened to blow the four walls apart and let in the empyrean upon the room's two occupants: Dermot, sitting in the bath, directly over the inlet, enjoying the secret feeling of warm water welling up beneath him, bubbling along his thighs and round at his back, tickling the inside of his legs, with its suggestion of strange, unlawful joy: suddenly forgetting this and everything else in the magnificent shock of sound that burst from the great figure in the window; Con, stropping his razor, rolling out the magnificent notes in challenge to the sunny colours of Vico Hill. Dermot caught his breath. No more, this year. That was all over. They had had their week at Delgany. This was the last proper time they would have of Con.

> *"Nor soon shall the tears of his country be dried,*
> *Nor long will his love stay behind him."*

Oh, would there ever be any escape from a world of good-byes! Why was everything so capriciously ordered that happiness could only last for a little at a time, and then one must be dragged away, protesting, looking backward, and flung into adversity? Home wasn't adversity—but school, the big new school? Why, this day fortnight, he would have been there several days already! Hold, hold on to the precious minutes. The chill will soon be stealing up from the grass, the sun will have sunk behind the trees. Con will stretch himself, and have to go. He has stayed away from evening church, already, as it's our last time, and he couldn't get down earlier, because of visitors at Delgany. Hold on, hold on.

The song ceased, and all three sat silent, watching the sun go down. For the two children, another golden day was added to the store that warmed them through the year. Con, when they were gone, would spend his Saturdays in racing and reliability trials, till the weather got too bad. On Sundays, he would play with other children, or go off for the day with Eileen, his favourite sister. Dermot and Eithne knew about the other children, but could not realise them. Con was so much a being of their world that they could not believe he did not hibernate until they came again.

"Well, childher—" He got up, and stretched his mighty frame, suddenly, and for no reason, putting a fist as large as a ham an inch from Dermot's nose. "Smell that! D'ye hear me? Smell that!"

He laughed, and let all his muscles go slack.

"Ye're goin'—when? Monda'—to-morrow week. And I'm off on Frida'." The good-natured creature had put off his own holiday, so as not to disappoint them. "But ye're comin' up on Thursda'? Y'are? Ah, well. Sure we don't have to say good-bye yet. We have a bit of divarsion in front of us still."

A bit of divarsion, yes, one bit, still. Divarsion so late, so final, as to be almost heartrending. The last bit of divarsion. Eithne clung tight to his arm, as they went slowly up the garden. He had to duck, laughing, under each pergola.

It was a fine bit of divarsion when it came, but dearly bought. A farewell visit to Dalkey Island, exploring round the fort, making faces at the goats, building a little cairn "till we all come again next year"; an afternoon so serene, so lovely that the promise seemed real, and they left in good spirits, already seeing ahead to the joys which should be theirs when they returned to dismantle the cairn and find the written message to themselves, signed with their three names, buried underneath it. The chill fell once or twice after that, the sudden sick weight on the heart, but feverishly they kept it at bay, till dinner-time. Then, as though to cheer them up, and make a laughing matter of the departure, the whole family from time to time uttered a kind of chant. "Aaah—aaah! the last meal till next year": which became, in Con's ferocious utterance, "Aaaaaaah! The last meal ye'll ever eat." This, which they received at first with laughter, grew too much for them. To the dismay of the company, Eithne's face suddenly puckered, and she slid out of sight under the table, to hide the bitterness of her sorrow.

There was a reaction after that, of course, and they left hilariously—not by tram, as usual, but in the sidecar: a last treat.

"We'll go a bit of a round home," explained Con. "Sure we've lots of time. We won't take longer than the walk and the tram."

The pair were clad in half the overcoats the house could muster, and sped off with happy cries. A ride under the full moon! Never had that happened before. Up Vico Road they sped, past houses washed pale in the moonlight, past secret, mysterious, smiling trees: along the while ribbon of road, under the great shadow of the hill, down, down between cool woods smelling of pine-needles, out on the levels beside the sea: past Ballybrack Station, past Brian's house: Brian, a married man now, settled in Killiney: inland then, through hedges grey in the moonlight, through sleepy, twinkling Loughlinstown, all strange and different at night, round by the big tree, and along the flat road home.

"Good night, Dermot boy. Good-bye. Good luck to ye at your new school. You'll write and tell me how you get on. Oh, sure, you'll get on all right. Good-bye. We had great divarsion, didn't we? Oh, but nothing to what we'll have next year, please God."

Dermot stood for a minute, waiting for Eithne. Then, suddenly wiser, he went in by himself.

CHAPTER XXX

Dᴇʀᴍᴏᴛ ᴀɴᴅ ᴘᴀᴅᴅʏ ᴡᴀʟᴋᴇᴅ ᴇᴀɢᴇʀʟʏ ᴜᴘ ᴛʜᴇ ꜱʟᴏᴘᴇ ᴛʜᴀᴛ led to the Forty Foot, Dermot holding the moist shillings in the palm of his hand. The slope was decorated with strips of bunting, which accorded strangely with its bare, forbidding rocks. Crowds were ascending it, gaily dressed crowds, ladies and girls treading where ladies and girls were permitted to tread once only in the year. Their unaccustomed voices and laughter rang happily up the steep walls and echoed back from the fat Martello Tower, above the bathing pool. Down Sandycove Avenue in a steady stream, past the little white dusty harbour, and up the rock they came, peopling its summer somnolence with footsteps, colour, and voices: while here and there a scarlet-coated bandsman, clasping some large instrument, added a vivid splash of colour for the eye, and promised as vivid music for the ear.

It was the afternoon of the Forty Foot Swimming Gala. This took place early in August, and Dermot never missed it. Now, having spent a year at a public school, and discovered that he could swim better than the average, he was madly keen on swimming and all to do with it: resolved to concentrate on his new ambition, to swim one day for his house, or even, possibly, long hence, for the school. Till this year, he had watched a spectacle. To-day, he would be a novice, receiving instruction in a mystery.

The love of boys for any form of athletics, and their veneration of the athlete, is a sound and natural thing: and those leaders are ill-advised who try to combat it. The

270

boy proceeds from enthusiasm to enthusiasm, and it is bad
psychology to try and force his transition from one phase to
another. All that is necessary is that the materials for his
successive enthusiasms should be within his reach, so that,
when he outgrows one, he may pass on easily to the next.
Athletics (or anything else) only become dangerous when
there is nothing to succeed them: when a boy's elders all
maintain with their prestige the same stage of arrested
development, and, by implication, disparage all further
stages. If, however, a boy must worship for a long time at one
altar only, it is hard to think of a better one than the altar
of skilled physical prowess. To play cricket or golf, to box
or swim, is an art. It demands sacrifices and incessant
practice. It requires a sound technique. Great artists in
this kind deserve more approbation from other artists than
they commonly receive, but that is because, as with some
musicians and many actors, the practice of their art has
taught them nothing outside it; they remain inarticulate
and undeveloped. So, fittingly, from the inarticulate and
undeveloped they receive their deepest worship. Pursuing
always a practical, tangible end—to strike more swiftly,
more accurately, or to cut a second off their time—they
exemplify in the simplest possible way the doctrine that
man is here to overcome difficulty and to perfect his powers:
and if there is a better lesson than that, the schools have yet
to find it.

When Paddy and Dermot reached the bathing pool, they
found that, as usual, rows and rows of chairs had been set
on the platforms and flatter portions of the rock. These
were filling rapidly. All the more precarious perches had
been filled long since by boys whose tickets entitled them to
any place of vantage except a chair. A few even sat with
their legs dangling from the edges of the diving boards;
but this was not considered a good position, as they had to
"come off ou' o' that" when the diving began, and huddle
upright against the rock as best they might, squeezing back

to let the wet bodies pass. Dermot's cousin, Desmond—younger son of the O'Dowda—was competing in the diving. He had blossomed out suddenly into one of the most expert divers on the coast, and taken seven first prizes the year before. The experts, swimmers and divers alike, attended every gala within their range. This was not from pot-hunting motives. They were favourites with the crowd, and their absence would be fatal to the gate.

A steward with a rosette showed the two to their chairs, and there was a burst of affectionate derision as some of Paddy's cronies recognised him from the "free rock" opposite. The Forty Foot authorities could only enclose the actual pool. The rocks outside it, commanding almost as good a view as the dearest seats, were black with all the ragamuffins in Kingstown.

"Ay, Wingman."

"Yeeow!"

"Ay, Paddy. What the hell a' you doin' there?"

Paddy waved at them—not too ostentatiously, for other occupants of the seats were showing faint signs of scandal.

"Oho," he muttered sardonically, "belt away, me lads. Belt away."

"Look," said Dermot, "there's Long Mike."

"Where?"

"There. Down near the water's edge."

"Oh, be the holy. Yes. I see'm. He'll have to come up ou' of' that, with the tide risin'."

As they watched, they saw Mike look up and apparently remonstrate with some boys on the rock above him, who were throwing down bits of seaweed. The boys grinned. Presently one of them, leaning over, aimed a winkle.

"I mind," said Paddy, "one day, on that rock, when the gala was on, there was a big boat passed close by, and the wash of her came up and gave them fellas on that rock a quare lick. A quare lick, it gave them."

"Were you there?"

"I was above. I do be always watchful for the tide. There's always some lads forgets that, and gets cot."

A few more minutes, and the band struck up. The Forty Foot Committee had every reason to congratulate themselves on the day. It was a glorious afternoon, the sea was calm, and they had a wonderful concourse of swimmers to amuse a record crowd.

The programme began with the usual club handicaps, for which none of the stars were entered. Yet even these lesser swimmers Dermot watched with envy. Even the outside handicap starters, those who leaped in at the word "go," were far faster, far more accomplished than he. Race after race he watched, all much alike, all serving to whet the appetite for the great events of the day, which should show the marvellous powers of the three best swimmers in Ireland. Dillon, Murray, and Mahony—with monotonous regularity the three finished first, second, third in every open event for which they entered. Murray you would pick out from any crowd of starters as a winner: a huge, genial, grinning man, with the deep chest and long arms of a giant. When one saw him in the water, it seemed inconceivable that any human being could travel faster. Mahony, too, was a fine big man, more of the swimmer's build, with flesh on him. But Dillon, who by some actual miracle did travel faster than either, was not remarkable in a crowd of athletes. He was muscular and well developed, but no judge of form on dry land would put him before the other two, or before many another splendid big athlete who had come to try his arm. Dermot had seen the three many times. He had seen them clean up all three places in the Open Quarter: he had seen them, individually, win a score of races: he had seen Dillon carry off the Hundred by a second from Haynes the Scotsman, beating the Amateur Record to that date. But neither he nor anyone else saw Dillon swim such a race as he swam that day, in the Two Hundred Yards Handicap which closed the meeting.

The Diving went off beautifully, according to plan. The star of those days, beginning already to wane, was a little pleasant man named Coldwell. A consistent and practised diver, with twenty years of success behind him, and a name for diving from all the most spectacular eminences along the coast, he was being challenged by the younger generation, and just managing to hold his own. This time, he had to be content with a second in the Standing Headers. One after another, in tense stillness, over the semicircular pit of upturned faces, the lonely figures walked to the end of the board, hesitated, stood poised, then rose in the air like birds, curving away downwards in a perfect arc, entering the water with hardly a splash, and reappearing almost before their twin feet had gone under. So high was the level that when any left the board ungracefully, or splashed with so much as an instep at fault, a kind of angry sigh went up from the crowd. Failure they would deride openly: not from cruelty, but because no one who was not a first class diver had any business to compete in such a show. In the end, the prize was won by a swarthy, tall, imperturbable man named M'Guinness. Desmond O'Dowda, after an extra dive, was awarded third.

"He's quare'n' souple, yeer cousin," commented Paddy. "Quare'n' souple."

He always said this. Certain ideas were linked together in Paddy's mind in a way that would delight those gentlemen who wish, at a moderate fee, to improve our memories for us. He could never think of one part of these composite associations without remembering, and proclaiming, the rest. In the same way, each rock along the coast had a story attached to it, permanently, as a part of its reality. Past and present co-existed in Paddy's mind. The new experience did not displace the old: it was just added to it. Paddy had but one scene, the landscape of the only place he had inhabited. He would go on filling it in, to the day of his death, adding more names and more ideas to the map, devoting to it the full force of a mind and a memory that had no burden and no distractions outside the range of immediate physical experience.

"Here th' come," cried Paddy eagerly. "Here th' come."

Chattering, laughing self-consciously, hugging their arms, shivering, hopping on their toes, the swimmers were coming down for the last race. There was a big crowd of them. It was half a minute before the great ones could be discerned, at the back of all: those who would have to stand at the top of the steps, and watch coolly the others leap in, one after another, till the sea was full of heads, of thrashing arms and feet, till there seemed no hope of catching even the nearest of those fast receding racers. M'Gulligan, Beatty, O'Dea: the onlookers ticked them off in whispers: Murray, Mahony, together, talking to one another, Murray grinning: a gap: then—Ah! a murmur ran round the packed mass: Dillon himself, holding his arms, quiet, aloof, looking no-where, seeing nobody. They gazed in awe at the famous and legendary figure. The fastest swimmer in Ireland! Swam in th' Olympic Games, agen a bloody big Swede! There—that man. Him.

Suddenly, before anyone but the first starters realised, the race had begun.

"A' ye ready? Get ready! Go!"

Crash! A solitary swimmer dived in and was making his way purposefully outwards. Four laps of fifty yards . . . "Three! Four! Five!"—two more joined him in the water— "Seven! Eight!"—then it became almost comic, for at every number one or two or three swimmers plunged in. The water was all broken. It was full of heads and foam.

"Forty-one! Forty-two! Forty-three!"

The splashes were fewer now. There were only four men left. Dillon moved slowly down the steps. Exquisitely, magnificently self-conscious, he looked away out to sea, to the horizon, taking no notice of the proceedings.

"Fifty!"

Crash! In went Mahony.

"Fifty-two!"

Murray shot forward like a great thunderbolt of flesh, and was yards out before one could gasp, his head under water, his great arms thrashing, his feet waving faintly on the surface. Astonishing to relate, Murray did not kick. He used his feet only for steering.

Dillon was alone. Slowly he leaned forward, and stretched out his arms from his sides. The first starters had finished one lap, and were heading inshore again. Oh, it was impossible that he—

"Fifty-eight!"

The tense body flung itself at the water like a stone from a catapult, and began, with an icy, controlled fury, to tear its way across the strait between it and the others. Cries, shudders of awe rose from the onlookers. This was not a man, but a projectile. When he passed the first incoming swimmer, he had halved the distance between Murray and himself. Then he was lost in a welter of heads and red thrashing arms. The crowd groaned angrily, to see such speed frustrated by the mere impenetrable mob of swimmers. But Dillon was not lost. Half way in, they caught sight of him again, no longer the last, nor near the last, tearing his way along, dodging in and out through the swimmers like an otter, but still impossibly far behind the leaders.

"Good man, Dillon! Stick to it! Good man! Good man!"

A roar of encouragement rose as he touched the steps, and was off again on his heroic, hopeless chase. The spectators sank back into their seats.

"Jasus," breathed Paddy, "there's a gait o' goin'!"

Dermot barely heard him. His nails were gripped into the sweating palms of his hands, and he breathed as if he too were racing. Then, suddenly, the crowd began to stir. Ludicrous, preposterous though it was—if he kept on like this —But no. He could never get through the mass of competitors. He—Yes! Look! Bedam, but there *was* a chance! There was just the outside edge of the cat's whisker of a bloody, immortal chance!

A murmur rose, fell to silence: rose again, and burst out suddenly into a roar. The bewitched, demoniac apparition of the swimmer was thrashing on, faster than ever, threading his way in and out through the brown heads like a needle through a sack. He reached the turn, and came back on the last lap. There were twenty in front of him; the furthest of them was already half way home. Oh, begod, begod, begod! The crowd was on its feet, yelling, clenching fists, beating downward with stiff arms, sending out the might of a thousand aching wills to animate those flail-like arms, those steel-spring thighs, with the last necessary superhuman burst of power. In he came, clawing the yards away, flinging them behind him, passing swimmers as if they were standing still. Twenty-five yards to go—twenty—fifteen—he's certain of a place—he's up—he's blocked—a twist, a leap in the foam, the flash of an outstretched hand—By God, he's HOME!

A yell arose, an explosion, a sheer flame of sound, that sent up every gull within two miles. Strangers turned, laughing enthusiastically, and caught strangers by the arm, shaking hands, punching them, tears of joy running down their faces. Then all leaned forward to roar blessings on the tired, white figure, as it pulled itself up slowly by the hand-rail, and climbed the steps, looking old and dazed. Two officious stewards bustled down, barging the crowds aside, and took each an arm. After a few yards, he disengaged himself with a smile, and straightened up. The marvellous vitality asserted itself again. When he reached the dressing room, safely out of sight of all the adoring girls and women, he sat down, and belched loudly, three times. It had cost him a great deal of inconvenience not to belch before, but he felt he owed it to the little green shamrock embroidered on the breast of his costume. As it happened, his scruples were unnecessary. The crowd were cheering so loudly that a salvo of belches would have passed unheard.

"Well, begod,' said a man behind Paddy and Dermot, as they went down to the harbour, "Say what ye will, whatever they give'm for that, he earned it.''

IT WAS ONLY NATURAL THAT, AS TIME WENT ON DERMOT should be less and less with Paddy. The Sea Wall belonged definitely to the past. An occasional hunt for a conger was all it could hope. Any fishing the two did now was in Kingstown Harbour. They fished for flatfish off the steps above the bandstand: they fished for pollack, smelts, and whiting from the mailboat pier. But now that Dermot spent most of every morning at the open air swimming baths, and Paddy had to put in three afternoons a week at his occupation as cleaner to the schools, the two had less chance to bear one another company. Dermot was experiencing the strange feeling which comes to all who mentally outgrow a companion: the uneasy sense of disloyalty, the self accusation, and, in Dermot's case, the fear of being thought snobbish, which had always troubled him since his meeting with the schoolmaster and the boys. He was as fond of Paddy as ever, but being with Paddy no longer satisfied him. An afternoon or an evening now and then he could look forward to: but a whole day palled. The Loughlinstown Walk had become a difficult engagement to fulfil. Paddy, with nothing to do but talk, became a burden before they reached Ballybrack. Dermot was at just the wrong age. A grown man would have asked nothing better than to provoke Paddy's tongue to comment and reminiscence. Dermot thought he had heard it all, and Paddy, conscious of a constraint somewhere, sought to ease it by volubly disinterring the past. The Dublin types whom Dermot met through Con seemed to him more interesting, because of their novelty: he could imitate Paddy in his sleep, and forecast, with high accuracy, in what terms or with what precise imprecation he would greet any given event. The fact had to be faced. Paddy, as guide, philosopher, and friend, was outmoded. This, Dermot obscurely felt, was fair and reasonable: but he looked back on his life, and saw it as a series of supersessions, his toy monkey superseded by Paddy-monkey, Paddy-monkey superseded by Paddy Kennedy, Paddy Kennedy now superseded by—whom? Did it matter? Looking back, he felt old, and faithless. He could not help changing, but felt the necessity as a weakness in his nature. Con was his idol: but he could not worship even Con in everything. In one or two ways, he felt older than Con. Was there something wrong with him, he wondered, something incurably shallow, which would prevent his ever being wholly faithful to anyone? He was neither wholly in his parents' camp, nor in Delgany—though far, far more in Delgany: not wholly anywhere. That had always been the trouble: as on the far distant but remembered occasion when he had taken the housemaid's part against his Mother, because the housemaid was in the right. That was an attitude not praised anywhere in life, that he could find. At school, you had to be all for your house, all for your school. In religion, you had (like the Delgany people) to be all for God. "He that is not with me," as Con so frequently repeated with emphasis, "is against me." Dermot seemed fated always to seek a place somewhere in the middle. He had never been able to believe any institution absolutely right, and he did not see how he was going to be either a complete free-thinker, like his father—a position growing daily less attractive to him; or an out and out believer like Con. He wanted to believe: but it was so difficult. Con and Eileen did not make it any easier. His father's arguments, which seemed to Dermot so convincing, which he had so often used at school, to the consternation or delight of his audience, simply slid off Delgany. If only Con and Eileen would answer them, smash them to smithereens, how happy he would be! But they would not answer them. They would not even admit that there was anything to answer. Dermot could not resist the treasonous thought that they did not answer them, simply because they did not understand: that their steadfastness was, from an intellectual point of view, the courage of those who do not realise danger. He suffered acutely from this. *They* said that reason should never be applied to faith: that to use it so was the temptation for reason, just as to get drunk was the temptation for thirst. And yet, to Dermot, reason seemed essential. While he brooded, circumstance took a hand.

It was a Saturday, fine, shining after early rain. Eileen was playing in a tennis tournament. Con and Dermot were to take her to Bray in the machine, and suit themselves whether they stayed to watch, or went off into the mountains and picked her up on their way home. They were starting early, for she had discovered that she must get a new pair of stockings, which meant making a long detour by the city.

"Good luck to ye, now!"

Aunt Patricia stood waving vaguely on the steps. Her family all played games passionately, but she hardly knew which game they were going out to play, or what result to enquire for when they came home.

"Thank you, Mummy darling! Go on in now, and don't be standing there getting your death."

Aunt Patricia looked startled, for the air was warm and gentle. Then she smiled wanly, recognising one of the many sayings of her own which her irreverent offspring delighted to turn against her.

"Oh," she said, "ye're a nice lot."

The roar of the engine drowned her voice, and she went in, still smiling, and shaking her head. She had a great deal to put up with, and much enjoyed putting up with it.

The roads were greasy, and Con, worming his way along

the tramlines, commented freely on the vanity and lack of foresight which made the detour necessary. Eileen replied with equanimity, finally slanging him in such vigorous Dublin that he grinned, and began treating the expedition as a game, whisking round the broad behinds of the trams, and sounding his horn at old women with shawls over their heads, who turned to curse, but broke reluctantly into smiles at sight of the good-natured handsome face laughing into their own. A slight skid, however, made him serious again: for, despite his impetuosity in other respects, Con was a very careful driver.

The stockings were bought, and soon they were making comfortable way along the Rock Road towards the scene of the tournament. For a while all three shouted happy conversation together, but gradually, oppressed by some strange uneasiness, they grew silent. Con made a few remarks, to try and lift the cloud: Eileen answered him shortly at first, then not at all. There was no possible reason to be seen for discomfort, yet it seemed to drop upon them from the trees, to reverberate back with their own echoes from the walls. Cursing softly to himself, Con slowed down, and proceeded with great care, almost in the gutter.

Suddenly he turned his face, and they saw that the sweat was standing on his forehead.

"I've felt this way before," he said, forcing a laugh.

"When was that?" asked Eileen.

"Down on the sands."

Dermot knew what he meant. It was on the sands near Portmarnock, where he raced.

"It was just before a bad smash," continued Con. "So, fuss or no fuss, I'm going to be on the safe side."

"You'll be in the ditch, if you go any closer," retorted Eileen, also forcing a laugh.

Con smiled, but he kept his way, bending intently forward, watching the road, and hooting tremendously before every turning. They bowled temperately along a straight

half mile, at the end of which loomed a pair of high stone
gateposts, the entrance to a drive. Immediately past them,
the road curved off to the right. As they were nearing the
end, they became aware of the roar of a powerful bicycle
behind them.

"Indian," said Con at once. He bent forward, hesitated,
then swung a rapid glance backwards. The pursuer, tearing
along at a tremendous pace, was three hundred yards behind. Con looked ahead at the gates, and calculated swiftly
that they would both arrive there at about the same time.
He hesitated, wrinkled up his face, and with sudden resolve
switched off the engine.

"What—" cried Eileen, raising herself in the sidecar:
but the roar of the approaching engine drowned her voice.
They were fifty yards from the gates. Acting upon another
impulse, Con put on the brakes. Though the speed was
nothing, the combination skidded slightly; the wheel of the
sidecar hit the grass edge of the ditch, and they stopped with
a bump, leaving the Indian a clear road. With a shattering
roar, he was up and past them: two riders, one behind on
the carrier. What happened then, they never knew. Maybe
the driver suddenly realised that the corner was sharper
than he thought, and tried to brake: maybe he tried to get
round as he was. The three horrified watchers saw the great
scarlet machine suddenly falter, and then shoot with the
speed of a shell smack into the second of the two stone pillars.
The driver struck the stone head on: his head burst, like a
tomato thrown at a wall. In an instant, there was nothing
but a wrecked machine and two motionless forms beside it.
One thing only moved: something red, dripping from the
gatepost.

For a few seconds the three sat, unable to move. They
simply could not believe their eyes. The thing had happened
in a flash. At one instant, two young men riding on a motor
bicycle: at the next instant, this. Dermot shut his eyes. He
was dreaming. When he opened them, there would be nothing

there. He opened them, but the horror was still there. A red pool was beginning to spread from the first crumpled shape.

With a groan, Con got off, and went forward. He said nothing, but kept waving a hand behind him, motioning Eileen not to follow. Very white, she climbed out of the sidecar, and went after him. A moment's hesitation, and Dermot followed.

Con reached the huddled shapes. His face had turned an indescribable colour, as if it were going to burst, and he was breathing loudly through his nose. He did not concern himself with the first figure, but bent over the pillion rider, and with infinite caution pulled at one of the lapels of his coat. Then, abruptly, he straightened up.

"He's alive, poor devil," he said, in a startled voice. For a moment he stood, staring at Eileen, the unnatural colour slowly draining from his face. "He's alive," he repeated, as they came closer. "What can we do?"

Trying to keep their eyes from the smashed, split thing a yard or two away, they came, and looked down on the survivor. He was obviously in a very bad way. Blood was trickling from one of his ears: his face was almost plum colour, and his chest seemed somehow to be crushed. He breathed slowly with a laboured, snoring sound.

"Couldn't we lift him in—or something."

Feeling themselves ineffectual and helpless, they stooped, and tried to raise the man's head. Though clearly unconscious, he groaned, and they desisted in something like panic.

"I wish I knew—"

Con, pale and anguished, stood, his legs wide apart, his great hands hanging down by his sides. Eileen looked into his face. Then, startling them into action, came the welcome sound of a car from the opposite direction. With a grasp of relief, Con bounded out into the roadway, holding up his hands.

The driver of the car slowed, saw the mess, swerved, and pulled up. He and a companion came running back.

"Still alive—this chap—he may have a chance—"

"Yes, yes."

The stranger, a dark middle-aged man with a black moustache, assented to Con's hurried explanation, and bent over the survivor. He examined him briefly, and pursed up his lips.

"No good, I'm *afraid*," he said, with a queer emphasis. "Still, if you'll help me into the car with him, I'll rush him to the nearest doctor. There's one a mile down the road. What the—?"

They all started, for a horrible hollow retching sound broke out behind them. Turning, they saw the stranger's companion staggering away to the roadside, trying to be sick. He had unwisely gone on to inspect the second victim.

The stranger swore at him, then stooped with Con to lift the living man. Eileen hastily made a bed of rugs, and together they laid him in the back of the car.

"Are you staying there, or coming with me?" called the stranger to his friend, callously.

"I'm—I'm all right now."

"Lep in, so."

The poor man made haste to climb in, giving Con a pitiful smile as he did so.

"Thanks. I'll get on quick. Sorry, but I must leave you to—"

He nodded towards the gatepost. The car jerked forward, collected itself, and shot off at a high speed. They stood, watching it go. It left the road very empty and very still. Almost lovingly they watched it out of sight, for no one could wish to turn round and face what lay there still untended.

Con and Eileen looked in each other's eyes. They did not speak. Then, with a single movement, they turned and went straight to the dead man.

Seeing them go, Dermot looked too. The sight was not really horrible, from where he was, for it did not look human.

That queer red spongy thing—was it a part of his face—what was it? He took a step forward, to see better; but the two cried out sharply to him to stay where he was. They were stooping over the shape. Eileen was down on one knee, beside the end that looked like its head.

The ground began to sway under Dermot, and the sky went dark, and the breeze on his forehead felt extraordinarily cold. This was the sort of thing he had always dreaded, yet half wanted to see. Better test himself. Better not be a coward.

"I'd better see, you know," he said steadily, and forced his feet one in front of the other. "I'd better see, don't you think." I'm not a child now, he was going to add, when Eileen looked up at him, and he stopped, transfixed by the extraordinary beauty of her face. It was still with exaltation and pity, like an angel's.

"Dermot," she said, "will you please get me my parcel out of the sidecar?"

He gazed at her. His lips opened three times before the words came.

"Th—the stockings?"

"Yes. Would you, please?"

He turned stupidly round, and went to the sidecar. She is keeping her voice calm for my benefit, he said to himself, because she is afraid I will break down. Here—the sidecar. Yes. In there. That is it. There. The stockings.

He took the parcel, and walked across to Eileen, keeping his eyes fixed upon her face.

"Here it is."

He gave it into her hand, and stood, still gazing at her.

"Now am I to go away again?"

"I think it would be better." She looked up at him, and saw his face, set and luminous. "Do as you like, Dermot boy," she said.

So Dermot stayed. Without horror, without fear, he saw her take out the new white stockings and with them bind together the shattered pieces that had been a head, winding them round and round, covering the poor unseemly ruin from casual eyes. When, at last, they came to lift him from the ground, Dermot saw that the top part of his body was crushed like a concertina. White splinters stuck through the dark wet bundle, and he realised, with academic surprise, that they were splinters of bone.

"One minute."

They laid him down again, and Con went over to the machine. From the back of the carrier he unstripped a roll, which proved to be a mackintosh ground sheet. Another minute, and they had tenderly rolled the dead man into it.

He looked strange and ungainly, when at last he was seated in the sidecar. The groundsheet was draped about his head and shoulders, and a corner of it stuck grotesquely forward, like a snout. Suddenly, Dermot thought of the Elephant's Child.

"I won't be long," said Con. They were talking, instinctively, almost in whispers.

"Do you know where to—"

"Yes."

The machine started up, and set off slowly down the road. Dermot and Eileen sat on a green bank. They felt tired, and shaky at the knees. Neither spoke. Dermot lifted up his face to a shaft of sun that came hot through the trees, and Eileen dreamily plucked at the grass by her side.

A car had come, and stopped. Eileen was speaking.

"There's been an accident," she repeated. "No, no. We're all right. One of the men has been taken off in a car, and my brother has taken the one who was killed. Yes. He's coming back for us. No, thanks. It's awfully good of you. Quite sure, thanks."

A second car stopped, and another. News of the accident had spread, and people, eager for excitement, began to arrive on foot.

"Here," said Eileen in a low voice, after the fifth or sixth explanation, "this is getting too much of a good thing. I vote we go on to meet Con."

Dermot glanced at the front of her frock and coat.

"You can't, very well, like that," he said. "Everyone'll stop you, just the same."

She looked down, and made a wry face. Then, catching his eye, she burst out laughing.

"The chance of a lifetime, for some of these chaps," she said, "to try and help a damsel in distress. I think we'll go on, all the same. You feel all right, don't you?" she added, with real concern.

"Perfectly all right, thanks."

With Eileen, as long as she felt all right, he knew he would feel all right anywhere.

"Come on, then."

They turned to go. Already a little crowd was standing round the wrecked machine and staring fascinated at the pool of blood.

"A' ye sure ye're all right to go on, now? A' ye sure—"

"Quite sure, thanks."

"Ah, I'd wait, miss. I'd wait a bit, till ye'd feel more steadier in yerself."

"Dig ye see what happened?" A big man, with a wet open mouth, fastened on Dermot. "Dig ye see—"

"Yes," he answered, with rising distaste. At once, three or four gathered round him.

"Ye seen it happen, is it? Ye seen it yerself?"

"How was it?"

"Eh, young lad?"

"What way was it, young fella?"

"Did he go full puck into the wall?"

A firm hand took his arm, and he saw it was Eileen's.

"Come on, Dermot. Will you let us pass, please? Thank you."

They walked on, leaving a murmur of surprise behind them. The road was getting full. People were running. As they caught sight of Eileen's frock and arms, their faces lit up with unholy eagerness. One after another, Dermot saw them decide to stop her, and fail at the last moment. The hand on his arm was tense and quivering. Stealing a glance at her face, he saw that it was set in a strange, cold smile.

Suddenly, to their relief, they caught sight of Con, making his way back in a veritable stream of traffic. He was very pale, but he grinned as he saw them coming.

"Thank the Lord," said Eileen, grinning back, as she jumped into the sidecar. "Here, son. Hop on, quick."

"I'll go on, and round. Quicker than going back."

Facing round once more to the scene of the smash, they saw that a small crowd had actually been following them down the road.

"Hey! Hey! Hey!"

Con sounded his horn and bellowed, as he approached the gates, and the crowd in the road jumped and scooted to either side. As they passed, Dermot, out of the corner of his eye, saw a man wiping the gatepost with a bit of newspaper. He called something over his shoulder as he did so, and grinned, the sun flashing on his teeth. Then they were gone.

As soon as they had got well away, on a side road, they pulled up, and sat on a sunny bank, facing the sea. Con wanted to "steady down," as he expressed it, before driving any further.

For a while they sat, looking out on the calm expanse of Killiney Bay. The sound of the breakers, sleepy and forgetful, came lazily to their ears. They ranged in series down the long curve of the strand, falling heaviest in front of the three, a little to their left, and passing gently down, like the slow opening of a vast blue fan with snowy edges.

The sun was hot. Eileen took off her mackintosh. The peace and warmth of it all made what had happened seem a nightmare. Only the stains on Eileen's frock attested to its reality. Even so, their avoidance of the subject was artificial, and they were glad when Con re-opened it.

"Thank God I pulled up," he said.

Dermot rolled over on to his stomach. He had been thinking about this very point.

"You mean that we would have been near the gates, and made it harder for them to turn?" he said.

"I mean a lot more," retorted Con, looking at him. "Do—"

"I thought you meant you'd be feeling perhaps to blame for the smash, if you'd been near," countered Dermot quickly, determined to get his thought out.

Con nodded impatiently.

"There's that too," he said, "and thank the Lord we've nothing like that on our minds. But we might very likely have no minds left for it to be on."

"No minds—?"

"Don't you realise that, if we'd carried on at the pace we were going, they'd have gone slap into us?"

CHAPTER XXXII

WE ARE PROUD OF OUR LOYALTIES, YET MOST OF THEM ARE determined by pure accident. The influence of a place or person is enough to range the majority of mankind under the green, the red, or any other banner. A cast in childhood, an angle of approach once learned, persuades the intellect to work in a given way, and exalt above all others a single facet of experience. When the loyalty is helped by a genuine antipathy to what appears to be on the other side, conversion can be violent.

The death of the two cyclists would not have been enough to make Dermot believe in the all-seeing providence of the Almighty, because the matter did not seem as simple to him as to the folk at Delgany. To assume that the two young men had met their end because they were irreligious, and that Con, Eileen, and he had been preserved for the contrary reason, seemed a little too easy. Doubts intruded; and he much resented his father's commentary on the accident, since it stated, forcibly and without reverence, his own secret feeling. While he wavered, circumstance again took charge, and saw to it that he made up his mind.

A joint expedition to the theatre in Dublin, light-heartedly proposed by Uncle Ben, was accepted by Walmer Villa for want of an excuse. The two parties did not mix well as a rule, and had few tastes in common: but there was a musical comedy running, *The Count of Luxemburg*, of which everyone spoke well, and Granny had not visited a theatre for years. Accordingly, after some misgivings, the Grays decided that the jaunt might be very pleasant for all concerned.

Only Grandpapa stood out. Wild horses, he declared, should not force him to enter a theatre at his age.

"And I wonder, Amelia," he added severely, "you to have no more sense."

The old lady looked across at him, the happiness fading from her face. It had taken them some time to persuade her.

"Well, now, maybe you're right, Alfred. I think I'd better stay."

"No, no, no backing out now, Granny. You've promised to come."

"If you don't go, *I* won't go. So there, Granny."

"Well, sure, I don't know . . ." She looked round, smiling vaguely on them all. Grandpapa got up, folding his paper.

"Ah, faith," he said. "You're all of a mind. You're all of a mind. I'd best leave you and me old woman together."

He paused by the door, chuckling with sardonic good-humour.

"A theatre, indeed," he said. "Why, the next thing, you'll want to be going to a dance."

So it was all settled, and the seats booked—nine of them, all in a row; parterre seats, close to the stage, so that Granny should see the faces and the dresses. A full three days before, Mr. Gray was up at Delgany, trying to organise the going-in and the getting-out-again. He returned to Walmer Villa, frowning at the Delgany lack of business sense. Only the most casual attention, he protested: nothing definite at all. "What's the hurry?" had been the best he could get out of them. Dermot saw perfectly well what had happened. The Delgany folk, delighted at "poor Ernest's fussing," had purposely withheld information. Nor could Mr. Gray get any from them, save a curt message, on the morning of the day itself, that the theatre train left at seven-twenty-five.

That evening was one which might well have been inscribed in the annals of Mr. Pooter. Con, who left the message, omitted to add that the theatre train, so called, was usually late, that most theatre goers did not trust it, and that

the Delgany contingent was travelling by tram. Little
imagination is needed to picture the state of Mr. Gray,
realising for half an hour that they would all be late, and
dumped finally, five minutes after the rise of the curtain,
some little distance from a theatre to which he did not know
the way. They were in their seats at sixteen minutes past,
met with unrepentant grins, and whispered expressions of
surprise at their late arrival. The only unruffled person was
poor Granny. Her eyes, from the first second, were fixed
upon the stage; and once she got her breath back, she proceeded to enjoy the piece whole-heartedly. Even Mr. Gray
presently forgot his anger, or put it into safe keeping till
afterwards.

> *"You and I, just we two*
> *Girl and boy, one hour of joy . . ."*

The rich voice of Bertram Wallis floated out into the
theatre, comforting them all, lulling them with its sense of
after-dinner romance. The production was a sumptuous one
for Dublin, as the company and most of the principals had
been imported immediately the London run was over.
Granny loved it all—but her favourite was Horace Mills,
the comedian. "'Is it necessary?'" she kept quoting, days
and days afterwards, from his song which, among other
matters, hit so neatly at "that horrid" Lloyd George.
It was an evening Dermot long remembered, apart from its
preliminary discomforts. It came back to him time and
again as a picture from a life which had vanished for ever.

"Disgustingly casual, and downright thoughtless," Mr.
Gray repeated, gazing round indignantly on his audience.
"Your Granny here, dragged about, and hurried from
pillar to post—to say nothing of our missing the first quarter
of an hour. After all, they know the place. This is their
town; and the whole outing was undertaken at their suggestion. They give me to understand that they are going in
by the theatre train—"

"They said the theatre train went at seven-twenty-five," put in Dermot. "They didn't say they were going by it."

"A mere quibble," snorted his father. "Of course, I naturally took it to mean that they intended to travel by it. How else was I—why, I didn't even know the way to the theatre. They knew we were utterly dependent on them."

An ugly little smile came across Dermot's mouth.

"Con said, since you were so particular, he made sure you'd have gone beforehand and drawn a map of the way."

Mr. Gray was so indignant he could hardly speak.

"If that's the way he looks at it, then, let me tell you, I don't think the better of him. Nor of you, for listening to him." He paused, and swallowed. "I might have known that, right or wrong, you'd side against your parents."

"It was for Granny's sake we were angry," put in his mother, more quietly. "It was thoughtless of them not to remember her."

"They made sure Daddy would have found it all out for himself," protested Dermot. "Even Aunt Patricia said they would none of them dare to make arrangements for *him*."

"I? I was in their hands entirely. This is their town . . . the expedition undertaken at their suggestion. . . ."

"We won't argue about it any more," said Dermot's mother. "Though, I must say, I am sorry to see you always against your parents."

Dermot's face contracted with irritation.

"It's all so silly," he said, and went out of the room. He did not tell them he had been arguing their side at Delgany, and been derided for his pains. The net result of it all was, quite unfairly, to increase his resentment against his father, for having put him in so inconvenient a position.

He was in this frame of mind when his father decided to take him on a trip round Ireland. Every year Mr. Gray combined business with pleasure by visiting a number of his firm's clients who lived in out of the way parts of Ireland. In consideration of these visits, he received a longer holiday.

He had wished for some time to take Dermot with him, but
Dermot did not want to leave the joys of Walmer Villa and
Delgany. This year, however, Con and Eileen went off for
their holiday in August: Con could not manage it later on:
and, in the blank period, Dermot let himself be carried off
on the tour. To make it more exciting, Mr. Gray had added
to his itinerary a visit to Killarney, as a grand finale.

The journey certainly amused Dermot, though he was
not really at ease with his father. At Waterford, they had to
share a bedroom, and this he disliked intensely. But the
riverside town left pleasant memories. They walked the
quays, visited an old theatre converted to a cinema, and
did not emerge into the cool streets till a few minutes before
ten.

"Now," said Mr. Gray unexpectedly, "we'll get a little
refreshment before we turn in."

And he led the way with confident steps to the bar of
one of the most palpable public houses Dermot had ever seen.

Dermot followed in amazement, hardly able to believe
his eyes. The bar, a low-ceilinged, timbered place thick
with blue smoke, was full of sea-faring men. They all turned
round to stare at the newcomers, but Mr. Gray showed not
the least concern, walking up boldly to the counter, de-
manding a Guinness for himself, a ginger beer for Dermot.
What was more, having received the drinks, he looked
around, and made for a vacant place at one of the tables,
Dermot following him in an agony of self-consciousness.

An old fat man, wearing a jersey with red lettering across
the bosom, looked Mr. Gray up and down for a moment.
Dermot was terrified that he would make some crushing
remark, and bring the whole crowd upon them. To his eyes,
the place looked a den of thieves. Instead, the fat man said,
with the greatest good humour:

"Good evenin', Colonel."

"Good evening," replied Mr. Gray, most cordially.

"Fine evenin'."

"Very fine."

Mr Gray took a short appreciative draught, while, quite casually, he glanced at the lettering on the man's jersey.

"Visitor to these parts?" enquired the man, after a short silence.

"Yes. I'm a Londoner, like yourself."

The old man raised his eyebrows. Dermot thought he was going to be angry.

"You can always tell a Londoner," said Mr. Gray, laughing. "I believe, if two London men met in the middle of a desert, they'd know one another straight off."

The old man smiled, and glanced around the bar. He was clearly flattered.

"Bein' here so regular, I'm often taken for Hirish," he said.

"That's a fact," put in another.

Mr. Gray turned round in his chair, laughing.

"*Is* there an Irishman here?" he asked.

"There is," replied a voice, in humorous disgust—the voice of the barman.

"You'll have to mind yourself," laughed Mr. Gray. "We're a dozen to one, or more."

"Oh, faith," grinned the barman, "I don't mind the lot of yez": and a most amiable conversation ensued, which ended in Mr. Gray's standing drinks to the entire company, and departing under a hail of the most cordial good-byes.

Dermot walked back to the hotel more astonished than he had ever been in the whole of his life. His father, so stiff, so starchy, so correct, had gone quite naturally into a pub, made friends with a lot of rough men, and been accepted by them, not with ridicule and sneers, but with obvious respect and liking.

"Decent fellows, those," said Mr. Gray, as they turned a corner. "Fancy finding a bar full of them here in Waterford."

Dermot learned a good many things about his father on

that trip. They visited Mullingar: they wandered down the streets of Ballina on fair day: they saw Sligo, Castlebar, and drove out to Bonnyconlon, the ancestral domain of the O'Dowdas: then, turning back on their tracks, they came down to Cork, and on to Macroom, from which they were to drive by motor coach to Killarney.

At Macroom, a difficulty arose. Their seats had been booked some time back, and the agent, ignoring this fact, had filled up all the places with latecomers, and told them they would have to wait. This Mr. Gray refused to do. The agent, knowing himself to be in the wrong, lost his temper.

"And what is it you expect me to do?" he cried. "Am I able to pull out the car like a bloody concertina, and fit in two places? Or do ye want a couple of ladies threw out on the road, to make room for the two of ye?"

Mr. Gray looked at him.

"Listen here," he said. "I'm a journalist. Either you carry out your contract with me, or I'll go back and blast your route to hell in every newspaper in Ireland."

The man's mouth fell open. His whole manner changed in an instant.

"Ah, sir," he said uneasily. "I wouldn't do that. I wouldn't do that."

"I will, though," said Dermot's father.

"Wait a minute, sir. Wait a minute." The agent disappeared into an inner room, and held colloquy with someone unseen.

"Look at here," he said, when he came back. "We can't put yez in the coach, because the seats is all full. But I tell ye what we'll do. We'll send yez on a car as far as the pass of Keim an Eigh, and there an auto shall come and pick yez up from the hotel. Will that do yez?"

"We don't have to pay anything extra?"

"Not a bloody halfpenny, sir. Not a bloody halfpenny."

"Then that'll do us very well."

And they were sent off, on an outside car, with the blessings of the agent and all his staff. More material for Dermot's wonder! He thought he knew all about his father. The idea that there were other sides to his character than those called out by home and Walmer Villa and Delgany was new and most disturbing. And—anyway—who was lying now?

"You have to bluff these fellows sometimes," said Mr. Gray, as if in answer to the thought. "It's wonderful how far a little bluff will take you."

Good, thought Dermot. Bluff: I'll remember the word.

The car jogged them twenty-six miles along the road, past the Lakes of Inchigeelah, past Lone Gougane Barra, to the pass of Keim an Eigh. There, in wild solitude, facing a barrier of mountains, the jarvey put them down, turned, and went clip-clopping his way home. Sitting on a bank of heather by the roadside, they watched him go. Slowly the valley was emptied of his sound. Loneliness poured down upon them from the mountains; it welled up from the heather underneath them. Eagerly, almost affectionately, their eyes followed the last living thing they could see. Far off now, he turned a corner, and the road was silent. The two raised their eyes to the mountains. Enormous, heather-covered slopes, fading away swiftly into the sheer mass of a great irregular wall, that would soon shut out the sun. Dermot moved his foot. It made a whispering sound in the heather. There was no other sound. Ahead of them, the road wound round a corner, and entered the pass. Behind them, it stretched empty. They were alone, in a huge, magnificent loneliness.

Mr. Gray broke it.

"I wonder how long this precious auto will be," he said.

"I don't know. Not long, do you think?"

"God knows. I daresay it was only a blind, to get us off their hands. No—they could hardly do that: dump us down here for the night. Yet I don't know. I wouldn't put it beyond them."

Silence fell again. There was something almost terrible in the way it came down, in the way nothing moved, not even a breath of air in the heather. The last few days, with all their bustle and quick, suspicious human contact, had not prepared them for the test of being left alone in such huge surroundings.

Suddenly Mr. Gray burst out with such violence as to make Dermot jump.

"God damn all Irishmen," he exploded bitterly. "A dirty, casual, dishonest, unbusinesslike set of cadgers."

Something in Dermot glowed with a cold, pale light.

"*All* Irishmen?" he said quietly.

"Yes. All. They're all tarred with the same brush. Even your precious Delgany crowd, that you're so fond of. They'll all let a man down as soon as look at him."

Suddenly Dermot knew that something terrible was going to happen.

"The Delgany people," he said, in a voice that came squeezed cold between great rocks of anger, "would never let anyone down. They are Christian people."

"Christian!—I dare say. So is that blighter who sold our seats to someone else. Does every kind of dirty trick during the week, and goes off slobbering to a priest on Sunday. My dear boy, they're all 'Christians,' the inhabitants of this blasted island. That what's the matter with them."

Dermot was shaking from head to foot. He had never known he could be so moved.

"Do you put t-the Delgany people in quite the same class? I don't think you—"

"Oh, you're going to tell me, I suppose, that they're Protestants, and that these other blackguards are Catholics. It's all the same in the long run. They're all too damned Christian to carry out their obligations in a decent and business-like fashion."

"Do you mean to say that Uncle B-Ben doesn't carry on his business in a decent and b-business-like fashion?"

"Now, look here, Dermot. You may think yourself very smart, trying to catch up everything I say. You're getting a bit above yourself, these days. Just because you do well at school, you think you can come home and lay down the law."

"I wasn't laying down the law. It was you, saying that the Delgany people were as bad as everyone else over here."

Mr. Gray compressed his lips for a moment before answering.

"You know perfectly well what I mean, and you needn't pretend that you don't. You know perfectly well—anybody but you would admit it at once—that the Delgany people let us down badly the other day over that theatre business. Being yourself, you prefer to take their side; out of cussedness, of course. You'd rather have your father labelled a fool and a fussy idiot than admit that, when I left all the arrangements to them, it was caddish and disgusting to mislead me, and then throw the blame on me. Or, leave me out of it: it was caddish and disgusting, when they knew Granny was coming, when they had persuaded her to come, not to make every possible arrangement for her comfort. I may not be a Christian, but I wouldn't have acted as they did, even to strangers."

Dermot sat, white with hatred, waiting an opportunity.

"I know, of course," his father went on, "that they didn't behave in that way on purpose. It's just that they don't think. They're casual, like the rest of the inhabitants of this infernal island. They're unbusiness-like. If they could extend their Christianity a little further, in the direction of a consideration for other people, they would be none the worse off, and those who come in contact with them would be the better."

"It's the first time I heard that Christianity and business ability were the same thing," said Dermot viciously.

"It is possible to be both a Christian and a good business man," replied Mr. Gray. "However, if I've got to choose, give me the business man, every time. I've had enough of Christians."

The steel rod snapped.

"And I've had enough of you," yelled Dermot suddenly, leaping to his feet, his face blazing. "For the last four years, you've done your best to run down religion to me, and destroy it. You've taught me arguments against the Bible, against God, against everything. You've filled me up with your cheap little tin-pot logic. I—I've heard all you've got to say: and I tell you, if I've got to choose between you and the Christians, I choose the Christians, every time."

Mr. Gray stared at him. He had not for an instant guessed the violence of the conflict. Dermot's outburst served at once to restore his dignity: he became the father Dermot had known before the trip began.

"Very well," he said quietly. "Now we know where we stand."

And, shifting his position, crossing one leg over the other, he took the guide-book from his pocket, and began to read it. Shaking from head to foot, unable to trust himself, Dermot wandered a few yards off. Already he was terrified at his outburst. He had behaved like a child, flown into a rage, said more than he meant, been ineffective: done everything the Delgany people would most deplore. He knew that, curiously enough, they would never countenance his being rude to his father. Still, under it all, there was a sort of awful pleasure, a sense of having burnt his boats: of having irrevocably cast in his spiritual lot with Con and Eileen and Uncle Ben.

As the minutes passed, this pleasure chilled. He felt conscious only of having spoken unforgivably to his father, who was spending time and money in taking him on a pleasure trip. Forlorn, he crept back to apologise. Before he could speak, Mr. Gray put away his book and stood up.

"I think I hear this precious auto," he said.

Dermot listened.

"Yes. I think I hear it too."

Sure enough, there came a hoot, and a big open tourer rushed round the corner, and pulled up at sight of them. Gathering their coats and belongings, they bundled in.

"Here—tuck this in round you."

Dermot's father leaned across, and helped him fix the rug. Then, catching his eye, he added with a smile.

"He came after all. One up to the Christians."

CHAPTER XXXIII

DERMOT SAT IN THE DRAWING-ROOM AT DELGANY, LOOKING
out over the bay. He had drawn a chair up beside the telescope. The hot August afternoon was hazy, though, close at
hand, the sun beat heavily upon the rocks and garden. A
patch of sea, close in, glittered and hurt his eyes. The telescope
was of little use for the long distances, for it could not pierce
the haze: it could only bring to him vague, enormous outlines,
the muzzy shapes of Kattygollagher and the Stack, lit by a
sleepy, imbecile sun: Killiney Strand, closer but still vague,
receiving its perpetual tribute of long soundless breakers:
Brian's house, remote and indistinct, with something
coloured hanging from one of the windows: a bemused,
half-nightmare world, depressing, tiring to the eye. But the
telescope was no longer trained on these far objects. It
pointed sharply downward, to a cove in the rocks, less than
half a mile away. From the window, one could see little
slow heads in the water, and hear faint, late cries. It was
an unofficial ladies' bathing place. At the foot of a steep
slope, it was hidden from above: and, unless a boat were
passing, there was nothing nearer to it than Delgany. Therefore the ladies undressed in the open, on the rocks. Naturally
enough, the idea of a lens which would bring them within
twenty yards of the windows did not enter their heads.

Dermot was not looking at them now. They were in the
water. He knew very well, however, that as soon as they
came out again, his eye would be glued to the telescope:
and he hated the knowledge. Every time he heard a step outside, he had been quick to swing the telescope away, and

303

point it at the distance; but no one had disturbed him. In England, at home, had there been a telescope, he would somehow have minded less: but here, the clamour of his instincts distressed him, turned sour the lazy afternoon. As the spasms of guilt and self-accusation rose miserably from his stomach, he tried to silence them, and bolster up his decision with an argument which all the time he knew to be false. A few days before, he had caught Con looking through the telescope. Con had been embarrassed, but had made a joke of it, and gone on looking. It can't be so wrong after all, then, he said to himself, if Con does it. You must take yourself in hand; you're getting in a regular state of nerves over it. Dermot began to walk up and down the room, speaking to himself roughly, bullying himself. Con is the best man you know. He wouldn't do a wrong thing. Look at that Opera business. (A couple of weeks earlier, Con had been offered the chief baritone part in an opera put on by society folk in Dublin, but had refused, since to accept would have meant rehearsing on a Sunday.) Doesn't that show you the sort of man he is? Well, if a man as particular as *that* looks at girls through a telescope, why shouldn't you?

But it was no use. Dermot was never able to deceive himself. He knew that, if there was any meaning in the terminology they used, it was wrong for both him and Con to look through the telescope. Con had never *done* anything, though he'd often had the chance: though he'd had more than one woman begging him to. Dermot knew that, for Con had told him. It hadn't been easy for Con, either, because he was only too apt by nature for that sort of thing. Dermot and he had had many talks together. It was nearly always the woman that started it, Con said: and this, to Dermot, was a new and terrifying idea. He had always thought that no woman could possibly be party to such a thing. He wondered how a man could ever persuade himself that a girl would let him. Con looking through the telescope had been a shock, a far greater shock, deep down, than Dermot was going to admit.

The girls were still in the water, splashing, and calling out. What a time they stayed in. There was one who looked as if she might be getting out in a minute. They were generally pretty cunning, even all that way off: put great towels like tents all over them.

A quick step sounded outside, and Eileen opened the door. Dermot swung round, confused, and stared at her.

"Hullo, Dermot." She came in, and shut the door. "What are you doing—looking at the girls?"

She asked the question lightly, and smiled at him. A hasty denial rose to his lips, but did not escape. Suffused, he gazed at her; like a guilty dog.

"Yes," he said.

She looked away, crossed the room, and sat down on a sofa.

"Well," she said, "don't let me disturb you."

And, putting her feet up with a quick gesture, she picked up a magazine, and began turning the pages.

"Eileen."

"Yes?"

"I want to ask you something."

She looked up.

"Well. Out with it."

"Do you think it's very beastly of me, to—to—"

"Look at the girls through the telescope?"

"Yes."

"Oh, no. Not particularly. It's your nature, I suppose. You can't help it."

"My nature? I—"

"Oh, sure, I don't mean yours in particular. You're no worse than the others, I dare say." She turned over several pages at once. "Sure, you men are all the same."

Dermot sat for a moment in silence. He was bewildered at her attitude: torn between a strong desire to protest, and a wry feeling of consolation at being lumped in with the rest of his sex.

"It's one of the things a woman has to take for granted about men, that's all," Eileen went on. "If all the handsomest men in the world were stripped under the window here, I wouldn't want to go peeping at them: no more would any girl I know. And yet men, decent men, will climb a tree in the rain to look at a housemaid taking off her clothes. If you're a girl, you've got to get used to it, that's all."

"D—don't you despise men frightfully, if that's so?"

"No. They're made differently, I suppose. At least—they all tell me it's harder for them than for us, and, judging by the things they let themselves do, it must be."

"I think it must be harder for them. It is to begin with, anyway. At school."

"Yes. So I believe."

"Eileen."

"Yes?"

"I wouldn't like you to have a false impression of me. I—"

"Oh, bless you, son, don't worry your head. You're a decent sort: anybody can see that."

"No, no, no. That's not what I mean at all."

"Well. What do you mean?"

"I mean . . . Eileen . . . I . . ." He struggled with himself. "I care very much what you think about me. More than anyone. That's why I don't want you to think I'm better than I am. I'm afraid you do."

Eileen said nothing. She laid the magazine on her lap, and looked at him with a half smile, encouraging him to go on.

"I've done wrong things, over in England, at school. I didn't know, soon enough, about what things really meant. Daddy didn't tell me till too late. I don't say I wouldn't have done it, even if he had: but I didn't have a proper chance, to begin with. But I've never done anything of that kind here in Ireland: never. It's different here. In this house, especially. And I haven't done anything of that sort for some time: more than two years, now."

"That's good, son."

She was serious, but her voice was very kind.

"The chief reason I was able to stop was because of . . . here: and because of you."

"Of me, Dermot?"

"Yes. I love you. I always have, since I was quite tiny. I felt I had no business . . . if I was doing that sort of thing . . . no business to let you kiss me, thinking I was a better sort of . . . I mean, I did so want to be fit to be allowed to love you. You've been my ideal. You've helped me more than you could ever guess."

There was a silence. He dared not look at Eileen.

"Dermot, my dear boy, of course, I'm only too delighted, and proud, if I've ever been any help. . . . But I'm a poor sort of ideal, I'm afraid. You'd better hurry up and find a better one. . . ."

Dermot raised his eyes, and looked at her steadfastly.

"I'd never believe any bad of you," he said.

She swung her feet down, sat up, and patted the sofa by her side.

"Well, that'll be something for me to live up to, too," she said, with a smile, as he hurried to sit beside her.

"Ah," she said presently, "it's a funny world, Dermot. You men have all the best of it. You go wherever you like, chase around after one little bit and the other, have a dozen affairs, go through the doctor's hands, and then, when you've had enough of it, come to some girl who's managed to keep herself straight, and ask her to marry you. Now, where's the sense of fairness in that?"

"There doesn't seem much," admitted Dermot.

"A girl has just as many chances of going wrong as a man, nowadays. But she mustn't take them. No matter how much she may want to."

"It must be easier for anyone in this house to keep straight, than for most people," declared Dermot.

"Because of our religion, do you mean?"

"Yes."

"Oh, that makes it easier, certainly." She spoke almost grimly. "We'd be lost without it."

"Tell me," said Dermot, "don't you find some of it a little boring, sometimes? All the church-going, and the sermons, and that side of it?"

"And supposing we do? Do you think Our Blessed Lord wasn't often bored by the things He had to do, and the stupid people He had to put up with? Surely we can endure a little boredom sometimes, for His sake?"

Dermot was going to ask why she was so sure it was for His sake, but, once more up against the blazing simplicity of the Delgany faith, he kept silent.

Shortly after this interview, he met the O'Dowda for the last time. That urbane cosmopolite seemed always the unlikeliest of guests for Delgany, but, actually, he fitted in very well. He did not attend prayers, nor accompany the family to church on Sunday. He used the place very much as an hotel, coming and going when he pleased: but everybody in the house was glad of his presence. His courtesy, as he grew older, became more and more effortless. He would make great play of consulting Aunt Patricia about his movements in the morning. Was she sure, now, this and that would be convenient to her? Because, if it put her out the smallest atom, she had only to say the word. . . . Eileen often wondered what would happen if anybody ever did say the word. One thing was certain, the O'Dowda would do what he wanted, all right. He would probably have a marvellous excuse afterwards. But then, the situation could not arise. He had everything so well in hand that acquiescence was certain. That knack of conveying, well before he would need to ask anything, that his hostess was a woman of exceptional understanding — she would go through untold inconvenience rather than jeopardise for an instant that estimate, conveyed less in words than in a tone of the voice, a deferential, flattering, intimate flash of the eyes. All is easy for the man who knows how to flatter a grown woman — though he needs certain physical attributes as well.

The O'Dowda knew how to flatter everyone; even an awkward public school-boy. Dermot came into the drawing-room after breakfast, and found him alone there, writing letters. For a full minute nothing was said: and, when the O'Dowda spoke, he did not stop writing or look up.

"Where is it you are at school now? Brighton?"

"Yes."

The O'Dowda paused for a second, screwing up his eyes against the smoke of his own cigarette.

"H'm. Damned immoral town, isn't it?"

One man of the world asking information of another. Dermot glowed.

"Yes," he said. "It *is* pretty stiff."

That was all: but many a man has been loved all his life for no more. The O'Dowda went on writing, and, having finished his letters, left the room without a word further, having added another devotee to a list scattered over half the world; one to whom, for the rest of his days, he never gave another thought.

CHAPTER XXXIV

THE O'DOWDA WAS ALWAYS THE MOST DAZZLING OF ALL THE
vivid characters who crowded Dermot's memories of Ireland.
Whether in fact or through his will to believe, it seemed
to Dermot that all the most interesting people he had ever
met lived there. Somehow, in Ireland, people gave fuller
expression to their quality. The odd were odder, the funny
funnier, the charming so very much more charming. Even
the lunatics had more scope. In England, Dermot had never
encountered anything better than a village idiot. But there
were lots of "mad ones" loose about Glasthule, and the
people treated them with the greatest kindness, holding
them in special awe, and never minding their tricks. Higher
up in the scale, Miss Tarbet, the friend of Granny's in whose
house they slept, kept an old mad lady under her care.
Dermot passed her, on the stairs, several times. She was a
tiny little old thing, with great sad eyes, which reminded
him of Paddy-monkey: but Miss Tarbet said she was quite
happy. The little old lady was very religious, and used to
keep Sunday with intense zeal, till she reached the stage of
thinking every day was Sunday. She would wake up all
right, obediently determined that it was a week-day, and go
through the morning with the air of an angel exiled from
home. By three in the afternoon she had grown fretful and
suspicious, believing that the people of the house were in un-
godly conspiracy to withhold the Sabbath from her. By five,
she was triumphantly seated at her old cracked piano, banging
weakly at the yellow keys, and singing in a mad old hollow

310

voice her favourite hymn. After a couple of verses, she repeated the chorus till she grew too tired to go on.

> "*YES we'll gather at the river,*"

sang the old mad lady,

> "*The beautiful, the beautiful, the river,*"

(She always made the same mistake:)

> "*Gather with the sai-haints at the river*
> *That flows by the throne of God.*"

You thought she had finished, for she had been singing it for a quarter of an hour on end: but with fresh emphasis she burst out again:

> "*YES we'll gather at the river . . .*"

Most people thought it funny, but Dermot did not. He would smile to Eithne when they heard her start off, but the mad happiness of the voice filled him with a different feeling. At the end of the holidays, when they were packing, it was unbearable. A few years afterwards, he sang that hymn in a service at the base, in France: and the sudden rush of memories came so clear, so poignant that for hours afterwards he was a man in a dream.

Then there was Miss O'Killikelly, who, according to Grandpapa, "would be better in a house of detention." Any word of Miss Tarbet's mad lady invariably provoked him to an attack upon the devoted and loquacious parish worker. Miss O'Killikelly still came in of an evening, to gossip with Granny: and Grandpapa was still obliged to throw down his boots into the hall as a hint for her to go. Increasing age had made him blunter in speech, and on some occasions he was downright rude to the lady, in a manner no goodnatured flutterings could ignore . . . Miss O'Killikelly would then lament to Granny, with great emotion.

"Ah, Amelia, it's trouble I'm always bringing on ye."

"Nonsense, Letitia. What possesses ye, to say a thing like that? Sure, you mustn't mind Alfred. His bark is worse than his bite. He doesn't mean the half he says."

"Ah now, he has a good right to be chasing me away out of the place, and I here, worrying ye, making a nuisance of meself to ye . . ."

"No such thing, Letitia, no such thing. It's a great pleasure to see ye."

"Ah, Amelia, it's too kind y'are, sure everybody knows that. You're too kind to me. Sure, I know well what everybody does be saying. It's a nuisance I am, and a worry to people. I'd be better under the sod."

"Letitia—such a thing to say! I wonder at ye. Ye ought to know better than to go—"

"And, faith, by the way things are going," sobbed Miss O'Killikelly, rising on the wings of her woe, "they won't have to wait long. Ye'll all be rid of me soon."

"Now that's nonsense, Letitia, and you know it is." Granny scolded her for a minute or so, then sat back in her chair. "It's too bad, Alfred to be conducting himself this way, and putting you in such a state," she said indignantly.

"Ah, there now, you see, what I do, what comes of me. I do be making trouble between husband and wife."

And Miss O'Killikelly would weep anew. Comforted at last, she would go off, sniffing, her bright eyes brighter than ever, and return next day with a peace-offering: a lemon pudding, which she made with great skill. Granny liked a lemon pudding, and even Grandpapa would grudgingly pass up his plate for a second help. He would disparage the maker of the pudding a good deal, to assert his principle: nevertheless, when Mr. Gray jocosely suggested that he affront Miss O'Killikelly every time she came, in order to secure a plentiful supply of the delicacy, the jest was not well received.

Dermot's public school summers passed very quickly.

His last, the summer of 1914, found him preparing hard for a scholarship at Oxford. Before he came over, it had been arranged that he should go in twice a week to Trinity, to work with one of the classical tutors there. He was to have a week's grace before starting; and during this week broke out the War.

The War at first made little serious impression in Ireland. It appeared in the light of a great sporting event, and the vast majority found themselves instinctively on England's side. In a Dublin theatre, a day or so after the declaration, three parts of the audience rose to their feet at "God Save the King." There are those who argue that prompt and confident handling of the situation by England then could have saved much bloodshed and much bitterness: but the Government behaved as if it expected to be struck, a dangerous attitude towards animals, men, and countries. Be these things as they may, the War did not disturb the holiday season. No one had at first believed it possible. At the baths, where Dermot spent his mornings, men talked of it idly: yet no one but an Englishman foresaw the certainty. When it did break out, there was no rush to volunteer. The adventurous spirits were all busy on their own, those who loved England preparing to resist her in the North, those who disliked Ulster running guns in the South. Like a boy who sees his acquaintance squabbling in a corner of the playground, they did not think the fight was serious, and looked to England to polish off her adversary inside a few weeks. News of a great naval victory, heavily placarded in the streets, confirmed this mood. Mr. Gray was jubilant.

"If it's true," he proclaimed impressively at lunch, "it means the Germans will never dare show their faces on the sea, for dread of the British Navy."

Unfortunately, the news was not true: but everyone took the line that it well might have been, and, anyway, that it would probably be true next week: and went on as before. It was this attitude, a sort of laziness, which kept hundreds of Irishmen from running to the colours. They did not dream that it was necessary. Neither side, indeed, those for England or those against, realised for some months the meaning of what had happened.

So all went peacefully as usual, and Dermot in due course visited Trinity, and was shown to the rooms of Mr. Stacpoole O'Hara. Mr. Stacpoole O'Hara did not at all fit in with Dermot's idea of a famous classical scholar. He looked as if he had come to mend the gas. His face, sad and dispirited, was ornamented by a drooping and draggled moustache. He wore a bowler hat a size too big for him, which was only saved from descending over his face by his ears, stuck out at right angles with the effort of supporting it. Over his chest and stomach he wore a dirty white waistcoat, with a gold watch chain. His suit was stained and shabby, the ends of the trousers frayed, one elbow shiny, and the other through. He wore canvas shoes. Dermot could not at first believe that he had found his man: but the pencil which scored his Greek prose was authoritative enough, and it did not take a dozen sentences to show him that he was going to learn a great deal. Mr. O'Hara affected a contempt for Oxford scholarship.

"I'll endeavour ta instil a little elementary accuracy inta ya," he said, "though maybe that'll be doing ya harm in the eyes of Oxford?"

And he proceeded to instil a great deal. Mr. O'Hara had no high falutin' notions about the classics. He approached them strictly on business. The cynical ease with which he extemporized the suavest and most admirable Latin verses confounded Dermot. Mr. O'Hara would sit back, picking his teeth, and dictate a version which more than held its own with any Dermot had met. Verses were Dermot's especial line, and he left Mr. O'Hara a sadder and wiser scholarship candidate. He was allowed to choose his own English, so there was no trickery about it. Mr. O'Hara, who seemed to have about as much poetry in him as a louse, could hash up a convincing version of anything.

"Ah," he said, when Dermot shyly asked the secret, "Sure, verses is a trick": and that was all that could be got out of him.

Dermot worked hard that summer. He got up early, and sat at a queer uncomfortable little table in Granny's drawing-room. He liked his new tutor from the first, and came to feel an affection towards him. O'Hara, too, evidently liked him, for often after the hour's work he would put on his monstrous bowler and walk with him to the tram.

One afternoon, as they were going out, they met a figure which instantly reminded Dermot of a clerical Dr. Johnson. Mr. O'Hara stood aside, showing every symptom of the greatest respect.

"Good afternoon, Doctor," he said.

The figure received the greeting very graciously. He peered quickly at Mr. O'Hara, and quickly at Dermot.

"This is Mr. Gray, a young English pupil I have," said Mr. O'Hara, with a wave of his dirty hand. Dermot was so used to the mistake, by now, that he did not bother to correct it.

The figure bowed slightly.

"How do you do," he said grimly. Dermot stammered an answer. Susceptible always to personal quality, he realised that he was in the presence of someone very considerable indeed.

Dr. Johnson looked away for a moment down the street.

"Will this war end soon?" he said abruptly.

"Ah, sure, I hope so."

"Well"—with a glance up at the big stone front of Trinity—"I hope you're right."

And he passed on inside.

"Who was that?" asked Dermot, in awestruck tones.

"That," replied Mr. O'Hara, well pleased, "is Doctor Mahaffy."

"Oh!" Dermot turned round, to stare once more after the famous figure.

When, a few days later, Mr. O'Hara interrupted the course of an unseen to point out the window and say "There goes a scholar you may have heard mentioned —Robert Yelverton Tyrrell," Dermot felt that his cup was full. Of all people on the earth, scholars and writers held his passionate admiration. He had discovered Synge, and went regularly to the Abbey Theatre. Con had been the unlikely introducer to this literary pasture: he always went there to hear the dialect, and, except for this, could not at all distinguish the plays from those he saw elsewhere. It was a great disappointment to Dermot that Mr. O'Hara did not share his enthusiasm.

"Did ya ever see any good thing come out of a place the like o' that?" he enquired derisively: and, "Ah, they've learned a pretty little trick. Take any old plot of any old play, and dress it up with a bit of talk from a pub back door."

Dermot looked at him, more shocked than he would admit.

"I think there's more in 'The Playboy of the Western World' than that," he said.

"There is," retorted his tutor. "A lot of sham poetry no corner-boy would soil his tongue with."

And Dermot, who was not yet hardened to differing in worship from those he liked, rode home in the tram hurt and dejected. He knew Mr. O'Hara was wrong; he hated to be laughed at for his enthusiasm: and he felt that, by not being able to silence and out-argue him, he had let down the cause in which he believed. More than anything, he resented the unspoken suggestion that he liked the Abbey because he was an Englishman and a tourist. It was desperately hard, to get himself accepted as Irish. Even his friends at the baths all thought of him as an Englishman.

"I'll tell you what you are," said one of them one morning, as they stood up and stretched, preparatory to swimming their length to the pier and back. "You're a quack Irishman."

It was not meant unkindly, but it stuck: Dermot never

forgot it. He swam savagely, and beat his traducer by many
yards: but the barb could not be washed out of his flesh.
"Begawrah!" Old mockeries rose up from the past. "The
quack Irishman." These obstinate brutes wouldn't have it
that anyone was Irish who didn't live there all the year
round, and go to school there. You might prove what you
like, argue what you like, do what you like. They just grinned
at you. They were like Mr. O'Hara, grinning at Synge and
the Abbey. A derisive grin: that was Dublin's answer to
most things, whether it understood them, or, as was more
likely, it had not the remotest idea what they signified.
Even Con was like that: he jeered at what he could not understand. Perhaps even that was one better than Uncle
Ben, who wouldn't allow that it existed. Dermot raged to
himself, sitting on the draughty covered top of the tram,
scowling at the big houses in their stately gardens, and the
long stretch of road to Monkstown.

Though he did not know it, he, and all the world, were
seeing them for the last time. Not the outward shell of
them, but all that gave them meaning. The eighteen-sixties
had received their death-blow. Even during the ten or
twelve years Dermot had known them, they were dying.
The slow pool in the river was breaking up; the eddies
found themselves in the grip of the current; they and their
circling lumber began to move, and were borne away. The
entrapped flotsam, which in the pool seemed so solid and
large, was swept into the main current, scattered, made
insignificant, and disappeared. Four years more, and those
big houses would be empty, staring in mournful incompre-
hension through their broken windows at an altered world.
Old newspapers would blow about the trim drives, the
orchards would be desolate and broken, the tennis lawns
dishevelled patches of rank grass. The broad peace and
security of an old order would be gone. When Bessie and
Dermot's mother had clapped the front door of Walmer
Villa after them for the last time, and faced one another on

the doorstep to say good-bye, the spirit of the old times fled from its last stronghold, the little alcove in the corner where the books had been, where the dark outline of the cuckoo clock showed still upon the wall paper: the corner sacred to Tom Moore, to Dickens, and to Vousden: the corner comforted by the shade of Henry Francis Lyte, and composed by the shade of James Mongan, Barrister-at-Law. That period died. The period enshrined at Delgany survived and suffered change. "Are ye right, there, Michael, are ye right?" sang Uncle Ben: and "When M'Carthy took the floor at Enniscorthy." These survived: but "The Private Still," which he also sang, was swept down the river with the years that owned it. The city Dermot had just left was to suffer change and violence. Gunfire and shells were to scar its face: Eithne was to come back ten years later, and search every stone of Middle Abbey Street to find, not the old offices, but some hint of where they stood. These tram-rides in to Trinity were Dermot's last chance to see a city which was about to disappear: "dear old, dirty Dublin," now no more, the despair of all who lived in her, whom all that knew her regret in their hearts, while thankful for the order and cleanliness that has taken her place: the old kindly, garrulous, amusing slattern, the old witty stinking fishwife, drink-sodden, paralysed in will, driven off, battered, given a black eye, kicked out, by a young hard-eyed woman who set to work scrubbing and setting things to rights: tottering off down the quayside of men's memories, with a hiccup and a joke flung over her shoulder, disappearing into the rain and the darkness, her uncertain steps growing fainter and fainter: lovable, disgusting, butt for the sentimentality of men remembering old days, forgetting old discomforts: a tub, a target, a smell of porter: a rotten social system: ignorant, credulous, gossiping, with fits of drunken generosity: dear old dirty Dublin, staggering away to limbo down the cobbled quays. The world is well rid of her: peace to her soul.

But Dermot, clanking away towards Sandycove, knew none of this. He saw, dimly, that there were changes: he appreciated the true meaning of the alcove by the cuckoo clock: but the city he had left, a city whose spirit was expressed for him in the jeers of Mr. O'Hara, seemed full of inimical health, in no wise on her deathbed. He loved Dublin, because Dublin usually meant Middle Abbey Street, the Abbey, and rides with Con. This new aspect distressed him. He did not recognise the old lady when she suddenly stuck out her tongue.

CHAPTER XXXV

"Dermot," said Con abruptly. "C'm here till i tell ye."

They had left the bicycle beside the mountain road, and clambered down the steep slope that leads to the Annamoe. For some time they wandered along the river, Con growing silent. He was subject to fits of silence, so Dermot took no notice of this. Well content, he looked up at the enormous hills that shut in the long still valley. A quick memory of Keim an Eigh came to his mind, and he dismissed it with a smile. Last year seemed a long time ago. He would not break out so crudely, and expose himself, nowadays.

They came to a place where round, smooth boulders stuck out from the bank, and there, without a word, Con sat down, and began moodily throwing pebbles into the water. Dermot found himself a rock a few yards off, and sat, dreaming. Con's voice, though it was not loud, made him jump.

"What?" he said, looking up startled.

"C'm here. I've something I want to say to ye."

Wondering, Dermot came across. Con shuffled along his rock, and made room. Then, without saying anything, he went on throwing pebbles.

"Can ye keep your mouth shut, if I tell ye something."

"I can."

"That's good. Well"—another stone, more viciously aimed. "I don't know what ye'll think of this, at all: but . . . maybe . . . I think, anyhow, ye'd better know. Only, mind, not a word to a soul."

"Not a word."

"Not a bloody word—" Con grinned, as they both remembered something they had heard in the street outside the office.

"—to a bloody soul," Dermot grinned back.

"Well. It's no laughing matter. It's—I'm in love with Eithne, and I always have been."

"I thought that," said Dermot. His eye, looking away, was caught by an agitated moorhen fussing about a hundred yards down on the opposite bank. Con glanced at him quickly out of the corners of his eyes.

"Well, I suppose you had as good a chance of noticing as the next person."

"Yes. I suppose so."

"Have any of the others noticed?" asked Con, with sudden apprehension.

"I heard Granny say, a long time ago, 'I believe Con will wait for Eithne.' But none of them took it at all seriously."

"That's good." Con blew with relief, and passed the back of his huge hand across his forehead. He surveyed the water for a moment, leaned down to one side, and threw two more pebbles.

"What will they think, do ye imagine?" he asked bluntly.

"They won't be too keen on it," answered Dermot, still watching the moorhen.

"No," said Con, slowly, "I was prepared for that." He scowled, and suddenly jerked his chin upward. "Why?" he demanded truculently. "What have they against me?"

His tone almost accused Dermot of the objection.

"They'll say, I suppose," said Dermot, not looking at him, "that you're too old, and that your prospects aren't good enough."

"My prospects—" began Con, in fighting mood; but stopped short. "Aye," he said, in a quieter tone. "I haven't much at the minute, I admit. But I've health, and strength, and the business is a good one. My Dad'll give me a bigger share in it, once I want to settle. Or, if he doesn't—"

"If he can't—" put in Dermot quietly. The moorhen, after much looking around, disappeared into a thicket.

Con gave his companion a sharp, surprised look. He saw a motionless and rather stolid profile, that belied its owner. Several times lately the quiet force of Dermot's personality had come suddenly out and surprised him.

"Well, aye, perhaps. If he can't—isn't the world full of jobs? And, anyhow—I have my faith in Almighty God, Who will find a way for me to carry out my heart's desire."

The sincerity of this unwonted eloquence moved Dermot. He waited a couple of seconds before replying.

"All the same, Con," he said, clearing his throat, "however much Daddy may appreciate that, you can't expect him to look upon it as a commercial asset."

"Commercial," said Con, picking up a fresh handful of stones, and beginning methodically to sling them after their predecessors. "Well, no. I daresay not. But is that the only view to take?"

Dermot swung round and confronted him.

"Don't ask me. *I'm* not saying it is. I'm only telling you what I expect they—Daddy—will say as soon as you tell them."

"I wouldn't tell him. Not at first. I'd tell your mother."

"She'd tell him."

"I'd ask her not to."

"She would, all the same. She's pretty much under his thumb, you know."

"Sure, she wouldn't tell him, once she'd promised not. I'd make her promise, before I let out a word."

"She'd be frightfully unhappy; and it would make a fearful row between them. I'd tackle him right away, if I were you. He'd be all the worse to deal with, if he saw he'd been sidetracked."

Con flung his last and biggest stone hard and true against a round stone in midstream.

"You may be right," he said gloomily. "I'll have to think it out. Anyway, I'm not going to say a word to them yet." He turned round, and faced Dermot. "What do *you* think of it, by the way?" he demanded bluntly.

Dermot smiled, and put out his hand.

"I'd ask no better, Con," he said.

Con wrung his hand in his enormous paw.

"Thanks, old chap," he said, with emotion. "It's good of ye to say that."

"It's a fact," answered Dermot awkwardly, "so why wouldn't I say it."

They sat happily together, watching the water. It ran dark and still. Only where the round stone stood up did it make any noise, embracing one side of it with a slow curved ripple, that set up a soft, thoughtful sound, unending, for a while unnoticed, then so distinct it filled the background of their consciousness, forcing them to realise it, and immediately forget.

"Does Eithne know?" asked Dermot presently.

"No. I didn't want to say a word to her, till I'd seen the others."

"Why?"

"Ah, sure, it's hardly fair on the girl. She's only a wee thing still."

"She's fourteen."

"Yes, I know. But what would anyone say, telling a child like that? Of course I know she's not a child in many things. But the world would say so. They'd say I was a cad."

Dermot got up. The rock was becoming hard to his behind.

"Well, Con, you know more about these things than I do, of course. But I'd say, if anyone's to hear about it, the first person ought to be the person whom it concerns. She'd far sooner know: that I'm sure."

"Maybe, do ye think, I'd better not say a word at all yet?" Con looked at him in woe-begone enquiry. "You see, Dermot boy, she's a lovely girl: and I don't want any damned fella in England getting in before me, for want of a word said."

"Don't you worry about that." Dermot was sure of his ground here. "You're the one person in the world she adores. There's nobody like you. Don't you worry."

"If I knew you were by, to keep an eye open, to give me the tip, if so be . . . ?"

"Well, now, what do you think I am? Of course I will."

"Dermot, old man, I—I don't know how to thank you. If ever a chap had a good friend—"

"Shut up. Do you think I'm not particular who I have for my only brother-in-law?"

"You're *only* one? Sure, what about when you marry yourself!"

"Ah, don't be a fool. You know what I mean. I've only the one sister."

"Aye." Con thumped his chest resoundingly. "And she's one in a hundred thousand of them."

"She is."

Dermot could not, for some reason, naturally praise Eithne. It violated an unconscious taboo.

"Then you think I'd better say nothing for a while?" asked Con, as they laboured up the slope.

"I think so, for everybody's sake."

But, for all that, the declaration was not long delayed. August nineteen-fourteen had set many a ball rolling, big and little. Great catastrophes are like cyclones, whose vast energies are expressed in the wrecking of cities and the dismembering of a butterfly. Nothing is too mighty for their influence, nothing too small.

Dermot kept the secret easily. Only once or twice, when he heard his family speculating about Con, did he feel the least temptation to blurt out his knowledge, and confound

Mr. Gray's facile diagnoses. There were times, however, when its magnitude suddenly struck him. Playing billiards one evening, looking across the room at Con, as he moodily watched Uncle Ben make a break: tall, powerful, handsome, brooding: he felt the sudden sense of power, the knowledge that he had but to blurt out a dozen words, and strike them all by lightning.

"Ah, me little darlin'—me little dar—Agh! now why didn't ye go in?"

Uncle Ben straightened up with a look of sorrow on his face. He gazed reproachfully at the ball, as if it had betrayed his confidence.

Dermot grimaced, went to the table, took quick but careful aim, and missed an all round the table cannon by a couple of inches.

"Hard luck, oh, hard luck indeed, little son."

Uncle Ben always treated his opponents as if they were children, exclaiming at the easiest of successes, condoling extravagantly upon the most obvious of errors. Age had emphasised this characteristic in him: he was now a bad man to play with.

"Now then, Ernest, me lad. A nice, easy, straightforward little shot for ye."

Mr. Gray came forward with a bad grace. He was a poor performer, and hated partnering Uncle Ben. Usually he refused to play. To-night he had unwillingly consented, to make a four. Worst of all, he disliked showing his want of skill in front of Dermot.

"Now, Ernest, boy. Get down, now: hit your own ball just a little to the left—no, not down there: *there. That's* it. Now, aim to catch me little red boy over yonder just about half ball."

Mr. Gray stooped, and rose.

"What is it you want me to *do*, Ben?" he asked, tartly.

"Just what I'm telling you, Ernest boy. Just what I'm telling you. Hit your own ball a little—"

"Yes. I heard all that. But what is the shot I'm supposed to be trying to make?"

Uncle Ben regarded him in mild reproach, as a saint might a disciple for want of faith.

"What we want to do is to go in, off red, into the top pocket. But if you'll just do what I tell you, now, ye'll see, it'll come out pat, without you worrying your head."

"Well then, I wish, if you don't mind, you'd tell me what I'm supposed to do first of all. Then you can tell me how to do it afterwards."

"Very well, Ernest boy. Very well." Uncle Ben crossed the room to chalk his cue. "Just what you like yourself," he said amiably.

"I mean—I may be a fool, but I do like to be told what I'm at."

"And so you shall. And so you shall."

Mr. Gray bent stiffly, took elaborate aim, and after a moment of anxious ridigity, miscued.

"Hard luck, Ernest. Hard luck indeed," cried the indomitable Ben, in tones so heartfelt they would have honoured a bereavement. Con hid a large grin, and Mr. Gray, rising, looked indignantly at Dermot, as much as to say, 'There, you see: that's what comes of following *his* advice."

"I think you'd better let me go my own silly way in future, Ben," he said, going over to chalk his cue, as Con, still grinning, got down and collected a slap-dash eighteen.

"*Eighteen!*" cried Uncle Ben. "*Eighteen*, the fella's mad. Oh, Ernest, Ernest, we're ruined. We're ruined entirely. Sure, what can the two of us do, against the like of that?"

He doubled round to the end of the table, and, stooping, anxiously scrutinised the leave.

"Ben boy, Ben boy, ye must see what ye can do. Ye must see what ye can do. Aye. Aye. Sure, they don't leave us much, Ernest. They don't leave us much. And we wanting every stiver we can lay our hands on. Aye, I wonder now, if

I hit that white fine, with just a touch of side, could
I—"

Con snorted. The shot was one Uncle Ben could make a
dozen times any night of the week.

"Oho—oho. That's me girl. Oh, but not too far. Not
too—ah. Now, maybe, if I could put down that red—"

Uncle Ben went on, doubling round the table after the
balls, addressing them affectionately, cajoling them, till
the exasperated Mr. Gray was ready to dance with rage.
Only the sight of its effect upon him kept the other two
from being irritated by the delighted monologue.

"Twenty-nine," recorded Uncle Ben, making a great
clatter on the marker. "Twenty-nine. Ah well. We must
take what we can get, Ernest boy. We must take what we
can get."

When, presently, Mr. Gray made seven, he was over-
whelmed with felicitations: and, such is the nature of the
novice, though he despised them, he was pleased, and had
to struggle in order to hide a smile.

"You're off form, Dermot boy," commented Uncle Ben
presently. "You're not playing your best to-night."

No one knew that better than Dermot. He could never
do anything naturally in front of his father. He became
nervous and uneasy. Indeed, any special occasion made him
nervous. That same summer, Brian had asked him to lunch
at his club. He liked and admired Brian, but was rather
afraid of him: and so, when after lunch Brian asked him
if he would care for a game of pills, he had not the courage
to refuse. They played a foursome, and Dermot, over anxious to do well, played execrably. Only towards the end of
the game was he able to bring off a shot or two that showed
he knew what he was about. The strange men intimidated
him, also. One of them, a little man in a bright pink shirt,
wearing a bow tie, was, Brian whispered, a celebrated painter,
by name Orpen. Dermot liked him at once: for he was very
amusing, very kind, and had more synonyms for the red ball

than Dermot had dreamed possible. The memory of that game was a nightmare, redeemed by him alone: and he, like the O'Dowda, received a devotion from a source he would speedily forget.

At a quarter to ten, Mr. Gray said they must be going. Dermot often got into hot water for coming home late from Delgany: nor were matters helped by a very decided difference between the Delgany and Walmer Villa interpretations of the word. Thus it was a good chance for Mr. Gray to finish an ordeal and assert a principle at the same time. When Uncle Ben riotously demurred, he could insist sadly, but firmly, as one whose duty compels him to give up a pleasure.

"I can't keep them waiting up," he finished, marshalling an added virtue: so Uncle Ben, putting on his coat, led him upstairs to say goodnight, leaving Con and Dermot to cover the table and put out the lights.

"It's an awful pity Father's got that way over his games," said Con, opening out his end of the long heavy cloth. "He usen't to do it. It's only the last two or three years. He's aged; there's no denying it."

"I don't mind it," said Dermot. "I'm used to it. I like him so much, I wouldn't mind what he did."

"Oh, sure, everyone likes him," said Con; "but it's harder to put up with things in your own people": a truth which Dermot most fervently endorsed.

CHAPTER XXXVI

THE END OF THE 1914 HOLIDAY PROVED TO DERMOT THAT HE was indeed grown up. Small outward and visible signs, such as increased pocket money, licence to go into Dublin to the theatre by himself, had not convinced him of his status, because he did not inwardly feel different. Even though (for instance) Mona now appeared as an untidy, heavy creature with a sulky expression and clothes not over-clean, he felt too much like the Dermot who had adored her to be disillusioned. The real Mona, *his* Mona, was not a creature of time. She was ageless and unfading. All his feelings about Walmer Villa, Delgany, and the place in general, were of the same quality. They dug deep back into his childhood, and kept him a child.

But, now that he had to say good-bye again, he felt a change. The good-bye was as poignant as ever, but he was far better able to bear it. He was emotionally stronger. A year was no longer a vast desert, in which anything might happen. He could see ahead. Years passed more quickly now. He had had, as always, a lovely time. Very well. He would go away thankful, work hard, get his scholarship at Oxford—this War would soon be over: there was nothing to worry about on that account—two glorious last terms, and then come over again. For longer, too, perhaps. Varsity terms did not begin till well into October. He and Con had a great plan, whereby he might stay at Delgany after the others had gone. He could work a bit, in the mornings. Oh, a great plan. And, after that—he hardly let his mind run ahead so far. Oxford terms ended in *June*. It was possible, just possible, mind you, that in the future, he might get over for a full three months. Oh, the future was full of hope: so full, he would be thankless indeed to grieve at going back now.

He packed in the room at Miss Tarbet's, during a waste hour of the afternoon, half hoping that the old mad lady would begin her chanting. Sure enough, just as he was filling the second case, the piano clanked feebly, and her unearthly voice struck up:

"YES we'll gather at the river . . ."

When he had finished, he paused at his parents' door, which stood open. Mr. Gray, in his shirtsleeves, looked up from the big trunk, and made a grimace. He was always sympathetic when they left, until they got into the train. Then, it was only a matter of time till he fished out his annual joke.

"Next station Sandycove! Isn't it lovely to think we have our whole holiday before us!"

Dermot did not enjoy the sympathy very much, as his father always managed to strike a jarring note: but he made a friendly grimace back.

"That old girl," said his father, jerking his head towards the unseen singer. "Wouldn't she drive you off your head? I was hoping to get through before she opened fire."

Dermot smiled.

"No," he said. "I don't mind her."

"H'm." Mr. Gray turned again to his task. "You're lucky, that's all I can say."

Dermot went on downstairs, stood while a tram went by, and crossed the road. Bessie let him in. The darkness of the tiny hall, the well-remembered, indefinable smell of Walmer Villa engulfed him. Queer, to reflect, when he seemed to be so deep, so firmly established in it all, that this time to-morrow he would be in a train, somewhere in Wales. He peered at the clock. In less than an hour, the Delgany folk were coming in to say good-bye.

The next morning dawned perfect. Dermot woke early. The bay was clear and calm. No fear of a rough crossing, anyway. With a sort of smiling composure, he dressed, carried his lighter stuff across, made a round of the rooms to see he had left nothing behind, and sat at the hurried, flustered breakfast, aloof and self-possessed as an iceberg. His mother, he noted regretfully, grew more and more easily flustered, and seemed angry if other people kept calm. He had to demonstrate, very politely, twice, that all his belongings were ready. Eithne sat, staring straight in front of her, inscrutable. Poor Eithne. It must be extra beastly for her. She would notice, and resent it, if he watched her. Had Con said anything? he wondered.

Five minutes before they need start, he remembered he had left a magazine in the summerhouse. Accordingly, without flurry, he went down the garden to get it. As he went, he looked at everything, with an eye that pretended it was simply interested. Determined not to be sentimental, nor to indulge to the old practice of saying good-bye to each place, he nevertheless welcomed the chance to see it all once more, and have a moment with it alone. If I hadn't left the book there, I wouldn't have come, he told himself: but he went slowly, even, at one corner, parting the long flags of an iris, to see if there were any snails, and smiling as he did so. He was grown up now, and a year soon went. It was merely a matter of patience. Sit tight, carry on, and presently the circle wheeled round, bringing one back. He crossed the lawn, all sparkling with dew, and stooped under the mass of creeper that overhung the summerhouse door. Inside, out of sight, smelling the old faint smell of mustiness and decay, he stood for a minute: and the treacherous tide of feeling flowed over his soul. He let it flow, then shook himself, and resolutely pushed it back. Yes, yes, he said to himself: it *is* a dear old place: but you'll be back soon. One more minute, fully savouring and exploring it all, and he went out.

At the top of the garden he turned, deliberately, for a long look back. One could always summon up a pretty accurate picture of it all: but nothing to the detail of the reality. (While, in the picture, one was remembering and placing this bush or that tuft of flowers, the rest of the picture blurred.) There it all was, standing patient and peaceful, in the early morning sun. A man, tiny in the distance, was walking along the road in front of the Glenageary houses. Down by the cottages on the right, someone was bawling fish. The Dublin Mountains curved, clear and beautiful, above the trees. The paint was almost all blistered off the cucumber frames. This is Ireland, this is Ireland. Well, he said to it lightly, as one who makes a concession to old customs, Goodbye, Ireland, till next year.

He turned resolutely, and went down the path. Suddenly he noticed the blank space, where Paddy-monkey's kennel had stood: and opened his eyes wide, in recognition of the garden's power, for there had been no kennel there this ten years. The times of leaving Walmer Villa were all one. Every year the circling orb ran again into that sorrowful patch. But Dermot was older now: he could master it all, watch himself, and study its effect upon him: and, as now, show himself manly and cheerful in the good-byes.

Granny was upstairs in bed. She had not been well, and was in great chagrin that she could not see them off. Dermot bounded up the stairs, and stooped over the bed.

"Good-bye, Granny darling."

"Good-bye, Dermot, pet." Granny was always tearful when they left. "Ta' care of yourself, now. Don't work *too* hard."

He put his head on one side, and smiled.

"I'll have to work *rather* hard, till December, I'm afraid, Then, please goodness, I'll be able to take it easy till I go up to Oxford."

"I hope so, darling. I hope so. And, once you're over your exam, sure, it won't be so long—"

"—till we'll all be over here again." He sat on the edge

of the bed. "It's not very long, once Christmas is past, Granny."

"Ah no, me child. But the winter seems very long, when you have it all before ye."

Granny began to cry again. He squeezed her hand, and got up gently from the bed.

"Get well quickly," he said gaily. "You talk of me taking care of *myself*. *You* take care of *yourself*. That's much more to the point at present."

Granny smiled weakly.

"Ah, son, I do. Sure, I take great care."

"Well, mind you do." He kissed her. "I'm afraid you're rather naughty, when there's no one about to see that you do what you're told."

"Good-bye, darling boy. Good-bye."

"Good-bye, Granny darling."

He ran down the stairs.

"Good-bye, Katie."

"Ah, sure, good-bye, Master Dermot. Ah, the blessing of—"

"Good-bye, Bessie. Not long till next year."

"Good-bye, Master Dermot. Good-bye."

The others had started. Grandpapa was standing at the gate.

"Don't go squeeze me hand, now," he adjured Dermot, suspiciously.

"I wouldn't," protested Dermot, taking it very gently.

"Faith, ye would, in a minute, " said the old gentleman. "Well, good-bye now."

Outside the gate, Dermot found Eithne waiting for him. They went down the road together, turning at the corner, and waving back to Grandpapa, who stood, leaning forward stiffly, looking after them.

"Poor old Grandpapa. He was afraid I'd squeeze his hand."

"Yes. He told me not to, too."

"I say. There's Paddy. Do you mind if I walk down with him."

"Of course not. I'll catch up with the rest."

That was a fiction, because they were well ahead: but Dermot did not stop to look into it. He crossed the road. Paddy, who had been sitting hopefully on a low wall, shambled to his feet.

"Well, Master Dermot."

"Well, Paddy. It's too fine a day to go."

"Oh, faith, indeed, it's grand." Dermot fell into step, as Paddy set off in his familiar shuffle, arms working, breath hissing between his teeth.

"P-lay up the music," he began, automatically, to hide his embarrassment: for he did not know what to say.

"I was sorry I couldn't get down to go after an eel, Paddy. But, somehow, there never seemed to be time."

"Oh, sure, I know. Ye do be busy now, and have lots to do. Sure I know. I wasn't expectin'."

To hear Paddy, one would have thought the idea almost a sinful indulgence. But Dermot had felt guilty. He had seen very little of the faithful old fellow, lately. It couldn't be helped. They weren't really at ease together, now. Whenever they met, they talked energetically of the past.

"Do you mind the day we got the big eel with a hook tied on to a swimp net?" Paddy asked suddenly.

"Indeed I do. I'll never forget it."

"And th' eel on Ballygihen Avena'; and all the little girls that did be watchin'."

"Yes, yes. Those were great days."

"Ah, the' were. We had great times."

"Paddy — we never had a dart at the mullet."

"No. No more we did. Ah well, if you're here, next year, please God, sure we might. . . . ."

"Indeed we might. We must. And do a Loughlinstown Walk."

Dermot's heart expanded towards Paddy. He would have promised anything, in the best of good faith.

They came out on the sea front, above the baths. There

was hardly anyone about. A couple of bathers taking their before-breakfast swim: a milkman or so: one or two people, like themselves, walking to catch the mailboat: no one else. A sudden sick pang shot up in his heart, as he recalled the look of the garden. Almost angrily, he thrust it down.

Hardly another word passed between them, as they went down in front of the Pavilion, across the wide dusty road, and reached the pier. No one was fishing. It was too early. The familiar sound of one's boots on the woodwork roused another pang, but he was prepared for it, and it had barely time to raise its head.

"Well. Good-bye, Paddy."

"Good-bye, Master Dermot. Thank you very much; thank you very much. The best of good luck to ye now. The height o' blessin'."

"Good-bye."

He went up the gangway, and joined the others. Con was coming, on his way in to town, to see them off. Eithne, leaning on the rail, kept an anxious lookout.

"There he is," she cried.

Sure enough, they saw the great galumphing figure, in his enormous overalls, charging up the pier. He was late, and the sailors at the gangway did not want to let him on: but he plunged past them like a mad elephant.

"Here, pet," he said, pressing some parcel into Eithne's hands. "And, if ye open that before ye get half-an-hour out, I'll have the behind off ye. Oh, sorry, Aunt Margaret! I didn't see ye!"

For a couple of minutes, the deck resounded with shouts of enormous laughter. Then, just in time, Con plunged down the gangway, and stood making faces, on the pier, He imitated in pantomime an old gentleman near him, and was caught doing it. He endeavoured to scandalise Mr. Gray, calling him to the rail, and bawling, in the coarsest Dublin accents, an intimate commission to some imaginary female relative. As the boat slid out, he ran along, blowing vast kisses. At the end of the pier, he climbed a great winch, and waved a scarf. But the boat slid fast, the scarf grew small astern, and soon the elbow of the harbour hid it.

Dermot was resolved again to be firm with himself, and not to spend all his time gazing religiously at the waning shore. He watched for a quarter of an hour: that first lovely but agonising quarter, when the coast opened out, when Delgany stood up fresh in the morning, with Vico and Killiney Hill behind it, to be hidden presently by Dalkey Island, and emerge again, smaller and different, when that was passed: when one could see the places in the mountains, the familiar runs, in one place, even, the tiny track of a road: the panorama of the holiday, like a drowning man's last glimpse of his life. After that quarter of an hour, he read the paper, looking up from time to time and noticing the changes. For a long while the spires of Kingstown stood up clearly. Each time he looked he expected to lose them, but there they were still. A haze came down over the mountains: their large outlines grew vague and dim, till, by some trick of light and matter, the last thing to be seen was little Killiney Hill, a tiny mound upon the horizon. Dermot looked at his paper, and read how women had been assaulted by Germans on tables in a Belgian market place. One woman testified to seven assaults. Dermot admired the presence of mind which had enabled her to count them, walked to the rail, and looked astern again. Yes: still there: little Killiney Hill; and the hump next to it must be Dalkey Hill. There, under the shelter of that mite of land, so far astern, was all he loved best in the world. Ah well: next year!

He turned, and looked ahead. From the ship's bow a great creaming wave, sparkling, thick, rich in the sunlight, rolled away outwards, solid as the sheets turned back from a bed. A vent in the ship's side was shooting out ashes, which only faintly discoloured the hissing, dancing glory of broken water. Yes: he was going away speedily from Ireland, to a new world, to new experience. He felt cheered, and strength rose in his heart. Ireland was lovely, but he must go now, and earn his next visit there. He looked back again, and could just make out, very faint and dim, the shape of Killiney Hill on the horizon.

EPILOGUE

TEN YEARS AFTERWARDS

THE FRONT DOOR OF DELGANY SWUNG OPEN, MAKING ITS well-remembered, indescribable noise, and a girl, stepping across the mat, softly thanked the maid who had let her in. It was dusk in the hall, but the girl's voice had not changed: and one who had not seen her since the events last told would have recognised her, with surprise, but little difficulty.

"Am I late?" she asked.

"No, Miss Eithne. It wants a quarter of an hour yet."

Eithne made a grimace.

"I must run," she said.

The maid smiled, and withdrew, her feet clattering on the uncarpeted stairs. Eithne hurried up to her room, to change for dinner. She turned left at the top of the landing, and left again. A breath of air from the sea met her as she opened the door, and she looked out upon the familiar perfect sight of the Bay. The Autumn evening was closing in. From the little town under the far headland a few small lights were beginning to twinkle resentfully. Eithne looked at it for an instant, and began to move with the purpose and directness of an efficient young woman who is in danger of being late for dinner.

Seven minutes afterwards, the danger past, she brushed her hair, frowning at herself in the mirror. She was thinner, and older: there were lines at the corners of her eyes: but the greatest change which had come over her was just that air of decision and purpose. She had a neatness, an efficiency, which told that, instead of following her mother's

road, she had hardened in a quicker, noisier school: a school
in which poise and grace were dearly bought. The girl who
now critically scanned her face in the mirror would be severe
with herself, and with others. Yet here, in this house, and
in this room, she might relax. Turning from the glass, her
eyes came to the mantelpiece. There, in all their remembered
disarray, stood the rows of cards and calendars, the invitations and the dance programmes. It gave her a shock
to find how clearly she remembered them after ten years.
A few weeks only might have passed since she last looked
at the ogling children, the dog with the tam o' shanter,
and the other tokens from Con's little girl friends. There,
smiling happily at her, was a snapshot of herself, sitting on
the bike, dressed in Con's overalls, in the pinewood on the
Lough Bray road. She moved along. "Lady O'Shea requests
the pleasure of Mr. Con McManus' company at a dance . . .
August 27th, 1912." Nineteen-twelve. She shivered suddenly,
turned off the light, and went downstairs. These things, all
there together, in fixed, gleeful refusal to admit all that had
happened — they were uncanny. She could well understand
Aunt Patricia's keeping them. She could not herself have
moved a single one: but, somehow, she was glad to know that
they would not stay there much longer. They refused to age,
like an old woman who has gone silly, and thinks she is still a
girl.

Eithne had looked forward almost with terror to the time
when she should first return, see the View again, and hear
the front door swing. She thought she would die of memory
and feeling. But when, yesterday, it had all opened effortlessly once more to her gaze, she had felt no emotion. Her
eyes had been expressionless. There it was, all as before,
the remembered wonder that was always more wonderful
than memory. The door scraped open, and Aunt Patricia
met her in the hall.

"Ah, Eithne child, welcome," she said, holding open her
arms. "Though it's to a sad, dull house now; not like it was."

Even that did not pierce the cold self-possession which had so unexpectedly encased her heart. She hugged Aunt Patricia and said:

"We're going to have a lovely time together."

And, strangely enough, they were. Aunt Patricia had laughed more, Eileen said, than she had for years.

The great gong banged, but without that exacerbating last crash which Con loved to beat from it, and the three women went in to dinner. They said little at first. A watcher would have felt that there was some subject which they were hesitating to approach. The table, shorn of a leaf, was lit by candles. They left the rest of the big room in shadow: but above the mantelpiece could be distinguished something new: a large frame with a portrait, and, inlet beneath it, a little inscribed panel.

"Well," said Eileen at last, "so you went to look over the old spot?"

Eithne looked up, grateful that the subject was delayed no longer.

"Yes," she said.

"Aah," said Aunt Patricia. "I never went round. I hadn't the heart. Sure, the front of it was enough for me."

"Yes. It has rather gone down, hasn't it? But I wanted to see if there was anything left of the garden."

Eithne's voice was quite steady. She took a sip from her glass.

"I went up the lane, at the side: you know, the one that passed the big tarred gate looking out by the manure heap. The gate was gone, and it was hard to see where the hedge used to be. The orchard is there all right—"

"That was all they left of the garden, when they let the house to the next tenant."

"— I know."

"They were going to build on it."

"Well," said Eithne shortly, "they haven't done so. It's all allotments. I went among them. There are the two trees still, on the left-hand side: the one at the top, and the big one where the seat used to be, opposite the summer-house. But the rest might never have been there at all."

There was a short silence.

"It's a funny feeling," said Eithne, in the same level voice, "to realise that a place has utterly ceased to exist: a place that was like a small world to the people who knew it."

"Like the country hedges that are swallowed up to make a town," said Eileen, making a warning face in the direction of her mother.

"Just like that," said Eithne gratefully, interpreting the glance. She pulled herself together. "I called in on Bessie, but she was out. So I left a message to say I'd be in to-morrow."

"She was terribly excited, to hear you were coming," said Eileen. "She comes up here once a week, to do some cleaning for us."

"Then I went and saw old Paddy."

Aunt Patricia looked up. There were tears in her eyes, but she ignored them.

"Is it the lame fella, that used to go about with Dermot?"

"Yes."

"Ah, a faithful poor fella. How is he?"

Eithne cleared her throat.

"Remarkably well. He has regular work at the schools. He lives with his sister, and they seem quite happy." She smiled. "We were very shy of one another at first, till I reminded him of one or two incidents. Then he sparked up splendidly."

A fresh course came, and they did not speak for a couple of minutes.

"It's a snug little place they have," said Eithne again.

"He thought the world of Dermot, did poor Paddy."

"They have a photograph of him, in uniform, on the best table."

"Dermot in uniform," said Aunt Patricia, musing. "D'ye know, I can never picture him like that. I never saw him in uniform. I can't imagine it suiting him."

"He changed very much," said Eithne. "But I know what you mean. He never looked quite at home in it."

"He was such a dreamy, thoughtful sort of a boy."

"Do you know, Aunt Patricia, this photo of him is just like that. It was the last he had taken. He looks just as I've often seen him look. As . . . as he looked the last time I saw him."

It was out. With a feeling almost of relief, the three women relaxed. Hitherto, they had not trusted themselves. Eithne and Eileen had talked together, sitting up late the night before, after Aunt Patricia had gone to bed: but they had been afraid to speak in front of her. Even now, by silent agreement, they did not talk at the meal. They waited till they were sitting round the fire at one end of the big drawing-room. Shadows leaped on the walls. The telescope, mysteriously shrouded, sent a fantastic broken bar leaping across the ceiling. A stray flicker, shooting under a chair, gleamed derisively on the nose of the wooden pig. Dimly guarding its secrets stood the glass cupboard which held the shark's jaws and the centipede. There were three people in the room. Eithne was too practical to fill empty chairs. She looked round seeing, not the room she knew, but a shell of it: useful to check one's memories.

She turned, and found Aunt Patricia looking at her across the hearth.

"Tell me about Dermot," said Aunt Patricia simply. "About the last time you saw him."

"Well . . . We went out as you know. . . . They didn't realise at first how bad he was. He had lost one leg, but seemed to be going on well. *He* thought so. We had a most cheerful letter from him: very characteristic, full of his sort of jokes. Dictated to a nurse, of course: but he had signed it, quite firmly. Then we were sent for, at short notice."

She sat back into the chair.

"We had two days with him. Most of the time, he was very sleepy and tired: but it made him happy to have us there."

"Did he know about—Con?"

"No, thank goodness. We kept that from him."

"You poor thing," cried Eileen suddenly. "You had a hard time."

"It wasn't very easy. I had one long happy talk with Dermot, the afternoon before he died. He talked a lot about here, and about Walmer Villa. About the garden. He remembered it in such detail."

"Did he seem unhappy . . . to know that it wasn't there any longer?"

"No. Quite serene and happy. He kept dozing for a few minutes, and then going on with the conversation. I didn't think he quite knew where he was: and then he'd say something, 'Are you still there?' or something like that, showing he knew just what was happening. He was perfectly happy."

"That's a blessing, anyway." Aunt Patricia paused. "You saw him again?"

"The next morning, with Mummy, for a few minutes only. They were going to operate at two o'clock. We left him at one. He was terribly tired. I turned round in the door, and saw him put his hand up to his forehead, very wearily; just the way he used to, when he was sleepy."

"He had no pain?"

"Very little. And he was gone before they could start operating."

No one spoke. Eithne sat back into the shadow of the deep chair, and blew her nose.

"One strange thing happened that afternoon. At about four, a letter came for Dermot from Con."

"Aah, Eithne, you don't say it."

Aunt Patricia started, and leaned forward.

"Yes. I can't tell you what I felt, when I saw his handwriting. I hesitated for some time, and at last I opened it. It was written the evening before Con was killed. He had just heard about Dermot, and was writing to buck him up." Her voice shook. "It—it was all about the rides in the mountains they'd have, when Dermot was well, and the War was over. It ended, 'We'll have great div*a*rsion.'"

Eileen drew in her breath. She was watching Eithne in a kind of wonder.

"For a while I felt absolutely torn inside, and then, suddenly, it seemed all right. The letter put it all right. I felt as if I could see them, together already, laughing at me for minding. For not understanding. And I determined not to mind. For their sakes, if they were anywhere where they could know about us, I determined to try and carry on. . . . It was extraordinary. I can't tell you how, but calmness and peace seemed to flow into me. I was quite composed. I went up to call for Mummy. I even let her take me to see Dermot."

"Did—"

"He looked just as I've seen him when he was a boy. Absolutely still and peaceful. . . . Well. There it was. They were gone. The two people I was most bound up in, gone together. Life was going to be different for us all, but perhaps even more different for me than for the others. I saw to everything, and took Mummy home. The rest you know."

There was a silence, and then Eileen began speaking, half in a dream.

"It was easier for us than for many people, because of what we believe. Neither you, nor Mother here, will misunderstand me when I say that the day I die will be the happiest day of my life. I have a very happy life: but I look forward more than anything to that lovely day on which I shall join my dear ones."

"In anyone else I'd think that morbid," said Eithne quietly, "but I know, with you, it's different."

"I'm that way, too, Eithne," said Aunt Patricia placidly.

"I don't care how soon the Lord calls me after my darling Ben and my two darling boys. But I'm quite contented, awaiting His word."

"Yes. It wasn't quite as easy as that, for me. Don't think I'm making light of the difficulty of holding on to such a faith as yours: or of leading the lives you do. It is just that—well, as a family, you see, we hadn't that faith. Daddy believes nothing: Mummy's not sure what she believes. Dermot and I learned all we know about your kind of faith here, in your house. We admired it, we wished we could imitate it."

"Why couldn't you imitate it, Eithne? That's what I never could understand. It's so simple. Just trust in God's providence, and leave all to Him."

"Yes. I know. It sounds simple, put like that. I can't explain, to you, Aunt Patricia, I'm afraid: nor to Eileen."

"I can see," said Eileen, "that Dermot might have met more obstacles to faith than we did. Though, I must say, in all humility, faith—the faith itself—seems easy enough to me. It's living by it that's hard."

Eithne said nothing. She knew only too well the impossibility of showing them where, for such as here and Dermot, the difficulty lay. They must reason, they must scrutinise. For them must be a faith which extended all their faculties, or no faith at all. Dermot had believed, hopefully, vaguely: the rush of events had given him no time to adjust his faith to his experience: but she knew that, had he lived, the faith of Delgany would have grown harder and harder for him.

After a silence, the three women went on talking, reviewing the happenings of the violent years. Walmer Villa had barely outlived the Gray's last visit. Three weeks after Dermot and Eithne had said their last farewell to him at the garden gate, Grandpapa had a seizure. For four days he lay, semi-conscious, singing to himself, in his husky ghost of a voice: praying loud and fervently: and reciting, hour after hour, without hesitation or fault, his favourite passages from Dickens. There, in that little room, in the mid-October of 1914, the last feeble spark of Victorian Ireland flared up and died. When the old man leaned back his head and uttered his last sigh, the long era of the eighteen-sixties passed for ever, and the bleak wind of a new Ireland blew down the street. Alfred Conroy had gone, and taken his world with him.

It was only fitting that Granny should soon follow. She had not been well, and took his death with composure —knowing, perhaps, how short the separation was to be. Dermot's mother was still with her. In spite of the doctor's assurances, she preferred to stay. Granny got better, and took to coming down for a few hours every day. Miss O'Killi-kelly called one morning, and was informed by Bessie that the mistress would soon be down. She came back in half an hour, and was met by a Bessie distraught, crying and wring-ing her hands.

"Oh, Miss O'Killikelly, Miss O'Killikelly, the mistress is dying."

Katie came out from the back regions somewhere, kneeled down in the hall, and began keening. Bessie turned and shook her.

"Will you whisht," she cried, almost fiercely.

Upstairs, Granny, an expression of surprise on her face, a half-smile at the suddenness of the trick played upon her, lay staring at the window that slowly blurred and darkened. Ten minutes later, Miss O'Killikelly, shaking her head from side to side, the tears streaming down her face, took home the lemon pudding that would not now be needed. When they heard the news, many wept with her: for the old lady was as near being universally beloved as it is possible to be. All, of every sect, called with their condolences: and Margaret met them all composedly. She and Aunt Patricia between them put the old house to sleep. Despite all it had meant to her, Margaret said afterwards that she

did it without bitterness or sorrow. It belonged to a world
that had passed away. Six weeks after Granny died, the
house was empty, and the garden wild with weeds.

Those two had gone in their fullness, for they were both
over eighty years of age: but the decade had taken others
whom it might well have spared. Uncle Ben was gone,
from one winter's bathe too many. Pneumonia set in, and
burned up the great strong man like a handful of shavings.

"It was better for him," wrote Eileen at the time. "He'd
never have put up with the need to take care of himself. He'd
just have gone on and killed himself the moment he was well
again. He hadn't the temperament for being an invalid."

But Ben was seventy, and so to be counted lucky in having
kept his strength of body so long. More cruel was the fate
of Brian, struck suddenly with appendicitis, and operated
on too late. Here, indeed, the will of God was hard to read,
for there were a great many good human reasons for leaving
Brian alive: but the few heads left at Delgany bowed in
unshaken trust. Anne was well, that was one comfort. She
and Topje were happy and prosperous. They came over
once a year to stay with Aunt Patricia, and she always
felt the better for their visit. They always asked her over
to stay with them, too: in fact, did all they could to take
the places of those she had lost.

One other death the three had to speak of at the fire, but
a death so splendidly in character that none of them could
regret it. During the War, the O'Dowda, cursing, proffered
unostentatious but valuable service to his King. As soon as
it was over, he went back to his beloved Vienna, and spent
four happy years there. The tall magnificent figure, erect
as ever, with its cloak, its broad-brimmed hat, its half-
humorous air of hauteur, became one of the best known
figures in that impoverished city. A connoisseur of guitar-
playing, he attended every small recital, private, semi-
private, and public, and to win his severe applause became
a mark at which the virtuosi aimed. One night, in a café,

it was noticed that when the player finished, the tall figure seated by himself gave no sign, but remained leaning forward, his head upon his hands. The waiter tip-toed up, and at last, greatly daring, touched his arm. Cornelius Conlon O'Dowda had died to music.

Eithne lay back in her chair, and looked at the ceiling.

"I've never quite understood about him," she said. "I don't know—but I believe Mummy was in love with him once, or very nearly."

Aunt Patricia sighed.

"Ah, sure," she said. "We were all in love with Corny." She got up, and smiled sleepily down at them.

"I'm going up to me bed," she observed. "Don't stay on, now, too late, the two of you."

They kissed her good night, and sat down again, to talk of things which many of their generation had to talk about: to look back to a childhood separated from their present by more than was good or wonted: to know themselves, like Grandpapa, relics of a past age, but an age fiercely, cruelly compressed: an age that budded, but never flowered.

And here we may leave them, and this story; for, by its very nature, it can never be completed. Yet, it if does no more than suggest to some, whose imagination will not run far backwards, that even in those distant years the sun shone warm, and the days were good, it will have served its purpose.

✑ ✑ ✑ ✑ ✑ ✑ ✑

A NOTE ON THE TYPE
IN WHICH THIS BOOK
·········· IS SET ··········

*This book is set on
the Monotype in a face called Scotch. There is a
divergence of opinion regarding the origin of this
face, some authorities holding that it was first
cut by Alexander Wilson & Son of Glasgow
in 1833. Whatever its origin, it is certain
that the type was widely used in Scotland
where it was called Modern Roman, and
since its introduction into America has
············ been known as Scotch. ············*

SET UP AND ELECTROTYPED BY THE
PLIMPTON PRESS, NORWOOD, MASS.
PRINTED AND BOUND BY H.
WOLFF ESTATE, NEW YORK.
PAPER MADE BY S. D. WARREN
CO., BOSTON. THE TITLE-
PAGE AND BINDING HAVE
BEEN DESIGNED BY
W. A. DWIGGINS